Praise for *To Die in Secret*

"Suspenseful and emotionally engaging, *To Die in Secret* is a compelling novel that considers the aftermath of tragedy and the cost of family secrets." — Amy Gottlieb, author of *The Beautiful Possible*

"*To Die in Secret* is full of complex, beautifully rendered characters who win your heart, settings that pull you into the New England countryside, and mysteries that keep you guessing. But more than that, it's a book that addresses the morally fraught issues of abuse, reconciliation, and the impossible goal of trying to be a perfect parent in an imperfect world." — Patricia Averbach, author of *Resurrecting Rain*

"*To Die in Secret* is a quiet build into a redemptive roar of a story that illuminates history, ethnicity, and spirituality into one beautiful weave." — Cynthia Neale, author of *Catharine, Queen of the Tumbling Waters*

D1667159

Other books by Haviva Ner-David

Yonah and the Mikveh Fish
Dreaming Against the Current: A Rabbi's Soul Journey
Hope Valley (A Novel)
Chanah's Voice: A Rabbi Wrestles with Gender, Commandment, and the Women's Rituals of Baking, Bathing, and Brightening
Life on the Fringes: A Feminist Journey Towards Traditional Rabbinic Ordination

To Die in Secret

a novel

Haviva Ner-David

Bink Books

Bedazzled Ink Publishing Company • Fairfield, California

978-1-960373-09-0 paperback

Cover Art
by
Meira Ner-David

Cover Design
by

Bink Books
a division of
Bedazzled Ink Publishing Company
Fairfield, California
http://www.bedazzledink.com

To the good enough parents of the world

To the good enough parents of the world

And to die—to die in secret, without asking what or why.
To close my heart's eyes while the world continues to exist . . .
For everything, everything is but a song that always ends suddenly,
Between being and not-being, on an evening that annuls everything.
And I—I am just the son of a mother who died once.
Nothing more.

— Abraham Chalfi (translated from the Hebrew by
Heather Silverman and Michael Bohnen)

ACKNOWLEDGMENTS

I would like to thank my beta-readers: Patricia Averbach, Debbie Jacobson-Maisels, Margalit Jakob, Julie Landau, Cynthia Neale, Dorothy Richman, and Frank Tipton. And especially Shoshana Lavan, who got to know the characters almost as well as I did while I was writing this book. Thank you to my parents for being the best good enough parents they can be, and to my children for letting me be the best good enough parent I can be. My eternal gratitude to my life partner, most constructive critic, and biggest fan, Jacob, not only for offering feedback on the manuscript, but for being my partner in good enough parenting and helping me make my dreams come true in so many ways.

CHAPTER 1

NOT TAKING UP much room in the world, perhaps no room at all, ephemeral and barely existing. That's how Nomi felt. She looked out the airplane window, at the clouds—floating, like she was. Suspended between here and there.

It had not been difficult to tie things up. She didn't own her house. Everything belonged to the kibbutz collective. She was lucky they let her leave with her jeans and tank top, thick hooded sweatshirt, and small carry-on suitcase with what she took from the contents of her and Avi's closet. The travel committee had bought her a one-way ticket to Logan Airport, given her two thousand dollars in spending money, and wished her well.

They had called an emergency meeting the week before, as soon as Nomi heard about her sister and nephew's sudden deaths. The head of the housing committee called to tell her their decision. She should be in touch when she was ready to return, he said. They would hold her house and membership for six months only, which should be enough time to be there for the ongoing investigation, sort through the deceased's belongings, and decide what to do with Nomi's elderly mother who was now totally alone.

"We'll buy you a ticket back when you're ready. In the meantime, foreign workers will sleep in the house," he added. Not, *do you mind if foreign workers sleep in your marriage bed of the past forty years just months after your beloved Avi has died?* That was how things were done on the kibbutz, which also had its benefits. Sometimes, she preferred being told what to do, since she did not always know what she wanted.

But kibbutz committees cared little for an individual's needs. The kibbutz was all about the common good, leaving little room for her personal trauma. This made it easier for her to lock the door to her two-room cottage and hand over the key, even after having lived there all her adult life.

Her repeated fate: leaving with practically nothing, not even much of a plan. The summer after her senior year of high school she had been running from the only place she knew—her childhood home in the Boston suburbs—on an airplane going in the opposite direction she was headed now. She had not liked that daunting—even terrifying—feeling then, and now, going back, she was too numb to think or feel.

Her parents had been barely speaking to her then. She and her shame had hidden behind her baggy clothing and shaggy hair; she could hardly eat and had lost almost twenty pounds before the school year ended.

"Your sister, maybe, but not you. What a waste. You were the smart one, the one with promise," her father had said, and Nomi understood her prospects for a worthwhile life in their eyes were gone. Her mother stood there shaking her head, as if there were no words that could convey the abomination of Nomi's sin. Her older sister, Judith—or Jude as she asked to be called, because of the Beatles song not the apostle—had gone off to live on a commune instead of college and had never been much of a student anyway.

Both girls had biblical names, but their parents had given Jude a Yiddish name as her Jewish one, named after her great grandmother—Yehudis Gittel, meaning good Jew, which turned out to be ironic. By the time Nomi was born, five years later, the fashion was to give Hebrew Jewish names, so Nomi got Naomi, meaning pleasant, which was her English name as well and should have been easy enough to emulate. But neither daughter managed to live up to their names in their parents' eyes.

Nomi, too, changed her name, but only after leaving home and never even told her parents or sister of the slight alteration. Whereas Jude had been bold enough to change hers while still living under her parents' roof.

Jude had always been bolder and braver than Nomi. And smarter, too, despite what her parents thought. But she was not interested in "schools and their rules." Jude was a source of vexation to her parents, whereas Nomi was the reliable one. Or at least she had been, before her life turned upside down. She was more studious than smart. She had known how to give her teachers what they wanted, because their expectations were clear, and she had the skills to meet them. She found boundaries, law, and order comforting.

Nomi remembered the day Jude had revealed her plan to leave home for the commune, established by a group attempting to build a collective on the grounds of a failed nineteenth-century transcendentalist self-sustaining Emersonian farm community. It was not far from the summer sleepover camp on the outskirts of Salem Nomi and Jude had both attended when they were younger. The original community had not lasted even a year, because of a scandal . . . or was it a murder . . . or both? The cabins had been deserted, and any later attempts to live on the land had been unsuccessful.

Legend had it there was a curse on the property—or maybe a witch's spell, considering its proximity to Salem—dating back to its original owners in colonial times. This was all Jude knew. Taking advantage of this "superstitious nonsense," a group of post-beatnik hippies had started squatting there and working the land. They were building a commune, and Jude was going to join them, she said, swearing Nomi to secrecy. She didn't mind rules if they were not authoritarian. Nomi listened, wide-eyed, in awe of her sister's nerve and sophistication.

They were sunning themselves by the pool when Jude confided in Nomi—a rare occasion, since Jude normally made no attempt to hide her resentment of her sister's favored status. Nomi felt privileged to be let into her older sister's world, mysterious and out-of-reach to Nomi. And frightening, too. Dangerous, even. It was not a world Nomi would have wanted to visit. She did not envy her sister's life on the edge; she was too fearful to venture there. But a part of her longed to stand in Jude's shoes for long enough to experience the thrill—with no trepidation, only abandon, like her sister.

It had always been that way. At the Jewish country club, Jude was the one who dove from the highest diving board, while Nomi had to muster all her courage just for the low one. Jews were not welcome at the other country club, her parents explained. And besides, it was "best to socialize with your own," in other words, with the young men the sisters would meet at the Jewish one.

Her parents were not especially religious, attending synagogue only during the High Holidays and for life cycle ceremonies, and sending Jude and Nomi to Hebrew school on Sunday mornings instead of full-time Jewish day school. But their Jewish identities were strong, their social circle all Jews, and it was understood their daughters marrying out of the faith would be unacceptable, disloyal, crossing a sacred cultural barrier. Besides, Jewish men made better husbands.

They did not necessarily make better boyfriends, Nomi discovered.

It was true Nomi was smitten with David and flattered by his attention, and there was chemistry between them. David was part of the cool crowd in her class who thought of school as more of a social opportunity. Nomi liked the positive attention of being a good student, but she did not fit in with the nerdy kids; she did not go to science fairs, was not a bookworm, and she did not like being teased by her classmates as a goody-goody or a teacher's pet. She fit in nowhere.

When she had started dating David, the teasing stopped. Especially when she began helping him and his friends with their schoolwork. Being with David was her bridge into another world, like the occasional peeks into her sister's life. He and his friends were not hippies, exactly. They dressed the part without taking the risks of living a life off the grid. *They* were not heading off to a commune any time soon, but they listened to *Live from Woodstock* and smoked joints when they could get their hands on them. It was like standing on the edge of the medium diving board, which was enough for Nomi. She was finally happy and had found her place.

Until the night that changed everything.

After that, she wouldn't take David's calls and walked through her days, half in her life and half still in the other place she had gone that night. She stopped talking to her friends—had they ever even been friends, anyway?—and caring about her schoolwork. She would have failed her final exams if she had not already worked so hard in school. But she did not do well, and her teachers were concerned, not only about her poor grades but also her changed behavior and dress and her loss of weight.

She had hoped for her parents' sympathy—especially from her mother, who was a woman, after all. Instead, she blamed Nomi, accused her of getting herself into "that situation." Even if her parents were right, she needed their support and assistance. It was clear she would get neither and could not stick around.

When Nomi saw the ad in the local Jewish newspaper advertising free one-way tickets to Israel for anyone interested in making the big move "upward"—*aliyah*, the Hebrew term for Jews moving to Israel—she grabbed the chance. "Making *aliyah*" was another medium diving board. She had visited Israel with her family some years before, after Israel won the Six-Day War. It was familiar ground, even if it was thousands of miles away. If she had a second home anywhere, it was there.

Going to live in Israel was a righteous choice. It was what good, loyal, proud Jews did—the ones who followed the rules, unlike her parents, who were only half-hearted Jews. It was what God wanted. She had read in Hebrew school Bible class how God had promised the land to the Israelite nation. And in Modern Jewish History, she had learned about the Zionist movement and the miracle of the establishment of the Jewish state.

Moving to Israel would not only get her back on the virtuous track; it would prove she was more principled than her parents, even if she had made this one horrible mistake. Maybe, despite her sins, God would answer her prayers.

Nomi went to the Israel office at the local Jewish Federation and arranged it all. She could volunteer on a kibbutz at first. There were plenty that offered *ulpan* to learn spoken Hebrew, and if she declared citizenship upon arrival, as any Jew could do, she would benefit from the country's socialized medical system and support for new immigrants.

After that she did not know what she would do. How would she manage on her own? But at least she could get away from her parents' judgmental and disapproving gaze. Her main objective was to run.

That is how she had ended up at Kibbutz Areivim in northern Israel, and never left.

She would not have been able to stay at the kibbutz if it hadn't been for Avi, who was not only a kibbutz member but the child of founders. They met that first summer, when she was working in the orchards picking cherries and peaches. Avi was her supervisor. She slipped and twisted her ankle and could not work for a few days. Avi came to check on her after work.

He knocked on her door, and when she answered and spoke to him on the threshold, not inviting him in, he sensed her unease. She was afraid to be alone in a room with a man, even if she was beginning to feel present in her life and body again. He said he'd be right back and brought two plastic chairs from the dining hall so they could sit and talk outside. His level-headed manner and sensitivity to her needs—in contrast to David's self-centered impulsiveness—won her over right away.

They took it slowly. Nomi could not suddenly trust again, and for Avi, slow was just his natural style. He took life slowly. He was patient—even with her awkward Hebrew—although she became fluent quickly. It was Avi who started calling her Nomi instead of Naomi. He said it felt lighter. She agreed. A new name for a new start, shedding her "A" along with some of her shame.

Avi did everything in a thoughtful, measured way, as if time was never an issue. It clearly was, as it turned out. No one thought someone in such good shape and health and not yet seventy could die of Covid. But he was dead within two weeks of having contracted the virus. The one thing in his life he did not do slowly was die. And she was left alone in a place she had never felt completely welcome.

Over the years, Nomi was slowly accepted by the kibbutzniks, but not fully. Forever an immigrant, she would never be part of the club. She wondered if she should go back there when she returned to Israel. But with no money or education beyond high school, she did not know how to support herself if she left the kibbutz. There, she worked in agriculture: in the fields, orchards, and hot houses. She knew her place; it was safe, even if not perfect.

So now here she was, over forty years after leaving the U.S., pressing reverse on her life. She had not been back in all that time; she had only called her parents to tell them of her whereabouts when she was engaged to be married. But they did not come to the wedding; they were cold on the phone, and Nomi had no strength to fight for her dignity or their love.

Nomi had wanted her parents' apology, and she had suspected they wanted one from her, too, for letting them down and then disappearing from their lives. She assumed her mother still wanted one from her now, but she was not ready to apologize then and was still not ready to now, even with so many years behind them.

Besides, visiting would have required asking the kibbutz travel committee to buy her a ticket, and the secretariat for time off from work. She would have had to explain why her parents didn't come visit instead of the kibbutz shelling out money and losing her work time so she could go. And if anyone objected, it would go to a general assembly vote, putting her personal business on display. Every kibbutz decision required committees, explanations, discussions, meetings, and votes.

The only person besides her parents and sister who knew about the shame she carried was Avi, and she told him at first only to explain her strange behaviors—like refusing to walk alone at night and checking for an exit any time she entered a closed space. She was not about to tell the whole kibbutz. Besides, she saw no reason to unearth that buried corpse.

There were many reasons—and excuses, she admitted—for not attempting to visit her parents. She had done nothing and let the years pass. It was easier that way.

Would her parents have finally come had she told them about the cancer and hysterectomy? Would they have sat in their comfortable life in the Boston suburbs knowing what their daughter was going through in her non-pampered kibbutz life in Israel? But she hadn't told them. Her parents might well have said it was divine retribution for ruining her chances at a life as charmed and privileged as theirs. Her heart could not have taken another beating from them. She did not make the effort to heal the relationship.

Nomi wondered what her mother would say when she arrived back, so many years later, a week or so after her daughter Jude, and her grandchild, Jonah, were found dead in their house. The police had found a note on Jude's refrigerator with Nomi's phone number and email address, the officer explained when he called. Nomi thought it was a prank call, because she rarely spoke to her sister on the phone and found it strange Jude would have her number on the fridge; most of their correspondence was by email. But when the officer emailed her the initial police report, she knew it was devastatingly true. Her sister and nephew were dead.

It had taken Nomi an hour or so to gather her equilibrium and courage and call the nursing home where her mother lived, to tell the staff. She asked them to inform her mother. The head nurse suggested Nomi do this herself and in person. After all, wouldn't she need to go through her sister's things and settle her affairs? It had not occurred to Nomi she would need to fly back.

"Your sister was your mother's only visitor," the nurse explained. "She came at least a few times a week." It was Jude who had chosen the home for their mother, so she would be close by. The nurse worried how she would take the news.

Thankfully, her mother was mostly living in the immediate present and distant past, without memory for much else, so she did not know how many days had passed since Jude's last visit. But she did often say, "When Judith comes . . ." and the nurse worried how she would react if they told her Jude was never coming again. Better to hear the news from her only remaining family member, the nurse added. That reality, too, had only hit Nomi when she heard the words on the phone: she and her mother were the only family left.

Nomi tried to convince the nurse she knew better than her how to break the news. She was not even sure she should tell her mother at all. Some things were better left unsaid when it came to her mother. Why upset her?

The news was shocking enough for Nomi, who had not seen her sister for as long as she had not seen her mother. Jude had not had the money for a trip to Israel. And they had never really been close. Jude was always on another orbit.

They did exchange letters—from the time Jude had left—which later turned into emails. The correspondence had been important to Nomi. Jude was the only person who could understand how she felt about her parents and the life both sisters had escaped.

But she did not really know Jude. She became more of a Dear Abby. It was easier to confide in someone so far away, and Jude answered with wise and thoughtful advice, carefully choosing her words, like Avi did. It was a shame Avi and Jude had never met. Perhaps now they would, in that timeless spaceless place of the soul.

That was something Jude would have written. At some point in her journey, Jude had become spiritual and discovered Buddhism.

Ever since Jude had re-entered her parents' lives, Nomi began to resent her older sister. When their father had a stroke, her mother swallowed her pride and called Jude, a home-care nurse. Jude became Ms. Compassion: helping him get proper care; moving them to an assisted living facility nearby; taking care of their father through rehabilitation, more strokes, and finally death; moving their mother to the nursing home when dementia set in. It was beyond Nomi how her sister could so easily forgive and forget after so many years of antagonism and damaging, hurtful parenting.

After Nomi's exit, the sisters had become equally persona non grata in their parents' eyes. Both had abandoned their parents' bourgeois lifestyle to live on agricultural communes—even if they were an ocean apart—and both had shamed their parents although only one had done so intentionally. Nomi had considered Jude an ally.

When Jude broke their unspoken sister pact united against their parents, she became the loyal daughter, while Nomi became the prodigal one. Nomi felt betrayed, and a little jealous. Jude had been the person she could turn to for commiseration. After she reconciled with their parents, Jude tried to convince

Nomi to do the same. Nomi could tell she was trying not to preach, but that was, essentially, what she was doing. The advice Nomi had once solicited from her sister kept coming, even though she stopped asking for it.

Jude sent Nomi emails with Buddhist teachings about non-attachment and compassion; about how forgiveness is for the one who is forgiving, not for the one who should apologize, how the apology is not even necessary; how good it feels to be free of resentment. And so on, and so on. How could Nomi forgive her parents if they did not even understand the damage and pain they had caused? Same went for David. And how could she forgive herself for letting David take advantage and upend her life?

As for Jonah, Nomi had met him only once, around ten, fifteen years before, when he came to stay with her on the kibbutz for a few weeks during a trip in the Middle East. He was the result of a relationship Jude had on the commune. When the commune failed—its members were more interested in philosophizing and smoking weed than farming—and they decided to try an urban commune instead, Jude did not go with them. She decided their free-love hippie lifestyle was not a good environment to raise a child and the rules of the commune were no better than those of the authorities of her youth, so she abandoned the idea altogether. That was the last she saw of Jonah's father, who had not been interested in fathering anyway.

Jude had continued squatting in one of the cabins and subsistence farming on her own. She worked her way through nursing school while raising Jonah, until he left for college. She remained estranged from their parents, who still did not accept her non-conformist lifestyle and choice to stay in such a gentile area— although they admitted relief she had left the commune and Jonah's non-Jewish father. Jonah had told Nomi all this when he had visited, filling in the gaps of her sister's story.

At some point, the county government took over the property and put the big farmhouse where the original landowners had lived, up for sale, and the surrounding cabins up for rent. Jude began renting until she saved enough money to buy the farmhouse. There had been a series of owners, none of whom stayed long. They all had bouts of bad luck—financial, health, and otherwise— reinforcing the notion of the legendary curse; the house then sat vacant until Jude bought it, did some renovating by hand, and took in boarders. It was around then Nomi and Jude's father became ill. Jude became a legitimate homeowner and came to their parents' rescue all within the same decade.

After college, where Jonah earned a degree in environmental studies, he went off to see the world. He was backpacking through life, returning home when he needed to recharge his batteries and earn money for his travels.

Nomi had gotten to know Jonah a bit when he visited that one time, and then moved on, to Egypt. When the Coronavirus surfaced, he had been living in Costa Rica. Then all U.S. citizens were called back home, so he moved in with his mother, doing climate crisis activism from his bedroom. That much Nomi had succeeded in getting out of her sister, between the lines of her gratuitous guidance.

Jude's emails were short, usually offering updates on her parents, and later, just her mother, a poem she thought would be helpful, or a quotation from a book. Nomi had needed to create a picture of her sister's life from these tidbits she dropped, like clues of a treasure hunt. Although Nomi had not yet found the treasure. Now, with both Jude and Jonah gone, was it too late?

"We're getting ready for landing. Please fasten your seat belts and close your food trays," the steward announced over the loudspeaker. "There's a fog over Logan Airport, so visibility is poor. We anticipate a bumpy but interesting landing."

CHAPTER 2

THERE WAS A fantastic burst of color from the trees as the El Al Dreamliner came in for a landing. And the cold air took Nomi's breath as she exited the international flights terminal. The sun was just coming up, burning away the fog. Autumn in Galilee meant olives ripening, not leaves changing color; the heat cooled off enough evenings and early mornings to be pleasant, requiring a light sweater, but certainly not a coat, hat, or gloves. It was lucky she had at least brought that hooded sweatshirt. She shivered her way to the rental car offices; she'd have to find warmer clothing when she got to her sister's house—a thought that made her shiver even more.

Once in the shiny red Chrysler, so clean it looked new—a fancy change from the kibbutz's communal old beat-up white Kango vans, full of wrappers and used coffee cups—she put the address of the police station into Waze. In their email correspondences, the police officer had written she should come to the station to be escorted to the house.

The investigation was not over, but the police could give her one set of keys, taken from the neighbors who had found the bodies. She shivered again. Those neighbors, an email said, had always kept a spare set, in case of emergencies, and suspected Jude's dog sitting outside next to her truck for two full days, barking and whining, was indeed an emergency. Especially since Jude was not answering her cell phone. It seemed she must have let the dog out when she and Jonah were feeling too ill to walk the poor creature the night of their deaths. Now, the police could hand the keys and the house over to Nomi, while they kept Jude's set, until the case was closed. They had taken what they needed for the investigation.

Waze said she would be there in a little over an hour. She adjusted the mirrors; her hair was a mess. She had not been on an airplane for over forty years and had forgotten how bedraggled she would look after the flight.

Nomi found a lipstick and hair clip in one of the pockets of her backpack. Avi had always told her she didn't need makeup. She only put it on when she had to make herself presentable to the outside world, which she found less generous and forgiving. She put her hands through her limp graying hair—once a lustrous wavy chestnut—to untangle and neaten it as best she could, and then coiled it up and fastened it with the hair clip.

Scowling at the wrinkles that had developed over the years around her gray eyes, Nomi put on her sunglasses. Despite the crow's feet, she looked youthful for her age, perhaps because she worked outside and wore sunglasses most of the time. Her rugged, unsophisticated dress and well-maintained figure must have had something to do with it, too.

Nomi followed the Hebrew instructions about kilometers and meters, which felt out of context, driving through a landscape reminding her of words like yards and miles she had not heard in decades. She made a mental note to try and figure out how to change the language setting on her phone.

As she drove, Nomi felt a pang of regret; the first time she was making this trip to Jude's house, her sister and Jonah would not be there. It had taken three deaths—her only beloved, her only sister, and her only nephew—to bring her here. It was too late for some things, and too soon for others. Nomi was not ready to say goodbye to any of them; there was more she wanted to say to them all, especially Avi. And she was not ready to contemplate what would be, now or later. She had come because someone had to do this job, and there was no one else.

She was glad to have some alone time and get a break from the kibbutz, though. Avi had been well-loved at Areivim. Many native kibbutz women had been interested in him, she discovered after they became a couple; an immigrant stealing his heart was no cause for celebration, so she was lucky they tolerated her. Avi explained there was never a chance he would have fallen for any of those women; it would have been like incest. But apparently not everyone agreed.

The organization and routine of life on the kibbutz was just what Nomi needed when she first arrived, though, and the security, too. And within that structure, she had begun to let go of some worry and guilt and been able to breathe again.

The kibbutz volunteer committee sent her to the fields and orchards with the fruit-pickers each day before the sun came up, until late morning, and then back again in the late afternoons as the sun dropped along the horizon, filling the sky and her being with color and light. In the mornings, as the sun rose, she felt its rays on her skin, waking her body from months of slumber.

She even began eating well and gained back the weight she had lost. It was then her periods returned, along with some sense of self-worth. At least she didn't have to suffer that consequence of her sin. She had been given a second chance. She was a withered plant coming back to life on new ground.

Nomi had enjoyed picking fruit that first summer when she met Avi. Then, through the years, he taught her everything he knew about working the land. He derived such satisfaction from planting seeds, watching them sprout into life, and nurturing them to fruition, it was contagious. It made her sad later, when her body did not prove to be fertile like the land he so loved. But at least he got that satisfaction from his work.

As Nomi fell in love with Avi, she fell in love with nature, a very small part of her life growing up, she recalled as she drove through the tunnel taking her from the airport into Boston—a tunnel not existing when she had lived here. The suburbs were not the country; sure, there had been trees and flowers, but everything was manicured. There was nothing growing wild—the weedkiller the gardener sprayed in season made sure of that—and plants were for decoration, not sustenance.

Her mother decided one summer it would be "cute" to have a vegetable garden. So, on a Sunday, Nomi's father took her and Jude to the local nursery and helped them choose seeds—tomatoes, peas, squash, and lettuce. They followed the instructions on the packages. It was exciting to watch the seeds peek up through the earth, transforming into food sweeter than candy because they had grown it themselves.

Nomi discovered peas grow in pods, not separately like when canned or frozen. Once she saw their natural state, it felt right they should grow that way, in little families, and she wondered why she had not realized it sooner. But how could she have known?

The vegetable garden, however, had been only a quaint project, supplementing what they bought in the supermarket. Living off the land was not something any Jews she knew did. It was not until moving to Israel Nomi discovered this was possible. Her whole kibbutz was full of nothing but Jews living off the land.

It was with Avi Nomi discovered she had a green thumb, and she loved being among plants who did not judge or hurt her. The work helped calm her nerves. It was hard for her to be around people—especially her peers, who reminded her of David and his reckless thoughtlessness. Avi was almost ten years older than she was—protective and doting, like a father. Or at least the one she wished she had.

She and Avi spent workdays together in the fields, and on Saturdays, their one full day off, they hiked the area, as far as they could by foot, as buses did not run on the Sabbath. One weekend a month, they were given use of a kibbutz vehicle and time off from Thursday to Saturday night, when they hiked the terrains of their tiny country—drivable from north to south in under eight hours even before more modern roads were built. Now it took only six.

In winters—more like a cool and wet summer in Massachusetts—they hiked forested and desert mountains, trails through wadis and fields; and in summers—hotter than anything she remembered from her childhood—they stuck to hikes that included springs along the way, or rugged beaches pleasant for walking and swimming. She wondered why there was even a Hebrew or Arabic word for the seasons spring or fall, since anything resembling these transitions happened too quickly to deserve recognition.

Avi's love of the land as a source of beauty, adventure, and nourishment never ceased to amaze Nomi. All through the Coronavirus lockdowns, they had continued walking the trails on the outskirts of the kibbutz. Regulations did not allow travelling outside their immediate locale. The first lockdown had been after an especially rainy winter, and the flowers—red and white poppies and anemones, lavender and pink cyclamens, purple irises, white orchids, and yellow and white narcissi—were a sign of hope in a period of despair.

They would chew on wild garlic as they walked and talked, marveling at the splendor around them, as if the pandemic was something "out there," happening to unlucky others living in densely populated cities and towns devoid of nature and fresh air.

Until it happened to them.

Avi had gotten it first. To this day, Nomi did not know how. Perhaps he had contracted it on one of his trips to Rambam Hospital to donate blood, something he had been doing regularly for thirty years. Nomi had tried to dissuade him from going when the pandemic started, but he said it was needed then more than ever.

Nomi had caught the virus from Avi. She waited it out at home, while his condition went from bad to worse in that same hospital. She was not allowed to visit. When the doctor called to ask if he had a living will, she knew it was the end.

Still lost in thought as she looked out the windshield at the road ahead, Nomi wondered if she should return to the kibbutz after this gruesome mission. Perhaps this could be an opportunity to break away, look for a job in agriculture and a house of her own somewhere else in Israel, but what and where? On the kibbutz, she was guaranteed shelter and food. She was taken care of. That was built into her membership, which had been granted her as a privilege of being married to Avi. It would be foolish to relinquish that.

Areivim was one of only about ten kibbutzim remaining communitarian instead of privatizing; they did well enough for everyone to live modestly but comfortably in that model, to which its members were still committed. The thought of going off on her own had its allure, but it was frightening. She had no savings or relatives to turn to. The kibbutz was her only safety net, even if it was not a source of emotional support.

Her in-laws, Amos and Hannah, had reluctantly accepted her into their lives, and they had the stereotypical polite distant sharpness of the *yekes*—Jewish Germans—they were. When she went back, she could expect more of the same. They had a common history that brought them together. They were both born in Berlin, both the sole survivors of their families after the Holocaust, and both had been on a Kindertransport from Germany to England and then sent on to Palestine, where they helped found Areivim.

Avi had been named for Hannah's baby brother, Brahm, short for Abraham. Throughout the war, Hannah had been jealous of Brahm, whom her parents had kept with them, while they had sent her away. Until the war ended, and she heard of her brother's fate. Had babies been allowed on the Kindertransport, her parents would have sent him, too, she later understood. What she had perceived as lack of parental love was really a selfless act to save her life, she had explained to Nomi.

Even *yekes* have hearts, Nomi knew. She imagined her in-laws' hearts like those British candies the kibbutz children were given as treats—the ones with the hard sour shells. If you worked hard enough to suck through the exterior, you were rewarded to discover a softer, sweeter interior. But the work needed to get to the center was not always worth the trouble.

Before Nomi boarded the bus to Ben Gurion Airport, Hannah and Amos—now in their early nineties—had said their goodbyes. There were no embraces, because of the Coronavirus, which was a relief to all of them, as they had never shown her physical affection. They did look, however, like they might be holding back tears. Although Nomi suspected those tears were more for their dead son and the grandchildren Nomi had been unable to give them, and less because they would miss their daughter-in-law.

Avi was his parents' only child, although they had wanted more, so, "cutting out Nomi's uterus"—the Hebrew term for a hysterectomy—meant cutting their family lines. This had pained her parents-in-law terribly. When they thought she was still out from the anesthesia in her post-op hospital bed, she had overheard Hannah say to Amos, "That doctor finished the job Hitler started."

Nomi and Avi did not argue often, but when they did, it was usually about his parents. He was unable to say no to them. When they asked for his help, he jumped to their rescue, even if it meant neglecting or disappointing her. She would understand, he explained, but he could not say the same for them.

Avi had not grown up in his parents' house. All the children on the kibbutz back then had lived in the Children's House. They had only spent an hour or two with their parents after dinner before bed. Avi had frequent nightmares but was not allowed to go to his parents. He would cry but the adult on duty would not let him leave. Sometimes, he would manage to sneak out and cry outside his parents' house; he knew if he knocked on the door, they would only bring him back. This broke Nomi's heart.

Avi seemed on a constant mission to please his parents, was afraid to cross them. The crying child standing outside his parents' door was still crying for their love, approval, and attention. This was at times suffocating.

Nomi knew Avi felt guilty about not continuing his parents' family lines, and his parents did not hide their feelings. At least not well. For the first few years after her hysterectomy, they found fault with Nomi's every move. She felt them critiquing her constantly with their eyes: when she let the water run while washing dishes; when she slept past seven am on vacation days; when she forgot to turn off the boiler after her shower in winter . . .

They could never hold themselves back—like all those years ago, when she had called Jude from the communal telephone after the surgery. She had badly needed to speak to someone removed from her kibbutz life, especially after overhearing Hannah's comment. The person on telephone duty had to pull the phone away when she refused to end the call—she had gone five minutes over the ten-minute time limit.

When her parents-in-law got wind of it, they gave her a talking to. Things like that were "against the communal spirit." They hadn't cared she needed support; they were probably hoping the marriage would fall apart because of her infertility and fragile emotional state.

Avi did stand up to them about that, though. Not the phone call, but the marriage.

"I married you, not your uterus," he told her, clearly upset at his parents. He then added in a playful tone, "That would certainly take all the pleasure out of sex," trying to make her smile. He had looked at her with that twinkle in his eye, and put his hand under her chin, lifting her face so she had to look at him.

She did smile, but she still wondered if he was truly okay with their new reality. When she asked him about this, he surprised her with his anger. She had never seen him so exasperated with her.

"Leave it alone, Nomi. Are you suggesting I find myself a concubine or something? Who do you think I am?" His face was red, the veins in his temples bulging. "My name may be Avraham, but I'd like to think we're a more functional couple than the biblical Avraham and Sarah were. If you don't agree, perhaps *you* want to look elsewhere. But don't project that onto me."

That was the last time she mentioned the issue, and Avi did seem, over the years, to become sincerely at peace with his lot. There were plenty of kids on the kibbutz for him to befriend. He was everyone's unofficial uncle, their *Dod* Avi. He played with the younger kids, let them climb on the tractors, took them for hayrides. And teenagers confided in him. He knew the kids in ways their parents couldn't. He got to be the one they all complained to about their parents.

Avi seemed content, and even his parents appeared to have resigned themselves to the marriage. Nomi was not sure what it was that had changed their minds, but they stopped rolling their eyes, which eased the tension between Avi and

Nomi as well. He still jumped to their aid whenever they called—more than once even interrupting Avi and Nomi's lovemaking—but Nomi came to resent that less, given they were trying as well.

Perhaps Nomi and Avi could have adopted a child, but they never investigated the possibility. They did not know anyone who had adopted. When Nomi did ask Avi if he knew anything about adopting in Israel, he said he saw no point; adopting would not continue his parents' blood lines. As far as he was concerned, he was happy being *Dod* Avi and having her all to himself. But if she really wanted to adopt, he was willing to ask around.

He reminded her that adopting would involve a kibbutz committee, though, since it would mean another mouth to feed. That fact put Nomi off the idea. She was surprised couples on the kibbutz didn't have to get permission not to use birth control. Sometimes, Nomi wondered if living on the kibbutz was worth the price.

Since Nomi was not even sure she wanted children, anyway, she had let the idea of adopting slide. The world was not a friendly place, and whereas Avi's reaction to his troubled childhood was to want to do better with his own kids, Nomi's rupture with her parents had made her wonder if she wanted children at all, considering the endless ways in which things could go wrong.

Her parents had messed up raising her, and she was not sure she could do much better with her own children. She liked to think she could. She liked to think she would not abandon her child in their biggest time of need. But she was not sure. How could one ever be sure? Perhaps this was God's way of letting her off the hook, she felt on a good day. On a bad day, it was God's way of punishing her for all the ways *she* had messed up. Beginning with agreeing to go to David's house that night.

Driving past the dorms of Boston University, where she would have gone to college had her life not taken such an unexpected turn, Nomi switched on the radio. Another voice in the car, besides the drone of directions, was welcome company.

As she drove past her childhood hometown, she considered taking a detour to the house where she grew up. But her parents had sold it and moved to an apartment when the five-bedroom Tudor became too hard to manage. Then they moved to the assisted living facility near Jude. Besides, she had not come back to this place out of nostalgia.

Nomi took in the sight of the fall foliage now on both sides of the highway, like the Israelites passing through the Red Sea with walls of water on each side. Only this looked more like walls of fire—with its power for both warmth and destruction. Either way, it was an awesome sight.

Nomi had not seen an autumn like this except in photographs since she had left the U.S. Kibbutz Areivim was not in the desert, but what passed for forest over there was like calling a chihuahua a dog, and the trees were mostly pine, not hardwood. It was a shame she had not appreciated it growing up. But she had not known anything different, and leaving the only place she knew, for such a foreign landscape and climate, had not been on her life agenda.

Passing exit after exit, Nomi sang along with the radio as she drove. She was used to hearing English songs on the radio, as even in Israel music from the U.S. and U.K. was aired often. But hearing the deejay speak in English sent her back in time, as did the sign to the Topsfield Fair she saw up ahead.

Nomi's family had gone to that fair every year, especially to see the fireworks. One year the only parking spot they found was in a lot far from the display, so they were in a rush to get there. Nomi, just four years old, had had trouble keeping up, so her father had put her on his shoulders, holding one of her feet with one hand and one of Jude's hands with his other. Her mother held her sister's other hand.

The walk felt like hours, as Nomi desperately needed to pee. She told her parents this, but they said she had to hold it in until they got to a proper bathroom. If she were a boy, perhaps going into the bushes could have been an emergency solution. Her mother did not approve of girls squatting on the side of the road to relieve themselves.

Nomi had feared her bladder would burst as she bounced up and down to the rhythm of her father's long strides, and her pubic bone pressed against the back of his neck. Then, when Jude said something that made Nomi laugh, she lost it. She could not hold back any longer.

Her father was furious when he felt the warm liquid begin to stream down his back. He practically threw her off his shoulders, so he barely got wet, but she had to spend the rest of the evening in drenched, smelly pants. She had tried to warn her father, but he was in such a hurry to catch the fireworks he had not paid attention.

"Let this be a lesson to you. Always go before you leave the house," her mother had scolded. "That's one of the drawbacks of being a woman, but you'll learn to live with it."

Nomi had wondered what the other drawbacks were, but she sensed it was best not to ask. Thirteen years later, she discovered the answer on her own.

And here she was, back in the place of those memories she would have preferred to forget. The highway narrowed from six lanes to four, and Nomi sensed she was approaching her destination. Waze confirmed it. Regret mixed with sorrow Jude and Jonah would never be there, nor anywhere else, ever again.

Nomi's eyes filled with tears as she pulled off the highway. So much death and loss in her life in such a short time. She believed in God but was not sure God believed in her anymore.

Waze told her she would be there in ten minutes. She was on a two-way single-lane road now, driving through one small town after another. A sign welcoming her to Northville was on her right. That was the name of her sister's town. She passed a church with a tall, pointy white steeple. When Waze told her she had reached her destination, she pulled into the small lot, put the car into park, and took a deep breath. She was here. Whatever that meant.

The police station was in the center of town—which appeared to be just this one street—with another church, a very modest grocery, post office, library, gas station, and a small but sweet sandwich and coffee shop with local charm and a few picnic tables out front. A sign read: "Takeout or Sit Out (and without a mask, none of the above)," which Nomi assumed was because of the Delta variant. She had read about the polarization in the U.S. over masks and vaccinations. She was used to Israel's polarization; it was strangely satisfying to see the U.S. was no better.

A chalkboard hanging behind the counter listed the day's sandwiches. Nomi bought herself a latte—the setting she used on the industrial sized coffee machine in the kibbutz dining hall, where she had gotten her morning coffee every day for the past forty-two years—with a local organic free-range egg sandwich. This sounded gourmet compared to the eggs from the kibbutz chickens, who were clean and treated well enough, but were not allowed to come and go as they pleased.

Nomi ate while sitting at a table outside. The sun had come out, and the air was warming up a bit. When she was done, she brought her dirty plate and cup inside and handed it to the young man behind the counter. He looked surprised and pronounced his "thank you" with extra gusto. Nomi blushed; she was a customer here, not a kibbutz member expected to pull her weight.

The police station looked so dormant Nomi wondered if they had opened yet. But the hours posted on the door—next to a sign, here too, warning people without masks they would not be admitted—showed it should be. Still, she was unsure, so she knocked.

"Door's not locked!" Nomi heard a male voice calling from inside.

Nomi entered slowly. What if there was only one officer inside? She still felt uncomfortable being alone in a room with a man. Although this was a police station, she reassured herself, as she stepped inside.

An attractive man about a head taller than Nomi and around her age stood to greet her. His hair looked like it had been shaved, with a bit of stubble growing in—a remedy to a receding hairline, Nomi suspected—and his midnight-navy uniform was tucked into his belted pants over a flat stomach. His shoulder patch read Essex County Police: Witch Territory, with a picture of a witch on a broom. His badge said Officer John Brooks, the name of the man who had called her.

"You're the sister. Naomi," he said with a nod, apparently still not handshaking despite the vaccine. "I'm sorry for your losses." He looked genuinely pained. "It must be hard."

When he had answered the door, Nomi thought she heard a trace of the accent she remembered from her childhood, and the way he said "hard" now left no room for doubt. He must have grown up here. Her own accent had never been this strong—somehow, the Jews in the area never had as strong accents as those whose ancestors went back to the Mayflower and the Speedwell, although her grandparents had come to Massachusetts at the turn of the nineteenth century, before the First World War even—but, anyway, hers had faded. It had been a long time since she had heard such a strong North Shore Massachusetts accent.

"Thank you" was all Nomi could think to say without having to explain her whole life to this man who also seemed at a loss for words.

This officer had not only the accent but also the look of a New Englander. It was hard to tell his hair color from his stubble, and whatever hair he had at their age was probably mostly gray, anyway, but she guessed it had been light, judging by his fair complexion and green eyes. His nose was not long but it was broad, as was his smile. Although that was the last sighting of either, as he quickly put on an official police department mask with the same logo as his shoulder patch.

"How was your flight? With Covid, and all. I haven't flown since the pandemic started. Not that I was much of a traveler before that, anyway." His eyes showed he was still smiling behind his mask. "I'm a homebody, I'm afraid."

"Me too. This was my first time on a plane since I flew to Israel over forty years ago."

Now his eyes showed surprise.

"It was easier than I thought it would be to get into the country," she went on. "In Israel, they're still being strict. Here there's no test required and no quarantine . . ." She was babbling out of nervousness. She hoped he wouldn't find her odd; this man did not know she had lost her husband to the virus.

"Yes, but we're proud of the numbers here in our county. They rose from June through October, when the summer residents and Halloween tourists were here. We are near Salem, after all. But now that we're getting back to being a sleepy town of ordinary local folk, they already started going down. There's some resistance to masks, but it's not too bad. And we have a good vaccination record, thank God."

Nomi was not sure how much God had to do with people wearing masks and getting vaccinated. She had once believed in a God who was more involved in the human realm, for good and for bad. Perhaps she still did. But that God had abandoned her when Avi was whisked away in an ambulance almost a year ago, disappearing out the kibbutz gate and of her life forever.

"That's good," Nomi mumbled and looked down at her Chelsea boots.

After an awkward silence the officer said, "Sorry. Forgot to introduce myself. I'm Officer Brooks. We spoke on the phone. We're a small operation here."

"Yes. I saw your badge. Nice to meet you, officer." Nomi felt she should do something with her hands in lieu of a handshake, so she reached out her elbow, hoping this was something they were doing here, too.

To Nomi's relief, Officer Brooks met her elbow with his. "Call me John."

"And you can call me Nomi. No one's called me Naomi to my face practically since I left this country—this same state, actually—years ago. I dropped the A soon after I left."

"Okay, Nomi."

Again, there was an awkward silence.

Nomi sensed John had more to say but was holding back.

"I didn't sleep much on the plane. Butterflies, I guess. When can we go?"

John took keys from a hook near the door. "Now, if you're ready. I'll take you"—he hesitated, as if trying to find the right word—"there." What was he avoiding saying? The deaths were an accident; nothing had indicated otherwise. In fact, on the phone John had said it looked like food poisoning, perhaps botulism; there were remnants of dinner in the kitchen when their bodies were found, and there were no signs of violence, a break-in, or foul play. But he was waiting for the coroner's report to confirm.

What would she find when she got to her sister's house? She wasn't sure she wanted to go, or even be here at all, but no one had asked her what she wanted. And she wasn't sure what she would have answered, anyway.

CHAPTER 3

NOMI RODE WITH John in his police car to Jude's house. His gentle manner and police uniform put her at ease. He and his deputy, Tom, would take care of returning her rental, he said. Jude had a truck at the house, and both truck and house, in fact everything Jude owned, was hers now—since Jonah was also gone, and their mother was not of sound mind. Jude had stipulated as much in her will.

Nomi was grateful for his help. How else would she return the rental car? She had no idea if there was public transportation here.

She looked out the window as they drove. After a few turns where houses were small, close to the road and to each other, John turned into more sparsely populated terrain. The longer they rode, the larger the plots grew and the further set back the houses became—until it was difficult to spot any at all. Driveways looking more like small country roads divided one neighbor from another, only sometimes leading to a visible house.

Kibbutz Areivim was in a rural area of Israel, but nothing like what she saw now. Israel was more like New Jersey: smaller than Massachusetts but more heavily populated.

Jude's house was one of those set so far back from the road, you might not know it existed. John drove them down the long dirt path, parked, and got out of the car. Nomi also got out, and seeing John take off his mask, she did too.

They looked up at the house.

It was a two-story Colonial. The façade was white painted clapboard, with a gabled slate roof and teal green shutters. It was so large. Kibbutz houses were tiny; she and Avi had shared a small, combined living room-dining-room-kitchen space with one bedroom and bathroom. This house looked like it must have at least six bedrooms. Jude was a widowed woman with only one adult child who had not lived at home properly for years, until the pandemic. She had once taken in boarders, though.

From the outside, the house did not look especially well-kept. But it was not run-down, either. Her sister had restored it to be functional. Impressive, seeing as she'd done most of it herself—and with some help from Jonah when he was around. There was nothing fancy or pretentious about the place, despite its size. This did not surprise Nomi, knowing what she did of her sister.

"It's bigger than I imagined," Nomi said.

"Yes. Your sister got a good deal. This is an original Colonial, not a Revival. It was once the main house of a large farm, built originally by a Puritan family in the seventeenth century. Although then it would not have been this large. The original Puritan owners would have had two or three rooms at most, and it would have had only one floor. Different owners must have added on to it over the years." John took on the tone of a knowledgeable tour guide as he spoke. "Now the house sits on an acre, only. The government turned the rest into a reserve, with woods, a pond. The smaller houses, on what was originally one property, have smaller plots and were dwellings for the farmhands, who could have been indentured servants, or even slaves."

Nomi's knowledge of U.S. history and politics was blurry and only at a high school level. She had grown up in Massachusetts but did not know much about this area. What was to the north of Boston had felt distant, even disconnected, from her upscale suburban life.

"I had no idea this kind of thing existed here. I thought the colonies were all about egalitarianism—for men, I mean—and freedom of religion, and slaves were only in the South. At least that's what they taught us in school, if I remember correctly."

"What they taught you wasn't untrue. But reality was not that black and white—no pun intended—life rarely is." John's voice sounded sad, and he frowned as his eyes closed to a squint. "Did you know Jews were not allowed to vote in the colonies? The first state to give Jewish men the right to vote was in 1790, in South Carolina, and the last was Maryland, not until 1824."

"No, I didn't know that." Unlike Nomi, John certainly had continued his education of American history. An interesting hobby for a police officer.

"The Puritans were escaping religious persecution in England, but they ended up persecuting others when they got here."

Nomi thought of Israel, where her own people had escaped persecution in other Middle Eastern countries—and even genocide, in Europe—to build a Jewish state, but were doing their fair share of oppressing Palestinians in the Occupied Territories, rather than annexing the land and giving its residents citizenship, or pulling out completely. Maintaining a Jewish majority in Israel, a Jewish state with an open-door policy to all Jews, and an Israeli military presence in the Territories, gave them a sense of security after their trauma.

Nomi knew from her in-laws and other Holocaust survivors the horrific details of this trauma, enough to justify their need of safety and fear of future persecution. Jew hatred was far from obliterated with the defeat of the Nazis, and the Palestinian leadership and terror cells were doing nothing to prove this theory wrong. Nomi knew from her own past what trauma does to your way of being in the world, and it cannot be easily shaken. Especially when danger still lurks around a dark corner. Feeling a sense of security had been essential for her. Still was.

Coming back to this part of the world had felt like a promise of some relief from the tension of the Middle East, the result of historic issues left unresolved. She deserved a break, a reprieve from the outer and inner conflict of the air she breathed in Israel. It filled the lungs and was pumped through the bloodstream of the entire population. But this place was not so different.

"The Puritans even executed Quakers back then," John added, shaking his head. "A woman named Mary Dyer was the first. Apparently, the original owners of this house, gentlemen farmers, were outspoken anti-Quakers." He took off his police hat, tossed it through the open front window of his car, and went to open the trunk. "The Puritans were not so pure. But the family got it back in spades, as I'm sure you know from your sister." He removed Nomi's bags.

"No . . ." she said, taking her backpack from him.

John raised his eyebrows, then peered at Nomi. "You don't know? She didn't tell you?"

Nomi shook her head, and John lowered his and sighed.

"The wife was the infamous Leah Marshall." He barely looked up.

Nomi did not recognize the name. "Who?"

He raised his head. "Leah Marshall," he answered, without enthusiasm, perhaps regretting what he had started. "She's a known historical figure around here. She killed her eighth child, her baby daughter, Despair."

"Did you say Despair?" Nomi threw her backpack over her shoulder.

"Yes. That was the girl's name. Names like that were not uncommon among the Puritans." John hesitated for a few moments. "Maybe it was a difficult birth. Maybe Leah never wanted another child. Maybe the idea of having another child threw her into despair." He rubbed his stubbly head as he shook it again.

"Yes. She could have had postpartum depression with her other births—you did say her eighth, child, right?—although I guess they didn't call it that back then."

"Exactly. Who knows? But it sure was a telling name. Leah broke the poor kid's neck." John clucked his tongue. "She claimed God told her to do it."

Nomi shuddered. "That's horrid." She covered her face, trying to block the story out like a scene on a movie screen. "How could she live with herself after that?"

John, hands in his jacket pockets, shifted his weight from one shiny black lace-up boot to the other. "Well, she didn't have to. The court said she was possessed by the devil, but that was not enough to release her from the death penalty. They went by biblical law in the colonies."

Nomi looked at her own boots, tan and scuffed. Fallen leaves were scattered on the lawn. They were still alive and vibrant with color but soon would become dry and brown.

"There was no such thing as an insanity plea in the Bible or in Leah Marshall's time," John continued to explain. "She was clearly mentally ill, but back then even being possessed by the devil was no excuse. That's why the house was empty on and off for so long. People believed she had put a curse on it, because her spirit was unsettled."

"Far from resting in peace." Nomi sighed as a cold wind blew around them, shaking branches and sending more leaves to the ground.

"Yes. That's why Jude got such a good deal."

"Well, my sister didn't believe in such things." Now Nomi remembered what Jude had said all those years ago about a curse on the house being silly superstition, even if she had not known the reason for the curse back then. She must have found out later but never thought to mention it. She had often called Jewish ritual superstition, too. She would not have let a legend of a haunted house stop her.

Nomi looked up at the house again and wondered if she did believe in such things, and if Jude still did not believe, later in her life, when she became a Buddhist. Didn't Buddhists believe in reincarnation? Was that different from believing spirits remain after death, taking care of unfinished business? If the soul could be reborn endless times until it learned life's lessons, if the spirit could hang around after the body dies, why couldn't it communicate with those who were still embodied?

John started toward the house with Nomi's carry-on in tow. She hesitantly followed him, wondering what it would be like to stay in that big house, alone, with all its deaths, and what Jude might have called bad karma.

Nomi noticed the sign "Pick and Pay" beside a lidded metal box—with no lock—on a table out front. John had not locked the car door, either. This small town was like her kibbutz in that way. Jude trusted others enough to use the honor system for what must have been one of her sources of income, offering berry picking to locals and passersby.

A blue pickup truck with plenty of dents and scratches was parked in the driveway. Nomi imagined her sister driving from home-care patient to home-care patient, probably spending much of her day in it.

How had Jude looked when she died? Neither sister had been good about sending photos, even as the rest of the world had gone image crazy with social media. That was something they had in common. Now it was a shame.

John followed Nomi's gaze and told her the truck's keys were inside the house, along with all her sister's and nephew's possessions. "It's all yours now. Even the dog. The neighbors are taking care of him, but they have their own—"

"I . . . I . . . I don't know how long I'll stay. This was all so sudden."

"No need to decide now. Take your time. He's happy there for now. Just saying he's yours if you want him. You'll probably want to go meet Jeff and Sam, anyway, and thank them for everything. They live over that way." He pointed to the left.

Nomi saw a house in the distance, behind a white picket fence. Jude hadn't mentioned a gay couple as neighbors. Then again, she hadn't told Nomi about any of her neighbors or friends.

"Theirs was one of those smaller houses for the farmhands—although it's nothing to sneeze at either. Those houses went up for sale not long after your sister bought this one."

"Thanks. I'll go over there."

"Your sister sure put everything in order. Not everyone would have had such foresight. I imagine being a single mother had something to do with that. And working in hospice, she knew a thing or two about the bureaucracy of dying." He practically whispered as he said those last words.

Nomi considered this. It *had* been smart of her sister. Jude may have had unconventional ideas, but she was practical, despite what their parents had thought of her when she was young. But Nomi couldn't help but perceive leaving everything to her as another of Jude's schemes to get her to face her past and reconcile with her mother. A last-ditch effort to persuade Nomi to follow the path Jude thought was right and would give Nomi peace. By forcing her to come here to deal with it all, she could control her from the grave.

Although not actually from the grave; she had asked in her will to be cremated. John had explained this, too, on the phone. It upset Nomi. She knew her sister was not a religious, or even practicing, Jew. Nomi herself was not especially religious. But she had loved Hebrew school and synagogue as a kid. And for her, some religious observances were sacred. She always fasted on Yom Kippur, heard the shofar blown on Rosh Hashanah, lit Chanukkah candles, and participated in the kibbutz Passover seder.

If Nomi had had a son, she would have had a brit ceremony—unlike Jude who had not even circumcised Jonah in the hospital. This had been the final straw that pushed her parents to stop helping Jude financially. And Nomi most certainly planned to be buried—beside Avi, in the kibbutz cemetery—when she died.

"May we go inside?" Nomi asked John, who was jingling a set of keys.

"Yes, of course. It's your place now. Just be prepared. Everything's as they left it. There's a lot of her in there. It might set off some emotions."

It was a thoughtful thing to say. And John had a sweet face. Sweet, but serious. Not bold and flirtatious, like Avi's, despite his measured ways. John had as many lines around his eyes as Nomi. He looked as worn by life. She wondered why.

"It's sensitive of you to think of that," Nomi said and wondered if John was married, had kids. He'd be a good husband and father. She'd look for a wedding ring when he took off his gloves. Avi, too, would have been a good father; he had been an exceptional husband. Her mother had been right about something. Jewish men did make good husbands. At least Avi did. However, John was clearly not Jewish.

Nomi and John approached the front steps of the house. There was another sign there, attached to a pole stuck in the ground: *You are on the traditional land of the first people of Massachusetts, the Wampanoag past and present. Please go no further unless you honor with gratitude the land itself and the Wampanoag tribe.*

Nomi had never seen a sign like this; the practice must have developed after she left the country. Of course, Jude would be one to adopt it.

Nomi only knew Kibbutz Areivim had been established on the land of a Palestinian village destroyed in the 1948 war of Israel's independence, because Jonah had asked about the ruins on the outskirts of the kibbutz when she and he were on a walk during his visit. She had, before, noticed the ruins, overgrown with weeds, and surrounded by cactuses, but assumed they were ancient. Or perhaps she had not given it much thought.

After her walk with Jonah, Nomi had asked Hannah and Amos about the ruins. They said they didn't know about what had been on the land before they were brought there as an army Nachal unit to build the kibbutz, back in 1949. They knew the land had been abandoned, but they did not ask by whom— although they did know it had been a Jewish town back in Roman times.

"Besides," Amos had added, "Jews are just as indigenous to this land as Palestinians are, if not more. It's a complex situation. If they abandoned their land, that's their problem. They were the ones who attacked us. Not the other way around."

Nomi suspected her parents-in-law knew more than they let on, and Hannah's next comment had confirmed her suspicion but also had given her pause.

"We were a bunch of war orphans with less than they had. No one today has a right to judge." Hannah threw Nomi a piercing look. "The world is totally different now than it was then. We were fighting for our survival, and the Arabs were no innocent victims. There was violence on both sides. It was a complicated time. Any attempts to understand it today only simplify and distort. You didn't live through it, so let it be."

Nomi felt bad she had raised the issue. She had no right to judge or even attempt to understand. She felt the same way about what had brought her to Israel.

Had she led David on? Had she not made herself clear? Had she wanted it, too?

Nomi pushed the thoughts from her mind. She and John were standing at the entrance to the house. The door was wide and tall.

As if he had read her mind, John said, "An oversized door like this is common in these parts. Big enough—I'm sorry to say in these circumstances—to fit a coffin."

Had Nomi heard correctly? "A coffin?"

"Yes," John answered. "Houses like these were built with a room called the parlor, to house the coffin when someone died. Until funeral homes came around and the parlor turned into what we call the living room today. That's why we call them funeral parlors. Death was a big part of colonial life. There was no penicillin, no vaccines. And conditions were harsh."

"Did I book the depressing tour, or are you always this upbeat?"

John laughed, but only half-heartedly. "Just telling it like it is. The realistic tour."

He opened the door into a foyer and waited for Nomi to enter ahead of him. "After you," he said, while putting his mask back on. She did the same but hesitated to enter.

He was being a gentleman, of course, but Nomi would have preferred he go in ahead. She was not concerned about being alone with him. But the house was another story.

CHAPTER 4

NOMI TOOK IN the earthy smell, and the inside of her sister's house. There were shoes for all seasons lined up on white painted wooden shelves; coats, sweaters, jackets, and vests were hanging on hooks above the shelves. She imagined Jude in this rugged clothing and these worn leather shoes, grabbing a key from one of the brass hooks on the back of the door, where a few hand-sewn masks hung as well. A message on a small chalkboard above read: *Don't forget a mask!*

Off the foyer, to the left, was the main living area—what had once been the coffin parlor—and a formal dining room was to the right. The walls were painted white, as were the wooden moldings around the windows and doors, and worn Persian carpets were placed around the hardwood floor. Couches in the living room faced a brick fireplace. The dining room also had a fireplace, and the long table was set with woven mats but did not look well-used.

Nomi walked through the dining room and into the kitchen. Here there was a smaller table, for two, also set with woven mats, a napkin holder, and a single candlestick with the remaining wax from a red candle. Nomi wondered if the candle had been lit when Jude and Jonah ate their last supper, if it had burnt out when they took their last breaths.

Trying to shake that image from her mind, she thought of Avi and her own cottage back on the kibbutz. They had also eaten their meals at a small kitchen table for two, and by candle-light for Shabbat dinner. One of the small rituals that made their life together feel sacred.

Nomi was spooked, and she had not exactly chosen to come. Her instincts had been right. It was too soon after their deaths to be in this house; it had been only a week since the bodies were found. Nomi felt her sister everywhere she looked.

"I cleaned out the fridge last time I was here," John said. "I came back after the coroner's office took the bodies and whatever else they needed away, and you informed me you were coming."

His voice came as if from another realm.

He opened the refrigerator. It looked pristine. Nomi wondered if it had looked that way before he cleaned it. "There wasn't much to throw out, though. No dairy products to go spoiled. Jude was a vegan, as I'm sure you know." That she did know.

Next, he opened a pantry. "She had already started pickling, canning, and storing food for winter, you'll see. And there are some dry goods here . . . rice and lentils, some nuts, and beans . . ." He made his way over to the counter. "I left this pumpkin out here for you." He patted it fondly, like a child's head.

Yes, Nomi decided. He did have children. But there was no wedding ring on his right hand, which was still resting on the pumpkin. His left one was in his jacket pocket, jiggling his keys.

"Looks like she was going to make soup," he continued, "which you might want to do for dinner. It'll stay good for a while, the pumpkin, if you don't open it—"

"Yes, I know. I work in agriculture back home."

He gave her an approving nod and looked out the kitchen window. "Well, in that case, there's still some fennel growing out back if you want to pick what's left. Cranberries, too. And those pears will stay on the trees for a while longer."

This intriguing man certainly had thought of everything. Either he was extraordinarily bored, or extraordinarily kind.

"Seems you and your sister had that in common," he added. "She grew a lot of her own fruits and vegetables. Most people in this part of town do."

The kitchen was warm and inviting, with its terra cotta floor, wooden cabinets, and granite counters—in sharp contrast to their parents' kitchen, with its linoleum, stainless steel, and shiny tiles. This kitchen projected a coziness lacking in their childhood home and belonging to someone who took pride in cooking and baking. Jude had a bread mixer on one counter, vegetables pickling on another, cast-iron pots hanging from hooks on an exposed brick wall, a set of professional-level knives next to the stove. A nut bag and cheese cloth were hanging over the sink as well.

"I remember her saying something about making her own tofu and almond milk, too," Nomi said when she saw John was also looking at the sink.

"Sure looks like it."

Their mother was not a cook. She had tried, but she could not get the hang of cooking, and did not enjoy it. Her kitchen was filled with whatever would make cooking, and cleaning up, more expedient. She liked to eat but did not like to prepare food. And at that time, the sixties and seventies, the idea that their father would cook was laughable. Besides, he was out at work all day in his law office, while their mother was mostly home, aside from her volunteer work, meetings, and social dates.

Nomi was somewhere between her mother and her sister. She did not spend much time in the kitchen, but when she did, she made salads and easily prepared dishes, with mostly grains and legumes. She was more likely to pick her own fruits and vegetables than bake her own bread—especially since the kibbutz had started buying whole wheat bread in addition to the standard white bread years ago—or try preparing complicated dishes. An avocado sandwich on toast with a salad on the side was a perfectly good dinner. Avi had loved to cook, though, so if someone would invest in preparing a more elaborate meal, it had usually been him.

The kibbutz provided breakfast and lunch in the dining room. Even during the height of the pandemic, before the vaccine, members did not have to cook those meals; they picked up food and took it home in plastic boxes during the lockdowns. All she need worry about was dinner, a light meal in Israeli culture—a lifestyle difference that suited Nomi. She liked going to sleep on a partially full stomach. She slept better, and it was better for sex, too.

Nomi missed sex, even if more often over the years she and Avi had gone straight to falling asleep in each other's arms when they got into bed. The hysterectomy had put Nomi through early menopause, and it had taken months for her to feel ready for penetrative sex again. The doctor did not want to give her hormones out of fear the cancer might return, but Jude had sent her Chinese herbs that helped manage that and other symptoms; when women her age were complaining of hot flashes, mood swings, and decreased libido, she was long past that and had settled into a peaceful relationship with her aging body.

But on the occasions she and Avi both had the energy and desire for making love, it was like renewing their commitment to each other without having to say a word. She could not imagine sex with anyone else. Even when she had found men handsome when Avi had been alive, she rarely felt attracted to them, and even now that Avi was gone, on the rare occasion she did feel an attraction she could not imagine being aroused by them. Or perhaps she could not imagine letting herself be aroused, even now with Avi gone. That would require relaxing, trusting, letting them into her private space.

This was something she could only imagine trusting Avi to do, because he was just so gentle and good. So generous and sensitive to her needs and apprehensions. The first time Avi had kissed her, he asked first. And he did the same with each new intimate step they took. He never started up with her in bed without asking, even after forty years of marriage. Even if she was half asleep. He knew her past and was sensitive to it. He never would have made her do anything she did not clearly want to do. He was her angel.

She knew she loved Avi like she had known nothing else so certainly in her life. With him, she had given herself completely. Nomi thanked God for sending him to her. But she did not forgive God for taking him away.

Perhaps one day she would be able to imagine being intimate with another man. Perhaps it was only a matter of time. But she was already toward the end of middle age. Even if she barely looked a day over forty-five, as people told her, by the time she could imagine letting another man touch her, who would even be interested? Besides, she didn't know if she had Avi's blessing. That felt essential, even if it was hard to explain why.

What distressed her most about his death, aside from her aching loneliness and feeling he had been cheated, was she did not know what Avi wanted of her now. There had been no chance to discuss anything, or even say goodbye. Just a few days after he tested positive for the virus, he complained he couldn't breathe. She called the kibbutz infirmary, and they called an ambulance, and that was the last time she saw him. She was not allowed onto the Corona ward, so they talked on the phone, until his situation got so bad, they had to put him on a ventilator, and she could only speak to him through the nurses.

She asked them to tell him how much she loved him and that he shouldn't worry, she'd be fine. She had said that only because she knew it would give him peace. But he couldn't talk then, so she had no way of knowing how he wanted her to continue without him.

Before she went under for her hysterectomy, she had asked Avi if he could imagine taking another lover if the surgery or the cancer killed her. She was shivering in her hospital gown and had asked a nurse to bring another blanket.

"How could I know? Why would you even ask such a thing?" he had said, rubbing her arms to warm her until the nurse returned.

"Because I don't think I could if you were the one who went first." She did not want to admit she was hoping he would say he felt the same way. It was an irrational thought, considering how young they both were. Of course, he would find someone after her. A thought that made her so sad, she had started crying on the gurney.

He had grinned. "More reason for you to stay alive longer than I do." He had stroked her hair and whispered into her ear like a lullaby, "Don't worry," squeezing her hand tightly. "I'm not letting you go so soon." That was the last thing she remembered, his whisper in her ear slowly fading away, as everything went black after that. Until she awoke after the surgery in a fog.

Now she played that scene over repeatedly in her head, trying to decipher his reaction, see if there was a hint between his words or in the expression on his face. Was his smile a teasing or an approving one? He had not said what he would do, and he had not told her what he would have wanted her to do if he died first. He had avoided a serious conversation. She was left with nothing, not even the faintest whisper in her ear.

Nomi opened the door to a screened-in-porch off the kitchen.

John followed. "You'll probably want to be alone now," she heard him say from behind her. "I'll just show you the porch and be on my way."

Nomi looked out at the backyard—overgrown grass with an assortment of trees and an old well; perhaps it was still functional. Beyond were orchards and fields, with woods to one side and smaller houses to the other.

"This was a regular porch that your sister screened in," John explained.

He sure knew a lot about the house.

"It looks lovely, for when the weather warms up." As these words escaped her lips, Nomi wondered if she'd be gone by then.

"There are glass windows, too, so you can even sit out here now if you want," he said, closing one sliding window after another. He picked up a space heater plugged into an electrical socket next to a swinging wicker love seat. Nomi noted its inviting thick cushion. "I assume she sat out here a lot."

Nomi looked around. She pictured her sister swinging while reading a book. There was even one on the table. "That wouldn't surprise me. She liked being outdoors as a kid. She didn't like being closed in. Not by walls and not by rules."

John chuckled but his eyes looked wistful and sad. He put his hand on the wrought iron handle of the springing door leading back to the kitchen. "I've outstayed my welcome. But I'm happy to help in any way I can."

Nomi followed him back into the kitchen. The door sprang shut behind her.

"You have the office number, but here's my cell," he said.

He wrote his number on a piece of notepaper and stuck it on the refrigerator with a magnet, one of those painted ceramic ones with an inspirational quote. Jude had a whole set of them, holding up various notes and photos of people Nomi did not recognize, except Jonah. There was one of Jude, too, with her arm around a snowperson it seemed she had built.

Now Nomi could see how her sister had looked as she neared sixty-five. She had not changed so much, considering the last time Nomi had seen her was when she was in her early twenties. The hair coming out from beneath her crocheted woolen hat was gray, and she had some wrinkles, but like Nomi, she had aged well.

There were a few pictures of a gray bearded man in a wheelchair, hanging on the fridge, too. He looked like a mix of hippie, lumberjack, and redneck, with a bear-like quality as well. Who was he?

While John was hanging the note, Nomi noticed her own name, phone number, and email stuck on the refrigerator, also with one of those magnets. This was the note John had been referring to which made it easy for him to reach her so quickly. There was a wedding ring on his left hand, the one he used to hang the note. Married with children. She wondered how many. What were their ages?

This was a game Nomi had started playing with herself when, about twenty years before, her ambivalences about having children had turned into regret, then longing. But she and Avi were too old by then to adopt, even if he had shown any interest and the kibbutz had approved. She imagined strangers' families instead. She played it to this day, only now she started adding grandchildren to the scenes. Her childlessness was no longer an open wound, but it was not yet closed, either.

"Give it a think before I go. If there's anything I can help with around here now. Do you know how to work the fireplace? It gets cold at night. I made the beds, changed the sheets, but there're extra blankets in the closet next to the bedrooms."

Again, she was touched by this man's thoughtfulness. Surely, preparing the house for her stay was not in his job description. "Thank you so much. But I don't think I can sleep in either of their bedrooms just yet. The couch looks comfortable enough for now."

"Your sister closed off all the house except this floor, to save on heating bills and maintenance. And she turned what was once a sitting room and a guest room on this floor into bedrooms. She did use the whole house once, for boarders."

So, he knew a lot about Jude, too. "Yes, so I understand."

"Those," he said, pointing to two doors next to the refrigerator which Nomi had assumed were a pantry and broom closet, "must lead to the staircases going up to the second floor and down to the Indian cellar."

"Indian cellar?"

"Yes. That's what they're called. Either they were built during the French and Indian War, or earlier, to hide from attack by the natives, who they called the Indians, as you know." He walked out of the kitchen, back through the dining room, and into the foyer.

Nomi followed.

"Shall I at least light you a fire? Especially if you're going to sleep out here," he said, turning his head toward the living room.

"I can manage the fireplace, I think."

"Up to you. I'm sure you'll have lots of questions, so don't hesitate to call. You'll have a lot to take care of. Things to sort through, the farm, the bills . . . Get death certificates. Meet with Jude's lawyer . . . Those matters."

John seemed distracted when he said this. Nomi wondered why.

"Consider me your go-to person, at least until you make some friends around here."

"Thank you."

"Everyone'll be happy to help. We're simple folk but friendly, and everyone knows everyone, even if these houses are far apart."

Nomi thought of the kibbutz, where the houses were close together and not only did everyone know everyone else, but they knew their business as well.

"Your sister was well liked," John continued. He looked down at his boots and then into her eyes. His were the green of a ripe olive still on the tree. "She helped a lot of people and families in the area, even if she kept mostly to herself after hours. Her name suited her."

Nomi did not understand. "How so?"

"Jude. It means praiseworthy. Saint Jude the Apostle—not to be confused with Judas, who betrayed Christ—is called the saint of lost causes. He took on the pain of others, like Jesus did."

Nomi winced at the words Jesus and Christ. Residue from her childhood when these were bad words. On the kibbutz, she could not remember hearing the words at all, not even in Hebrew.

So, John was a religious Christian, not surprising considering all the churches around. Her parents had never approved of her sister's choice of residence. "Living among the gentiles," they had called it, which was why it was especially ironic they had ended up living here as well. Nomi wondered if John frequented a church, and if Jude had found a synagogue to attend, at least on the High Holidays. Although even that would probably not have interested her, unless she had changed her views on organized religion over the years, which did not seem likely considering her request to be cremated.

"My sister was not a religious person. She chose the nickname because Judith sounded too religious—Jewish religious, I mean—and parochial. She considered herself a universalist."

"Maybe so. But she seemed quite spiritual, from what I could see. And principled."

"Yes. She was both."

Nomi felt familiar jealousy rising in her chest when John spoke of Jude this way. She had accomplished here what Nomi had been unable to accomplish on the kibbutz. Her sister was not only respected in this town, but she was accepted and appreciated to the point of admiration. From the way John spoke, she had perhaps even felt at home.

Nomi tried to imagine Jude living here among these people. As she had that thought, she knew it was her mother's voice she heard in her head. Her mother's words: "those people." Still, it was, indeed, such a gentile area. Full of what they had called WASPs and "townies" when she was a kid.

Hers and Jude's childhood sleepover camp had been around here. It was a Jewish camp, traditionally but not strictly religiously observant. It had attracted a mix of Jewish families from the greater Boston area; the one thing they had in common, besides being Jewish, was they were all wealthy enough to afford sleepover camp. There had been a gate to enter the camp and a fence around the campus. It was an upper middle class Jewish white-collar enclave amid a middle-to-lower-middle-class mostly blue-collar farming area. The people who lived on the other side of the fence were considered not just foreign, but inferior.

Like a self-imposed ghetto, Nomi thought to herself. It was the people on the inside who saw those on the outside as somehow lesser humans, not the other way around. She had experienced a similarly ironic sense of elitism on the kibbutz, but there it was toward "those capitalists" outside the kibbutz gates, despite the fact the kibbutz cooperated with that capitalist system in order to survive.

As much as her parents' "us" and "them" attitude irked her, she understood it, and even empathized with it. Of all places her sister could have chosen to live, this was an odd one. Was she a glutton for punishment, as her father liked to say? Or was she just so oblivious to the cultural differences that set her apart from these people? Nomi silently berated herself for thinking in her mother's terms again.

Nomi saw John to the door. She noticed him putting his hand on his revolver, which sat in a holster around his waist. It was hard to believe this gentle man carried a gun, let alone used it. But Avi had done the same when he went on military reserve duty every year. She imagined it was that same quality in Avi, his desire to protect what he loved, that had drawn this man to his line of work.

Being a drafted soldier, though, was different than choosing to be a police officer. Perhaps this had something to do with why she had known no Jewish police officers growing up. Or perhaps it had more to do with the relationship of the Jews in her town to where they lived. Not feeling it was totally theirs to protect, and not being certain they would be protected by their country and neighbors, either.

Like she had never met a Jewish farmer until she moved to Israel, she had never met a Jewish police officer, either, until then. At least, not that she knew.

John showed her where the keys to her sister's truck were hanging. "There's no security code. It's an old model. I checked the tank. There's plenty of gas. She's showing her age, though. It took me a few tries to get her started. I suggest you bring her in for a check."

Nomi had only the spending money the kibbutz had given her for the trip, and she had already used some to rent the car. The truck was a blessing. "I'll be sure to do that. Where do you recommend?"

"I'd trust Bill and Bill Junior with anything with wheels and a motor. They're next to the gas station in town."

When John was gone, Nomi took a quick look around the rest of the house—at least the part of it not closed off—and found the bedrooms that had once been a study and sitting room. The original owners of this house had slept upstairs, but she found it hard to imagine sleeping even in the downstairs bedrooms all alone in this house that had seen so much death.

Nomi found a fleece jacket hanging in the foyer. She took it from the hook and held it to her nose. It smelled of vinegar and rosemary. She hesitated. Jude may have worn it only ten days before, the day she died. But Nomi would have to get used to using her sister's things if she was going to be here and accomplish what she had been called upon to do. She took a deep breath and put on the jacket. It warmed her instantly, although far less than the hug she wanted to have received from Jude after walking through her front door. She let out her breath with a heavy sigh and closed her eyes to hold back tears.

Nomi went out to examine the grounds. There were a few steps leading down to the grass—covered in red, yellow, and orange leaves—which she crossed to examine the well. The fresh crisp air lifted her spirits, as did the sheer beauty of the place—the expanse, the vibrant colors. The well had a pump and a bucket. Nomi tried the pump, and water came out. "Cool!" she said aloud to no one. She wondered if the water was safe for drinking. Already, she had questions to ask John. It was good he had left his cellphone number.

In the orchards, Nomi identified peach and plum trees, as well as various strains of apple and pear. John had been right; there were still pears on a few trees, so she grabbed a basket next to a tree and filled it with fruit. She walked through Jude's extensive garden, where she was growing vegetables, squashes, and tubers. Nomi spotted the fennel. She'd have to come back to get what was left of it all before the first snow—something they did not have to worry about in the Israeli climate. A rake leaned against a tree; Nomi had used one to clean after the olive harvest before leaving for here but had not used one to rake autumn leaves since she was a teenager.

Next, she went out to the blueberry and cranberry patches and walked through the rows, examining the bushes turned crimson from the change of season. She'd come back out to pick what was left of the cranberries, but blueberry season was over. Behind the patches were woods to one side and farmland to the other, with smaller houses scattered on the land. These were the houses John mentioned had been for farmhands once.

She wondered if there were hiking trails in those woods, but she had not been hiking since Avi died. She was afraid to hike alone. Maybe she'd make a friend here to hike with.

The sun was setting, and Nomi's eyes were practically closing; her limbs were heavy from exhaustion. She had barely and only sporadically slept over the past forty-eight hours. At sixty, she couldn't abuse her body like she used to. It was time to go inside and rest.

Nomi brought the basket of pears up to the porch and placed it on the table. She'd start looking through her sister's closets and drawers later. She collapsed on the wicker swing, took off her boots, and put her feet up on a footrest. She imagined Jude coming in from outside, carrying a basketful of potatoes right from the ground to bake for dinner. Seeking a distraction, Nomi lifted the book on the glass table to examine it.

It was a hardback, titled *Life in a Box: A Mother's Journal in Hiding*. The plastic covering the book jacket, and the empty card-pocket inside, indicated it had once been a library book; Jude must have bought it in a neighborhood sale. Nomi opened the jacket and read the introductory pages. It was published in 1976 by a small press specializing in Holocaust memoir.

When she flipped through, she noticed just about every page had extensive underlining in pencil and a variety of placeholders: photographs, cards, magazine and newspaper clippings, and pieces of paper with writing and drawings. It looked like Jude, or Jonah, had been studying this volume, like a textbook or sacred document.

Perhaps one of them had been reading this book right before they sat down to their fatal meal. Goosebumps spread from Nomi's neck down her arms and back. She hoped their deaths were more peaceful than Avi's had been. Imagining him dying alone in that hospital was unbearable. At least Jude and Jonah had been together.

Nomi covered her feet and legs with a hand-knitted blanket—surely Jude's creation—she found on a wicker chair that matched the swing. She turned on the space heater and started reading. The book was a diary, written by a Jewish woman in hiding with her six-year-old son in Lwów during World War II, translated from Polish. The diary had been found in the mother and son's hiding place, an attic crawlspace so small there was no room for an adult to stand or even lay down, the introduction explained.

Batja and her son had hidden there for almost two years. But the diary began in September of 1939, before they went into hiding, when the Russians invaded Poland from the East and the Germans from the West.

> *Someone must document what is happening to our beloved Lwów, so I have decided to put pen to paper. The Russians invaded and Jakub has gone into hiding, lest he be sent to a work camp in Siberia, or even executed. My*

*hand is shaking as I write that word. I am so afraid for him, and I don't
know if I can manage this all on my own.*

Nomi knew what that was like, to be left on her own. And she did not even
have a child to keep her company. It would have been a huge responsibility to
care for a young child in such trying circumstances during the war, but at least
this woman, like Jude, had someone to care for, was not completely alone.

Nomi tried to continue reading but kept nodding off. She was woken a few
times by a scratching noise coming from below, although she was not sure if
it was real or just a disturbing dream. With all the talk of coffin parlors and
haunted houses, it would not be surprising for her to have nightmares. Each time
she awoke, she started reading again, but her eyelids were so heavy, she finally let
herself fully succumb to sleep's sweet relief.

CHAPTER 5

WHEN NOMI AWOKE, the book was on her stomach and the blanket pulled up to her neck. She was not on the porch. She was on the couch, in the living room. The coffin parlor, she thought, and grimaced. She did not remember having moved in the night; she had been so exhausted. And John had been right; it was cold in the house with no fire going.

She sat up and noticed pain in her neck and lower back. Sleeping on the couch had perhaps not been the best idea, but she was not about to sleep in one of the two bedrooms. She stood and stretched, touching her toes and moving her head around to relieve some of the stiffness. She looked at her watch: six am. She had slept until morning. At least she had avoided jet lag. She was famished and needed coffee and a shower, but first she went back out to the porch to make sure she had turned off the space heater.

There was only one full bathroom in this accessible part of the house, so she had no choice but to use it, even if it contained Jude and Jonah's intimate items: used wooden toothbrushes, all-natural creams and oils, a non-disposable bath sponge hanging in the shower. There was nothing resembling soap or shampoo, though. Only a glass bottle filled with a liquid that smelled of vinegar and rosemary, like the fleece jacket. Nomi had a vague memory of reading something somewhere about washing with vinegar. She tried it, while holding her breath.

In the kitchen, the closest thing to coffee was cocoa; the tea was all herbal, with no caffeine. She didn't care for instant coffee, anyway, and wouldn't have known how to work a coffee or espresso machine, even if Jude had one. So, she made a cup of cocoa with raw cane sugar she found in the cabinet. She ate oatmeal bars from a jar on the counter; that would tide her over until she could get a good cup of coffee in town. She would give the truck a try and drive back to where she had gotten that latte and sandwich and do some grocery shopping at the same time.

It was early, though. Things would not be open yet, and there was that pumpkin on the counter, sitting next to the crock pot. She could not find a cutting board, so she used a plate. Nomi cut the pumpkin into squares while frying onions on the stove-top, then put the pumpkin and onions into the pot with water, cinnamon bark, and fresh ginger she found in the freezer and grated into the mix.

By the time she finished, it was seven am. With any luck, the coffee shop would be open when she got there. She grabbed a couple of the pears she had picked the day before and headed out.

It took a few tries to get the truck started, and there was almost a full tank of gas, like John had said. Her sister's daily planner sat on the passenger seat beside her. She picked it up and opened it to the day's date. Tuesday November 30, 2021. Jude had three home-care patients. The names were clearly written, and Nomi easily found them listed with their phone numbers in the phonebook section.

Had anyone informed Jude's patients of her death? It had been a long holiday weekend for Thanksgiving, so any patients since last Wednesday probably had not expected her to show, anyway.

Someone should inform them. She'd call each one. Although some were probably not able to speak on the phone. Hopefully at least some had aides or relatives there to answer. She should call her mother's facility, too. As much as she dreaded it, she would have to make that trip. The thought made her heart race and her lungs tight.

Over a large latte, Nomi tried the first patient's number, her sister's eight am appointment. There was no answer. She decided to drive to the house. She put the address into Waze. It was only fifteen minutes away.

The house was in a more densely populated area. There was no farm, and there were no seasonal flowers out front, either, as opposed to the neighboring houses, which all had a nice display. It was a brick house with weathered wooden trimmings. The blue paint on the door was peeling. There was a mangled motorcycle in the driveway with flowerpots decoratively placed around and on it with a sign that read: *Harley Davidson (1982-2019), Man's Best Friend.*

Nomi lifted the brass knocker and knocked twice. No answer. She tried again. Still no answer. Her sister's patients all needed home visits, even if some were not terminally ill. She went back to her car to warm up and decide what to do. Back in the driver's seat, she moved her head around to relieve her neck muscles, still sore, while considering her options. After listening to a few songs on the radio and rubbing her hands together to keep them warm—she'd have to start taking gloves when she went out—she called the next patient, the ten am. A woman picked up.

"Hello."

"Hello. Am I speaking to Anne Williams?"

"This is Beth Williams, her daughter. My mother's not able to come to the phone." This woman, too, had that strong accent Nomi remembered from her childhood.

"Yes, of course. I'm calling about her nurse, Jude. Judith Rappaport. She . . . well, she won't be able to come today, or anymore at all. You see, she died. Tragically." Nomi hadn't expected to blurt it out like this, but she had not had to say these words yet to anyone who knew her sister, except the nurse at her mother's facility.

"Yes, I know. It was all over the local news. Terrible story. I can't imagine. She was such a special woman."

Nomi closed her eyes and took in a breath. "She was my sister."

"Oh, poor dear," Beth said after a moment of silence. "She told me she had a sister. In Israel."

"Yes. That's me. I came to sort through her things. It's all mine now, it seems."

"That would make sense, with her son gone, too, and her mother in that home."

Nomi leaned forward and rested her elbow on the steering wheel. "You seem to know a lot."

"She'd been taking care of my mother for over a year now. My mother had a stroke. She can't talk. It's not easy to be around her. When Jude came, I was happy for the company. Especially during Covid lockdown." That explained the woman's chattiness. And with the same last name as her mother, maybe she had never married or moved out. "She didn't talk about herself much. But when I asked, she told me. Mostly, she listened. Your sister was a good listener."

Despite John's respect for her sister, this surprised Nomi. Their correspondences were not conversations. Jude sent out information and snippets of wisdom but never asked how Nomi felt and never shared how she felt, either. "I hadn't seen her for many years. I knew her mostly as a teenager. And an email correspondent. She was a good listener?"

"Yes, she was. Even though my mother couldn't talk, Jude listened to her, too. She could sit and listen through the silence. Or even *to* the silence. She's the only one besides me who was able to get through to my mother. It'll be hard to find a replacement. The agency said they'd send someone new this week. But it won't be the same."

"Agency?"

"Yes. She worked with a home hospice agency. I called them as soon as I saw the news. They said they'd send someone over after the holiday weekend. I assume they would have called me if I hadn't called them first."

"Right." Of course. Jude had worked with an agency who would inform her patients if they hadn't already seen the story somewhere. She hadn't thought of that, either. "I guess you didn't need me to call, then. I wasn't sure her patients would know."

"That was kind of you."

Was she being kind? Or was she just doing what needed to be done?

"You're welcome to call any time if you need help with anything. You must be here alone. I just remembered now, about your husband. Jude told me when it happened. This virus, it's cruel. Come over some time, even, for tea. You'll need a mask. I'm being careful with my mother. I'm sure I don't need to tell you about that. Please don't hesitate to call. You have my number."

"Thank you," she said, but she doubted she would.

And Nomi would not need to call her sister's patients to inform them of her sister's death, after all. That was a relief. Or was it?

As much as it irked her to hear about her "special" sister, she found herself wanting to hear more. Her sister was dead, and so was her father. And her mother was losing her faculties. Perhaps she didn't need to feel threatened by them anymore. Making Nomi an heir was a generosity. Why did she perceive it as an attempt to control her life?

So, she did not need to bother this Frank person, or any of Jude's patients. She looked at her sister's afternoon appointments, anyway—was she avoiding the inevitable visit to her mother?—and then flipped to the next day. Frank was listed again at eight am. She looked to the day after that and saw his name there, too. He was down nearly every day of the month at eight am, and many evenings as well. She'd try knocking on his door one more time. This man must have known her sister well. If he didn't answer, she'd leave it at that, although she did want to talk to him.

Nomi went back to the door and knocked again. Still no answer. If he was expecting Jude, shouldn't he be home? Or had he, too, heard the story from the local news?

She walked on the front lawn, overgrown and full of weeds, to the closest window. She leaned in over neglected hydrangea and juniper shrubbery and peeked through the glass. A man was sitting in the living room with a knitted blanket over his lap and legs. He looked familiar, but Nomi could not place where she had seen him. It looked as if he was meditating, with headphones on.

No wonder he wasn't answering. He looked okay, so she decided she could go and leave a note in the mailbox. She found a pen and scrap of paper in the car and wrote a note, but while she was putting it into the mailbox, she heard a voice from inside. "Coming. Just a minute. Who's there?"

"I'm Nomi Erez, or Naomi Rappaport . . . Judith Rappaport, Jude's sister. I came to see if you're okay."

There was the sound of a lock being unbolted, and then the door opened. The man with the headphones was sitting in an electric wheelchair in front of her. "Not easy to maneuver the door in this thing."

His accent was not as strong as John's. More hick, less refined. His tattoos and ear piercing suggested that as well.

"Did you say you're Jude's sister? The one who lives in Israel?" he asked. He had bags under his blood-shot eyes.

This man, too, knew about Nomi. She wasn't sure why it surprised her Jude had spoken about her with patients. "Yes. I came back to the U.S. to go through her things."

"I see. I suppose someone should. It's not like I could do it."

What did he mean by that? Nomi looked more closely at him. He was broad shouldered, with a full gray beard and long gray hair, pulled back into a ponytail. He had a red bandana tied on like a hat. His skin was wrinkled, rough and worn, as if he had spent much time out in the wind and sun.

Nomi realized where she had seen him before. He was the one on Jude's refrigerator. What was this man's relationship with her sister?

"May I come in?"

The man—Frank, Nomi reminded herself—rolled back in his wheelchair so Nomi could enter. She put on her mask and walked over the threshold. The house smelled of burning incense and hickory wood. There was a fire in the woodburning stove in the living room.

Frank fumbled for his mask. It matched the red bandana on his head, and Nomi saw it was hand-sewn, probably from an old bandana. "It makes sense you showed up. But I'm still somewhat in shock." He put the mask on with shaking hands.

Nomi saw his chest heave beneath his Harley sweatshirt. His eyes filled with tears. "I shouldn't be surprised. We all go when it's time. And Jude was even preparing for it. But it's still hard to digest."

Nomi blinked, not sure she had heard correctly. "Preparing for it? I don't understand."

"That was part of the work we did together." His hands were in his lap. He was wringing them.

"Work? Is that why you're on her calendar every morning?"

"Yes. We did our morning meditation together. She was my nurse after I had the accident—"

"Accident?" He was speaking as if she knew—or should know—more than she did.

"A motorcycle accident. I was a serious biker before this," Frank said, spreading his arms to reveal his inert and atrophied legs. He pointed to the photos hanging on the wall. There was one of him on a Harley-Davidson with a smiling red-haired woman next to him, on her own bike. There was also a photograph of

Frank in a firefighter uniform. "I was a firefighter, too. Since the accident, I can't do either."

"So, my sister was your nurse?"

"Yes. But now she's more like a friend." He caught himself. "I mean, she *was* more like a friend. But more than a friend, really. A special friend. If you know what I mean." His voice choked and the tears started flowing and were absorbed into his mask. "I know it may come as a surprise to you, at our age and me like this." He looked down at his lap.

Nomi wasn't certain what he was implying. Were they lovers? His legs were clearly paralyzed. She wondered if he could move or feel at all from the waist down.

"You were a couple?" Nomi asked, and added without thinking, "Jude never mentioned you to me." At least not more than any part of her life. There were the photographs on the refrigerator, though.

Frank collected himself. "We hadn't made a formal commitment or anything, but we were very fond of each other."

"I understand. I'm sorry. I didn't mean to be hurtful." Nomi approached this man who had apparently been her sister's companion and lover. She wanted to comfort him but didn't know how.

"As I said, I'm still taking it in. I've been doing inner work to learn to accept things as they are. We worked on that together. But I really don't know how I'll manage it without Jude." He wiped his teary eyes with his sweatshirt. "I'm sorry I'm crying like a baby, but—"

"No need to apologize. Really. I didn't realize you were companions. I lost my husband this year, too. To Covid. I know how hard it is. Here, let me bring you a glass of water."

Nomi went to the kitchen, not a separate room, but a section of the main living area. The counters were unusually low. She filled a glass with water from the sink, brought the water back to Frank, and watched him drink it down quickly, his Adam's apple undulating as he swallowed. His hands were large, his fingers thick, and his sweatshirt sleeves pushed up to his elbows. His muscular, hairy forearms were covered with tattoos.

If he had been Jewish, he would not have put tattoos there—because of the numbers tattooed onto the forearms of concentration camp inmates; at least not if he were a Jew with any sensitivity, which it seemed he had.

"Do you want to sit down?" Frank asked.

He wheeled himself to the living area, and Nomi hesitated, wondering if he had a preferred place to sit. Would he bother to lift himself from his chair to sit on a piece of furniture? He did not make a move to transfer himself, so Nomi chose the lounge chair directly across from him and sat down. He stayed in his wheelchair.

"So, you meditated together? Can you tell me more about that? About Jude. We'd lived so far apart all these years . . ."

Frank sighed. "When I came back home after rehab, Jude was my nurse. But even then, she was more than a nurse. More like a therapist. Both, really." He choked on his words, then composed himself.

She scanned the room as he talked, looking for traces of Jude.

"I was depressed. I didn't want to keep living. But I was also afraid of death. I was in a terrible state. She introduced me to Buddhist meditation. I joined her sangha, too. It meets once a week. We have a teacher who lives in India. It's online. He has students around the world. The sangha changed my life. *Jude* changed my life."

She spotted, folded on the couch, the knitted blanket she had seen through the window draped on Frank's legs. Now that she thought of it, it looked like the one she had slept with the night before. She wondered if Jude had slept here sometimes, and if Frank had slept at her house.

Then she saw a photograph of Jude, in a frame on the fireplace. Jude in her pickup truck, with her hand against the window, apparently trying to stop Frank from snapping the picture. Laughing. She looked so alive it was hard to believe she was really gone. Nomi wondered how it was for Frank to look at that photo now.

After Avi had died, Nomi could not look at his photo without crying. Even now it was hard.

"I'm so sorry. She was my sister, but I didn't know her like you did."

"That doesn't surprise me. Jude was a private person. I never saw her house. She told me about it, but I never went there. I never even met her son."

"Really?" That was odd. It was strange for her sister to have a secret tryst. Why would she have needed to keep Frank from Jonah? Or was it just because of Covid he had never been to her house?

"Jude wasn't your typical person. It's hard to explain. She didn't talk for the sake of talking—if you know what I mean. When she told you something, it was for a reason. And when she didn't, it was for a reason, too. You could sense that about her."

Had Nomi misjudged her sister? This description did fit, but the things she found irritating were the very things this man had appreciated.

Frank wiped his eyes again. "I'm sorry I can't offer you anything. I'm not really in a condition for company now."

She leaned forward and put her hand on the poor man's knee, which felt bony, even beneath his jeans. "Do you need anything? What can I do to help?"

"No, nothing. She wasn't really my nurse anymore. I'm self-sufficient now. She helped me get the house set up for that—" His arms did look very strong.

"I didn't mean to imply—" He had misunderstood. She would have offered help even if he was not disabled. At least she thought she would.

"I'd like to be alone now if you don't mind. I know I invited you to sit, but I really can't face anyone just yet."

Nomi knew how he felt. She still felt that way to some extent.

"Of course." Nomi stood and started towards the front door. "But give me a call if you think of anything. Please. I'd like to stay in touch."

Frank rolled after her. "Sure. I'll see you out."

At the door, Nomi gave Frank her number. He saved it in his phone. She left and heard the door close behind her.

Like her, Frank was alone. Should Nomi have let her sister help her, too, when she had the chance?

As she tried starting the truck a few times, Nomi decided it was time to see her mother.

When the engine finally caught, she put the address into Waze.

CHAPTER 6

NOMI'S MOTHER WAS sitting on her bed. She was looking out the window, her back to Nomi, her hair white and thin and pulled up into a small bun. She wore black slacks, a magenta sweater with the collar of a print blouse folded over it at the neckline, and sneakers—something Nomi had never seen her wear.

"Mom," she said.

Her mother turned her head.

Nomi would not have picked this woman out of a crowd as the mother she had last seen over forty years ago, but when she examined her face, she saw traces; that woman had been glamorous and well-pruned: the fine features, thin lips, gray eyes, and defined chin. She was even wearing the pearl necklace Nomi remembered her grandmother, Nomi's great-grandmother, Jude's namesake Yehudis Gittel, had bequeathed her, with an amethyst brooch pinned to her collar, and matching earrings. Either the nurses were especially attentive, or her mother still had enough of her faculties to accessorize.

Nomi looked more like their mother, and Jude their father, even if people had often confused them. Jude had her father's brown eyes and fuller, rounder features. But they had shared the same wavy chestnut hair and body type—thin but sturdy, medium height, muscular-yet-still-feminine build. The shape of their faces was the same, too. They even shared certain movements and gestures; or so people had said. She wondered if that would still have been true. She would never know.

Nomi understood why people had mistaken her for Jude, yet her parents said they did not understand. "You're like night and day," they'd say, implying Jude was night and Nomi day—like the bad witch and the good witch from *The Wizard of Oz*, one of her favorite childhood films. Until she shattered their image, that is; then she and Jude began to meld, until, eventually, they swapped places.

Her mother looked at her quizzically, then her eyes brightened. "You're finally here. I've been waiting for you to come back. How long has it been? Come, sit down," she said, gesturing to the chair by her bed.

Nomi made her way, slowly, to her mother's bedside. It was hard to tell how lucid she was. On the phone, some days she seemed totally with it, and others she could barely remember who or where she was. She was also good at faking it.

"You should put up your mask first," she told her mother, who looked around, confused. "It's around your neck."

Her mother put her hand to her neck and felt the mask but still looked perplexed. "Mask? Why would I need a mask of all things? And why on earth are you wearing one?"

Her mother had to be reminded constantly about anything that had not happened either decades or minutes ago. "It's for germs. It's the regulation here." She would not mention the pandemic; that would only alarm her. "Here, let me help you." Nomi leaned over to help her mother. Then she added, "It's been a long time, Mom. Too long. But it's not just my fault, you know."

Nomi was surprised by an urge to crack her knuckles, a habit she had broken years ago, after marrying Avi. Her mother had hated it. Nomi stopped herself.

"Well, no need to be so dramatic. I managed. Where have you been, anyway?"

Nomi sat in the chair her mother had indicated. It was metal-framed, and had a plastic seat covered with an embroidered cushion, which Nomi assumed Jude had made. "You know, Mom. Israel. On the kibbutz."

"Visiting your sister?"

Nomi's heart missed a beat. She hesitated. With the mask and her mother's dementia, it was not so surprising. This would buy her more time. "I was with Naomi. Yes."

"How is she?" She asked automatically, with no emotion Nomi could detect.

Nomi had gotten into the routine of calling her mother at least once a week, yet she seemed to have no recollection of their recent conversations. Nomi wondered if she even remembered Avi had died.

Nomi put her hair behind her ears and felt the straps of the mask, so let the hair fall back in her face. She must look a mess to her mother. But at least in her mother's head it would be Jude who would receive the criticism.

"Not so good, since Avi died." She looked at her mother but could not tell what she was thinking. She had always been good at putting on various masks—but not the literal kind—depending on her surroundings.

"It's been hard for her," Nomi went on. "He wasn't just her husband. He was her best friend. Her only real friend." She shifted in her chair. "With no kids, and no family in Israel, he's really all she had. It's a shame you never visited her, Mom. The kibbutz is nice. I think you'd like some things about it."

Nomi's mother shifted her position too. "Maybe so—"

Now that she'd started, she couldn't stop. "I mean, you had many years when you could have gone to visit. You never even met her husband, Mom. And now it's too late." She felt childish and wished she could have taken back that last comment. But it was too late for that, too.

Perhaps if there had been grandchildren, her parents would have put the past aside, gotten on a plane, and visited. As if providing legitimate offspring would have proven her purity or innocence, or at least acted as a consolation prize or gesture toward reconciliation. But there weren't—not even an "illegitimate" one. And Nomi herself was still so traumatized by her sudden fall from grace that even she thought her childlessness could be a punishment from God.

Her mother put on her reading glasses, hanging on a chain around her neck, and took a better look at Nomi, who thought this would be the end of her charade. "This doesn't sound like you at all. Your sister is the judgmental one."

Nomi let out a sigh of relief. Her mother still did not recognize her. Yet, it stung to know her mother had Nomi stamped this way indelibly in her memory. Any real relationship between them had ended when Nomi left, whereas her mother's relationship with Jude had developed since then.

"There you go, typecasting us again. Will it never end?" Where had that come from?

It baffled Nomi how her parents had packaged and labeled their daughters like products for sale. Although, truth be told, their tendency toward this had rubbed off on Nomi. The more she heard of her sister's virtues, the more she became convinced she could never live up to her example.

Jude had put resentments aside and cared for their parents. And despite her difficult financial circumstances and responsibilities as a single mother, she had not only become self-sufficient and built a rich life for herself, but she was Glinda—or rather, Gittel—the Good Witch of Northville who flew in to save the day; her sister had lived up to her middle name after all.

"Did visiting your sister affect you, Judith? Anyway, I'm in no condition to jump on a plane. I don't even know if they let us out of this place," she said, looking around in confusion.

Did her mother even know where she was? Or was she just keeping up a good face—another one of her talents? These traits were serving her especially well now.

"If someone should make the trip, it should be your sister."

Nomi was tempted to reveal her identity and tell her mother she had, in fact, made the trip. But she could not bring herself to face her mother, let alone reveal her favored daughter, Judith, was gone. "Well, you can call her. Why does she always have to call you?" she said, instead. She was ashamed of the whine in her voice. Besides, could her mother even manage making a phone call now? Nomi knew she was reverting to teenagerhood, but she could not help herself.

Her mother shook her head. "You know I'm not one to pick up the phone."

Nomi kept pushing. "You could even apologize. Naomi told me how hurt she is you never did that. It's never too late, you know." She looked directly at her mother.

Her mother's cheeks grew red, and Nomi recognized that defensive look. "Apologize? I refuse to take all the blame. She never came to visit. Not once. Not even when your father was dying. She didn't even come to his funeral!"

It was difficult to predict what her mother would recall on any given day, but apparently, she remembered Nomi's shortcomings. Selective memory, perhaps. Was there such a thing with dementia? Was it possible her mother was only remembering what served her conscience?

Her mother was shaking. She was wringing her wrinkled, gnarled hands with their loose-fitting rings and becoming increasingly agitated as she spoke, not what Nomi had wanted. She put her hand on her mother's, which was cold but soft to the touch. Veins bulged beneath her fingers. Then Nomi remembered the Coronavirus and took her hand away. As much as she resented her mother, she did not want to make her sick.

"Naomi has her reasons." Nomi sighed. "She has no money, and she has a life on the kibbutz. And responsibilities. Besides, it's not so easy to get permission and funds to travel." She paused. The kibbutz would have paid her airfare for a parent's funeral, and yet, she had not even asked. Now, she wanted to stop talking, but she couldn't. "She's still upset at you, Mom. And at Dad. For abandoning her. She never forgave you for that. She still doesn't."

"Well, then. It's mutual," her mother said, fingering the buttons on her cardigan nervously. "Now please fetch me some tea. You can bring yourself some, too, Judith. Don't forget the sugar. You know I like it with two teaspoons."

Relieved to get a break from her mother, Nomi stood. "Sure, Mom. Anything else?" She tried not to show the hurt in her voice.

"No. That'll do just fine."

Nomi went to ask for tea at the nurse's station. She found the restroom as well and washed her hands thoroughly with antiseptic. Her mother was right. There was resentment and hurt on both sides. Better to leave it alone. Better to let her mother think she was Jude, whom her parents had not only forgiven completely but who had become their savior. She may not have been religious, but she was certainly better at the Fifth Commandment than Nomi was. Why upset her mother?

When Nomi came back with two cups of tea on a tray, her mother looked at her quizzically again. Then she seemed angry.

"Judith, where have you been? Your father just called and said it was time for me to come home. How long have I been in this place? I don't need a vacation anymore. The service is terrible, and I don't know anyone here. I want to go home."

"I'm sorry, Mom. I don't know how to take you home." Where was home, anyway? "I don't think I can. Here. Have some tea."

Nomi placed the teacup on a small bedside table. Her mother's hands were shaking. She tried lifting the cup, but her hands were too unsteady.

Nomi helped her drink. Her mother dabbed at her lips with a handkerchief she had in the pocket of her sweater. It had her initials embroidered onto it: E.R. Edith Rappaport. More of Jude's handiwork.

"Now, how's that? Any better?" Nomi asked.

"It does taste good. A little tea always hits the spot." She looked at Nomi again, but this time blankly. "I don't think I know you, but I am grateful for the service. I don't remember ordering tea, but I guess it must be teatime here now. If it's no bother, just sit with me for a while. I'm feeling a little lightheaded. I don't think I should be alone."

CHAPTER 7

NOMI SMILED AT the smell of the pumpkin soup when she walked in. The aroma reminded her of Thanksgivings from her childhood, an American holiday, not celebrated in Israel. Her last Thanksgiving dinner had been the year she left, when her relationship with her parents was still good. It was Jude they had been angry with then.

They had asked Jude to come home for the holiday, but they had not expected her to show up with her boyfriend Greg (who later became Jonah's father) from the commune—both in flair jeans, he in an "Anita Bryant Needs Cunt" T-shirt and she in a "Harvey Milk for President" one. Nomi had been quiet during most of the meal, while her father argued politics with Jude and Greg, and her mother tried to change the subject.

When her parents had seen the last relatives out the door, her mother said, "Well, that was some position to put us in, bringing him here like that." She looked as if she had just eaten a lemon.

"Like what?" Jude and Nomi were clearing the table, and each had brought a stack of plates to the kitchen.

Their parents followed them. Nomi did not know where Greg had gone. Perhaps to find a place to smoke a joint.

"You know what your mother means, young lady," their father had grunted.

Jude practically dropped the stack of plates onto the kitchen counter and turned to face her parents, who were moving in on her. "You asked me to come home. Greg is my boyfriend." She put her hands on her hips. "If he's not welcome here, we'll both be going."

Their father answered while their mother pursed her lips. "You know how we feel about you dating outside the faith. The least you could do is show up without the show. This is our house, and that was our family. Your family. You embarrassed us and yourselves."

"Well, if I'm an embarrassment, I don't need to stick around. This is who I am. Take it or leave it."

Their mother looked at their father before answering. "You heard your father. This is our house. When you're here, you live by our rules. No smoking, no drinking, no profanity on your clothing."

"Rules. That's all you care about around here. Rules and what everyone will think. I have more important things on my mind. I can't live that way. I'm out of here," Jude said as she exited the kitchen without even a glance back at their parents.

"Why are you wasting your time with this low-life gentile, Judith?" their mother called after her. "When are you going to come to your senses and realize what's really important?"

But Jude just grabbed her bag and left, with her mother's question hanging in the air. Nomi assumed her sister had gone out to find Greg and hitchhike back to Northville. That was Jude's last Thanksgiving with their parents, until their reconciliation when their father's health issues began, and she took charge of his care. She had answered her mother's rhetorical question and "come back to her senses" in the end.

Nomi placed the bag of groceries she had bought at the local convenience market on the counter and put them away. She had not gotten the truck checked nor called Jude's lawyer, but it had been a draining enough day without either.

With a bowl of soup and what looked like home-made crackers from the pantry, she went out to the porch. She plugged in the heater, picked up Batja's diary, and started where she had left off.

October 23, 1939

Izaak and I had to leave the apartment on Plac Smolki and everything in it. It was generous of cousins Chawa and Nachszon to offer us shelter. I never imagined I'd one day be turning to my poor working-class relatives for help. Russian soldiers have moved into our beautiful home by now. I can only imagine what they will do to our furniture, our china. Poor Ada and Ninka helped me pack up Izaak and some clothing for our move, and that was the last we saw of them and our charmed life.

Luckily Jakub had been smart enough to give our silver, jewelry, and savings to someone he trusts for safe keeping. If something happens to Jakub, he says (I tried to be strong when he said that but I broke down nonetheless) and the Russians leave and it is safe to be a bourgeois property owner again, this person will find me and Izaak. It is dangerous for me to know who and where this person is, like I cannot know where Jakub is. He has always been so smart that way. Precautious yet courageous, too. I don't deserve him. I am not nearly as brave or shrewd as he is. What would I do without him? What WILL I do without him? I don't know.

<u>Perhaps we should have gone to Palestine like Jozef when we still could.</u> <u>But I am not as hearty or adventurous as my Halutz brother.</u> There's malaria there, and I am not cut out for kibbutz farm work. That was always the

difference between us. I liked the city, culture. He liked to be outdoors and work with his hands.

How I wish everything could be like it was on Plac Smolki. Not only do I not have Jakub, but no governess or housekeeper, either. I don't know if I will be able to manage. How I miss our dinner parties, the theater, the opera, museums. How quickly things can change, before one even has a chance to appreciate them while one has them. I loved our life, and now it is gone. That is the life I was made for. Not working the land in Palestine, and not stuck in this tiny, shabby apartment in the poor part of town. Certainly not without Jakub to take charge when I can't handle things.

It was hard for Nomi to continue reading, not only because she knew the horror to come, but also because she found Batja grating. Nomi empathized more with the woman's brother, Jozef, who apparently had left to join a kibbutz in Palestine before the Russians even invaded. Batja reminded Nomi more of herself before she had left her pampered life for the kibbutz.

Had Batja really considered her elitist bourgeois status in Poland worth risking her and her child's life? Couldn't she see what was coming? Was it so beneath her to go to Palestine and get her hands dirty? Nomi could not fathom why her sister or nephew had found this diary worth annotating. But they had, so there must be something to it.

Nomi, too, had been comfortable in her upper-middleclass life. Like her parents, she had envisioned a house in the suburbs with a husband who had at least two post-high school degrees. Avi had gone straight from high school to the army and back to working in the kibbutz fields after he was released from service. He was not the husband she had envisioned for herself; her kibbutz cottage was not the house she had envisioned for herself, either.

Would Nomi, too, have stayed, trying to cling to her disintegrating life, had she lived in Europe when Batja did? She had only left home because she felt she had no choice. But once she was on the kibbutz, living a life not so different from Batja's brother's, she saw how privileged her childhood had been, and how wasteful and elitist. Of course, no one deserved to be murdered by the Nazis, but it was hard for her to muster sympathy for this woman.

There was more to it than that. Nomi caught herself these past two days wondering what could have been had she not left in such a hurry, even regressing to the Nomi she had left behind in the suburbs so many years ago. It made her wonder if she had fully left her behind. Had the possibility she might rediscover this abandoned self—a thought lingering somewhere in her unconscious—been one of the factors preventing her from returning to visit sooner? Had she been afraid she, Nomi Erez, might turn back into Naomi Rappaport—or at the very least miss her—if she set foot again on Massachusetts soil?

Nomi heard that scratching noise from below. Even if there was no spirit haunting the house, there did seem to be an animal in the space beneath the porch. There was a floor under this one—the Indian Cellar John had called it—and a whole upper floor Nomi had not yet explored. She put the book down and went to the kitchen.

The two locked doors in the kitchen were of wood, painted white. Beneath the brass doorknobs were old keyholes, for a skeleton housekey. Nomi rummaged through the kitchen drawers to no avail. She'd have to call a locksmith. She added that to her to-do list.

Now was a good time as any to look through some of her sister's clothing. She could just about manage it. Not like when Avi died; she had gone to the communal clothing exchange and taken from there, instead of from their shared closet. Over these past nine months, she had only gone into their bedroom to fetch the most necessary items, and she had avoided looking around. She had kept her eyes closed or shielded, could not face their bed without him in it. She had slept on the couch, like she was doing now. Finally, when she had been packing to leave for the airport, she forced herself to go to their closet. If not for this trip, she would not have done it.

Nomi went to her sister's bedroom. She and Jude had once shared shoe and clothing sizes, although their tastes in both were different back then. On the kibbutz, the clothing was practically one-size-fits-all. Avi had joked it was more like "one size fits none," which became their private code any time a kibbutz committee or general assembly meeting took a decision best for the collective but bad for the individual.

Nomi approached the closet and opened the door. It smelled of cedar and moth balls, which uncannily felt like a kind of communication from her sister. Some of her breath remaining in the house. She shoved that irrational thought aside as she pushed her sister's nursing uniforms, hanging in the closet, aside. There was no such thing as ghosts.

Nomi undressed and chose a flannel shirt from the rack. It was soft and comfortable. Next, she chose a pair of her sister's jeans, which slipped on easily and were so worn they were starting to fray.

Instead of Jude wearing the jeans to death, it had been the other way around. What a depressing thought. But Nomi was used to depressing thoughts and second-hand clothing—and third-, fourth-, and fifth-hand clothing as well—some of which had been worn by dead kibbutz members. Although not Avi's.

She'd left his clothing in their closet for the foreign workers. It had been too painful to remove it.

The only item she had taken was the work shirt Avi had worn that day he came to check on her with her twisted ankle and they had sat outside her cabin talking. That was her favorite. Often when he wore that shirt, she waited impatiently for their workday to be over so she could take him to bed.

Nomi's eyes welled up at the mere thought of Avi; yet going through her sister's clothing did not have that effect. She had not had a real cry yet for her sister. She had not seen her in so long, so looking at her clothing now brought Jude to life, in a way, more than it made Nomi miss her.

Drying her eyes with her sister's shirt sleeve, she spotted a pair of good hiking boots, necessary if she did find a hiking partner or get up the courage to venture into the woods alone—an unlikely scenario. She tried them on. Her image in a full-length mirror on the closet door came into focus as she blinked away what was left of her tears.

Nomi examined her reflection. After a proper shower, even with vinegar, her graying hair looked thicker and wavier, more like she remembered Jude's. Her own hair had been thicker and wavier back when she had last seen Jude, too. No matter what her parents said, she and Jude had looked alike.

Nomi's hips were wider now, but her figure looked especially good for her age. Perhaps because she had never been pregnant or given birth. Yet, Jude's jeans fit perfectly. Her sister had retained her figure as well, it seemed. She had only had one child, and she was such a health nut. Her clothing fit Nomi perfectly and was just what she was used to wearing.

Working out in the fields and orchards, Nomi dressed in what was durable and practical. She did not feel a need to dress up, and Avi said he preferred her with casual clothing or no clothing at all.

Nomi smiled to herself, remembering how he'd say that. Would she always be able to access memories of him so easily?

Is this how Jude had looked standing here in front of this very mirror? Nomi started to tremble, literally quivering in her sister's boots. She had aspired to stand in her sister's shoes when she was younger. Now, however, she was not sure she wanted to.

Nomi leaned her back against the closet wall and slid down; she sat on the floor weeping into her sister's shirt. Was she crying for Avi, or for Jude and Jonah? Maybe for all three.

When Nomi finished, her head was pounding. She stood up. That was enough crying for now.

She would not need to shop for winter clothing; she would not pack up her sister's clothing to donate to the Salvation Army. She would simply wear it now and worry about what to do with it later, when she left.

She could imagine leaving, but she could not imagine anywhere she'd want to go.

CHAPTER 8

NOMI SPENT THE next few days getting her morning coffee in town and visiting her sister's patients—to hear more about the adult sister she never knew, but also because she felt most comfortable these days with others to whom life had not been kind.

She met Liz, a forty-five-year-old woman with terminal lung cancer; Jo, who was recovering from triple bypass surgery; Sue, with Parkinson's; Ed, with Alzheimer's. Some were on their way to at least partial recovery, while others were on their way out of this life. She even visited Anne and her chatty daughter Beth, who, indeed, had never married or had kids and was lonely caring for her mother.

She had not understood how her sister chose this profession. Nomi preferred working with plants. But now she felt drawn to these people, who were living life at its most raw, as she was. The sick, the dying, and the grieving and lonely club.

Nomi was living on a different plane now that Avi was gone. She had already felt different on the kibbutz, being the only English speaker. Then, later, as the only childless married woman. While there were plenty of other widows on the kibbutz—Israel was a society that went from war to war—being the childless American widow put her so far outside the realm of anyone else's experience that she had retreated even more into herself.

Jude's patients were suffering, the same club's criteria for entry. And Jude had been their bridge to the world of the not-yet-suffering, or to the world of those who had made it through and were waiting for the next wave to hit.

Despite her resentments, Nomi found she welcomed hearing about her sister from these people. It was filling in a picture of Jude beyond her emails. All her patients shared a deep appreciation for Jude, which must have been affirming for her sister, after not receiving that from their parents growing up. Although her mother had since relied on Jude, Nomi doubted she showed gratitude or affection. More likely, she considered this Jude's duty.

Nomi would go back to visit her mother soon. Perhaps this time her mother would recognize her. But what if she didn't? What if she again mistook her for Jude? Would Nomi have the courage to reveal her identity? Was that even the best thing to do? The news of Jude's death would likely confuse her more, make her lucid moments less frequent. Who would it serve to tell the truth? Why not let her go on thinking Jude was alive and Nomi still far away?

Nomi drank the last bit of her latte and put the number into her phone to call "Lisa," a name she had seen on Jude's schedule already a couple of times, but "John Police Officer" appeared on her screen. She hung up. Assuming it was a mistake, she tried again. But the same thing happened. She checked the numbers; they were identical. Strange. Maybe numbers around here were similar, and she had made a mistake while putting his number into her phone.

These past few days, John had sat with her briefly when he spotted her sitting at the coffee shop, on his way into the station. He rode up on his police motorcycle—apparently, the police car stayed parked at the station overnight—took off his helmet, put on his police hat, and sat down at her table, as if they had planned to meet. He seemed as happy for the company as she was. But she had not seen him today. Maybe he had come in early and was already in his office working. She'd knock on the door of the police station to get his actual number. Then she'd call Lisa's number again.

But John was not at the station. Another man opened the door. When he introduced himself as John's deputy, Tom, Nomi thanked him for returning her rental car.

"Is John here?" she asked. Should she have called him Officer Brooks?

"No. He's still at home this morning. His wife, Lisa, is very ill. Until he can get a replacement for your sister, he and his kids are taking care of her."

That explained why John seemed to know Jude. Nomi wondered why he had not told her about his wife. He must have had his reasons. She did not like when people questioned her own ways of coping with Avi's illness and death.

Nomi wrote to John when she was back in the truck.

> Good morning. This is Nomi. So sorry to hear your wife's ill. Jude was her nurse?

A few minutes later, John answered.

> Yes. They were very close.

Nomi wrote back:

> Do you mind if I come over to meet her? Is she up for that?

If he did not want her to come, he would tell her. There was no harm in asking. This was not something she would have done back when she lived in this place. But Israelis were not ones for manners; they said what they meant. Over the years, Nomi grew to appreciate that. At least most of the time. But when John did not answer she wondered if she had been too forward. Then, an hour later, he wrote.

> Lisa was sleeping when you wrote. But she's up now and really wants to meet you.
>
> Thank you both. When can I come?
>
> Now is good. I'm with her. My kids couldn't cover today. A new nurse is coming later.

John and Lisa's house was not far from the station, close to the center of town. It was a small white Colonial, with a terra cotta tiled roof, wooden shutters painted black, and a brick walkway, lined with flowers, leading to the front door. Modest. Nothing showy, but sweet, sturdy, well-kept and -built. What Nomi would have expected.

Nomi rang the bell, and John came to the door almost immediately. He was already wearing a mask. Nomi had hers on too.

"Hi, come in." John was not in uniform, but in running shorts and a dry-fit T-shirt. He was sweaty. "My apologies. I was getting in a run while Lisa rested after breakfast. I need to stay in shape, for the job, but I can't leave her alone. So, I bought one of those." He gestured toward a treadmill in the living room.

John was trim yet muscular, something she had not noticed when he was in uniform. Not stocky or especially broad, but he had strong biceps and thigh muscles. A runner, not a weightlifter. Avi had been neither; his had been a farmer's body. Muscular in a rugged outdoors kind of way. His skin had always been colored or textured by the natural elements, whereas John's could be the color it was the day he was born. And with not much more hair, either. Avi had had more hair on his body than John had on his head. Although it was hard to know for sure with his hair shaved so close to the scalp.

"This was one of Jude's slots—"

"I—"

"I know what you're going to ask. I'm sorry I didn't tell you Jude was Lisa's nurse. I didn't want to mix my job with my personal life."

"I had a feeling you knew Jude more than you let on, but I thought it had to do with your professional position and the investigation." She felt a need to explain her unusual and forward request to meet Lisa. "It's been helpful for me to meet people who knew Jude. Maybe you can also help me fill in some details."

"Our pleasure." He paused, put his hand to his chin over his mask. "And what I just said is only partially true. I didn't tell you about Lisa also because I don't always feel like talking about it. It's private. Not secret, just private. If you know what I mean."

"Yes, I do. Really, I do." Nomi had told John about Avi's death that first morning he had joined her at the coffee shop; even then John had never mentioned his wife's condition.

John looked at her, and their eyes locked. They had not talked about her feelings around Avi's death. She had not known he was part of the club. Now that it was out in the open, perhaps she would feel comfortable talking about it. Perhaps he welcomed the idea of sharing his feelings, because he went on.

"The kids help. We have two. Although they're not kids anymore. They're grown and they each have a kid of their own—a one-year-old and a two-year-old—so I don't want to burden them."

That familiar pang of jealousy arose in Nomi's chest.

"Thankfully, they live nearby," John continued. "I'm here all evenings. And all mornings, until someone comes to take over so I can go to work. I think it's time to get someone in full time. That's what I told the agency."

"That seems wise."

John seemed to have everything under control, but Nomi sensed the business of caring for his wife was also a distraction from dealing with his pain. Perhaps now, too, he preferred not to unleash any emotions.

"Please make yourself comfortable for a few minutes. I was about to jump in the shower," he said while heading up the stairs.

Nomi walked around the main area of the house. It was tidy and simple. Sports medals hung on one wall, and on an adjacent wall hung a certificate of appreciation to Lisa from the school where she must have worked as a teacher before she got sick. Another wall was filled with family photos.

There was one of the whole family, minus the grandchildren. Those must have come only after Lisa's illness. In the photo, she had a warm smile, rosy cheeks that seemed naturally so, and thick, long salt-and-pepper hair tied into a braid. She was strikingly healthy, strong, and alive. Everyone looked cheerful. Nomi felt those familiar tears coming on.

There was their wedding photo. They were facing each other, gazing into each other's eyes. Lisa had a white flower lei around the crown of her head, with a veil hanging down her back. Her hair was dark and loose in this photo. John's was light, the color of wheat, as Nomi had guessed. They both looked so young, so hopeful. Life before, Nomi thought.

She sat in a chair in the living room and had picked up a photography coffee table book about the history of Salem, when John emerged. He took quick showers—like everyone on the kibbutz, as water was rationed there. That had taken Nomi a long time to get used to. Avi had confessed although he grew up with five-minute showers and turning the water off while lathering soap and shampoo, he had dreamed of longer ones.

Nomi wondered if John would have taken a longer shower if she had not been there. Although maybe not, if he was the only one home with his wife. She shook her head to shake her thoughts away. After all, why did she care?

John was dressed for work, but his shirt was buttoned only half-way, so his black undershirt was showing. He put on a mask, sat on a loveseat across from Nomi, and leaned in with his elbows on his knees, ready to talk.

Nomi closed the book. "Do you mind my asking what Lisa has?" She twirled her hair with her finger.

"She's in the final stages of cancer." John's tone took on the weight of his answer. "She had breast cancer over ten years ago. They did surgery and radiation, and she was cancer-free since then, until it came back several months ago." His face and voice fell. "It had metastasized already. She's had chemo, which gave her more time, but there's nothing they can do at this point, they say. We just stopped the chemo. It could be weeks or months, but years would be a miracle," he choked.

Nomi let out a sigh. "That is very hard."

"Yes, it is." He lowered his eyes.

"Avi, my husband, he died relatively quickly." Now she knew he could commiserate with her grief; before it was only his manner that put her at ease. "I have nightmares about those two weeks he spent alone in the hospital, in isolation, but at least it was only two weeks. That gives me some comfort."

John looked up again and Nomi caught his eyes. They looked pained and tired. "I feel grateful I can be here for her. I don't know how you managed, knowing he was suffering alone."

"I was a wreck, actually," Nomi said, shifting in her seat. "When he could still talk, before they put him on the machines, he kept reassuring me he was okay. But I'll never know for sure." She sighed. "He would have said that anyway. He was protective. He had to see me through a hysterectomy when I was only in my twenties—"

"Oh, wow. I hadn't realized—"

"No, I didn't tell you. How could you know?"

"Cancer?"

"Yes. That's why I don't have children. Thankfully, I've been in remission ever since, but it's always hanging over me." Although Nomi knew it was more her childlessness, the outcome of her cancer, than the threat the cancer may return, that hung over her most. "I know what cancer is like, although I was lucky. We caught it early, so no chemo. It was a hard time, with the surgery and radiation and what it meant for our future. Avi was my pillar. My only real support. Then and all our years together. We only had each other. And now he's gone."

"But you're still standing, I see." John's expression brightened a bit, as his eyes crinkled at the edges. He was trying to be positive.

"Well, sitting, actually." She laughed.

He did, too. "I meant figuratively."

"And I mean figuratively and literally. I'm not standing quite yet. I think that will take a long while."

"I get that." John stood up from the loveseat. "I'm going to check on Lisa," he said, as he opened the door to what seemed a study now substituting as a makeshift hospital room. He went inside and Nomi waited.

John peeked his head through the doorway. "She's getting tired, but she'd like to meet you for a few minutes. She sleeps a lot now."

"Before we go in, I should tell you she was attached to Jude. Jude was her home-care nurse on and off since she was diagnosed the first time. And since she's been unable to be at home alone, your sister was coming three times a week. It'll take someone very special to fill her shoes."

Nomi had heard that before.

"She took Jude's death hard at first. But she seems much better now."

The first thing Nomi noticed when she walked into Lisa's room was the crucifix hanging on the wall above her bed. What a gruesome thing to hang in a dying woman's room. A bouquet of fresh flowers would have been more appropriate. Something to bring some cheer instead of that bloody limp body on the cross. How had Jude managed to sit here day after day with that hanging there? Nomi assumed it brought this woman comfort somehow, even if she could not understand it.

Lisa's eyes were closed. Her face was sallow, and her head covered with a scarf. Perhaps John's shaved head was not to hide his receding hairline after all, but rather in solidarity with his wife.

Three cats were curled up around Lisa on the bed. They looked healthy, well-fed, and very comfortable. There was a cot folded up against the wall. Nomi assumed John was sleeping on it now, next to his wife. When he could sleep at all.

Nomi wished she could have slept beside Avi when he was dying in the hospital. She had also wished his death had not been so quick. But now she was not sure. Seeing the contrast between the woman in the photos hanging on the wall and the woman lying here on the bed was heartbreaking.

"Lisa, honey," John said.

Lisa opened her eyes. There were dark circles around them.

John walked over to his wife's bedside. "I'm here with Jude's sister," he said, sitting in a seat beside her bed and taking her hand in his. They looked at each other, like they had in their wedding photo.

"Nice to meet you," Nomi said, approaching the bed. "I hear you had a special relationship with my sister."

Lisa smiled with dried lips. "Yes." Her voice was soft and hoarse. She pressed a button and her bed raised her to sitting position.

"I'm glad to hear so many people loved her. Our family dynamics were complicated. Love and support were not forthcoming. She escaped to a commune when I was in high school, and I escaped to Israel after that."

Lisa took a sip of water from a glass on a night table next to her bed. She pulled the blue hospital mask on her chin up over her mouth and nose. "Yes, I know. We shared a lot." Tears formed in her eyes. "I'm just so sad she's gone. I assumed I'd be first."

What did that mean? But Nomi simply said, "I'm sad, too," to Lisa, and to John, "But more for what I missed, not being near my own sister."

"She was like a sister to me," Lisa whispered.

That stung, but it was good Jude had found that in her absence. Nomi hadn't. She had not found even one sister-like friend on the kibbutz all those years. But it hadn't mattered, because she had Avi. Now, with him gone, it mattered a lot.

She approached Lisa's bed. "Please tell me something about her. Anything you think I should know."

Lisa thought for a moment. "It really is a shame you didn't know your sister. She was an exceptional woman, and so good at what she did. She calmed me, helped me accept and prepare."

Frank had said the same thing. Did someone help Avi prepare for his death when he was in the hospital? Would that have lessened the tragedy? Would it have made it easier for Nomi, too? Would she miss him any less had she sat watching him suffer the way John was doing for his wife now?

"Lisa told Jude things she wouldn't even tell me," John said, taking his wife's hand in his.

His gentleness moved Nomi.

"Jude told me it was important for Lisa to have someone like that in her life, even if it made me feel excluded. Your sister was wise that way. She was not only a nurse. She was a chaplain, too, really." Jude the atheist, a chaplain. The thought made Nomi smile.

"It's hard not to have that now," Lisa said. "But she's still with me. I was that for her, too, I think. I can still listen. The cancer hasn't taken that from me."

Jude had opened to this woman. "Is there anything Jude would have wanted me to know?"

Lisa looked softly at Nomi. "Your sister was strong. Her life was not easy, but she was always there for others. May her and her son's souls rest in peace."

At that, Lisa's eyes closed. Jude had not had an easy life, and she was strong. Much stronger than Nomi. That even Nomi knew. But what else had her sister shared with Lisa?

John released his wife's hand as he stood. "She needs to rest. I'll see you out."

Nomi thanked Lisa and told her she'd come again if Lisa wanted. She hoped Lisa heard.

At the front door, Nomi thanked John for letting her visit. "I hope I was not intruding. Time must be so precious for you both now."

"Yes. When she's awake, she still has meaningful moments. I read to her; we watch films together. Sometimes I just sit with her and hold her hand. I treasure whatever time we can be together now."

If only Nomi had been able to do that. "Is she in pain?"

John shook his head. "She's on pain killers and seems comfortable enough. But the psychological pain was hardest in the beginning. The frustration and grief, mourning what she couldn't do and what she would miss. She was an exceptionally active and lively woman. Hardly ever sat down. It was because of her I took up running, to be able to spend more time with her. She was a runner. I literally had to catch her on the run." He looked like he was smiling again beneath his mask. "I had to force her to sit with me sometimes. Now she has no choice."

Avi and Nomi had been suited in pace and temperament. "That must be so frustrating. For her, I mean."

They stopped in front of the door.

"It was hard for her at first, to calm that part of herself." John looked at Nomi with sad yet resigned eyes. "But with no choice, she's had to learn to ask others for help. God has a cruel way of teaching us what we need to learn."

John opened the door, and Nomi slipped by him. He smelled of Irish Spring soap, the brand her father had used. It had been years since she'd smelled that particular fragrance.

Nomi paused to take in John's words and turned to face him. "So true. I'm still trying to figure out what I'm meant to learn right now, what direction I'm meant to take. This may sound callous, but Jude and Jonah's deaths have at least been a distraction from the grief of losing Avi."

"I've played out the scenario too many times in my head. It's so close to home." He paused and then said in a whisper, "How can you stand it?"

The cold air from outside wasn't what made Nomi shiver. "The grief goes so deep it feels bottomless," she admitted.

John looked at Nomi with eyes as bloodshot as those of a drunk with a hangover.

They stood in silence, taking in their shared reality.

"Have you considered a support group?" John asked, finally.

"No. That's not something kibbutzniks do."

"Well, you're not in Kansas anymore," he said.

Nomi grinned beneath her mask. She missed being able to use cultural references from her childhood. If he was about her age, as it seemed, perhaps that had been one of his favorite films, too, as a kid. Even if John was a townie, a police officer, and not even Jewish, there was something more familiar about him than anyone on the kibbutz.

"I go to a support group near here, for caregivers," John said. "I saw a sign for a bereaved partners group starting this week in another room at the same time—"

"An advanced level? The sequel?"

"Something like that . . ." John let out an almost chuckle. "Would you like to come along with me and try it out while I'm at my meeting?"

Nomi welcomed the thought of spending more time with John, beyond their semi-chance meetings outside the police station, and he seemed to genuinely want her company. Maybe he was also hungry for others who were in mourning in one way or another. "I don't know . . ."

"Both meetings are on Tuesday evenings. Eight o'clock. I'll pick you up at seven-thirty. It'll do you good."

CHAPTER 9

NOMI SAT ON the porch reading while she waited. She had continued with Batja's diary only because she was curious to see what Jude or Jonah had found so interesting. When the Germans invaded, Batja was still in the dark, or in denial, as to the danger of her situation. She was even relieved that a more "cultured" people were taking over, hopeful Jakub could return, and they could resume their bourgeois life now that the Communists were gone.

But soon the woman woke up to reality. When the Germans marched through Lwów, with a celebratory victory parade, Batja watched with Izaak and her cousins from the window as Gestapo beat Jews on the street and her gentile neighbors stood by.

Jakub returned that night to see Batja and Izaak after two years of hiding from the Russians, only to tell them he was going off to join the Resistance against the Nazis. "Before we were undesirables because we were bourgeois property owners. Now we are undesirables because we are Jews."

Batja broke down when he told her. She understood why he had to leave before, when only his life was in danger. But now that all their lives were in danger, how could he leave her? He said it was his moral duty to try to save others and fight the Nazis. Nomi liked Jakub, although she understood Batja's feelings of abandonment as well.

Nomi read some parts and skimmed others, looking for notes and underlinings, and slowly, she started to understand why this reader had felt drawn to Batja—she was growing.

December 5, 1941

We were given an order to move to the ghetto. They gave us only three hours to pack what we could carry. Luckily, when the police came, Chawa, Nachszon, and I were not at the factory, where I now work with them every day, or Izaak would have had to face the Gestapo alone. We packed whatever necessities we could into two suitcases and left the rest for our gentile neighbors to pillage. I saw them coming with empty bags, like vultures after the kill, as we pulled our suitcases to the ghetto while trying to keep our hats from flying off in the wind.

Leaving was not as hard as when we left Plac Smolki, with so much less to leave. Why did I even find all that so important? Life now is about

surviving from one day to the next and savoring every moment I have with
my son, because no one knows what will be tomorrow.

So here we are, in this tiny ghetto apartment we share with three other
families. I don't know how I will manage here. But at least Izaak has some
playmates now. Here the children can even go outside. In the ghetto, everyone
is Jewish, so there's no way to hide. God has an ironic sense of humor!!

The last line was something Jude would have written in her emails, and it
was likely she, like Batja, would have wanted to savor each moment with her
son. As an essential medical worker, she must have been especially afraid of
contracting Covid. Nomi guessed it had been Jude reading this book and doing
the underlining. But she could not be sure.

Again, Nomi was distracted by the noise beneath her. It sounded like nails—
or claws?—scratching against stone. She didn't know how to get underneath the
porch. If an animal had gotten inside, it was not through a human-sized hole.
She'd have to find a locksmith and call pest control.

A horn honked outside, and Nomi grabbed her sister's fleece jacket. Frank
was already in the front passenger seat. Nomi had invited him to come along,
but she was surprised he had agreed. Now she wondered if it was a good idea.
Would she feel comfortable sharing in the group with Jude's bereaved partner?
She couldn't very well uninvite him now.

John's family car was handicapped-equipped, which suited Frank and his
wheelchair. John's daughter had come over with her husband and toddler to be
with Lisa while he was out. Both support groups were at a local hospital, John
said as he drove down the dirt path leading to the main road. They drove with
the radio playing, an "oldies" station. They were doing a Beatles mix. "Hey Jude"
came on.

"Should I turn this off?" John asked, reaching for the radio knob.

"No, please," Frank said. "I like it. It's like she's with us."

Nomi did not argue; she, too, liked hearing the song. She envied Frank his
ability to feel Jude with him. When the song was over, Nomi saw Frank wipe his
eyes with his sleeve. They pulled up to the hospital.

This was the first meeting, so the time was spent with each person sharing their
grief story. There were ten people. Participants sat two seats apart, wearing masks.
At first it was hard for Nomi to connect. But as people spoke, they removed their
masks, and with them their inhibitions.

There was a variety of ages. A few had lost their partners to different types of
cancer, another to suicide. There were three other participants whose partners

had died of Covid. The last in a car accident. Frank's story was certainly the most unique. Many in the room had heard it on the local news.

Frank told the group he had been on the verge of suicide when he met Jude and had certainly given up any hope of finding love again. What he had not told Nomi was that his long-time girlfriend, Susan, had died in the same accident that had crippled him. She was his riding partner, leading on her bike and hit head-on by a car whose driver was drunk and had lost control of the wheel.

Frank was not hit by the car, but by Susan's motorcycle, so he and his bike had survived—although both had been severely damaged—which explained how the bike was still sitting, laid to rest, in front of his house. He spoke about the guilt he had for letting Susan ride in front of him. Then he shared how Jude had saved him from ending his own life, gotten him out of his depression when he couldn't ride anymore. Riding had been his passion, aside from his work as a firefighter.

"But what I wouldn't give to ride again! That would be my best medicine. I feel most alive when I'm riding." Frank's face lit up. "But Jude taught me ways to deal with what life is trying to teach me and accept things as they are. It was one thing to accept my own fate, though." His peaceful voice suddenly turned bitter. "It's another to accept what happened to Susan, and then Jude. That is much harder."

There were sounds of agreement around the circle. Nomi nodded too.

"Even with all the inner work, it's hard not to feel tested. Two women, so alive, both gone, and me, half living, still left here, all alone," he ended and then put his mask back on.

Nomi was glad she had come. But now it was her turn; she did not know where to begin. Did she even need to tell these people why she had left home all those years ago?

Nomi removed her mask, crossed her ankles, leaned forward, and took in a breath. She looked around the room. The other faces were masked, which made it easier, as did the knowledge they were all grieving. Their eyes were fixed patiently on her.

She began her story with when she met Avi, of how she had always been studious and had never imagined herself working with her hands. But Avi had brought out another side of her that loved being out in nature, planting and watching things grow. The work soothed her.

She talked about her cancer and hysterectomy and not being able to carry children, and her regrets, now that she was alone in the world, about never having adopted. She and Avi had been happy, content, and she had reconciled with her childlessness, she had thought. But now, with Avi gone, her feelings of loss were resurfacing, making her realize she had not dealt with them sufficiently, nor given herself space to mourn what she had lost. She didn't know how to approach mourning something she had never had.

Part of her still wanted a child. And more than anything, she wanted Avi back. But neither were possible, she knew, so she had to find purpose elsewhere.

"I have nothing and no one. Not even a career. I'm completely unmoored. All I have is a mother with dementia, my sister's truck, and her house with everything in it." She was about to stop talking when she remembered what John had said about the neighbors and the dog. "And her dog, too, apparently, if I want it."

Nomi stopped there.

"Well, that is something," Frank said. He was sitting in the seat two over from hers and looked at her with big round eyes above his bandana mask. Nomi had not noticed his thick lashes before. She was beginning to see Jude's attraction and how he and Jude were suited. Like Jude, he spoke his mind and was not easy to put in a box.

Nomi nodded at Frank. "I guess. But it came so suddenly and is kind of, well, overwhelming."

Frank's eyebrows furrowed. "Maybe Jude was trying to help you—"

"That was my sister," Nomi interrupted. She wondered if people detected the sarcasm in her voice. Nomi had no doubt Jude had always been trying to help. But it was what she thought Nomi needed to hear, what she thought would be best for Nomi. Why hadn't Jude been the kind of listener people out here described? Why had Jude always been trying to change her? Fix her?

"Maybe she still is," he added.

"Excuse me?" Nomi wasn't sure what he meant.

"Trying to help, I mean. Her spirit. I feel her energy with me now. It comforts me to know she's still around."

There he went again, talking of feeling Jude's presence. Nomi heard others from the circle agreeing. They too still felt their partners with them, they said. Why was it only Nomi seemed unable to do this? There was so much she wanted to tell Avi, to ask him. So much had been left unsaid. She wanted him to tell her what to do. Guide her. But he was inaccessible.

Nomi had even tried conjuring Avi before bed, asking him to appear to her in a dream. But nothing. He was silent. Or gone. By her side one minute and the next swept off in an ambulance, disappeared into the black hole of a Corona ward, never to be seen again except as a corpse being buried in the ground by a bunch of men in full-body anti-Covid gear. But he was already gone by then. His body was not him.

After the meeting, Joan, the social worker who was facilitating the group, approached Nomi.

"Have you considered doing volunteer work while you're here? That might give you some sense of purpose." Joan looked to be about Nomi's age. She was plump with curly gray hair, wearing round wire-rimmed glasses and a loose-fitting sweater dress and boots.

"I have no plans except to get my sister's things in order and see about my mother. Volunteering could be nice. I wouldn't have any idea how to find something, though. I might have grown up in this state, but I feel like a fish out of water."

"Why did you leave?" Joan asked, cocking her head. "What brought you to go so far away, to Israel? If you don't mind my asking."

"No, it's okay. I had a kind of falling out with my parents at the end of high school."

"Falling out?"

Should she tell this woman more? It would be easier than in front of the whole group. "You see, I thought I was pregnant," she finally said, although practically under her breath. Her face turned warm even after all these years, her heart beat loudly in her chest. "A false alarm, but neither I nor my parents knew that yet. I let them down. They had higher hopes for me than getting myself into that kind of mess."

Nomi, too, had higher hopes for herself back then. And as much as she tried to forget that night, the memories kept returning.

They had been down in David's finished basement—where there was a pool table and a record player—when it happened. They were listening to The Beatles and The Rolling Stones; he had asked her to dance. It was romantic.

She was enjoying herself and swept up in her feelings for him—*Could it be love?* She wondered, as John Lennon sang "It's only love" in the background—and how adult she felt. He told her how beautiful she was. He was handsome, too, but she was shy to say. She loved his sky-blue eyes and his toothy smile, and she liked touching his shoulders when they danced. His hand on her back felt good, too.

He started to kiss her, and then led her to the leather couch. They had kissed before, even made out, so she was happy to go along. Although that had been in the backs of movie theaters and in the used Ford Mustang his parents had bought him for his seventeenth birthday, so this time was more serious.

She had felt herself being carried away by his affection and her desire, by wanting to please him and pleasure herself. It had felt good to want him, to be in touch with that place inside herself.

But she had not wanted to "go all the way," as they called it then. Yet, they had.

Soon after that night with David, remembering the verses in Deuteronomy read aloud from the weekly Torah portion in synagogue—after her bat mitzvah, Nomi had decided to start going to synagogue on her own, despite her parents' disinterest—Nomi had found the verses again to double check. She had remembered correctly. Because Nomi was a non-betrothed virgin, she and David would have had to marry. Even if she was not living in biblical times, that thought was enough to make her run. She could not even speak to him, let alone marry him.

"And I'm not sure I blame them. At least not about that," Nomi added. "I couldn't face them, my boyfriend, or myself. So I left."

"We all make mistakes. You were so young. And sometimes what feels like a mistake can even be a necessary part of our growth process."

"Yeah, well." She was about to crack her knuckles but stopped herself.

Joan put her pen to her mask. "I know a woman who's been trying to get a community gardening project off the ground not too far from here. For teens at risk. I'll give you her number. Maybe you can help her." She wrote a number on a piece of paper as she spoke. "Tell her Joan sent you."

"I don't know—"

"It's just a suggestion." Joan handed Nomi the slip of paper with the name "Diane" and a number written on it. "You may want to give it some thought. Or not. Up to you."

CHAPTER 10

NOMI WAS HAVING herbal tea on the porch before heading into town. She liked going for coffee at the sandwich shop—and when John joined her on his way into work. But she would have to watch her spending, or she'd be forced to return to the kibbutz before she finished what needed to be done here.

Which reminded her she intended to call Jude's lawyer to set up a meeting. She didn't even know Jude's bank details. But for now, she just wanted to drink and read. Things were getting worse for Batja and Izaak.

March 15, 1942

We cannot stay in the ghetto anymore. Gestapo have started rounding up Jews and putting them on trains. Word is they are being sent to camps. Some say labor camps, some say death camps. I wish I could not believe that is true. But I do. Once I would have broken down at the thought, but I am stronger now. Jakub said so, too, when he came to me in the middle of the night.

He came to the mattress where I sleep on the floor, next to Izaak. We have our own room, a luxury here. Jakub woke me and covered my mouth so I wouldn't wake the others. He whispered he is looking for a place for me and Izaak to hide. He is working as quickly as he can, he said. We must not get on those trains. If the Nazis come for us before he finds us a place, we must run and hide anywhere we can.

I urged him to stay the night, not to leave me. Or at least to find a place for us all to hide together. I told him I can't do this alone anymore, that I need him. I know it was selfish of me, as he is risking his life to save others. But having him with me after being apart for so long, and with the world going to pieces around us, I broke. I just wanted to be held, to be taken care of. Like before. I am tired of being strong.

He told me I'll manage, that I don't know my own inner strength, that one reason he fell in love with me was because of it. I find that hard to believe.

He begged me to recognize it in myself, find it and draw from it now, that our son's life depends on it. I told him I am trying, that I will try even harder. For him, and for Izaak.

He kissed me, as though it might be our last. It felt good to be touched again, to have my senses awakened, to let myself relax into the touch of my beloved. <u>With life as fragile as it is now, I feel more alive these days than ever before. Each moment is so precious, and real.</u>

We made love without a sound, so as not to wake Izaak, but Jakub did not finish inside me. I am just after my time of the month. As little as I get to eat here, I still bleed every month. It's a curse. Neither of us will risk my becoming with child. As much as we've always wanted more children, that is not meant to be now, with the world the hell it is.

I tried not to cry when he left. Jakub is right, <u>I do feel my own strength growing inside me</u>. <u>But I am not that strong.</u>

Nomi would have underlined that last line had Jude—or was Jonah the reader?—not already done so. In fact, there was much in the diary she, too, would have underlined, and there was much she wished she could have told Batja—like to risk it all to bring a life into this world, even if the future looks grim.

While she was putting her mug on the dishrack, Nomi heard a knock. She grabbed a mask and put it on while she opened the door to a woman who looked to be in her thirties—although it was hard to tell with her mask, which was cloth with a flower print and looked hand sewn. On her back was a baby in a carrier.

"Hi. I'm your neighbor, Samantha. Sam." So, Sam the neighbor was a woman. "This is Hope," she said, holding the baby's moccasin-ed little foot.

She was a miniature version of her mother. Both had big brown eyes and blonde curls peeking out from hand-knitted hats, perhaps a present from Jude the giver. Maybe the mask was, too. Unless Sam was also good with her hands.

"Say hi, Hope," she said, tickling her daughter's foot. Hope lifted her pudgy hand and opened and closed her fingers in an almost-wave.

"How old is she?" Nomi asked. She had no experience with babies; she had never even worked in the kibbutz nursery. Perhaps a kibbutz committee's attempt to be sensitive to her childlessness—although no one had asked her if that was what she wanted.

She had spent some time with teenagers, though, since the teens were expected to pitch in during school vacations. Some worked with her in the fields. She managed all the English-speaking volunteer groups, too, many of which included teenagers. She had graduated to manager, like Avi was when she had volunteered the summer they met.

"She's almost a year already. Hard to believe. A Covid baby. People walking around in masks is totally normal for her. She's never seen different. Born soon after Biden and Harris were elected. That's why we named her Hope."

Nomi could see Jude and this woman being friends. Progressive, and upbeat. And if she was also into crafts, that was something they could have discussed. She thought of the name of the baby whose mother—Leah, John had said her name was—broke her neck. Despair. The poor kid had never even had a chance.

"Sweet name. Do you want to come in?" Perhaps she was hoping to be asked, and that was why she had a mask on. Or maybe just to be careful, even if it wasn't required outdoors. Or maybe it was a political statement.

"No. I have the dogs with me," she said, indicating two dogs tied to a tree in the front yard. "And Hope's tired. She needs a nap. We're out for a walk. She'll fall asleep when I get moving. But I thought I'd come by first, to tell you how sorry I am. Jude was very special."

"Thank you. I didn't know her so well." Nomi twirled her hair. "I've lived in Israel since right out of high school."

"Yes, she mentioned that."

"So, you did know her well?"

"I knew her, but not so well, either. She kept to herself, but what I did know of her, I liked. She was friendly and helpful, but private. We couldn't have asked for a better neighbor. She'll be hard to replace."

That phrase was becoming a town mantra.

"It's just so terribly sad she's gone. And tragic how it happened," Sam said, lowering her face and voice.

It was interesting no one seemed to mention Jonah.

Changing the mood, Sam smiled. "I love her dog. I thought maybe you'd like to meet him. He's super friendly."

"Oh, thank you. I would." Nomi stepped outside. It was chilly, but she would only be out for a few minutes.

They walked across the yard to the dogs. Both were large: one a retriever, and the other a hound.

"That one's your sister's. Elvis," Sam said, pointing to the latter. He had shiny black fur with brown patches.

"Makes sense the hound would be Elvis." Nomi laughed. "He even looks a bit like him."

"Yes. That was Jude's sense of humor."

"Hi there, Elvis," Nomi said, petting the dog, who started wagging his tail and jumping up to greet her.

"He likes you. Maybe he can tell you're Jude's sister. You do look alike."

"That's what people used to say." Nomi thought of her mother's recent mistake. "And I am in her house. It must be confusing for him not to be here. She had him a long time. No?"

"Yes. She adopted him when he was a puppy. He was a rescue—"

"Of course, he was." She hugged herself for warmth.

"Excuse me?"

"I mean, given who Jude was—"

"Yes, of course. She did like to be of service. He must be around seven, eight years old now, which is middle age in dog years. He's a calm dog, easy to manage. But I would love to hand him over to you. We have our own, as you see. And Hope is our third. Kid, that is. We have our hands full." As if on cue, the baby started to whine. "Yes, we're going, sweetie. Just a few more minutes." Sam bounced up and down.

"Oh, I'm sorry for burdening you. And I'm so grateful for your help. I hear you're the one who found them . . ."

"It was Jeff, not me. I had an intuition I should send him, and not with the kids. It wasn't like your sister to neglect Elvis. They were buddies." She smiled, perhaps at a memory. "Did you ever have a dog?"

"No. But there are lots of dogs on the kibbutz where I live. Also rescues. They're communal dogs, we all take care of them. I do love dogs, but Jude and I never had one when we were kids. We wanted one, but our parents wouldn't allow it. They said they'd be the ones who'd end up having to deal with it."

"There's a lot of truth in that. It's the parents who do most of the work." She rubbed Hope's feet with her gloved hands. "And we already have a lot on our plates. The things we do for our kids . . . Luckily, Jeff and I are both dog lovers. We both had dogs, growing up. But two is a lot to handle. Taking them on walks, for example."

Hope started whining again.

"I should go." Sam bounced the baby more.

"Well, why don't I join you?" Here was a walking partner to explore those woods. "I can get to know Elvis and help you out, too. On the walk. Then we can see what to do after that."

Sam's eyes lit up. "I was hoping you'd ask." She untied her dog from the tree. "How long are you here?"

Nomi untied Elvis. "I don't know. I'm taking it day by day."

"I know you live in Israel. And I heard about your husband. I'm so sorry. I didn't mean to make light of Covid before, with what I said about Hope and masks." Sam fingered Elvis' floppy ears as she said this.

If she had heard about Avi's death, she probably knew they had no children, too, so Nomi wouldn't have to tell her and suffer her pity. "No, it's okay. I can't expect the world to tip-toe around me." She started to hand the leash to Sam. "Here. Can you hold him while I run inside to get a jacket? You manage okay with both?"

Sam took the leash from Nomi. "Manage is a good word for it. I admit it's a bit much."

Nomi felt bad she couldn't commit to taking Elvis, but she had no idea how long she was staying.

She emerged within minutes, and they set out.

The dogs walked side by side, pulling Nomi and Sam along and seemingly knowing where they were going.

They took Nomi and Sam down to the end of the road and onto a dirt path that led into the forest. It was early December, where the first rains would be falling in Israel and the landscape starting to wake up from its summer slumber. But here, it had been raining all summer long, so the forest had never totally dried out, and the blanket of fallen leaves covering the forest bed was even moist from more recent colder rains.

They took off their masks and let the dogs off their leashes once they entered the forest. The dogs ran up ahead together, scampering and playing as they went. Nomi walked behind Sam, who led the way.

The forest bed was covered with leaves that Nomi could practically feel drying out as she tread. The smell reminded her of the black Wissotzky tea bags in the Kibbutz dining room—her afternoon drink of choice. Nomi glanced beneath a pine tree and spotted a wild mushroom.

"I see you have mushrooms already here," she called out. "Our foraging season in Israel only begins later in the winter."

"Nope. This isn't the beginning of the mushroom season, it's the end."

"Right, of course. It's been so long . . ."

"Foraging season in general is winding down now."

They walked in silence for a few moments.

"I used to see your nephew out foraging, with Elvis. Sometimes with your sister, sometimes on his own. He usually walked in the direction of the pond."

John had mentioned a pond, too. "Is it big? The pond."

"Not small, but not huge, either."

"Where is it?"

"Further that way," Sam said, pointing.

What had they been talking about before she mentioned the pond? Ah, Jonah. "So, Jonah liked to forage?"

"Yes. But he wasn't a big talker when I'd see him. A cerebral type, I'd say. Kept even more to himself than Jude did. I didn't see him for a while out here. We must have gotten onto different dog walking schedules. And then I started seeing him out a lot more again. Until, well, you know . . ."

"Hmmm."

"When Jonah showed up to shelter in place with Jude, I guess it was nice for her to have his company, and the help with Elvis—her being an essential worker and all."

Nomi looked over at Hope, who was fast asleep in her carrier.

"You were right. Hope's sleeping already. She's precious," Nomi said. A child of hers and Avi's would have spent countless hours sleeping in hiking back carriers. She felt the tears coming on and hoped Sam would assume it was the cold.

They followed a marked hiking trail alongside and over a stream by way of a small wooden walking bridge, with cattails and poplars on both sides.

As they continued walking, Nomi was transported back in time to when Jude would take her to explore the woods not far from their home, on summer days when her parents and school were both out and Jude had been left in charge. Now, as she looked around, Nomi could practically smell the mushrooms and other fungi growing back then, while she and Jude collected earthworms in glass jars to bring home as pets in lieu of the dog, cat, or even rabbits or hamsters their parents would not allow. Even the earthworms had to stay outside on the back porch.

Now that she thought of it, those woods had been a hangout for David and his friends, too. They went there sometimes to smoke weed out of sight of their parents. That was the first time David had kissed her in front of their friends. She had been shy, and the others had teased her and winked at David and patted his back.

The trail looped back to the other end of Jude's and Sam's street, and Nomi found herself in familiar territory again. She spotted Jude's driveway up ahead. Nomi pictured herself taking Elvis on this walk every morning. She hadn't imagined a dog as her hiking partner, but why not? She'd feel safe enough with Elvis along. Perhaps she could help with the dog just until she went back.

When they stopped in front of Jude's house, Nomi offered to take Elvis. She heard the relief in Sam's voice when she said she'd send Jeff over with dog food later.

Home, Elvis went right to the imitation fur rug next to the fireplace and curled up for a nap. If this dog could talk, would he, too, tell Nomi no one could fill her sister's shoes? Since he had no other choice, he seemed content settling for Nomi.

She looked around the house, wondering what to do next. Too anxious to sit and read, she went outside to pick what was left of the cranberries on their vines. That took a good couple of hours, and when she came back inside with a few baskets, she brought them to the kitchen and started boiling some to make sauce. She'd put it in jars for winter, like Jude had already started doing.

As she waited for the berries to come to a boil, the slip of paper from Joan the social worker caught her eye. She had put it on the fridge with one of Jude's inspirational quote magnets. This one said:

Carpe Diem!
Seize the day!
–Horace

She decided to call. Just for some information. Taking in a dog was enough of a commitment for one day.

"Hello. Teen Crisis Center. This is Diane speaking. Can I help you?"

"No, no. I'm not a teen. Far from it. I'm calling about volunteering." She had not intended to suggest that right away, but she had not called for help, either. Not exactly.

"How did you hear about us?" Diane sounded hesitant.

"From Joan, a social worker. She said she knows you. I met her at a bereaved spouse support group she runs, at the hospital."

"Ah. Wonderful. If Joan sent you . . ." The woman sounded friendly but business-like. "Why don't you come visit the center? We can sit and discuss the options."

"I'm not sure it's for me."

"You're welcome to come see the place to help you decide."

"I don't want to waste your time."

"Don't give it a second thought. I'm here every day. How about tomorrow at nine? I'll show you around. No commitments."

CHAPTER 11

NOMI WAS ON the porch, eating fresh cranberry sauce with yogurt. What would her sister think of her bringing dairy products into the house? But then again, it was Nomi's house now. The dog was resting at her feet.

September 25, 1942

Jakub found us a hiding place in the Catholic part of the city, and just in time. God must be watching over us. The Gestapo let us alone during the "Great Aktion" last month, when they emptied most of the ghetto. Every day, they came through, knocking on doors. Somehow, they passed by ours, like the Angel of Death in Egypt. They shot people in the street.

Then, today, the Gestapo hanged the head of the Judenrat and members of the Jewish police from balconies of the Judenrat's building. How can I raise a child in this horror? I used to censor the scary parts when I read storybooks aloud to Izaak. Now there is no point. Much worse is happening outside our window.

It is hell here. There is no running water, and come winter, there will be no heat. We cannot stay any longer. If Jakub had not come in the dark to take us into hiding, I would have taken Izaak and run. But what does that even mean? I don't have shoes for running. What good do my heels do me now? I'd be better off cutting them from my shoes and boots, but Jakub said that would only arouse suspicion.

We will take our yellow stars off, though, for the walk to our hiding place. Otherwise, if we are caught, we'll be shot on the spot, being out after the Jewish curfew. But if they realize we're Jews without stars, we'll be shot too. I am like a mouse trying to avoid a series of traps. If not that one, the next. It is inevitable we'll get caught in one eventually. If not for Izaak, I don't think I could go on.

I must go, but I am writing this now in case we are caught. I will take this journal with me, so if I don't survive, I can at least be a witness to this nightmare.

Again, that scratching noise below. There must be a way to get underneath the porch and see what was living down there. She put the book down, grabbed a flashlight hanging on the wall, and went outside.

The property was on a slope, so the porch was above ground. It was supported by walls from all around, and chances were, it was hollow in there. A good place for rodents to live. But Nomi could not find where they were going in and coming out; everything looked shut tight and solid. If something was there, perhaps it was not coming out at all.

Defeated, she went back inside. Elvis was still sleeping on the floor. She decided to continue reading, intrigued to follow mother and son in hiding.

November 1942

We begin our stay here today, Izaak and I, in this attic crawlspace now our new home, although it is barely big enough. Where Jakub has brought us is worse than the ghetto. We will have to relieve ourselves in buckets and wait for those hiding us to take away our waste and bring us food. But at least we feel a bit safer here.

If someone had told me this would be my fate (my last chance at survival living like an animal in a hole in the wall) I would say I could not stand it. But I have learned to adjust to what felt impossible every step of the way. If this is what we must do, I will do it. If not for my own wretched life, at least for my son.

Nomi thought of the space beneath her, the "Indian Cellar," as John had called it. What if she had to hide down there for months, even years? Alone. Like Batja, she had adjusted to a life she had never imagined. But could she have managed in such an extreme situation?

The elderly Polish couple who are hiding us, Pan and Pani Zacharczak, look pleasant enough. They say they have nothing to lose. He is a Communist who hates the Germans. (They don't know we were bourgeois before this country fell apart.) She is a devout Catholic who says Hitler has it wrong, the Jews did not kill Jesus. And Jesus was a Jew!

I assume we can trust them, but it is so hard to know. Perhaps they are hiding us only for the money; they are poor and without much food. Jakub has asked his trusted friend who has our jewelry, silver, and money, to pay them a monthly sum to hide us, feed us, and pass us messages. Through an underground of some sort, but I do not know any details. Jakub says it's safer that way.

When Izaak asked me how long we would have to stay in this "box," I told him, until the war is over. When would that be? he asked. I had no answer for him. It could be weeks, months, even years. And in here, with no window, only slits in the wooden planks, it will be hard to know when a day begins or ends.

I told him the war will be over when God hears our prayers. I told him this box will be our ark, like Noah and the flood. We will float here and pray for the flood to stop. We will wait for the rainbow. That is what I told him.

But my boy is smart. He asked me where the animals are. I told him they are in our imaginations, that we will have to live much of our lives in our imaginations now. He smiled and went back to sleep.

When Izaak was sleeping, I took out this journal. I brought a lantern, candles, and matches, writing and art supplies, my knitting, and a traveling set of chess with us. When Pan and Pani Zacharczak bring us food and news from the outside, I will ask them about library books.

I told Izaak not to worry about his father, but I do. My heart wants to believe he will be okay. He is tough. He survived hiding from the Russians. But the Nazis are so much worse, and joining the Resistance is more dangerous than being in hiding. I asked him again to find a place for three to hide, but he said he would not save only himself and his family. I knew that was what he would say. And I love him for it. But I wish he would go against his principles just this once.

With more Aktions every day and the ghetto emptying out into a ghost town (I shudder to say it, but it is true, as I suspect most of those taken away are ghosts by now) we knew we had to run. We saw what the Nazis did down Peltewna Street to the ghetto, killing Jews as they marched. We heard about the camp in Belzec. It's not a work camp like Janowska. It's a death camp, a killing center. Jakub confirmed the rumors, told me everything when he visited. Fighting or hiding are the only options. We will not agree to be taken and murdered by the Nazis. I will not send my precious Izaak into their hands.

Oh, God: If you created us in your image, you must be a very complicated being, tearing yourself apart from inside, as we humans are. Either that, or you are crying like a parent whose children have lost their way. Or worse yet, gone off to hurt themselves. Perhaps even to hurt you.

Nomi found herself reading not only to find out what had happened, but for Batja's inspiring insights about facing life when it felt impossible to go on. It seemed either Jude or Jonah, whoever had been reading this diary with pencil in hand, had felt the same.

If only she knew what had been going on in this house leading up to Jude and Jonah's deaths; the most she could do was guess. How frustrating the only witness was now lying by her feet but couldn't say a word.

CHAPTER 12

AT SIX AM Nomi awoke to the sound of a dog barking. It was still dark outside, and cold. She pulled the blanket over her head, but the barking only became louder and closer until it seemed it was right next to her ear.

Elvis!

She pulled herself off the couch but kept the blanket around her. The fire she had lit the night before had burnt out. She did her usual stretches and would have loved a cup of coffee but needed to deal with the dog. And she'd probably not make it to the coffee shop since she had agreed to meet that woman, Diane, at the center, the opposite direction, at nine.

Perhaps she had been hasty about agreeing to visit the teen crisis center, and about the dog. She was enjoying her morning lattes at the coffee shop, and John's company gave her a good reason to get up and out.

Elvis seemed eager to fill that role in her life, and he was hers now. She should just invest in a coffee maker. But how long would she be staying, anyway? Maybe she'd look for one on her outing today, and do a big shop at a proper supermarket, instead of just picking up a few things at the local convenience store to supplement the fennel, squash, and tubers she had harvested from Jude's garden. She'd try to stop by the car mechanic tomorrow if she made it into town. Surely, Bill and his son knew of a good locksmith, too.

Nomi quickly put some cocoa and sugar in a thermos, added hot water, packed her backpack, went to the foyer, and opened the front door. There was no sun yet, but the sky was beginning to show signs of light, and the cold morning air woke her enough for now. She looked through a basket with an assortment of gloves, hats, and scarves, found herself a set, and left with the dog on a leash.

Sam had let Elvis off the leash, but Nomi was afraid to do that on their first day out alone. She didn't know yet if he'd stay with her, didn't want to risk losing him.

Elvis was strong and stubborn—as hounds can be—and pulled Nomi where he wanted to go. He took her on the same route as the day before. Nomi let him; she had wanted to go back there.

She breathed in the crisp cold air and the smell of fallen leaves damp from dew. The forest bed was a carpet of crimson and gold, and the only sound was the faint crunch and squish of leaves beneath her boots and Elvis' paws. There was a definite sharpness to the cold, this early in the morning.

For the first twenty minutes, Elvis kept them on the same trail. But then he took a different turn, off the blue trail onto the yellow. Nomi hoped he knew what he was doing. She had a forty-minute drive to the center and wanted to find a coffee shop nearby.

Elvis came to a halt. He peed onto a spruce tree, covered with lichen, and turned off the trail. He was sniffing the ground with his wet black nose, his long brown ears dragging along the dirt.

Elvis pulled her through the woods, and, finally, to a clearing. Off in the distance she saw the pond. It was bigger than she had pictured, as were most things in this place. There was a mist over the water, creating a dreamlike effect. Nomi wondered when it would freeze over, reminding her of ice skating on the lake near their childhood home. Jude had broken her arm one winter trying to do a twirl on the ice, like Dorothy Hamill. Nomi had not been ice skating since moving to Israel—it was not cold enough there for lakes to freeze over—and doubted she still knew how.

Elvis kept walking, pulling Nomi along. A few moments later, a small cabin suddenly came into view, about ten meters square, made from branches laid skillfully like the Lincoln Logs of her childhood, and tied together with an intricate web of knots and crisscrosses.

Elvis pulled her to the door. Nomi knocked, but no one answered. She opened the door. Elvis quickly found what he was looking for: a well-gnawed animal bone. He settled in on a rug, much like at Jude's house, and started working on the bone. She was glad he was here.

There were sparce furnishings inside the cabin: a small bench, a bong for smoking weed, a makeshift table from a piece of wood laid across plastic cartons, and more plastic cartons supporting wooden planks that served as bookshelves holding an interesting collection of fiction, poetry, and non-fiction—mostly philosophy and political thought.

She didn't have much time, but she sat on the bench, poured hot cocoa into her thermos cup, and scanned the shelves: *Anna Karenina, Crime and Punishment, War and Peace, Call of the Wild, Walden, the Journal of Henry David Thoreau*, titles by Ralph Waldo Emerson, Marx and Engels, Rousseau, Nietzsche, Robert Frost, John Burnside, Walt Whitman, and more. There was a book sitting on the table, a paperback: *Into the Wild*, by Jon Krakauer. Jonah's name was written inside. This must have been his hideaway.

She had seen the film *Into the Wild* but not read the book. She was not as big a reader as her sister. Or her nephew, it seemed. She took a sip of hot cocoa and read the back to jog her memory.

A young man, Chris McCandless, had left society to live alone in the wilderness of Alaska. He was escaping materialism and social constructs to live a pure and simple life. But he died, tragically. Nomi now remembered how—from mold on seeds he had foraged that made his body unable to turn nutrients into usable energy; he slowly starved to death. How ironic if Jonah had been reading this book when he died of food poisoning.

The book was written by a journalist who had traced Chris' footsteps and even visited the abandoned bus where the young man had spent his last weeks in the wild and left a journal of those last weeks, written across the last two pages of a field guide to edible plants.

Nomi put down her cup and flipped through the pages. The end quotation in the film had been memorable and poignant: *Happiness is only real when shared.* But she also remembered reading in a review how those had not been his last written words. Nomi flipped through the pages more, reading passages and reminding herself of the film while trying to find the page quoting Chris' actual final note. Eventually, she found it. He had written his last words on the back of a page ripped from a book of poems by Robinson Jeffers, "Wise Men in Their Bad Hours."

Nomi read Jeffers' poem; it seemed Chris had chosen this poem intentionally for his final note. She read aloud from the poem the verse she found most resonant, "Death's a fierce meadowlark; but to die having made something more equal to the centuries than muscle and bone, is mostly to shed weakness." Would shedding weakness make her life more than just muscle and bone? Had it made Avi's?

Nomi read on in the book, as she heard Elvis snoring on the rug. Apparently, Chris' note on the back of the page with the poem read: I HAVE HAD A HAPPY LIFE AND THANK THE LORD. GOODBYE AND MAY GOD BLESS ALL. A happy life. Had Avi's life been happy enough to make it that easy for him, too, to say goodbye? Or had the happiness made it harder?

So, what had been the final last words in Chris' journal? This had been his last note, but it was not from his journal. She flipped through the book more to find where Krakauer had shared Chris' last journal entry. What she found made her smile: "Beautiful Blueberries."

Nomi placed the book on her lap and cupped her cocoa in her hands. Her smile widened at the smell of bitter chocolate made sweet with raw cane sugar. She took a sip, warming her insides. With so little strength left, Chris must have chosen his words carefully. What did these two words, juxtaposed, mean to him? What was he trying to tell the world?

Again, she thought of the film's final words: "Happiness is only real when shared." Had he wished he had someone to share his beautiful blueberries? Writing about them was one way of sharing them, at least.

She had read in that same book review that not only were these not his final written words, but he had not actually written those exact words at all; rather, something similar.

Nomi flipped through the paperback and found the actual sentence Chris had written: "He was right in saying the only certain happiness in life is to live for others." He was referring to Leo Tolstoy's *Family Happiness,* which Krakauer also quotes in the book:

> I have lived through much, and now I think I have found what is needed for happiness. A quiet secluded life in the country, with the possibility of being useful to people to whom it is easy to do good, and who are not accustomed to have it done to them; then work which one hopes may be of some use; then rest, nature, books, music, love for one's neighbor—such is my idea of happiness. And then, on top of all that, you for a mate, and children, perhaps—what more can the heart of a man desire?

A tear dropped from Nomi's eye onto the opened book. She wiped the page and her eyes with the sleave of her coat and closed the book.

Tolstoy's description had been her life—minus the children—and now it was gone. She knew what it was like to share a simple life in the country. She knew she should be grateful. Some people never experience that at all. But if she had never had it, she wouldn't miss it. She might have longed for it, as she did for children, but not mourned its absence, leaving a gaping cavity where her heart had once been.

It was the little things about life with Avi: the way they'd touch toes while reading on both ends of the beat-up sofa; the way they'd stumble into the bedroom after too much cheap wine to make love on the thin army mattress into which their entwined aging bodies sank; the feel of Avi's scratchy stubble against her face, her breasts, her stomach, and eventually, finally, between her legs; the way he looked at her with those black-coffee eyes, lit up with mischief and wonder, as if he was falling in love with her again each time he saw her.

The mere knowledge he existed and would be there for her when she needed him. Until he wasn't anymore. Just muscle and bone under the ground. Had he made his life more? Had he shed his weaknesses? If only she could reach him, she could ask. Or perhaps just knowing his spirit was still alive would be proof enough his life had been more than a decaying body returning to the earth.

But she did not even know that.

Nomi finished her hot cocoa, put the book and empty thermos into her backpack, and woke Elvis. It was time to head back.

CHAPTER 13

NOMI WAS WORRIED when Waze—in Hebrew, as she had not figured out how to change the language on her phone—took her into an upscale residential area. She hoped she was not lost, had expected the center to be in a business zone. She drove past grand and less grand houses, clearly a wealthier neighborhood than Jude's. It was closer to Salem, too. More like a suburb. If this was the right place, she was fifteen minutes early. She had assumed there would be a coffee shop. No such luck here.

She parked in the driveway of the address given to her by Diane, the woman on the phone. There was no sign out front marking the building in any way. Nomi double-checked the address she had written.

Perhaps the center was inside the house, which was a Colonial like Jude's, and about the same size, but restored on a more upscale level. It looked like what John had referred to as a Colonial Revival. It had a slate roof and gray shutters to match; the turquoise clapboard looked new and freshly painted, and the front lawn and flowerbeds well-tended. She ascended steps leading to a covered awning supported by white pillars, like a welcome to a worthy guest, and rang the doorbell. After identifying herself, she was buzzed in.

Nomi found the lower-level interior had been renovated as an office, with a warm aura and an aroma of freshly ground coffee beans. The floor was covered in wall-to-wall carpeting, and the walls with textured wallpaper—both things Nomi had not seen since she left the U.S. There was a waiting room in the entrance and a front desk with a receptionist who put on a mask with the number of the center's hotline printed on it, as Nomi approached her.

The receptionist told her Diane would be off a call soon and would come out to meet her. In the meantime, would Nomi like a cup of coffee?

Nomi spotted the espresso machine behind the receptionist and said she would love a latte.

Some minutes later, after Nomi's coffee was ready, a woman came out from a hallway off the reception area. She had short dark hair and was in black jeans and a powder blue sweater—matching her eyes, which smiled at Nomi from above a mask identical to the receptionist's. It was hard to tell for sure, but she seemed younger than Nomi, maybe in her forties.

"Hi. I'm Diane. You can bring your coffee to my office. I had mine earlier."

Nomi followed her into a tidy carpeted room with painted wooden moldings, where Diane sat at her desk and invited Nomi to sit opposite in an upholstered chair. There was a photograph on the wall of Diane, maskless, self-assured and attractive, speaking from a podium. A newspaper article was framed beside it. Nomi could only make out the headline announcing the opening of the center, with a photo of the house, too. She wondered how long this place had been around.

Diane cleared her throat. "So how can I help you? Or was it that you said you might be interested in seeing how you can help us?"

Nomi crossed her feet and leaned forward in her chair. "Maybe. But first I'd like to know about this place. It looks lovely. But what exactly do you do here?"

Diane chuckled. "Well, that would be important information to help you decide." She handed Nomi her business card with the center's website highlighted in fluorescent yellow. "It's all on the internet, but in short, we're a safe space for teens at risk, a place where they can come for support and guidance. We run groups, provide individual counseling, activities, and in some cases even shelter."

If such a place had been around back when Nomi was in trouble, perhaps she never would have ended up on a plane to Israel. But that would have meant no Avi. "Are there a lot of places like this here? I grew up in Massachusetts but moved to Israel over forty years ago."

"Yes. Things have changed a lot since we were teenagers."

Nomi wondered how old this woman thought she was.

Diane stood and pushed back her chair. "Let me show you around. Then you can tell me more about yourself, and we can see if it feels like a good fit on both ends."

Diane began the tour on the bottom floor, which contained offices and the reception area; the back was a clinic for social workers and therapists to meet with the teens and hold support groups and workshops. The top floor was a safe space for them to eat, relax, and talk, and where some even slept.

As she climbed the stairs, Nomi's nostrils filled with a delicious smell reminding her of breakfasts at the local IHOP when she was a kid. A young woman in a gray sweatsuit with an abundance of curly dark hair was standing in the kitchen, her back to Nomi, making waffles. Homemade, not like the frozen ones Nomi's mother used to buy in the supermarket and pop into the toaster for breakfast. This young cook was wearing earphones, singing, and dancing along. Nomi thought the lyrics were Hebrew, but the girl's accent was American, so it was hard to tell.

A group of teens were seated around a table with hot drinks in ceramic mugs. Others were sitting in the lounge watching something on a big screen. There was a white board displaying the day's schedule in black dry marker.

"Fresh buttermilk waffles! Get 'em while they're hot!" the curly-haired young woman called, carrying a plateful as she emerged from the kitchen.

When she put the plate on the table, Nomi saw she was almost certainly pregnant.

Diane greeted the teens with a warm "Good morning," which they returned. "I'm making a trip to the supermarket this afternoon, so prepare a list. Okay?"

A few replied. Others raised a hand or nodded a head. It was a warm, friendly place, but not cheerful, with the exception, perhaps, of the young woman with the waffles. Was she staff?

Diane took her through a hallway to some rooms with doors closed. "These are bedrooms for those who need a temporary place to shelter."

"Shelter?" Nomi asked. "For how long?"

"Let's go back downstairs, and I'll explain it to you there," Diane said, leading the way.

Back in her office, she closed the door, sat, and invited Nomi to sit.

"Some of our teens need a place to stay for a while," Diane explained. "If they're being abused, for example, or their parents threw them out for one reason or another."

"Like what?"

Diane tapped a pen on her desk. "Like pregnancy. We even get pregnant teens who were raped and carrying the child but who do not want to have an abortion. We usually do advise it, but it's up to them to decide."

"What an awful dilemma," Nomi said, fighting an urge to crack her knuckles.

"Yes." Diane sighed. She leaned back in her chair. "So why did you choose here to consider volunteering?"

"Well, as I said on the phone, it was suggested to me by Joan, the social worker at a bereaved partners group I attended. My husband died less than a year ago. Of Covid."

"That's so hard."

"Yes, it is." What else could she say?

"Do you mind if I ask why Joan suggested here, exactly?"

"Well, she said something about a community garden project. I've been living on a kibbutz in Israel for the past forty years. I work in agriculture." Nomi looked down at her hands clasped in her lap. "And I suspect she thought of the teens at risk angle as well, since I left home when I was barely eighteen."

"Oh, really? Why so?"

Nomi took a deep breath. "I thought I was pregnant."

"Thought?"

"It turned out I wasn't, but I could have been." She still couldn't talk about this without heat rising up her neck, her heart palpitating. "He was my boyfriend at the time. I . . . well . . . he . . . Well, see . . . My parents were not sympathetic when I told them. They acted as if it was all my fault, so I ran away from home. To Israel, which is where I've lived ever since, as I said. This is my first time back."

"That's a long time to be away." Although she must have heard countless teen runaway stories, Diane's eyes showed genuine sympathy. And no judgment. Not in her voice, either. She apparently understood how trauma can make you do such drastic things.

Diane leaned in now, over her desk. "Did you ever get any emotional help?"

Nomi's shoulders tensed. "If you mean a psychologist or support group, no. Those were different times."

"Yes, I know." Diane sighed. "But it's never too late to deal with old wounds."

An old wound. Is that what this was? If so, did that mean it could be healed?

"So, what brought you back now?" Diane asked.

Nomi's voice dropped. "Well, my husband died, and I was left alone. We didn't have any children." She had a lump in her throat.

"That could make it even harder."

Nomi closed her eyes, took another deep breath. "Yes. We lived on his childhood kibbutz. His parents are still there. But without him, it's hard to be there. Although there are things I love about it, I never felt totally at home, even before he died." She had not planned to be this vulnerable with a stranger.

"So, you came back . . . home?"

"Well, it's not that simple. This place doesn't feel like home anymore, either. I would never have come back, if not for my sister's death. She left me her house nearby, in Northville. I needed to come here to sort through her things and decide what to do with the house. And with my mother, who lives in a nursing home in the area."

"Wow." She let out a whistle. "That's a lot of pain you're carrying around."

"My sister's son died with her. They were together. Food poisoning, the police think. But they're waiting for the forensic report."

Diane's eyes widened. "Oh. You're Jude's sister . . ."

"You knew her?"

"Yes. What a tragic, devastating story. I still can't believe it. I'm so sorry for your loss. Your losses, I mean. You must have been shocked. I know I was. She volunteered for our hotline, answering calls. She had a rotation . . ." Diane looked more closely at Nomi, as if trying to find signs of her sister in her face. "Come to think of it, she told me your story. She volunteered here because of what happened to you."

Jude hadn't missed any charitable opportunity. She had left her mark everywhere. Even here. Nomi did not know her story had affected her sister so deeply. "Really?"

"Yes. Jude was special."

Nomi stiffened and let out a snort under her breath. Enough. She was tired of hearing that line. Here she was, a mere mortal—jealous, resentful, angry, unforgiving, and worn down by her own life—showing up on her sister, Saint Jude's, turf.

Diane continued unfazed, a relief to Nomi, who felt somewhat ashamed by her reaction. Perhaps she had not noticed.

"Before the pandemic, and before her son came to live with her, she even took in some of our young women who had nowhere to go. Mostly pregnant teens whose parents had kicked them out."

"I didn't know. She told me she had boarders, but she didn't say what kind."

"Yes. My sense is she did her charitable works quietly."

"I see."

"Jude volunteered to take these young women in until after the birth, when they could go back to their parents."

"Go back?" Going back in time would have been the only way such a thing could have happened with her parents.

"Yes. Often, in those cases, the parents are willing to take their daughters back as long as there are no traces of the pregnancy."

"You mean no baby."

"Exactly."

"That's awful."

"Maybe so, but even that's a stretch for a lot of these parents."

Nomi made a face.

"Jude was considering turning her home into a halfway house for pregnant teens," Diane added, "and a place for some to even stay more long term if their parents would not take them back."

Jude had never mentioned this to Nomi. She couldn't help but be moved by this gesture, even if it had not come to fruition. Especially if her story had been the impetus for Jude's plans. As maddening as it was to be Jude's sister, she could see why she was so valued. Nomi would have been in awe of her, too. And being her sister had almost celebrity status.

"Jude said it was a good way to repair some of the tragic history of the house." Diane cringed. "You know—that terrible Leah Marshall story."

Jude had given weight to the house's history, after all. "Yes, I do know about it. Just awful."

They sat in silence for a moment.

"What happened with that idea of Jude's?" Nomi asked.

"It went on hold when Jude's son came to live with her." Diane shook her head. "It just wasn't a good idea anymore to take in young female boarders in such a sensitive state with him there. And besides, there was Covid by then."

Diane must have meant having a young single man around was not a good idea. Or was there more to it than that?

"Makes sense. It was a good idea, though, the halfway house. Do you get cases like that often? Young pregnant women with no place to go?"

"Too often, unfortunately. There is one living here now. Temporarily. She's only seventeen—"

"Like I was when it happened."

"Excuse me?"

"I mean, when I thought I was pregnant."

"You know from experience how much she needs guidance and support. And she'll need it even more when she gets closer to her delivery date. She's six months in. That's why she came to us. She couldn't hide it anymore, and she couldn't be at home anymore. It's a tricky situation."

"How so?" Nomi hoped she wasn't prying.

Diane sighed. "She's a rabbi's daughter. Her social worker is trying to help her decide what to do. It's too late for an abortion. She's someone I would have sent to your sister back when she was taking women in. With her Jewish background and nursing experience, it would have been a perfect fit."

Nomi pictured a pregnant teenager lounging on the couch by the fire in her sister's living room, reading aloud from a book, her feet resting on Jude, knitting a blanket. "Yes. But can she stay here?"

Diane put her pen to her masked chin. "We provide a room for her, and from our donations, we're able to help pay her expenses for now. We have a grant to help young women like her through the pregnancy and birth; after that, they're more-or-less on their own." She paused. "There's an assumption they won't keep the baby."

Nomi's stomach fluttered. "You mean adoption?" The word still flustered her. "When it's too late for abortion?"

"Yes. We encourage adoption in cases like that, when the parents are not on board."

"Makes sense." Nomi's heart started beating more quickly.

"She wants to keep a low profile," Diane added, "so she left her part-time after-school job—"

"Did she have to drop out of school?"

"No. We help her keep up with her classes online. Luckily, because of Covid, that's an option. She's been a real trooper. But as the birth gets closer, it would be better for her to be in a home with an adult around. I don't live here. We're not a halfway house. We provide services and temporary shelter, but nothing as long term or intense as this young woman needs."

"Well, maybe I can take her in," Nomi heard herself saying before she had time to think it through. Was she trying to prove she could be as righteous and generous as her sister?

Diane's eyes brightened. She straightened her chair again and leaned in over the desk, with her hands folded in front of her. "That would be fabulous. You did come here to volunteer . . ." She brought her excitement down a notch. "But that is an extreme way to start. And, of course, we'll need a few references. Although you are Jude's sister . . . And Joan sent you . . . Why don't you take some time to think it over? Go back to the house, feel out what it might be like to share the space with a stranger. She is lovely, though. And she'd help, of course. Whatever you need."

"I don't need anything. Except company, maybe." Her sought-after alone time was starting to feel lonely.

"Well, whether you need it or not, she's a great cook. In fact, she'd like to go to cooking school one day."

Nomi wondered if she had been the one making waffles in the kitchen, with all that hair, not on the staff, after all.

"It might work out beautifully if you want company. She's serious but fun. A strong personality."

That had been her impression of the curly-haired young woman.

"She's intelligent, too. Go home and call me back in a few days once you've had a chance to sit with it. I wouldn't want her to go through another rejection."

"Yes, I understand completely." She looked Diane in the eye. "Again, from personal experience."

Diane nodded. "Of course. And, again, we will need to check your references."

"I'll get those to you and think it over." She'd have to rely on the kibbutz for one reference. Who else? And she had forgotten to ask for more information about the community garden.

CHAPTER 14

NOMI AND ELVIS went out to the porch while soup simmered on the stove top. She sat on the swing and Elvis on the matching loveseat, where he immediately fell asleep. Captivated by both *Into the Wild* and *Life in a Box*, Nomi had been alternating between the two books. She picked up the diary. Mother and son had already been in hiding for nine months.

1943

> *We've been here forever. Know it's still summer, feels like a sauna in here. Did not think Izaak would be raising my spirits. Precious child. Try not to let Izaak see me crying, but tonight he did and asked why.*
>
> *Didn't want to tell him I worry about Jakub. The Nazis cleared the ghetto and shot the last Judenrat. Thank God Jakub had sense not to join. Ghetto is now a labor camp, say the Zacharczaks. Miserable life, but at least <u>I have this box to protect my son.</u>*
>
> *I said nothing to Iz. Wish I could reassure him but <u>cannot lie to my son.</u>*
>
> *Try to keep to a schedule. Pray the Modeh Ani when we think it's morning. Hard to be grateful, but I insist. Before we sleep, say the Sh'ma, but how could God be out there still?*
>
> *Try to sleep, leaning against each other. Neck hurts, wake to rotate my head, change positions. Try to stretch, squat daily. Cannot stand, but Iz can. Make him march in place, will need to walk, run, be strong, when he's free.*
>
> *Tell Iz stories and give him lessons. We talk in whispers, play word games, chess. Iz will be a champion when this ends.*
>
> *Zs bring us library books, one a week, more would be suspicious. One for us, one for them, then switch. Tolstoy, Gorki, Dostoyevsky. Explain them to Iz, keeps us busy, minds sharp. No children's books, too risky.*
>
> *<u>Iz loves American adventurists—London, Verne. Thoreau. Imagine living in cabin in woods instead of crawlspace in attic, say lessons learning from living in box—blessings in disguise. Hugged Iz when said he gets me not governess all day.</u>*
>
> *Charcoals and paper—<u>to imagine better life and world, saves sanity.</u>*
>
> *But mind wanders . . . Nazis want to wipe us out, are doing good job. Zs bring old newspapers wrapping food. Nazi propaganda, but I guess truth. Nazis may not be winning but treat us like vermin.*

Trust the news from Zs. Nazis marched in and burned remains of ghetto, scared Jews out of hiding or burned them to death—their fate anyway.

Only other option to hide in sewers, many Jews there already. Could not imagine living with rats, pipes of human waste. Makes me feel fortunate. And they're not in death camps at least. Or ashes.

<u>*What has humanity become? People like rats. If not for people like Zs, God would bring another flood. Trying to keep faith in God and humanity but can't see rainbow from here.*</u>

<u>*Two forces at war now—good and evil. Zs are so good, risking their lives for us. Don't know I would for them but would like to believe. Am growing stronger inside, but not as selfless as Zs or Jb. Am I evil or less good? Maybe world not so black and white. Maybe a continuum, and most fall in gray area.*</u>

<u>*Extreme times means choosing sides. Drastic times make heroes and villains. I stay here to protect my son, waiting to see which force wins. Even that too much but have no choice.*</u>

<u>*Prayer only weapon now. Love and hope forces keeping me alive.*</u>

Nomi had also felt an urge to underline that last section. Batja now was not only a wise friend, but a guiding angel.

Here someone—Jude or Jonah?—had placed a newspaper clipping like a bookmark. It was about conspiracy theorists predicting the world's destruction from Covid-19, global warming, the internet, 5G, Bill Gates, and the Illuminati. That was odd.

There was another article, from a mental health journal, about personality disorders, depressive disorders, and psychoses. In that article, someone had underlined "Avoidant Personality Disorder," "Paranoid Personality Disorder," "Borderline Personality Disorder," "Schizophrenia," "Clinical Depression," and "Bipolar Disorder."

Nomi closed the book. Frank had mentioned he struggled with depression. Jude had helped him overcome that. Maybe he was on medication, going to online therapy. Nomi hoped so. She hoped Jude had not been his only support.

She dialed his number, had not seen him since the support group.

"How are you, Frank? This is Nomi. I wanted to check in. See how you're doing."

Nomi tried not to sound pitying as she pictured him sitting in his wheelchair, alone in his living room.

"I'm okay. I've continued my meditation practice. That helps. And the sangha."

Had she been projecting? She had forgotten about his online sangha; she didn't even have that.

"They miss Jude, too." He sighed but did not sound on the verge of tears.

"Are you getting out at all?" Nomi looked at the book on her lap. "Since the support group?"

"Not really. That's one benefit of Covid. Everyone delivers now. No need to leave the house."

Frank sounded like he would very much like to leave the house. Nomi's outings were keeping her from falling into a depression.

"That's not healthy, Frank. You need to get out. Do you drive?" Nomi didn't remember seeing a car in his driveway, although she knew there were cars for paraplegics.

"I never liked the car. Motorcycles are my thing."

She could have predicted he'd say that. "You live out here all by yourself with no car?"

"Yeah, well, Jude took me around in her truck. My chair fit on the back nicely. And I don't need much. There are vans to take me to doctor's appointments and physiotherapy. What I miss is the feeling of riding. The freedom of it, and the speed." His voice was more animated. "But Jude helped me realize I don't need all that." His excitement abated. "I can be happy without it."

Nomi remembered what Frank had said almost word for word at the meeting. "Didn't you say riding again would help you cope with Jude's death? In the support group."

"Did I say that?" He was quiet for a few moments. "I guess I did, and it would. I don't need it, but it sure would feel good."

Nomi thought she had heard of motorcycles, too, for paraplegics, not just cars. "Did you ever look into a bike you could ride?"

"I assumed I couldn't. And at the beginning, after the accident, I was afraid to get on a bike again. I couldn't even look at a bike." He paused. "Because of Susan . . ."

Nomi certainly knew about avoiding any reminder of your deceased loved one. And Frank had the guilt on top of it. "And now?"

"I got over that. I can look at my bike and remember the good times. It was Jude's idea to put my bike out on the lawn. We did a ceremony. It's a memorial."

She liked that idea.

"Yes. But now, with Jude gone, I have nothing left to lose. Or live for, either. If I'm going to die, it may as well be on a Harley. Do you know what I mean?"

"I don't know. I've never ridden."

"I didn't think so. I meant metaphorically."

Of course, he did. "Right."

What was Nomi's metaphorical Harley, the thing that made her feel most alive? There was planting and being outdoors. But with Avi gone, none of that filled her up like it used to. She was trying, but it was one thing to live; it was another to feel alive.

CHAPTER 15

NOMI PULLED UP to her mother's facility and put the truck in park. The few times she had gone now to visit her mother, she had been "Jude." Today would she have the courage to go in as herself? Was it even a good idea?

Had her mother noticed Nomi had stopped calling? She decided to before going in to visit.

Her mother picked up the phone quickly. "Naomi?" she asked.

"Yes. It's me," she said as she turned off the truck and took the key out of the ignition. "I know I haven't called in a while." As the words came out, Nomi regretted them. Chances were, her mother did not even have a concept of time. She was lucky her mother remembered who she was. Or was she more of an idea in her mother's head? Or, worse yet, did she not even know who she was and just pretended, saying the name that appeared on her cellphone?

"Naomi?" she repeated, sounding more like she was asking who the caller was, than why she was calling. But before Nomi could clarify, her mother added, "How are you?"

She sounded distant and confused, but when was the last time her mother had asked her how she was? She held back tears. "Not so good. Not since Avi died."

"Sorry to hear that."

"He was all I had you know."

"Yes, that is hard."

Was her mother using pleasantries because she had no idea with whom she was speaking?

"What will you do now?"

Nomi pushed back her car seat to give her legs more stretching space. "What do you mean?"

"It's no fun to be alone. Who will take care of you?"

Nomi shivered. "The kibbutz takes care of its members. That's the biggest benefit of being there." She quickly corrected herself. "I mean here."

"They take care of me here. Wherever I am. But I feel so alone. It's sad to be alone. I have no one to take care of. I can't even take care of myself anymore." Her mother sounded as if she might cry. But it was still hard for Nomi to muster compassion for her.

"Well, I can take care of myself, thank God. I've managed all these years." With no help from you, Nomi thought. But there had been Avi, and that had made all the difference. Could she manage without him? And, like her mother said, with no one to care for? She, too, did not want to be alone. And she certainly did not want to discuss this with a mother who did not even remember who her daughter was. "I should go now."

"Thank you for calling," her mother sniffled and ended the call.

Nomi put on her mask, went into the building, and stood in front of the door to her mother's room while cleaning her hands with Alco-Gel from her backpack.

She entered as Jude.

Her mother was wearing the same cardigan as with each of "Jude's" visits, only with a different shirt and pair of slacks. She was crying.

"What's wrong, Mom? Why are you crying?"

Her mother looked up. "It's good you're here, Judith. I had a call. I don't know who, but she made me sad. It reminded me of when your father got sick."

Nomi handed her mother a tissue.

"I pushed you and your sister away. I felt so alone. But you came back, Judith. You are so good to me."

Nomi leaned over to embrace her mother but remembered the Coronavirus and quickly pulled away. She had never heard her admit to pushing her daughters away, let alone regretting having done so.

"What did you tell the woman?" Nomi asked. She felt guilty for playing with her mother's dementia, but she was curious what her mother remembered. She seemed more lucid now than she had been on the phone. Apparently, seeing "Judith" in person had that effect.

"I told her she should find someone to take care of her, like you are doing for me. Or someone she can take care of. I know I'm not much help to anyone now, but I like to think I can still be a mother to you, Judith. Even just by letting you take care of me and teaching you to learn from my mistakes."

This was getting even more interesting. "What mistakes, Mom?"

"Oh, it's no secret I failed as a mother. I had no idea what I was doing. I was fumbling through. I didn't mean to hurt either of you. I did my best. No one taught me how to be a parent. I'm not even sure I ever wanted to be one."

This was news to Nomi.

"That's what we did back then. Got married, had kids. It wasn't like in your day when everyone felt the sky was the limit. Although I'm not sure how much happier that made you, either. With all that trouble Jonah is giving you."

This, too, was news. "What trouble, Mom?"

"You know. I don't understand half of what you tell me, but that son of yours is causing you as much of a headache as you and your sister caused me. Maybe more."

Was her mother confused, or had Jonah been a source of worry for Jude? If so, that would explain much of the underlining in the diary. If it had been Jude who was reading it.

She tried to feel into what Jude would have replied, what Nomi herself would have done if she had children. "I'm doing my best, Mom. He's my son. I'm the only parent he's got. He needs me. I'll see him through this."

"You're a much better mother than I ever was, Jude. You don't push him away. You stand by him. My mistakes taught you a thing or two. Although we'll see how much good that does you. The whole thing's a mess."

"What whole thing?"

"Parenting. You're pretty much doomed to make mistakes any way you play it. But maybe it's better than being alone."

Nomi reached out and took her mother's hands in hers.

CHAPTER 16

THAT NIGHT IN the kitchen, Nomi continued reading.

1944

So cold. Winter. Can't sleep. Iz keeping me warm. Woolen blankets from the Zs. Snow and ice melting into our box. Rubbing my hands together. Must get blood flowing to write.

Must be strong for Iz. Stay alive. Need sleep. Afraid to sleep. May not wake up. What will happen to my boy?

Cannot move. Iz stretches and marches. Jewish boy must run.

The more Nomi read now, the more she was becoming convinced it had been Jude reading this diary. There was a photograph of snow piled up behind the house. On the flipside was written: *Winter 2021, snowed in during lockdown. Doubly stuck.* A year ago. Nomi wondered how Frank had managed then, and Jude's other patients. Most seemed to have other caregivers, like Lisa had. But Frank was totally alone.

It was nine am, late enough to call Diane. With her mother's words, "It's better than being alone," echoing in her head, Nomi dialed her number.

"Good morning."

"Diane? This is Nomi. Jude's sister. I've given it some thought. I'd like to take that young woman in. I'm so sorry, though, I can't remember her name."

"That's because I didn't tell you. We protect the identities of our teens."

"Yes, of course."

"If you come to the center, I'll tell you more about her, and you can meet each other. The final decision is hers. I already checked your references. It's hard to get a better reference than a police officer." She laughed. "Officer Brooks has nothing but glowing things to say about you."

John had been the only person in the U.S. she could think of. She had given the secretary of the kibbutz as the other, revealing her plan to do volunteer work. But that was not an issue as far as the kibbutz was concerned, as she would not be earning any money.

"And they have a lot of respect for you over at the kibbutz, from what I could understand." That was nice to hear, but respect was not affection. "So let's have you two meet, and if you both agree, she can move in with you immediately."

WHEN NOMI ARRIVED, she first sat with Diane, who told her the young woman's name and more of her story. Ruth had grown up in a Chassidic home. Her father was the local Chabad rabbi. He and his wife had moved to the area to do what they called "outreach" to Jews who were not religiously observant. In summers they catered to the wealthy Jews who came for the culture within an hour's radius of the county, as well as for the fresh air, lakes, and hiking trails; in winters, they played to the needs of the local Jewish population, which had grown over the years, although not enough to support a proper synagogue.

They competed with the liberal synagogues in the more general area at least half an hour's drive away. But Ruth's parents, and Chabad in general, saw themselves as bringing a more authentic Judaism. They hosted Orthodox services and Friday night meals at the "Chabad House," also their home. Ruth was the oldest of nine siblings. Her mother was pregnant with their tenth.

But Ruth had rebelled against her parents. She refused to dress in the long skirts and sleeves her mother and sisters wore. She kept her hair loose instead of tying it in braids, and she went out with friends and got a job after school so she could buy herself a smartphone, something her parents did not approve and refused to subsidize.

Ruth infuriated her parents. She was outspoken and sharp, but still somewhat innocent; she was not sexually active. When she was raped by a big donor who came to stay with the family in the summer, she had been afraid to tell her parents. But when she discovered she was pregnant, she told her mother.

"But her mother didn't believe her," Diane said. "She assumed she was sleeping around and said she deserved it. She told her to pack her things and leave before her father found out. She said she would tell Ruth's father she had run away."

Nomi thought of her own mother. At least her parents had not kicked her out, although they had alienated her and made living with them so unbearable Nomi couldn't stay any longer. And at least Nomi was not the child of a Chabad rabbi and had not been pregnant, even if she had thought she was. And her mother had not been pregnant, either. Mother and daughter was a complex enough relationship.

"She roamed from friend to friend for a while, until the pregnancy started to show. And that's when she came to us," Diane concluded. "She didn't want to abort, and she was too far along for that, anyway, by then, as I told you last time we met. She's been here for about a month and is just beginning her third trimester."

"That's some story. What does she plan to do with the baby?"

"She sees a counselor here, but she hasn't decided yet. She can't bring the baby home, so if she keeps him—"

"It's a him? She knows the baby's sex?" Nomi suddenly knew if she had been pregnant with David's baby, she, too, would not have had an abortion. Or was her current childlessness making her think that?

"Yes. She saw that in the ultrasound. You can tell the sex quite early these days . . ."

That familiar feeling of loss crept up again. As if she ever knew anything about prenatal ultrasounds.

"If she keeps him," Diane continued, "she'll have a rough time of it. She hasn't even graduated high school. And she has no family support. Nothing. She's a smart young woman, with promise." Nomi had heard that before. "And there are plenty of couples who would love to adopt the baby. But she's stubborn. She isn't ready to give up this baby."

"Can I meet her?"

"Sure. She's upstairs." Diane stood. "Let's go see what she's up to."

Ruth was sitting in the lounge. Nomi's hunch had been correct. She was the young woman who had been making waffles. Then she had been wearing a baggy sweatsuit. Now she was dressed in a tight-fitting turtleneck sweater and hip-hugger jeans below her pregnant belly, sticking out like a honeydew melon from her narrow sturdy build. Nomi had hidden behind oversized clothing for months, even without a pregnant belly. She admired this young woman's courage.

But it was her wild hair that had first caught Nomi's attention and did again. Ruth's nest of wiry bottle curls had a life of its own, surrounding her head and face like a crown. And Nomi was especially taken now with how instead of playing down her large aquiline nose, she drew more attention to it with a hoop ring with turquoise beads.

Ruth looked up at Nomi with big, round chocolate brown eyes surrounded by thick, dark lashes. Her lips were naturally red, set off by her olive skin.

Nomi extended her elbow to her. "So, you're Ruth? I'm Nomi."

"Ruth and Nomi. I've read that story before," Ruth said, meeting Nomi's elbow with hers. Her smile was open yet reserved.

Nomi had not thought of the biblical characters. "Nice to meet you, Ruth."

"Nice to meet you, too. Should I put on a mask?" Ruth asked, looking at Diane.

"We don't wear masks in the house," Diane explained to Nomi. "We're family. A pod."

Nomi liked the sound of that. Like peas. She had not been indoors with someone without a mask since Avi died. She thought of Tolstoy's description of family happiness she had read in *Into the Wild*: a spouse, children, meaningful work, communal service.

"But when visitors come, it's required." She turned to Ruth. "So, yes, that's the rule."

Ruth went back to her room and came out wearing a mask with a smiley face. Nomi could not tell if it was meant ironically.

"So, Diane tells me you wanted to meet me. That you're thinking of letting me stay with you until the baby comes. I'm homeless now." She tried to say this in an off-hand manner, but Nomi detected a slight sharpness.

After that night with David, Nomi had wanted more than anything to disappear. Ruth did not seem ashamed or afraid to take up space. Yet she was probably hurting inside, just trying to be brave.

"That makes two of us," Nomi said. "I'm staying in my sister's house. She died and left the house to me. I don't know how long I'll be here or what to do with it. My husband died less than a year ago, too. We had no children."

Ruth let out a long whistle. "Sounds like we're a match made in heaven. A better *shiduch* than even my parents could find." She snickered.

Perhaps the smiley mask was ironic. Yet, she had seemed cheerful that first day.

"Could be . . ." Nomi wondered if Ruth's parents had tried to find her a husband already.

Ruth switched to business. "Are you staying at least until the end of March? That's when I'm due."

Diane looked at Nomi. "Yes, Nomi agreed she would commit to staying at least until the baby comes, and even after, so you can figure out what to do next. Right, Nomi?"

She had said that. But she quickly calculated the months in her head, to be sure it could work. She had left in November. The kibbutz committee told her they'd hold her house for six months. That meant she could say yes without committing to anything long term. She should put Jude's house on the market by then, anyway.

Nomi nodded. "Right." She looked at Diane, wondering how to proceed.

"So, what else do we need to do before we close the deal?" Ruth asked. She looked at Diane, too.

Diane looked at Nomi.

Taking in Ruth would give Nomi a sense of purpose. And company. It would give her two ingredients in Tolstoy's recipe all at once. Accompanying Ruth in the pregnancy and birth process would be emotionally challenging, no doubt. But as she had said to Sam, she could not expect the world to tip-toe around her.

Could she ever be happy again? She didn't know, but she felt ready to take steps in that direction. Like Frank had said, she had nothing left to lose.

"Well, then. Shall we pack your things? I have a truck. There's lots of room."

Ruth sighed with relief and her eyes shone. "Really? Wow! Thanks. I don't have much."

"She came with a small bag of things," Diane explained. "And she took more from our donation supply."

"Well, I came without much, either. But my sister, Jude, left enough for the two of us," she said. "You're a bit smaller than us . . . I mean, smaller than she was, and I am. We were the same size. Similar in many ways, but different in others." Nomi looked at Ruth and her round belly. "Let's get what you have and head home."

It was the first time Nomi had referred to Jude's house as her home, she realized, as she followed Ruth to help her pack up and bring whatever little she owned out to the truck.

CHAPTER 17

WHEN NOMI AND Ruth got back to the house, they looked for clothing for Ruth, who said it was spooky to wear the clothing of a dead person, but then again, why shouldn't it go to good use? If Nomi could do it, so could she. After all, she had never met Jude or Jonah.

Then Ruth said she was starved and headed for the kitchen. She loved to cook, she said. And, indeed, she did look very much at home pulling ingredients off the shelves, examining the knives, pots, and pans, finding the cutting board Nomi hadn't been able to find.

"I cooked more meals for my family than I can remember," Ruth said, turning to Nomi with a frown. "The oldest of nine doesn't get much chance to be a child."

Nomi began cutting vegetables—which she'd had to get from a supermarket—for a salad. She had gone to where the farmer's market was supposed to be, only to find just a few winter-squash sitting out for people to take for free. She had already eaten what had been left in the garden.

In Israel, winter was a time of sprouting and growth. The kibbutz farm was abundant with leafy greens of all types—lettuces, kale, cilantro, spinach, collard greens. Everything was coming alive after being dormant from lack of hydration all summer and fall. Here, there was little life now and nothing growing. Except what was under the surface, Nomi thought. Like Ruth's baby.

When they were sitting and eating the salad Nomi had prepared and a delicious vegetable stew Ruth had pulled together, Ruth asked Nomi why she had no children. Evidently, she wasn't one for small talk.

"I couldn't," Nomi answered, looking into the darkness outside the window. It was a cold winter evening, and she had lit a fire in the fireplace. "I had cancer in my uterus. They took it out to save my life. I gave up my ability to give life to save my own."

"Was it hard for you to decide?" Ruth asked.

"No. Not at all. There was no choice. I would not have survived if I had not done the surgery."

Ruth moved her food around on her plate with her fork. She had eaten her first portion quickly and taken another, which she had almost finished.

"Mine isn't such an easy decision. I don't know for sure I can manage with a baby. I'll have no support or help, but I could find a job."

Ruth looked up at Nomi, wide-eyed and hopeful. Innocent. She was still a child in some respects, despite her apparent maturity and tough, independent demeanor.

"At least he'll know I wanted him, that I didn't abandon him." She placed her fork on the table and took a sip of water from her glass, then filled her plate with salad and started eating again.

Nomi's own feelings of abandonment collected in her chest and rose to her throat, making it hard for her to get her words out. She took a breath and shared from her heart: "Listen, Ruth. I know how you feel. I came to volunteer at the center because my parents didn't want me around, either, when I was your age."

Ruth put her fork down. She leaned in over the table. "No kidding."

Nomi put her fork down, too, and sat up in her chair. She had finished eating. "I kid you not. At least that's what I thought, from the way they accused me. I wasn't pregnant, but I thought I was. And instead of helping me, they pushed me away," she said, echoing her mother's own words. "My mother said I had brought it upon myself—"

"Like mine—"

"And then neither of them could look at me." Nomi knew she had also encouraged her invisibility, but if her parents had made the effort to see her, to draw her out of her retreat, given her room to deal with her trauma and her confusion around it, its emotional ramifications, that could have made all the difference. Instead, they pushed her further away and inside herself.

"My father doesn't even know. My mother kicked me out before I could tell him. *Baruch Hashem* for the center."

Nomi smiled at Ruth's use of the Hebrew words for "Thank God"; sprinkling in Hebrew and Jewish terms was clearly part of her Chabad upbringing. "I wish there had been something like that for me back then. I escaped to Israel. I wanted to run as far as possible without getting lost."

Ruth's face lit up. "Israel? I'd love to go there. Sounds like a place you can be Jewish without being a freak." She picked up her fork and ate more salad.

Nomi laughed. "I never thought of it that way, exactly. But yes. Being Jewish there is normal. Jews are the majority. But it's not all rosy, either. There are sacrifices for security."

"You mean the wars?" Ruth asked while chewing.

"Yes, but not only. There's also the moral sacrifice of maintaining a Jewish majority. Thousands of Palestinians in exile who are not allowed to return. Occupied territories with residents who do not have citizenship."

"Why not?" Ruth swallowed and asked.

"Well, there's this feeling Israel's survival is always at risk. The Palestinian leadership doesn't accept a Jewish state. They and the surrounding Arab states attacked the Jews instead of accepting the Partition Plan in 1948, and they keep attacking. Terrorism, missiles. Do you follow the news there?"

Ruth put down her fork. "Yes. But my parents didn't talk much about modern Israel when I was growing up. They talked about Jerusalem as a place to dream about going one day, when the *Mashiach* comes. An idealized Israel, I guess. The promised land."

"Yes. Real Israel is complicated. And this conflict goes back to the Torah, with Yitzhak and Yishmael. Siblings who never found a way to get along. Even if modern history exacerbated it."

"It does sound complicated."

"But coming back here as an adult, I realize this place is also complicated, with a dark history behind its brave one. Slavery, the Civil War, the natives who lived here before the colonists. The colonists themselves. There's still resentment and trauma. I feel it in the air here, too, and see it on the news, for sure. If history is not dealt with properly, the ramifications come back to haunt you, no matter where you are."

Ruth took another forkful of salad, nodding as she brought it to her mouth.

"In Israel," Nomi continued, "there's such recent history still playing itself out to this day, which is why it feels so raw, I think. Like a fresh and open wound."

Nomi wondered: Could whole societies have wounds, too?

Ruth swallowed. "Well, I don't care. An old wound is not so different than a fresh one if you haven't treated it properly, as you said. I'd love to be on a plane to Israel now. Anywhere far from here."

"I thought that too back then. But being back here is making me see there's no place to run. It's here. It's there. It's everywhere."

"What is?" Ruth was chewing again.

"Moral ambiguity."

Ruth swallowed her mouthful. "I thought you were going to say God. Do you know the kids' song? *Hashem* is here. *Hashem* is there. *Hashem* is truly everywhere." Nomi had not heard that song since Hebrew school.

Ruth stood and pointed to the ceiling, even taking a little jump as she did. "Up, up." And then down to the kitchen floor as she bent over. "Down, down." Her curls bounced with her as she sang.

Nomi joined in. She pointed to her right and left. "Right, left, and all around," they sang in unison, spreading their arms out to their sides and then bringing them in, embracing the air. They both chuckled.

Ruth became serious and sat back at the table. "I hear what you mean by moral ambiguity, though, but some things are not morally ambiguous at all." She shivered. "Like what that guy did to me."

Nomi, too, sat down, her body suddenly feeling heavy like her heart. "Agreed."

She thought of what she and David had done, and how she was still struggling to understand what had happened. She caught herself wishing her story was as black and white as Ruth's, and then was ashamed of herself for being jealous of someone else's trauma. Victimhood envy. Did that term exist?

Ruth finished the salad on her plate and put down her fork. "I *am* confused about what to do with this baby, though. Maybe you can help me sort it out."

Nomi hoped she could. She was not sure she was the best person, though, considering. "Sure. I can try."

"I don't want to give this baby up for adoption, but I also don't want to be a mother right now. Especially not a single one. But I am certainly not interested in getting married, although my parents have lots of men in mind. They were already in touch with the *shadchan* before this happened," she said, looking down at her belly.

"Oh my. Well, of course you're not ready"— Nomi had met Avi when she was just a bit older than Ruth and had married him a year later, when she was only nineteen, but theirs had not been an arranged marriage, a totally different story—"to be a mother, I mean. You need to think of yourself and what's best for this baby. How could you possibly take care of a baby on your own? And with no family support."

Nomi regretted her words as soon as they came out of her mouth. She sounded like Jude, offering advice instead of doing what Ruth had asked her to do, to help her sort it out for herself. Besides, she was not even sure she agreed with what she had just said. Sometimes she wished she had gotten pregnant that night from David. She and Avi could have raised the baby together.

Ruth sat up in her chair, gathering her defenses. "You of all people should understand why I don't want to give him up."

Nomi knew she had come across as authoritarian. She'd have to be more careful. "I do understand. Really, I do. Believe me, I still walk around with that scar from my own mother, both my parents, not wanting me around." She paused, listening to the wind making the shutters bang outside. "I'm sorry if I was insensitive or bossy."

"No. I'm sorry. I have trouble with authority. I shouldn't have snapped at you like that. I know you're trying to help. I do want to know what you think. I'm so confused."

Nomi could not express what she was feeling, in her heart. She did not grab Ruth by the shoulders and tell her not to give up this chance to be a mother, no matter what the costs, because this might be her only chance.

She took a deep breath. "Listen, Ruth. I won't tell you what to do, but I should tell you this. My parents rejected me. But I found unconditional love elsewhere, from someone who was more equipped to give it. And so will your baby. Anyone who would adopt your baby would love him, too. Perhaps even extra, if it's a couple who can't have biological children. Trust me. I know. If Avi and I had adopted, we would have loved that child big time."

Ruth's face, her whole being, softened. "So why didn't you adopt?"

Nomi tried to explain, although she was not sure even she understood. "This was more than thirty years ago. Adoption was different back then, especially in Israel. Maybe there were families with adopted children in Israel in the eighties and early nineties, but we didn't know of any. We only knew of institutions for orphans, youth villages and kibbutzim who took them in as a community. But not private families."

"You didn't even try to find out?"

Now it was Nomi's turn to feel attacked. Taken aback yet impressed by Ruth's audacity, she considered her challenge. "Okay, I admit, I was ambivalent about becoming a parent, especially after being rejected by my own parents."

"I can see that, but my experience makes me want to do better with my kid."

Nomi thought of Avi. He had felt the same. "I feel that way now, but it's too late."

"Do you regret not adopting?" Ruth asked.

"Yes." She had said as much in the support group. "If you can give a child to a couple who otherwise couldn't have one, and a stable home to a kid whose teenage mother is not ready to be a parent . . ." She looked at Ruth, hoping she would not take offense or feel cornered. "What is a better gift to be able to give to all of them?"

Ruth put her elbows on the table and cupped her chin in the palms of her hands. "I wouldn't have chosen to have a child this way, but he is mine." She rested her free hand on her belly. "I already feel that. Even if I give him to others to raise, I'll always think of him as my child, I think. Is that fair to the adoptive parents? To my child? To me?"

Nomi looked at the kitchen walls that had witnessed Jude and Jonah's last meal. She thought of her own cottage back on the kibbutz, now housing foreign workers compelled to leave their wives and children to send them money to live. She thought of Avi, dying so abruptly and alone. She thought of Lisa and John.

The messy painful unfairness of life. Like in the song they had just sung, that, too, was everywhere. And adult that she was, Nomi was not sure she could navigate it any better than this seventeen- year-old sitting across the table from her.

CHAPTER 18

DINNER HAD GONE well. Ruth had opened to her, and she to Ruth. *It's a good match*, Nomi thought and smiled to herself.

Batja's diary was open on her lap and she was about to start reading when her phone rang.

It was John. She was used to seeing him in person. Although now, with Elvis, she had not been making it to the coffee shop in time to catch him before he went into the station, they still went on Tuesdays to the hospital for their support groups. But then Frank was along, and she sat in back. They also exchanged text messages, but they had not spoken on the phone since he called to inform her of Jude and Jonah's deaths when she was still in Israel. She had not known him then; he was just Officer Brooks.

"Hello, John. Is everything okay?" She looked out the window. It was dark, with a sliver of a moon. He must have been calling from home.

"Yes. Well, as good as it can be, I guess."

"Right. How is Lisa doing?" Was John sitting in his living room, where she and he had talked that day? Was Lisa sleeping? How was he passing his time?

"She's sliding physically but in good spirits. She's keeping me strong."

Nomi thought of Batja and Izaak.

"Please send her my regards. I wanted to come back to see her again, but I've been busy."

"The dog? Elvis, right?"

"Yes, but he's only part of it."

"Did it all work out with Diane at the teen crisis center?" Of course. She had used him as a reference. He must be calling to find out what had happened with that.

"Yes—I'm sorry. I should have thanked you. Your reference was such a help. So now I have a pregnant teenager living with me. She just moved in today. Her name's Ruth. A rabbi's daughter. She was raped by someone staying with her family. She'll be here until the birth, in March."

"Wow. Terrible story. Is it that Chabad rabbi's daughter? Schwartzman?" he asked, although he struggled to pronounce the guttural sound at the beginning of the word "Chabad." Nomi let out a slight giggle but held back, not wanting to insult him. At least he was trying.

"Yes! How did you know?"

"He called the station a while ago with a missing person's report, but then he called back to say everything was okay."

"Well, it wasn't. Her mother sent her away, but her father doesn't know."

"Sheesh." He whistled through his teeth. "Ruth doesn't want to report it, press charges?"

"No. Not yet at least. It's complicated, with her parents and all."

"I respect her privacy, but he shouldn't get away—"

"It's her decision—"

"Well, you know I'm here if you need my help with this, or anything else."

"Thank you."

There was a slight pause, and she pictured John rubbing his stubbly head.

"Good of you to take her in. That's a big step."

Talking to him now made her realize she missed their conversations. Perhaps he did too. "I know. But I think it's a good step. A step in the right direction."

"Sounds like it. And it means you'll be here until then."

"Yes. I'll try to come by soon, to see Lisa."

"Thank you. That's not why I called, though," he quickly added.

"No?"

He paused and took a deep breath. "I called to tell you we got the lab results."

Nomi closed the book and put it on the coffee table. She leaned forward and gripped the phone. "And . . . ?"

"They found a lot of cicutoxin in both their systems, and in samples from the food. That's the toxin in water hemlock, plentiful around here. It's found on water beds and is the most common cause of accidental poisoning from foraging. It looks a lot like other wild root vegetables, wild carrots, parsnips . . ."

Nomi remembered her walk with Sam. "That makes sense. They must have cooked with it that night. Sam, Jude's neighbor, told me she saw them out foraging a lot."

"Them?" Was there a trace of concern in John's voice?

"Yes. But I think more Jonah than Jude. In fact, I found a cabin in the woods where I think Jonah used to go a lot. Near the pond—"

"Water hemlock—"

"Oh my. You're right."

"A cabin?"

"Yes. He had books there." She did not mention the bong.

"I see . . . A regular Thoreau." Again, that same lilt in his tone.

"Yes. In fact, he had some of Thoreau's books there. And Dostoevsky, Emerson, Walt Whitman . . . It seems he was reading *Into the Wild* when he was last there. Ironic, right? You know the book?"

"Hmm . . . Yes . . ."

"I took it back with me to Jude's house. I'd only seen the film, so I've been dipping into it." She was reading Batja's diary more slowly now, knowing it would not end well. Although neither would this book. Like life itself. "Tragic story of ideology taken too far."

"Yes. And a stroke of bad luck. The best laid plans, as they say . . . Maybe I'll go have a look, at the cabin."

"I can take you there if you like. I walk the dog that way every morning."

"Sure. I'd like that." His tone sounded sincere, and sad. "But I'm with Lisa in the mornings before I go to the station."

"Right, of course. I'll take you whenever it works for you. Elvis is always up for a walk."

"Ok. I'll talk to Sam first. It seems likely that's what happened . . . A foraging . . . accident."

There it was again. That tone and now the hesitation.

"So sad. Doesn't seem right to go like that . . ." John's voice trailed off, and Nomi assumed he was thinking about Lisa. "Listen, I should get back to work. It piles up here with me in and out like this now."

"Of course. Don't give it a second thought. Thank you so much for letting me know. It's good to have some closure."

"Well, we can't close the case yet, but I wanted to share the results."

Nomi sat up, stretching her back muscles that had gone tight. "I appreciate you keeping me in the loop. It means a lot to me. And with so much on your mind."

"I'll tell you as much as I can. Whatever information I'm allowed to release."

"You're so kind."

"That's part of the job."

"I'm not sure all investigators would take the trouble to keep the family posted."

"Maybe not. I wouldn't know. I'm just doing the job as I see fit."

"Well, thank you."

"I should go now." He paused. "I'll be in touch. And please do come by."

Nomi held the phone in her lap for a few moments after John hung up. A mistake in foraging. She wondered if it had been a painful death. How much had they suffered?

She googled water hemlock.

Water hemlock is the most poisonous plant growing in North America. All parts of the water hemlock are toxic and can cause death in as little as 15 minutes. It contains cicutoxin, which acts on the central nervous system and causes convulsions, seizures, and respiratory failure.

Water hemlock grows in marshy, swampy areas of meadows; and along banks of streams, pools, and rivers. Accidental poisonings usually occur when water hemlock is mistaken for edible plants such as artichokes, celery, sweet potatoes, sweet anise, or wild parsnip or carrots.

That confirmed John's theory. Poor Jude and Jonah. They would not have even had enough time to get to an emergency room. What a horrible way to die. But at least it was quick, and they had been together.

Nomi put her phone aside.

Spring 1944
Zs brought potatoes and bread. More than usual. Saying goodbye. Arrests of Resistance agents. Please not Jb. Zs not safe, must hide.
Iz asked re food. No need. <u>Not much longer. Grateful for every day.</u>
Tried to give back food to Zs. Rotten potatoes are gold. Choosing humanity over life. Zs insisted. I took, for Iz.
Zs gone. Must sit and wait. Too weak to move. <u>Cannot send Iz off alone.</u> No shoes even. <u>Will not abandon my son. Have each other. Love. Will not have to face cruel world or death alone.</u>

Here was a handwritten page ripped from a notebook:

My dream from last night, August 15, 2021:
Jonah is standing on a cliff with a parachute on his back. He is singing Bob McFerrin's "Don't Worry, Be Happy." He walks to the edge of the cliff and jumps.
I wake up feeling anxious. Did the parachute open? Did he pull the release string? Did he even want the parachute to catch his fall? Why did he jump?
The parachute did its job by being there on Jonah's back. That is all it could do. It is Jonah's choice whether he will pull the string or not. And even if he does, there is no guarantee the parachute will open. Even if it wants to open, it cannot control whether it will open or not. That is up to fate.
It is out of our hands.

I am the parachute. I can only be there to have Jonah's back. I cannot be sure I will open to catch his fall, even if I am there doing my job. My job is to be there ready to open, but the rest is out of my hands.

Jude was the one who had been annotating, and she was concerned about Jonah. Her mother had not been confused. That was now clear.

Poor Jude, parenting her only child alone. She was surrounded by people who appreciated her, yet was so isolated; she helped many, but who helped her? Parenting had to be complicated, like her mother had said. Perhaps it was a good thing Nomi had no children.

Ruth and Nomi had gone through everything in Jude's closet, even her socks and underclothes. Now Nomi was privy to Jude's dreamscape as well. The most intimate parts of her sister.

CHAPTER 19

THE FIRST WEEK of Ruth's stay, Nomi awoke early each morning with Elvis and took him for a long walk in the woods. When she returned, she knocked on Jonah's—now Ruth's—bedroom door to wake her.

Ruth spent her time keeping up with schoolwork. She was in her senior year—like Nomi had been. Watching Ruth come out of Jonah's bedroom in Jude's slippers and sweats with her pregnant belly, listening to classes online, doing her assignments, taking breaks to listen to music and podcasts on her phone, made Nomi think back over forty years to those few months before her escape to Israel.

She had not managed to function like Ruth.

If online school had been an option, it might have helped her cope. As it was, she could barely get out of bed or leave her room, which was why she had lost so much weight and her periods had stopped—not because she was pregnant, but she only understood that later, when she had already left. Besides, the fact she could be pregnant was enough to make her parents stop talking to her. Nomi had skipped most of her classes and it took all the inner strength she could muster to drag herself out to her final exams, or she would have failed high school altogether.

Ruth's focus inspired Nomi to take care of her own to-do list. First, she brought the truck to Bill the mechanic, finally, after putting it off for weeks. He said the ignition should be replaced, and other repairs were needed as well, so Nomi should decide if it was worth investing in the truck rather than selling it. In the meantime, he said, she could keep driving until it simply refused to start.

While at the car mechanic, she noticed a locksmith next door and arranged for her to come to the house the next day.

It turned out that changing the locks would ruin the decor of the doors. No one carried those old locks these days; they were the equivalent of antiques. The locksmith's suggestion to Nomi was to keep looking for the keys and call back if she couldn't find them.

Next, Nomi bought a small stovetop moka pot coffee maker, as Ruth had suggested. If she was going to be staying at least through March, she needed to create a more affordable and practical routine. Ruth taught her how to use it, and how to change the language on her Waze app to English.

She wanted to be around the house more for Ruth. They had their coffee together with whatever Ruth prepared: pancakes, waffles, eggs, oatmeal, and other comfort foods Nomi had not had for breakfast in years. Kibbutz breakfasts were salad, cheese, and toast.

On Thursday, Nomi drove Ruth to the center to meet with her psychologist and support group. Friday, she spoke with Jude's lawyer and confirmed that Jude's house and truck did legally belong to her. She discovered she had full access to her sister's bank account, too. There was not much there, the lawyer said. Her sister, apparently, had been living hand to mouth, because she had bought the house cash down, with no mortgage, especially since it seemed her boarders were not the paying kind. The clerk at the bank said it had been important to her to own it.

Jude had been so efficient it gave Nomi goosebumps. What had her sister been thinking as she made these arrangements? She had put everything in place to make it easy for Nomi to take over her life.

For the Sabbath, Friday night and Saturday, Ruth made a special dinner of potato kugel, vegetable soup, cabbage salad, and sauteed broccoli with rice and marinated tofu. Before dinner, Ruth said she wanted to light the Shabbat candles.

Nomi and Avi would light the candles together each Friday evening; they also attended services at the kibbutz synagogue. The kibbutz was not a religious one, but a group of members had become interested in Reform Judaism, and the kibbutz had agreed to send an especially enthusiastic member to rabbinical school in Jerusalem, on the condition she come back and serve as the kibbutz rabbi, which she did.

Nomi became a regular participant at services. She had even said the mourner's kaddish for Avi regularly. She missed doing that. Then, when she heard of Jude and Jonah's deaths, she had said the kaddish for them, too.

But Nomi had not been able to bring herself to light the candles alone since Avi's death. Now, she agreed to let Ruth lead them in the ritual.

Nomi wondered if Jude had special Shabbat candlesticks and candles in the house. They searched but could not find any. Instead, she took the candlestick from the kitchen table and found another on the mantlepiece in the dining room, above the fireplace. Both were with candles.

"Two is perfect. In my parents' house they light one candle for each member of the household. For a *s'gulah*. You know, Jewish good luck."

Ruth looked away, and Nomi wondered if she was thinking about her parents, her siblings, and whether they were still lighting a candle for her.

Then she looked back at Nomi and tried to smile. "And it would be tempting the evil eye to light for this guy," she said, patting her belly.

Ruth lit the candles and waved her hands over the flames, singing the blessing in a sweet melodic voice. She looked in a trance, while she covered her eyes with her hands, chanting and swaying.

Nomi covered her eyes, too, but found it hard to concentrate. Ruth had altered the words of the blessing. Instead of the traditional language calling God King of the Universe, she called God Spirit of the Universe and invoked the *Shechinah*, as well.

Nomi knew from sermons of the Reform rabbi at her kibbutz, in Kabbalistic theology the *Shechinah* is the feminine nurturing earthly aspect of God. But she had never heard the term substituted for the traditional male aspects of God in the liturgy. At most on the kibbutz, they included the foremothers when they prayed, but they never dared to change God's name. Surely, this was not something Ruth knew from her ultra-Orthodox upbringing either.

This understanding of God appealed to Nomi but did not ring true. God was judging her from the heavens, not dwelling with her here on earth, holding her hand or feeling her pain. Nomi longed for a compassionate God who would embrace her with her faults, make her life just a bit more bearable, but that was not the God she knew now. Nomi wondered where Ruth had encountered Her.

"Welcome *Shabbos* angels," Ruth was singing.

Nomi still had her hands over her eyes, so she peeked from between two fingers to see if Ruth had uncovered hers yet. She hadn't.

"We are pleased to have you here with us this *Shabbos*, our first together in this new home. Oh, *Shechinah*, I am so grateful you sent Nomi to me. Thank you. Now please watch over me and Nomi and the baby growing inside me. I hope it's not too much to ask, but we're all especially vulnerable now."

There was silence, and then Ruth, with her eyes still covered, added, "Do you want to say anything, Nomi? When *Shabbos* is entering, the gates of prayer are open more than usual."

Nomi did have a lot to say to God, but she felt awkward. "No. I think you covered it pretty well."

"Up to you—"

"Well, actually." Suddenly, she felt brave behind her hands, and perhaps even a bit hopeful. Even if she did not believe in this *Shechinah* God, perhaps Avi's spirit was out there somewhere, still, in this earthly realm. "Avi, if you're listening, please let me know. I could use some help here finding my way without you." She felt the tears coming on, so she stopped there.

There was silence for a few moments, and then Ruth sang the biblical Priestly Blessing, in Hebrew, only instead of blessing others, she blessed herself and Nomi.

Yivarcheinu Adonai viyismireinu
Yaer Adonai panav eleinu viyichuneinu.
Yisa Adonai panav eleinu
Viyasem lanu shalom.

May God bless us and keep us.
May God shine light on us and be gracious to us.
May God turn toward us
and grant us peace.

Nomi was impressed with Ruth's poise and charisma. Perhaps some had been inherited from her rabbi father, but some must have been learned as well.

"Amen," Nomi said in response. She peeked and saw Ruth uncovering her eyes, so she did the same.

"Good *Shabbos*!" A good Sabbath, Ruth said with a delighted smile.

"*Shabbat Shalom*." A peaceful Sabbath, Nomi replied.

And, at least for the moment, she felt some potential—a tiny glimmer of a spark—for inner peace.

CHAPTER 20

NOMI CAME BACK from her morning walk with Elvis and knocked on Ruth's door.

"Rise and shine sleepyhead! We're going on an outing today. After breakfast." Nomi opened the door.

"But it's Sunday! I need my sleep. I'm growing a baby," Ruth groaned from her bed.

Nomi peeked into the room. Ruth put her blanket over her head.

"It's a beautiful winter's day outside," Nomi said, stepping in and pulling the blanket back. Ruth was wearing a pair of flannel pajamas she had found in Jonah's closet. "Blue skies, the sun is shining. The day is short. It'll be dark by five. Up you go!"

"Okay, okay. I'm getting up."

An hour later, Nomi and Ruth were in the kitchen eating a pancake breakfast with local maple syrup.

"Have you been to the Salem Witch Museum?" Nomi asked, adding more syrup, a luxury in Israel. "Salem is so close by, but I haven't been yet."

Ruth shook her head with her mouth full.

"Really?" Nomi asked.

Ruth swallowed. "Really. Hard to believe. But my parents were focused on my Jewish education for extra-curricular activities. Local history was not a high priority."

"No school trip?"

"Actually, we're learning about the witch hunts in American History class this year. We're doing colonial times now. The Puritans and all that stuff. My teacher is taking my class on a trip to the museum and other historic sites throughout the year." She looked down at her stomach. "But I'm not showing up in person, as you know."

"Let's go, then. Today. It's open on weekends. I checked."

The museum was a Tudor building, with eaves ironically resembling a pointy black witch hat. A sign said it used to be a church. A statue of author Nathaniel Hawthorne sat out front, as well as one of Roger Conant, founder of Salem. With his cloak and typical Puritan hat, he looked like an illustration of a warlock from a children's book.

Nomi had read Hawthorne's *The Scarlet Letter* in high school. It was required reading, but she remembered it to this day. She felt for Salem Puritan Hester Prynne, whose elderly husband sent her to the colonies but never joined her nor divorced her. She gives birth to the child of a man not her husband, the minister of the town parish, and is made to wear a scarlet A as a mark of her shame.

Nomi had let go of the A in her name and built a new life for herself with the love of her life, while Hester wore her scarlet A to the grave and only in death was able to lay in peace beside her lover. At least Nomi had not lived in New England in colonial times. The 1970s was bad enough.

New England in the 1970s, when Nomi had been a teen here, was not as progressive as it was in 2022, but at least she had not lived in this place in colonial times. Even now, there was still much room for improvement.

There was a pumpkin next to the museum's front door and a sign: *Masks required for entry.* Lines taped onto the front walk and sidewalk were meant to keep people in order and standing apart while waiting to buy tickets, but a commotion erupted at the front of the line. A man was being escorted by security guards out of the museum. He was yelling, "You can't force me to wear a mask!"

"I'm sorry, sir, but that's the museum's rule, and Massachusetts state regulations," one security guard was politely explaining while firmly taking the man away.

"We're in the middle of a pandemic here, sir," the other security guard added.

The man was resisting. People were moving back to avoid being in the middle of a confrontation, or worse.

Nomi wondered if security guards in the U.S. carried guns, like in Israel. If so, she hoped they were the only ones here with guns. Gun laws were much looser in the U.S. than in Israel. She had heard a news story where someone in a convenience store had shot dead the security guard who'd asked him to put on a mask.

"What a jerk!" Nomi said, shaking her head. "Why not just wear the stupid mask? It's a pain in the neck, but if it can save lives, why not?" Although it had not saved Avi.

"I agree," Ruth said, "but this masked against the non-masked stuff also pisses me off."

The museum guards took the struggling man away, then came back and started letting people into the museum again.

The exhibit inside told the story of the Salem Witch Trials, how strange symptoms in some of the Massachusetts Bay colonists were blamed on people—

mostly women—who were accused of practicing witchcraft, communing with the devil, and casting spells on other colonists. Symptoms included hallucinations, delusions, muscle spasms, convulsions, and a sensation something was crawling under the skin.

Nomi read an article hanging on the wall with theories as to what the true ailment could have been. One was rye-induced ergotism—fungal poisoning by the same substance used to make LSD. Historical evidence showed weather conditions in the winter and spring leading up to the witch trials may have caused the rye crop to produce this fungus. That also explained why the symptoms ceased when the witch trials ended—not because the witches were gone, but because the crop ran out.

That, one of the exhibit's posters explained, combined with mass hysteria, groupthink, the political climate, societal pressure, difficult living conditions, and a fear of smallpox, all led to the witch hunt.

Twenty people were executed. Nineteen by hanging and one, eighty-one-year-old Giles Corey, by pressing, which meant crushing his chest with stones. Corey, who had been tried in the past for beating his indentured farm servant, refused to stand trial because he did not want to turn his estate over to the court.

Corey may not have been guilty of this "crime," but he did not seem a sympathetic character. Nomi thought of Leah Marshall. If she had been suffering from postpartum depression, did she deserve to be hanged? Where did she fit into this witch hunt phenomenon, if at all?

Corey was executed without a trial, Nomi continued to read, but his estate remained in his name and went to his heirs. His wife, Martha, was hanged as a witch. Nomi wondered who lived in his house today, if it was still standing.

Nomi and Ruth stopped in front of two paintings from colonial times: one depicting a group of Puritan women being hanged in the town square, and another of a man—presumably Corey—lying beneath a wooden board chest-up with large stones piled on the board.

"What a way to go!" Nomi exclaimed.

"I learned about that from my father," Ruth said.

"About the witch hunts?" This surprised Nomi. "I thought you said your parents weren't interested in American history."

"No. About pressing." Ruth indicated the painting of Corey's execution. "My father said that's what *s'kilah* means in the Torah—not throwing stones at someone but crushing them with stones. It was one of the forms of capital punishment. For sins like not keeping *Shabbos,* adultery—and for witchcraft. Rape, too, come to think of it."

Yes, Nomi knew those verses well. The man forced himself on the woman, and she called for help, but to no avail. In that case, his punishment was stoning. Only his punishment—because the woman had screamed. If she had not screamed, they both would have been stoned.

"I admit it gives me pleasure imagining the jerk who did this to me underneath that board," Ruth added, frowning.

An announcement came over a loudspeaker: a tour was beginning in a few minutes. Ruth and Nomi joined.

The museum docent, a young African American woman with cornrows, the name tag Khadijah, and a clear plastic face guard, explained the mission of the museum: to keep the history alive so people would learn from it, not repeat it. She pointed to other similar events that followed, like the McCarthy trials where Americans accused of being Communists were tried, and some executed. The Rosenbergs, for example—a Jewish couple, with children who had been left orphans.

"Are there still witches today?" one girl, about ten years old, asked.

Her mother bent over and whispered in her daughter's ear loudly enough for others to hear, "Of course not, Jenny."

But Khadijah said it was a good question. She explained there were, indeed, still witches today. Back then, those trying the witches considered a witch someone who cast spells on others to cause them harm. But there were still people today proud to call themselves witches. They believed in the occult, communicated with other realms, healed with energy, practiced magic, cast spells, and even rid houses of phantoms, spirits, and ghosts.

"They use their magic to do good in the world," Khadijah continued. She was animated, passionate. "There are witches who consider their witchcraft a way to connect to their truth or inner power. Especially people who feel like outsiders or are frustrated with more conventional avenues of social change."

Khadijah addressed the whole group now, switching back into formal docent mode. "The rise of witchcraft usually coincides with the rise of feminist and anti-establishment movements. This was true during the transcendentalist and suffragette periods, during Woodstock and second-wave feminism, after the Anita Hill hearings, and then again after Trump's election and the MeToo movement took off."

Khadijah looked again at Jenny and smiled. "That was a long and complicated way of answering your question. Yes, there are witches today, even more, in fact, than there have been in a while. Witchcraft is on the rise. As Emily Dickinson wrote, witchcraft was hung, in history, but history and I find all the witchcraft that we need, around us, every day."

The tour continued to a display of racist, homophobic, anti-Semitic, and other hate propaganda. Also in the showcase were statistics of the relationship between hate crimes and hate rhetoric on social media, which was a kind of witch hunt, too, the explanation said. A propaganda cartoon from Nazi Germany of Jews with yellow stars, black hats, and long noses standing around a witch's cauldron caught Nomi's eye. She saw Ruth looking at it, too.

"Witch hunts of all kinds are an attempt to subjugate alternative energy and power," Khadijah continued. "It's about the people—usually women, as well as LGBTQs, people of color, and other disenfranchised groups—who don't do what the church or patriarchy, or whoever is in power, want. Sometimes it can be specifically about controlling women, but that's not always the case."

Khadijah stopped in front of another display case showing domestic life in colonial times. There was a loom, a spinning wheel, a laundry washing board, a grinding mill.

"Life was hard for everyone in the colonies," she explained. "But especially women, who carried the burden of keeping the house running, and some also worked on their farms. Women were subjugated to their husbands, without much of a voice, let alone a vote. Conditions were harsh here, and Puritan life was strict and dreary."

Khadija ended the tour on a hopeful note. "Salem means peace. Like the Hebrew shalom, or the Arabic salaam. After hearing all this shameful history, when you go outside, look around you. Where the witches were hanged, people gather to protest injustice. You can even find signs reminding us of this place's original name when it was a native fishing village, Naumkeag."

After the tour, Nomi and Ruth went to the Witch Trials Memorial, adjacent to the Old Burying Point, where the graves of two of the trial magistrates were found. On a stone threshold to the memorial, there were inscriptions of words the accused had said at their trials. Nomi was struck by Elizabeth Howe's plea for justice: "God knows I am innocent!" she had said before she was hanged. Little good that did her, though.

The memorial was a row of twenty benches built into the stone wall surrounding the cemetery, one for each victim of the trials. Those hanged for witchcraft were cremated and had no graves. Unlike Jude, they were Christian, not Buddhists, and this had not been their choice. It was the court's decision. In that society, cremation was a terrible disgrace. This memorial was a corrective of that.

Nomi and Ruth walked along the dirt path parallel to the benches and read each engraved name. Nomi wondered if Leah Marshall was buried in the Old Burial Point. Or was she, too, cremated?

A row of locust trees lined the benches, and a sign explained it was the type of tree used for hangings back then. People had left behind offerings all along the benches and trees: flowers, coins, amulets. Nomi and Ruth sat on a bench. Nomi put down the cardboard carrier with the two cups of hot apple cider they'd bought at a café on their walk over.

Nomi told Ruth about Leah Marshall as they removed their gloves and clutched their cups, warming their hands as steam rose from their drinks.

"What a gruesome story," Ruth said, grimacing. "It'll give me nightmares. How can I sleep in your sister's house with that energy floating around?" She shook her head.

"I didn't mean to scare you. It *was* four hundred years ago." Nomi tried to take a sip from her cider, but it scorched the tip of her tongue. "Be careful. Cider's still hot."

Ruth was wearing one of the knitted hats from the basket in Jude's foyer, so her wild curls stuck out from the bottom and around her neck and shoulders like a black lion's mane. "Didn't you say something about history coming back to haunt us if we don't deal with it correctly?"

"Yes. But I didn't mean with ghosts."

"You heard what Khadijah said, witch hunts continue to this day. Witchcraft, too. So that means spirits are alive and well. If not, witches would be out of business."

"You mean, without the alive part." Nomi was poking fun, but then she thought of the legendary curse on the house, of that noise beneath the porch. "But seriously, do you really think Jude's house could be haunted?" She felt silly even saying it.

Ruth lifted her cider to her lips and blew, her breath mingling with the steam rising from the liquid. "Seriously, Nomi. I've been attending Zoom events with a women's community who call themselves Jewish priestesses. This is real stuff. We do alternative ceremonies based on the traditional ones, but with a feminist pagan twist. I found them online when I was searching for something to make it feel like *Shabbos* at the center, but something different than how I grew up. I was the only Jew there. It was lonely on *Shabbos*."

Nomi knew how that felt. She had never heard of Jewish priestesses, though. "How are these priestesses different from witches?"

"I'm not sure they are. It seems like a fine line to me. The priests in Temple times, the *kohanim*, did some pretty pagan rituals."

Nomi considered this. "Is that how you learned to light Shabbat candles like you did on Friday night? It stretched me, but it was nice."

"Sort of. It's a combination of my mother's candle lighting routine and some things I've learned from the priestesses. The feminine God language, for example."

"Okay. But ghosts?"

"Listen, Nomi. Even my father believes in ghosts. Or demons. He just calls them by their Hebrew name, *sheidim*. And spirits, *ruchot*. If you look closely at a lot of the traditional Jewish rituals, you'll see their pagan origins. I didn't realize it myself until I was exposed to this online community. It's fascinating stuff." She blew on her drink again. "Why do you think Jews put mezuzahs on our doorposts? For protection. When people are having a stroke of bad luck, my father tells them to check the parchment inside the mezuzah, to make sure there's no mistake in the writing. He has all kinds of stories about people who were healed or changed their luck that way."

Nomi put down her drink and picked up a metal pendant someone had left as an offering on the low wall next to her bench. It was five-pointed, not the six-pointed Jewish Star of David Nomi knew. She wondered about its significance. "You're saying a mezuzah's like this?" she said, showing Ruth. "An amulet? I never thought of it that way."

"I hadn't thought of it that way either until recently. And now, hearing Kadijah today, it makes even more sense."

There were *mezuzot* on all the kibbutz buildings, even if it was a secular kibbutz; this was a well-engrained Jewish practice that had become part of the culture, even if its origins were pagan. But it just occurred to Nomi now that Jude's house had none, which did not surprise her. Her parents had hung a mezuzah on their front door when she was a kid, though. The rabbi of their synagogue had come over to say a blessing. What was the difference between a blessing and an incantation?

"Your father's a warlock?" Nomi mused, with a bit of a chuckle.

Ruth looked pensive. "You saw that picture of the Jews around the witch's cauldron . . . Maybe, by some definitions of the word, he is. But I don't know if I'd call him disenfranchised. At least I never thought of him that way . . ."

"You did use the word freak, if I remember correctly." She picked up her drink with one hand while still holding the amulet in the other.

"I guess I did." Ruth crinkled her eyebrows. "Well, I was embarrassed as a kid by his long black coat and his black hat with *peyos* stuck behind his ears. It was mortifying to be seen with him at parents' meetings. The other fathers were in jeans and sweatshirts, or at the most a suit and tie, and there he was, with his warlock costume!"

"I can only imagine. My parents were the opposite. All about fitting in." She paused and reconsidered. "Actually, about conforming only as much as society would let them, and only to an extent." It was a strange mix of wanting to be accepted in mainstream Christian society and keeping a safe and superior distance.

Ruth took a tentative sip of cider. "Well, now that I'm out of there, I see things differently. I didn't like my parents' rules and restrictions, but they are good people. They believe they're serving God. And they've helped many."

She looked past Nomi, her eyes somewhere else. "Problem is they consider their path the only way to help, the only thing anyone could need." She sniffled, her large nose turning pink from the cold. Or was it emotion? "I had a special relationship with my father. He's strict, but he has a soft side, too. When I was a little girl, I sat on his lap for hours, listening to his stories and *niggunim*. I miss that."

Nomi had heard Ruth singing along in Hebrew to music through her headphones, like that day she first saw her. Was that what she was singing? Her father's *niggunim?*

Nomi tried her cider again. It warmed her insides, and the cinnamon and cloves reminded her of childhood New England winters when life seemed simpler. "Hot apple cider. That's something *I* miss from *my* childhood. This is delicious."

Ruth looked lost in thought as she drank. "Believe it or not, I understand why my mother told me to leave. She was worried about my siblings, that what happened to me might taint my family's reputation. And concerned about the family's financial security, too. She has other kids to protect, and I'm the oldest. I can manage." She sat up tall. "Besides, we hadn't gotten along for years. She couldn't accept me for who I am. So maybe it was time for me to go. I can't live the way they do. My mother wears dark stockings all year round. She covers her hair with a wig, a proper married religious Jewish woman." She pulled off her winter hat and ruffled her abundant curls, making them look even more wild. "Can you imagine me doing that?"

Nomi shook her head. She had heard some Chassidic women even shaved their hair off completely underneath their wigs. There were whole neighborhoods full of them in Israel. "No. Definitely not."

"And having this *mamzer*"—Ruth made quotation marks with her fingers for the Hebrew word for bastard—"baby not long after she has her legitimate one was not going to be good for anyone involved. She should be due just around now, in fact." She looked like she might cry.

Nomi had looked up the definition of *mamzer*, too, when she had thought she could be pregnant with David's child. Technically, Ruth's child was not a *mamzer*, because she was not married and therefore not committing adultery. And although her rapist was married, a man is allowed more than one sexual partner according to biblical law, which stipulates that Ruth's rapist should have married her. But, like Hester Prynn's lover, he did not own up to his responsibility for the pregnancy, let alone admit to having raped her.

Like Hester and her child, Ruth and her baby would be ostracized if she brought him home to her parents—just as Nomi would have had she been pregnant, whether the child was technically a *mamzer* or not.

"I'm sorry, Ruth. That's so hard," she said, putting her hand on Ruth's knee.

Ruth collected herself. "And my father would feel awful if he knew. This guy is his biggest donor. He'd feel torn between defending me and keeping the Chabad House going. My mother's the more practical one, and less sentimental. She did what needed to be done . . . Come to think of it, I guess my mother's a witch, too." She spun her hand in the air. "She waved her magic wand and made me disappear."

Nomi imagined her parents dressed in witch costumes, waving their magic wands, and reciting their incantation: *But you were the good one. You had promise.*

Nomi fingered the amulet; the metal was cold. "My parents did the same to me forty years ago, and they were not Chabad. We were High Holiday Jews, and I appreciated whatever Jewish ritual we did. I was no rebel. I liked rules as a kid. They gave life meaning, and structure. It was the gray areas that unsettled me, the thought that perhaps there was no rhyme or reason for it all."

Nomi looked at the row of locust trees, their branches blowing in the wind. Sun shone down on the faded green grass beneath them. The air was frigid, but the sky deceptively blue.

"That's one reason I had such a hard time after what happened to me," she continued, looking now at Ruth, who shook her cup to mix in the remaining spices, and finished her cider.

"What do you mean, what happened to you? You slept with your boyfriend and thought you were pregnant, and your parents treated you like a criminal. How is that a gray area? They should have supported you."

"I mean what happened with my boyfriend, not my parents. I didn't want to sleep with him. I really liked him, even fantasized about marrying him one day. But I was not ready for sex. Maybe I didn't make it clear enough, or I wasn't forceful enough. Or it was too late."

"You mean *you* were raped, too?"

"I didn't say that."

"But he did it when he knew you didn't want to?"

Nomi's stomach tightened; her body grew suddenly hot despite the cold. "He was my boyfriend. I was at his house."

"You mean, date rape."

"I don't know," Nomi hesitated.

"Did you tell him you weren't ready? Did you tell him to stop?"

They had been making out, and she was aroused . . . until he started trying to stick his hand in her underpants. They had never gone below the belt before. She kept pushing his hand away, but he kept rubbing his erection against her. Part of her had wanted to continue, but she did not want to go all the way. As much as she felt herself becoming wet and warm, she knew she was not ready. The idea of it scared her. Her head was telling her no, even if her body was telling her yes.

She kept pushing his hand away. He told her he loved her. Didn't she love him, too? She didn't know. She needed more time—to sort out what she wanted, to seek advice, to talk it through. Her usual instinct to try and please others was at odds with her instinct to save herself. And pleasing him would be displeasing her parents. She was confused. She tried to tell him between his kisses, but he shushed her, told her she was ruining the moment.

He reached for his zipper. Then her body, not just her mind, began to rebel. She tried to push him off her as he slid her underpants down to her knees, pushed up her skirt, and pulled his erection out of his briefs. She had never even seen it before, and now he wanted her to touch it.

She had turned away, shaken her head, and insisted, "No, David, no," punching him as he forced it between her legs. And then inside her. She had been surprised at how easily it slipped in—because she did not want it there, her desire had shut down; but it was too late.

"Did you resist?" Ruth asked, when Nomi didn't answer.

She had cringed, closed her eyes, with tears rolling down her cheeks, but she had not screamed. She had wanted to, but the sound just sat there, stuck in her throat. It had all happened so fast yet taken forever. Exhausted and defeated, she had inhabited another place until he was done.

"Yes, I did. But I didn't scream for help."

"You've been reading too much Torah," Ruth said. "I don't care what it says there. I didn't scream either. I didn't want my parents to find me like that. I just wanted it to end as quickly as possible. Now I know better. The support group and psychologist at the center helped me see that. I had nothing to be ashamed of."

Was that it? Yes. She had just wanted to get it over with. She had thought she deserved it, that it was her fault somehow. "But I was there with him willingly. Part of me even wanted his attention. Just not like that . . ."

"It was not your fault," Ruth said with total conviction. "If you told him you weren't ready, you were raped."

Nomi looked blankly at Ruth's face, as if she could find the answer there.

"Nomi, did you tell him no?"

Yes, she had; aroused or not, she knew she did not want it and she had told him so. "Yes, I did. I said no. I said it twice." Of that she was certain.

"Then it was rape."

It was, wasn't it? She had been raped, whether David had been her boyfriend or not. She had said no, and he had not respected that. He had forced her, even if she had been wet with desire. She had not wanted him inside her, and he had gone there anyway.

It was rape. Rape. Saying that peeled away layers of shame, covering her, like a heavy blanket, for all these years, but now where did that leave her? Exposed and vulnerable, with not even that blanket to protect her.

Where had God been while David was forcing himself inside her? Cheering him on, one of the good old boys? Or was there really a *Shechinah*, a God with a womb, crying along with her as the Universe betrayed her?

"I was so confused and alone," Nomi whispered, looking down into her cup; she had only drunk half the cider. "And my parents reinforced that with their accusations and rejections."

"That's really shitty," Ruth said, putting her hand on Nomi's, which was still resting on her knee. "Parents should be there to see us through this stuff. That's what they're for. Right? I won't do that to my kids. Never."

Nomi only wished she could say the same, but she had missed her chance. Her womb, whatever trace of the creative nurturing divine she had left inside her, had been cut out long ago.

CHAPTER 21

NOMI AWOKE GROGGILY to beeping, a message from John on her cell phone:

Lisa would like you to come. She wants to speak with you.

Her head immediately lost its awakening fog. Even if she did feel sorry for herself, Lisa was dying. Nomi knew how quickly that could happen.

I will come this morning.

Good. I'm running over to the station for a while. The new nurse is here.

Nomi took Elvis for a quick walk, grabbed breakfast, and left a note for Ruth, still sleeping. She was out in less than an hour.

A woman in a nursing uniform opened the door and let Nomi into Lisa's room. "She's having a relatively good day."

Lisa, her face more emaciated and her middle more bloated, had her eyes closed and was surrounded by her cats. She looked so peaceful it was a shame to disturb her. Nomi went to her bedside and sat in a chair. The crucifix had been moved to the wall across from the sick bed. Nomi couldn't stop gazing at it.

Lisa opened her eyes. "You like my crucifix," she whispered. "I had John move it so I could see it from here. But you must see a lot of them. Jude told me you live near Nazareth."

Nomi looked at Lisa and shook her head. "Actually, I rarely see any. Israel's a predominantly Jewish country. And I don't make it to Nazareth much—"

Lisa raised the fuzz of hair growing back in as eyebrows.

"And even when I do, I don't go into any churches." She looked at the crucifix again. She couldn't lie to a dying woman. "And like is not the word."

Lisa struggled to smile. "You don't?"

"Honestly? I find it depressing."

"Depressing?" Lisa looked up at the crucifix. "It's a sign of hope. Redemption. God's reconciliation with humanity even after we continue to sin, again and again."

Nomi followed Lisa's gaze. Jesus hanging, lifeless, on the cross, blood dripping from his hands and feet. Where was the hope there? "How so?"

"The vertical line is the divine realm, and the horizontal is the human one. But they come together to create the cross," she explained.

Nomi tried to see what Lisa saw. "If it were just the cross, maybe, without all the gore."

"It's the same message, just a cleaner look. But as we both know life isn't that easy. You can't just cut out the suffering."

"I do know." She looked at Jesus, and for a moment his suffering was hers, and her suffering was his. The feeling unsettled her, and she looked away and then back down at Lisa. "But still. It doesn't have to be front and center."

"You're more the plain gold cross type?" Lisa smiled.

Nomi laughed. "Actually, I'm more the Star of David type, since you're asking." She reached into her sweater, leaned over Lisa's bed, and showed her the Star of David necklace she was wearing. It had been a present from the kibbutz when she and Avi had become engaged all those years ago.

"Of course, you are." Lisa's eyes were sunken but kind. "But that, too, has a similar message, as I'm sure you know."

"Really? It's a national symbol."

"It has a spiritual message, too. If you look at it closely, it's really two triangles. One pointing upward and one pointing downward. They overlap to form one symbol. Like the cross."

She examined the pendant. "You're right." She doubted the kibbutz committee knew this interpretation. "It's a lovely idea." But she was not sure she believed in redemption anymore. Or divine providence. At least not for her. Or Avi.

Lisa closed her eyes to rest from the exertion of speaking.

After a few minutes, Nomi touched Lisa's hand, cold and dry like a desert stone at night. "John said you wanted to tell me something."

Lisa opened her eyes. "Yes. It's about John. I worry about him. He'll be lonely after I'm gone. You know."

Of course, Nomi knew. The thought of the days, months, years, stretching on like this. "Yes, I do," was all she said.

Lisa looked at Nomi with pleading eyes. "I want him to find someone. I don't want him to be alone."

"Did you tell him?"

"He refuses to talk about it." She turned her face to the wall.

Nomi was still touching Lisa's hand. She squeezed lightly. "Oh, but you must tell him, Lisa. Avi and I never properly discussed it. His death was rapid, and they would not let me on the Covid ward. But anyway, Avi didn't like to discuss death.

He had so much tragic death in his family history, he wouldn't go there. Both his parents are Holocaust survivors. When I tried to discuss our eventual deaths, he made light. And now, well, I don't know what he would have wanted."

Lisa turned her head back to Nomi. She coughed and cleared her throat. "Why does it matter what he would have wanted? He's gone now. I don't believe I'll have human desires or needs once I die. I can assure you Avi is not feeling them, either. Feelings are connected to the body, to mortality, to the human condition. His soul gives his blessing."

Nomi took in Lisa's words. She wanted to believe they were coming from Avi, too, that Lisa was a channel to her beloved. But she didn't know. "How can you be so sure?"

"Because I'm close to death myself. I can already feel that emotional letting go as I'm slipping away. I'm leaving this world for another heavenly realm, and I have a clear sense I will not feel jealousy or anything of the sort when I'm there."

Nomi did not have a sense Avi would feel the way Lisa did. Hadn't he said it would be better for her to live longer than him since she had no intention of taking a new lover? He had been teasing, but perhaps it really was what he had wanted. Even with his body underground, she could not bear the thought of him with another woman.

Lisa and John had children and separate lives. Nomi and Avi had had only each other, and their lives had been entwined from day to night. Besides, Nomi was not ready to move on. She was grateful to Lisa for trying to make her feel better, but no one could understand her and Avi's relationship. It was just between them. "Thank you, Lisa. I don't know if Avi would agree, though."

Lisa closed her eyes again and lay quietly. Nomi wondered if she should leave.

Then Lisa opened her eyes and found the strength to continue. "But even that's not why I asked you to come here. I have my selfish reasons."

"Selfish? How could anything you ask of me now be selfish?" Nomi hoped she would not let Lisa down. Even if she felt a piece of herself had been ripped from her being, even if she felt raw and alone, she was still alive. She did not take that for granted.

"Because I'm not dead yet, and I feel myself still holding on. I want to be able to let go in peace." She coughed again, and Nomi looked around for water. She spotted a glassful on the table, and helped Lisa take a sip.

"John will throw himself into his work and his fitness when I'm gone," Lisa went on. "And helping with the grandchildren, our church community, the town. I know him." She struggled to speak. "But he'll resist looking for love. He'll think he doesn't need it. Or that it would hurt me in some way. And maybe he doesn't need it. But it won't hurt me. The thought of him alone for the next twenty or more years breaks my heart."

"Lisa." Nomi had tears in her eyes; she squeezed Lisa's hand.

"Let me finish." Nomi was surprised at Lisa's resources of strength. "John deserves more than to be okay. He deserves to be happy. And another woman who is worthy of his love deserves to be happy, too. He has been a stellar partner and lover. He's been so good to me."

Nomi had sensed this from the first time she met John. "He's a lovely man."

Lisa's eyes locked with Nomi's. Why was Lisa telling her this?

As if she could read Nomi's thoughts, Lisa added, "I was planning to ask Jude to take care of John, to make sure he found someone. Now she's gone. But Jude brought you here. Will *you* make sure John doesn't sit at home moping when I'm gone? You've become friends. Knowing he'll be taken care of will help me leave this world in peace."

Nomi released her grip on Lisa's hand. Her cheeks were becoming warm. She looked down, avoiding Lisa's other-worldly gaze. What was Lisa suggesting?

"I don't know how long I'll stay here, Lisa. I came to get Jude's things in order and figure out what to do with my mother. But this is not my home. This is not my life. I'm not Jude. I have my own life."

"Of course, you do, Nomi. I know that. I'm not suggesting you take over for Jude. But don't let trying to prove you're not Jude prevent you from doing what you were meant to do here. I trust you'll find your own way."

The problem was, Lisa trusted Nomi much more than Nomi trusted herself.

CHAPTER 22

"DO YOU BELIEVE in miracles?" Ruth asked Nomi as they sat watching the Chanukkah candles burn.

They had decided to light the candles on the dining room windowsill, the custom for this winter solstice holiday. Everyone walking by could see and be reminded of the potential for light and miracles even in the most dark, cold, and portentous of times. According to Jewish legend, after the Jewish military victory over the Greeks—the few against the many—when the Holy Temple had been desecrated, the oil in the Temple's menorah was only enough to last for one day, but it lasted for eight. The miracle of Chanukkah.

Ruth had officiated this candle lighting ceremony, too, pointing out its pagan origins. She used feminine God language for the blessings on the candles and reflected on the light and miracles in her life despite the darkness.

When Ruth had asked her if she'd like to share, Nomi said she was having trouble seeing the light in her life. But she was trying.

Ruth then guided them both in a visualization, imagining the *Shechinah* an orb of divine light shining inside themselves and then expanding slowly to include even those they have trouble seeing in that light. Nomi tried to expand her circle to include her mother, and she was able to see some rays of light reaching her, even if not enveloping her entirely; but that was as far as the orb would reach. And David was outside its limits completely.

After the candle lighting ceremony, they had sat at one end of the long oak dining room table to eat the traditional fried potato patties—a reminder of the oil miracle—with apple sauce, only they were using Nomi's homemade cranberry sauce instead. Ruth had added sweet potato, leeks, and zucchini to her potato patties, her personal interpretation of the age-old custom. Snow was falling heavily outside, but Ruth and Nomi were warm and cozy.

"Miracles?" Nomi said in a low voice. She paused in dipping a crispy patty in cranberry sauce and put it down. "I don't believe in a God who's involved in the human realm. At least not in my life. Not anymore. I mean, I want to believe, but it makes no sense Avi would die so tragically. He was so good. And where was that God when David did what he did?" She was still having trouble using the word rape.

Ruth looked at Nomi with intense sharpness. "I don't believe all my parents' rules are from God, but I do believe there is some divine force out there. Not the old man in the sky judging us if we are good or bad, or even preventing bad things from happening to us, but more like spirit flowing through everything, connecting everything, giving life meaning. It's just too depressing otherwise."

"I hear your point," Nomi said. "But how can there be meaning in Avi's death?"

"I don't know if there's meaning, exactly. But it's more about trust, I think. Trusting that things happen the way they're meant to. I know you've been dealt a shitty deal. So have I. But if we hadn't, we wouldn't be sitting here together right now. That means a lot to me."

Nomi felt happy tears emerging, the first in a long time. "To me, too." She reached across the table and put her hand on Ruth's. "A lot." She looked past Ruth at the candles, their warm flames shining against the backdrop of the dark cold outside.

Ruth took a bite from a patty with cranberry sauce and washed it down with water from her glass. "Well, I do believe in miracles. At least I did. There were times I could really feel that divine force I'm talking about. It's hard to explain, but I did feel watched over by God when I was a kid."

Nomi had also felt divine presence in her life, even after that night with David. Perhaps not understanding the full extent of what had happened had helped her keep God with her. Until Avi died. "I felt the same way. God even saved me a few times. So, I guess I did believe in miracles once." She dipped her patty in cranberry sauce and took a bite. Ruth had spiced it with cinnamon and nutmeg.

"Tell me more." Ruth put her elbows on the table and rested her chin on her clasped hands. Her dark eyes were wide and sparkled like the candles behind her. "How did God save you?"

Nomi told Ruth about the ad in the paper and the relief of not being pregnant with David's child. "Then, God sent me an angel when Avi knocked on my door. No divine intervention since then, though." She sighed. "Only three angels for me, it seems."

"I wouldn't be so sure." Ruth leaned into Nomi over the table. "There are four *m'lachim*, you know."

"No. I didn't know. They didn't teach us that in Hebrew school."

"Maybe your school was more *misnagdish*."

Nomi still had trouble understanding the mix of Yiddish, Hebrew, and English in Ruth's speech. "You mean the *mitnagdim*? The rationalists?" She was aware of the historic split between the rationalist and the Chassidic Jews, who had a more mystical approach; although she also knew over time the distinctions between the two communities had blurred, at least in the ultra-Orthodox Jewish world.

"Yes. My family is *chassidish*, although my mother grew up in a *misnagdish* family. So she's the more rational of my parents. Stricter, too. But she became *chassidish* when she married my father, and that's how they raised me. Things don't have to make sense where I come from."

"They did where I came from."

Ruth put a few more patties on her plate. "Eating for two," she said as she saw Nomi watching her.

"Enjoy! I think I'm full."

"You know, it wasn't from my Jewish priestess community I first learned about the archangels. My parents sang me to sleep every night when I was a kid, with a prayer asking the angels to protect me. It's actually a traditional *t'fillah* before bed. You say it with the *Sh'ma*."

"We didn't in my house."

Her parents had not had a bedtime ritual with her. They would send her and Jude off to sleep, regardless of whether they were tired or it was dark outside, and there was no tucking in, reading aloud, or singing of lullabies. The sisters would have to occupy themselves before falling asleep. That was the rule: if you are not tired, stay in bed until you are. No leaving the room allowed, not even for the bathroom.

Relieving herself before leaving the house and before bed became so engrained in Nomi's routine from childhood, she still did both to this day. Once as a kid she had forgotten and had to pee into her piggy bank; she couldn't wait until her parents were asleep to sneak out to the bathroom.

"So, tell me more about these four *m'lachim*," Nomi said.

"The archangels. There's one in each direction."

"Like in the God song?" She started to sing, "*Hashem* is here, *Hashem* is there—"

"Right. Michael, Uriel, Raphael, and Gabriel," Ruth said, pointing her fork in the four directions as she said each angel's name. "They guard us when we're asleep and guide us when we're awake. So be on the lookout for another one." She winked. "Your fourth angel may even be here already, waiting to see how to help." She popped what was on her fork into her mouth.

Nomi had heard about the Sabbath angels, but not the archangels. "Like your father's *sheidim* and *ruchot*?"

"Yes. But *sheidim* cause trouble and were never embodied. They're just evil spirits. *Ruchot* were once embodied and are more neutral, or could go either way.

M'lachim are embodied but are not human, and they are always good. They come to help."

"Well, I would welcome an angel about now."

"Me, too," Ruth said. "It's been a while since I felt God's presence like I used to."

"What do you mean?"

"When I was a kid, I didn't feel God saving me, exactly. But I did feel God guiding me. Even in small decisions, like which cereal to eat or which way to go when I was walking and got lost."

"Cereal?"

"Do you think that's silly?"

"No. Not at all. You were just a kid." Nomi thought of Jiminy Cricket in Disney's *Pinocchio*. "You mean like a kind of inner voice?"

"I guess. But it really felt like God speaking to me. Then, after the rape, that voice was gone." She snapped her fingers. "Just like that. Until now," she said, her face lighting up.

"How so?"

"Well, that's why I asked you about miracles, because I feel it coming back. When I heard you talk about how you regret not having adopted, I felt God in the room again, like I used to. I felt God guiding me. It made it easier for me to decide what to do. I've been wanting to tell you this, ask you about it."

"What?" Nomi leaned in over the table and held her breath. Would Ruth say she had decided to keep the baby? She did not want to take responsibility for having inspired that. Even if her heart felt that could be the right thing to do.

"Give up this baby for adoption. I see now how someone who could not have biological children might even appreciate this child more, give him more love than most parents. Like you said."

Nomi exhaled. "I know this is hard for you, Ruth, but it's for the best."

"That's not all, Nomi. I wouldn't give my baby to just anyone. God sent you to me for a reason. I see it now." She looked into Nomi's eyes. "I want you to adopt my baby." Her eyes were pleading. "Would you do that? Not just for me. For you, too. You must know the word *bashert*, right? Do they speak Yiddish in Israel? This was meant to be."

Nomi stared at Ruth with her mouth open. It pained her to think of Ruth giving up this baby to strangers. What if this was Ruth's only chance to have a child? Nomi, too, had grown attached to the life growing inside this young woman who had become like a foster daughter to her in such a short time. It was not as if she had not imagined herself with this baby. She had even dreamt about it. But it didn't really make sense.

"I'm sixty years old, Ruth. How could I adopt a baby? I'd be nearly eighty when he graduates high school. If I live that long."

"I'd like to still be involved, and at some point I could even take over. I want to know he's in good hands until I can. You said you regretted not adopting. Don't you wish you had a child?"

Of course. And how many times! But she had also given up any hopes of that. Why was Ruth stirring up those feelings? Nomi had opened Jude's house to this young woman, and she felt affection for her. They were meant to come together now, here in this place. She, too, believed this. She wanted to help her. But she was not about to adopt her baby. Surely that was going too far.

First Lisa's request, and now Ruth's. She did not want to be this town's Dorothy, fallen from the sky to save them from the Wicked Witch . . . especially if that witch was God in disguise.

Nomi looked over at the Chanukkah candles. They had burned down and were flickering out. She was not Jude. She was not going to take on everyone else's pain. She had enough of her own.

CHAPTER 23

NOMI NEEDED SPACE. Straight after dinner, she went to the porch to read. Ruth's request, especially on the heels of Lisa's—which Nomi wasn't even sure she understood—had been too big. And yet, she felt guilty. But it was impossible, certainly for someone as broken as she was. What did she have left to give?

So why was she still thinking about it? And about Lisa, and John.

Reading would be a distraction.

She had not sat out on the porch in a few weeks, even with the heater, because it had gotten too cold. But she felt the porch beckoning. She would brave the chill.

There was no date on the next entry, not even the year. Batja must have been starving and half-delirious.

Nothing from Resistance. Rationing food and water. Will not last. <u>*Almost end*</u>.

And then this one:

Knitting scissors. <u>*Tonight, our hair*</u>. *Will not let Nzs do it.* <u>*And then . . . ?*</u> <u>*Must listen to heart*</u>.

At this page, there was a photograph, dated September 2021. It was of Jude kneeling among her blueberry bushes, her hands in a namaste gesture, with her hair cut close to the scalp—along with a page on which was copied a long excerpt from the *Bhagavad Ghita*:

Why do you worry without cause? Whom do you fear without reason? Who can kill you? The soul is neither born, nor does it die.

Whatever happened, happened for the good; whatever is happening, is happening for the good; whatever will happen, will also happen for the good only. You need not have any regrets for the past. You need not worry for the future. The present is happening . . .

What did you lose that you cry about? What did you bring with you, which you think you have lost? What did you produce, which you think got destroyed? You did not bring anything—whatever you have, you received from here. Whatever you have given, you have given only here. Whatever you took, you took from God. Whatever you gave, you gave to God. You came empty-handed, you will leave empty-handed. What is yours today, belonged to someone else yesterday, and will belong to someone else the day after tomorrow. You are mistakenly enjoying the thought that this is yours. It is this false happiness that is the cause of your sorrows.

Change is the law of the universe. What you think of as death, is indeed life. In one instance you can be a millionaire, and in the other instance you can be steeped in poverty. Yours and mine, big and small—erase these ideas from your mind. Then everything is yours and you belong to everyone.

This body is not yours, neither are you of the body. The body is made of fire, water, air, earth, and ether, and will disappear into these elements. But the soul is permanent—so who are you?

Dedicate your being to God. He is the one to be ultimately relied upon. Those who know of his support are forever free from fear, worry and sorrow.

Whatever you do, do it as a dedication to God. This will bring you the tremendous experience of joy and life-freedom forever.

Nomi gazed into her sister's eyes. She exuded serenity, as if thanking the Universe, as if enlightened. Nomi remembered what Frank had said about her sister preparing for death. Lisa had said it, too. Something on Jude's face, coupled with these words from the Buddha, suggested this photograph was part of that journey. Nomi thought now of Jon Krakauer's description of the peaceful look in Chris McCandless' eyes in the final photograph he took before he died of starvation.

Nomi flipped through the book now to find that passage. She read it aloud.

"Some people who have been brought back from the far edge of starvation . . . report that near the end the hunger vanishes, the terrible pain dissolves, and the suffering is replaced by a sublime euphoria, a sense of calm accompanied by transcendent mental clarity. It would be nice to think McCandless experienced a similar rapture."

Nomi put down *Into the Wild* and picked up *Life in a Box*. She read the next entry:

Fading. Will die or they will kill me, but <u>not my son!</u>

Nomi turned the page. But that was it. The end of the diary. There were acknowledgments and photographs of the journal in which Batja had written and of the crawlspace where it had been found. Sheared human hair lay between the pages.

Nomi already knew Batja had not survived, yet her eyes filled with tears as she read this last entry. Batja's death felt like a personal loss. And how had she died? Nomi hoped it was from starvation, or even by her own hands, not at the hands of the Nazis. Then they would not have gained the satisfaction, and like with McCandless' death, she would have experienced those serene final days.

And what about Izaak? There was no postscript telling what had happened to him. Had Batja killed her son? Like Leah Marshall, she would not have been in her right mind, after days of starvation and months of living in that crawlspace. She had given him life; she certainly had every right to take it before the Nazis did.

Yet the thought of it made Nomi want to stop her somehow. God had also been a partner in giving him life, and no one knows what plans God had in store for the child, what the future, what the next moment, would bring. She was starting to see that now. Did she believe in miracles? No one had saved Avi. She could not judge Batja, but she also could not imagine going through with such an act, no matter how bleak the future might seem.

If possible, she needed to find out what had happened to them. She took out her phone and searched on Amazon. There was a new edition, published by a large mainstream press, with more information, it seemed. She ordered it.

Nomi stood to take the book and her tea mug back inside, and that was when she heard the scratching noise again. She would return to the locksmith and then call pest control. As much as she hated to resort to that, she saw no other option.

NOMI CHECKED THE mailbox a couple days later. No book, but there was a large manilla envelope from the kibbutz containing some letters. They had forwarded them on to her. She sat down at the kitchen table with the envelope and opened the one that looked most interesting. It was from Rambam Hospital, where Avi had died.

> Ms. Erez,
>
> We were saddened to hear of your husband's death from the Coronavirus. As you know, he was a regular donor at our hospital for twenty years.

It was thoughtful of them to write, after all those years Avi had donated blood. Especially since that was probably where he had caught the virus.

She read on:

> We were so moved by his story, wanting to help in this way, and how unlike other donors, he refused to take money.

Money? Nomi had never heard of blood donors receiving money.

> His mission to help increase the Jewish population after the Holocaust and continue his parents' blood lines, especially since they are both survivors, was inspiring. It was wonderful of them to send us such a beautiful letter telling us how proud you all are of his legacy.
> Please accept our heartfelt condolences from the entire Rambam Fertility Clinic.

Fertility clinic? There must have been some mistake. Nomi read the letter again. And again. And again.

Avi had been lying to her all those years. He had been donating sperm when he said he was donating blood.

He had said he didn't need children. He had said she was enough for him. He had said he didn't want a concubine. What was the difference between spreading his sperm this way and spreading it through a concubine or two? Where was the rational, careful, thoughtful Avi she knew?

They had shared everything, been the centers of each other's worlds. And yet he had not shared this.

Nomi was adrift in a storm with nothing to hold onto. Where had her anchor of a husband gone? She gasped for breath, drowning in this whirlpool of thoughts and emotions, flooding her like a divine punishment. How could she have been so blind? So stupid? Even Avi's parents knew about this. He had told them but not her. What was going on?

She checked her watch. It was two pm, nine pm in Israel. Only just not too late to call her in-laws.

"Nomi," Hannah answered. She and Amos were probably sitting over tea and Petit Beurre biscuits. "Is everything okay?"

Nomi had not called her in-laws since she had left. She had emailed them to say she arrived safely and would let them know her plans. But since she did not know her plans, she hadn't written again.

She didn't know what to say. Normally she would try a bit of small talk. But she could only think of one thing. "I got a letter from Rambam, the fertility clinic. I don't understand. Avi was donating sperm?"

"They wrote you a letter?" Hannah's voice was as composed as ever. Nomi had never seen her flustered.

"Yes. I guess Avi never thought to tell them he was keeping this from me." Nomi couldn't help her sarcasm; her anger was sharp. She had never spoken to her mother-in-law this way, never spoken this way of Avi, either.

Hannah cleared her throat. "This was not about you, Nomi. It was a family matter. Between us and Hitler. We didn't survive and bring Avi into this world for nothing."

Was she serious? Had this been Avi's idea or his parents'? "Avi was my husband, my life. He said he didn't need children."

"He didn't want to hurt you, Nomi. But he also had a duty as a son, a Jew, and an Israeli. We are survivors. I don't expect you to understand."

She found it difficult to breathe. She had never been accepted. The spoiled American who knew nothing of suffering was how they saw her, but this confirmed it.

"The arrangement benefited everyone," her mother-in-law added.

"Everyone except me!"

"Nomi, you know better than anyone what a giving man our son was," Hannah said after a long silence. "He loved you dearly. But he had this need, too. And we have ours. Why should his love for you prevent us from continuing our blood lines? Think about it. He was not unfaithful, and he was helping others."

Hannah made this seem like the only logical thing Avi could have done. So why was Nomi's head spinning, her heart beating like it might burst her chest open? "But he was deceiving me!"

"He was deceiving you to protect you. You are only upset because you found out. Had you not, there would be no harm done. That is how he wanted it to be. He didn't want it to change anything between you."

Nomi remembered what Avi had told her: they were not like Abraham and Sarah in the Bible. He had wanted to retain their special intimate connection, their beautiful life. He didn't want to ruin it. She understood that. But keeping this from her was ruining it in a different way, tainting it with his betrayal. He did not want to hurt her, Hannah had said, so why did he do it? He knew her. It *did* hurt, discovering now what they had shared had not been enough for him. All those years she had thought it was. But it wasn't.

And even more than that, he had acted as if it was. He had kept this from her. He had been with her without his full self, while she had taken the risk of giving her full self to him, always.

Hannah was right. What she hadn't known hadn't hurt her. But now she did know, and it hurt like someone was throwing the gift of her whole heart into the sea.

CHAPTER 24

NOMI HAD LIKED going to synagogue when she was a child. Her parents took her and Jude every year on the High Holidays. Back then, she did not speak Hebrew, so she did not know what the prayers meant. But she liked the music and reverence of the service. She did wonder, though, why God only visited the Jews on Rosh Hashanah and Yom Kippur.

Then she started Hebrew School at the synagogue and asked her teacher, Rebecca, a young woman teaching her way through college, who explained that traditionally Jews pray three times a day. Even at their Reform synagogue, there were services every Friday night and Saturday morning, she explained, and a few times a week, on the New Moon, and on other holidays, like Passover and Sukkoth, as well. That had been a relief for Nomi, discovering there were more opportunities to speak to God.

Nomi had asked her parents if the family could go to services more often. Her parents said they were not interested, twice a year was enough for them. But Rebecca offered to take her to Friday night services, and that became their routine. Her teacher would pick her up and take her along to synagogue every Friday night before dinner. Nomi loved the service. She especially liked the part when everyone stood, turned to the door, and bowed, welcoming the Sabbath Queen. She pictured a spirit queen blowing in like the wind, turning the day into Shabbat.

Then, after her bat mitzvah, Nomi decided she wanted to go every Shabbat morning as well. She especially liked the Torah service; that is how she had remembered those verses from Deuteronomy. But the Friday night service was always her favorite; she was glad when the kibbutz started having them. She missed that now. She had not said the mourners kaddish for Avi or her sister and nephew since leaving Israel.

But she wanted to go to synagogue now not just to say kaddish. She had a lot to say to the God who had disappeared from her life. Not only had that God taken Avi from her, but her life with him was not as she had thought.

And not only had her parents reinforced her shame, but they had reinforced her guilt, instead of helping her see what it had taken a seventeen-year-old to show her: she had been raped. Whether she screamed or not, she had told him no, and he had had no right to force her.

And not only was she going to disappoint Lisa by leaving, but she was going to disappoint Ruth, too, by not agreeing to adopt her baby.

That day she first met Lisa, John had mistaken her stance for standing, when, really, she had barely been sitting. And now, whatever chair had been holding her even in that position was pulled out from under her.

And there was a new strain of Covid now. Omicron, they called it. What was God trying to tell her and the world?

The only synagogue she knew of in the more immediate area was Ruth's father's Chabad House. She decided to go; she could get a glimpse of him at the same time. She was curious about this warlock Ruth had described with such mixed feelings. He was not to blame for Ruth being ousted from the house; it was her mother who had told her to leave. He believed in miracles and magic, but sounded grounded, too. Perhaps he could be of help to Nomi now.

She looked online for the location. She would tell Ruth she was going to Frank's house to check on him.

The only dress or skirt Nomi found in Jude's closet was a long summer sundress, which she put on over a pair of corduroys and a turtleneck sweater. When she found the address, she parked the truck a block away and walked to the building. She did not want to be seen coming out of her car; Orthodox Jews did not drive on the Sabbath.

Nomi walked into the synagogue and sat in the women's section, behind a carved wooden partition. The other seats in this section were empty, except for an elderly woman in a wig who was dozing off, and a young woman in a long skirt and baggy turtleneck sweater who was swaying with fervor, the prayer book pushed up against her face.

This suited Nomi fine. She just wanted to sit with God. If God was willing to sit with her. She took a prayer book and held it on her lap, unopened. Although she spoke Hebrew fluently, she was used to modern Hebrew spoken by Israelis, not liturgical Hebrew sung by an American in melodies she did not recognize.

She listened to the drone and murmur of the men praying on the other side of the partition and was at peace with not being able to decipher what they were saying. It brought her back to those outings with Rebecca, a highlight of her week. Besides, she didn't need other people's words to talk to God. Relying on others in her life had only backfired.

Nomi closed her eyes and let the singing wash over her as she threw a silent request out into the Universe: *God, I believe you exist. The beauty in nature is just too perfect and intricate to be a fluke. But you feel so far away. I'm lost, need your guidance. If there really are four guardian angels, I have one more coming. Please. I need my fourth angel now.*

Suddenly, the singing stopped, and the room quietened to a hush. Nomi opened her eyes and looked through the latticework in the partition.

A tall man with a dark beard, wearing a black fedora and a long black silk coat, stepped up to the pulpit. He was thin and well-groomed, not what Nomi was expecting. She had pictured Ruth's father hefty and disheveled. And old. This man was younger than Nomi, which made sense, now that Nomi did the math. Ruth was the oldest child in her family, and in her world, they still married young.

This rabbi also had a strong presence, despite his strange outfit. Like the statue of Roger Conant outside the witch museum.

He removed his mask. "Good Shabbos," he said, looking around at his audience and fingering his beard. It had been hard to see with the mask, but he had the same large nose and big round eyes as Ruth.

It had been hard to see at first, but he had the same large nose and big round eyes as Ruth.

"In this week's *parshah*, we read of the Children of Israel, *B'nai Yisroel*, who cried out to *Hakadosh Baruch Hu*, The Holy One Blessed May He Be, to save them from *avdus*, from slavery. They cried and they cried," he continued, "and *Hakadosh Baruch Hu* kept sending them miracles. One miracle after another, but it was not enough for them. This time, just as the Holy One was about to give them the biggest gift of all, the *shnei luchos habris*, the tablets of the covenant, they were so blind to their good fortune that they built a golden calf." He waved his hands in the air. "Imagine that. They thought a *pesel*, a statue, could save them more than the Almighty."

The rabbi paced the podium. "Were they just crazy? How could they not see what was right in front of their faces?" He raised his arms, looking up as if at God. This man did not need an intermediary, an idol, a golden calf. He seemed to have a direct line to the divine.

"It reminds me of a story the *Rebbe* liked to tell, of a pious man who is on a sinking ship. He keeps calling out to God to save him. First a lifeboat goes by and the man on board offers to save him, but he says he is waiting for *Hakadosh Baruch Hu*, that he has faith. The lifeboat leaves. Then a rowboat goes by, and the rower, too, offers to take him, but again, he says he has faith in *Hakadosh Baruch Hu*, so the rowboat leaves, too."

"When only his face is above water, a big steam liner goes by and someone on board throws this pious man a rope, but the man says he believes *Hakadosh Baruch Hu* will save him at the last minute, so that boat passes, too. The pious man drowns. He goes to heaven and asks God: 'Why didn't you save me? I was pious, I believed.' God answers: 'I tried! I sent you a lifeboat, a rowboat, and a ship. Why didn't you let me save you?'"

There were chuckles from the men's section.

"Yes, it's humorous, isn't it? And the man on the sinking ship is a fool. But we are all on a sinking ship. No one gets out of this life alive, as they say. But *Hakadosh Baruch Hu* is sending us a lifeline every minute of every day. Just like He did to *B'nai Yisroel* back then. Those *mishugena*s who won't be vaccinated or wear masks, they're as bad as the man on the sinking ship who refuses to get on the lifeboat."

There was a din of murmuring among the audience, and Nomi wondered if they were agreeing or disagreeing. According to what she had read and heard on the news, most ultra-Orthodox rabbis were encouraging their communities not to be vaccinated or wear masks. In fact, from what she could see through the latticework of the partition, only about half the men were wearing masks. Ruth was right; her father was an exceptional character.

"And just as foolish is any Jew who passes up the opportunity to live a life of *Yiddishkeit*," the rabbi added. "The *Toyra*, the *shnei luchos habris*, is our lifeline. It won't make us live forever, but it will make this life a meaningful one. I know it's not easy always to keep the *mitzvos*. Sometimes our *yetzer harah* tries to steer us away from doing what we know is best. We run away from the embrace of *Hakdosh Baruch Hu* who loves us, who wants us to come home to Him. But we refuse, and in the end, we're only hurting ourselves."

Nomi was sitting on the edge of her seat. Perhaps this was what she needed. To come home to God through religious observance. She had always been attracted to the comfort of rules, a clear structure of appropriate behavior, a coherent understanding of what was expected of her, and a plain idea of what was right and wrong.

She sat through the rest of the service with her eyes closed, taking in the calming atmosphere. Could this be a home for her? When she heard the words of the mourner's kaddish, she stood and recited it too.

Suddenly, she heard a shushing noise to her right. It was coming from the elderly woman in the wig, who had awoken and was shaking her head at Nomi. Then she started clucking her tongue. What was she trying to tell her? Nomi lowered her voice but continued reciting.

The young woman to her left came over and whispered, "Women don't say kaddish here. Only men do that. It's *asur*. A woman's voice is *ervah*. It's immodest. If you're interested in that kind of Judaism, go to the Reform. Not here. This is the real thing."

Nomi, her face turning warm, stopped saying the kaddish. She looked between the latticework and saw the rabbi looking toward the women's section from the corner of his eye, but he said nothing. He could not see the women from his side, but he must have heard her start and stop reciting. Apparently, these women were right. How could she have thought this might be a home for her? It had not even been a home for this rabbi's own daughter.

This rabbi and his synagogue—*shuls* and their rules, Nomi thought, remembering what Jude had said about schools and their rules so many years ago—were not going to provide the comfort or salvation she was seeking.

People would only let her down. Humanity would only let her and God down. She left as anonymously as she had come.

CHAPTER 25

NOMI FILLED A thermos with coffee, made a *tehina* sandwich, grabbed some carrots, a green apple, and left a note for Ruth saying she'd be gone most of the day. She put on her sister's hiking boots, threw on a down jacket, knitted hat and gloves, a fleece neck warmer, and started out the door.

"Come on boy!" she said, grabbing Elvis' leash and heading out to the truck.

It was a gray day, but temperate, and no rain. A gloomy winter morning. The clouds hung low and long. There was still snow on the ground, but it seemed to be melting, and there was no ice at least.

Nomi got in the driver's seat. She needed to clear her head in the fresh air. John had told her about a mountain less than an hour away with beautiful views from a fire tower at the peak. It was in a state park over the New Hampshire border. She put the location into Waze and turned her key in the ignition, but the engine didn't catch. She tried again. Still nothing.

"Damn truck!" she growled and hit the dashboard. Elvis, who was sitting in the front seat next to her, barked at the ignition. It suddenly started.

The drive was almost straight north on the highway. Elvis had his head out the window, and his long ears flapped in the wind. Nomi kept her gloves on, with the cold air coming in, but Elvis was enjoying himself too much for her to close the window.

At least one of them was having fun.

The trees were empty of leaves and looked cold in their naked state: black trunks in snow-covered earth against a gray sky with white clouds. As though someone had turned a color photo into black-and-white, like Oz into Kansas. Her life.

When Nomi reached the state park, she asked the ranger in the office where she could find the trailhead.

She parked, let Elvis out of the car, put him on his leash, and made her way to the trail. She let him off and they started to walk.

Elvis stopped.

"Come on!" she called.

Their walks were usually leisurely and level; he was a hound—stubborn and lazy. He sat down.

"I'm going up, Elvis. Please come."

He stood, yawned, and followed, keeping pace behind her, although he stopped and signaled with his head in the opposite direction whenever she looked back to check he was there.

She began on a marked trail, which wound around the mountain base. She walked quickly, practically jogging. Something was pulling her upward. She had not moved this quickly in years.

The trees—Nomi spotted maple, pine, hemlock, fir, oak, spruce, birch, and beech—were so tall she could barely make out any sky above her. The ground was covered with pine needles, acorns, and fermenting leaves, which stuck to the soles of her hiking boots as she treaded through mulch, creating compost as she packed the fallen leaves into the ground.

Sloshing through puddles of mud and melting ice, she reached a sign for the Tower Trail. She followed the path and continued walking, at her fast pace. Suddenly, the trail became steep. She looked up, longing to be at a height where she could get some perspective, but her boots were caked with mud, weighing her down. She took one off at a time, balancing on one leg, scraping and banging the sole against a rock, to release the claylike muck from the rubber. She would need her footing to continue.

The climb was challenging with everything so cold and wet. She heard her own determined breath, heavy but quick, and saw it, too, turning into mist when it hit the cold air.

Elvis was not used to climbing, but when he slipped, he continued forward, which surprised Nomi. While he had his stubborn and lazy side, he also had his protective and loyal one. A true hound. He felt her sense of urgency.

When Nomi reached the top, her hands numb even beneath her gloves, she was breathing heavily from the altitude and exertion. Lightheaded and a bit dizzy, she needed some food in her body. She'd only had a few sips of coffee from her thermos while waiting at a traffic light before getting on the highway, and again after getting off.

The wind was strong on the summit. She surveyed the territory—shaking out her arms and hands, sore from climbing—and looked for a good spot to sit and rest. But there was no unexposed place, no protection from the elements. Up here the wind came at her mercilessly, like needles against her cheeks. She put her neck warmer over her mouth and nose.

Perhaps this had not been the best idea.

Then she saw the fire tower. She had imagined a lighthouse more than a tower. This structure was a wooden booth on metal stilts, with a narrow staircase zigzagging upwards. With the mist and low-lying clouds, this could be a stairway to heaven, or a portal to the divine, only it was devoid of any such signs. If there had ever been angels ascending and descending, they had long gone. Unless they were up at the lookout point. The desire to climb still higher, and perhaps find shelter, propelled Nomi forward.

Up she climbed, fighting the wind and ignoring her aches and pains, her watery eyes blurring her vision. When she reached the booth, it occurred to her perhaps someone was inside. She knocked. No answer. She tried the door. It was locked. She turned to head down, teetering on the ledge of the platform, but the view caught her eye. She looked past snow-brushed pine trees out to the landscape in the distance. Filmy clouds, stretched thin along the horizon, hung suspended. Floating vapors and condensation. Did they even exist at all, or were they a figment of the human imagination?

Everything was an illusion. A creation of the human mind. Even those purple mountains beneath the clouds. Purple mountain majesties. But where was God's grace now? God's wrath and rage were more like it. Even America, the Land of the Free, was an illusion. So were good Jewish boyfriends, perfect marriages, blameless founding fathers and mothers, and parents who protect their children. There was nowhere to run or hide. No escaping life.

Nomi let go of the railing and opened her arms to her sides. This is what it felt like to be on the high diving board. She had never had the courage to make the climb. Yet here she was, literally standing in her sister's shoes, feeling reckless. With no grounding, no direction, and utterly alone.

She felt her body swaying with the wind. She could jump. Who would know? Who would care? Like the Buddha, she had no attachments. No one was worrying about her, no one depending on her. She had Ruth, but their relationship was temporary, as fleeting as the vapors making the clouds, and as the breath coming out of her mouth as her chest heaved and her lungs worked extra hard to do their life-sustaining work.

Ruth would give birth, and when Nomi did not adopt her baby, their time together would pass, a memory evaporating slowly into thin air. Like her mother said, there was no one to take care of her and no one for her to care for. There was just her mother left, and that was painful. And she was fading, too.

Even her memories of the charmed life she had thought she shared with Avi were no longer sacred. She did not doubt his love for her. She did not doubt he kept his enormous secret from her out of a desire to protect her. But with no past, no present, and no future, she no longer saw the point of going on. Even Batja had stayed alive only for Izaak. And then she, too, had given up hope and most likely taken her own son's life. Like Leah Marshall, giving in to despair. If they could, Nomi could, too. She had nothing and no one.

If Tolstoy's recipe for happiness was correct, what were her chances of finding it? What was her purpose on this earth? Why was she even here at all?

The wind swayed Nomi to-and-fro as she inched her way closer to the edge. She closed her eyes and found herself in her sister's dream. No one was her parachute. She could jump, and no one would catch her. How would it feel to fly, before she hit the cold harsh ground? She had read somewhere, when jumping from such a height, death happens before impact; the air pressure breaks you first. Dying in flight did not scare Nomi; there was an allure to it. She could die quietly, like she had lived, leaving this galaxy like a cloud.

She opened her eyes and stepped further to the edge of the platform, the wind blowing in her face. But as she looked out at the endless expanse around her, she knew what she wanted was not to jump, but to be lifted away. She wanted a parachute. She did not want to die. She wanted to be saved. She wanted God to save her, to send her an angel. God had done it before. Where was God now? Tears were streaming down her cheeks, and she heard whimpering. Was it coming from that bottomless empty place inside her?

It was Elvis. He had followed her up to the fire tower. She had forgotten about the poor dog. He, too, had no one. Nomi was his angel. How would he get home without her? There *was* a being on this earth who needed her.

And Ruth, too?

What if Ruth asking Nomi to adopt her baby was the lifeline God was sending? Had she been too blind, or too absorbed in self-pity, to notice? She could help Ruth. As Ruth's rabbi father had said, doing good deeds is what makes life meaningful. That is what Tolstoy, too, had said, as well as being surrounded by those you love. She had imagined a quiet life in the country could only be with Avi. Had she been shortsighted?

Nomi could do it. She could adopt Ruth's baby. She could take the baby back to the kibbutz, where she had security, a safety net and support system, and a framework to raise the boy. And she'd stay in touch with Ruth, so she could still be part of her son's life and maybe even join them at some point; that's what she wanted. They'd figure it out. If she adopted the child in the U.S., it would be a fait accompli. The kibbutz wouldn't dare protest if he was already legally hers. And if they did, she would fight them on it. She was not the timid newcomer she had been when she and Avi had talked about adoption.

Nomi did not have to play the role of Jonah in the parachute dream. She could play the role of the parachute if she chose. Could she be a parent? Could she be a parachute ready to open? It was more than her own parents had done, and here she was, not only surviving, but making a difference in the world. Despite the mistakes her own parents had made. Or perhaps even because of them.

Nomi had let Avi's lack of interest in adoption, her own ambivalences around becoming a parent, and her doubts about her ability to do a good job, dissuade her from pursuing that possibility. She did not have to be a perfect parent, she was learning in her new role supporting Ruth. She could be present and do her best, and that was already a lot.

She did not have to be a superhuman spouse to her dead husband, either. Avi had not been to her. He had seemed so content with just their shared life, she had not wanted to admit she wanted more. But he had not been contented, and she too had wanted more, even if she understood that only now.

She had a choice. As deceitful as Avi's actions had been, his intentions had been generous; he had, in fact, been doing a good deed. But he had not consulted with her. He had acted without her consent. If he could fulfill his needs and dreams behind her back, she could do so, too, now, with him gone. He was not showing up to guide her, so she would have to act unilaterally, as he had. She wanted love in her life. She was only human, after all.

Nomi had love to give and a heart open to receiving it. That was all she had expected from her own parents, and it was all she needed to be a good enough parent herself. Even her own parents had managed that much. And it had been enough. Enough to bring her to this point, standing on this platform on the peak of this mountain—the wind rattling her but not knocking her down—ready to dive into the next stage of her life.

The letter from the hospital was God's way of telling her we all have choices. Even she had back then—although she hadn't been aware or awake enough to realize it. God was sending her a lifeline, even if she had been too myopic to see there are many ways to communicate with God. Now all she need do was grab it. The thought of adopting Ruth's baby made Nomi's stomach fill with butterflies, but rather than quiet them, she would give them freedom to fly.

Nomi squatted and buried her face in Elvis' fur. He licked her cheeks, the kiss of unconditional love bringing her back to the land of the living. "I'm sorry, boy. I forgot about you. There are lots of dogs on the kibbutz. You'll like it there. I promise."

Elvis wagged his tail excitedly.

Nomi took hold of the shaky banister and found her bearings. The wind had died down a bit, and she had Elvis by her side to accompany her down. She began her descent, an angel carrying herself to sturdier, even if not safe, ground.

CHAPTER 26

REMEMBERING HER CONVERSATION with Ruth from the night before, Nomi set out with Elvis. She had promised to speak to Diane about adopting the baby, and Ruth had literally jumped up from her chair, come over to Nomi, and given her a long, firm hug. As she felt her arms around her, her coarse hair against her cheek, Nomi realized she had not hugged anyone but Avi since the pandemic had started. It was her first human embrace since Avi had died. She had held on for a few moments even after she felt Ruth's grasp loosening.

With all that excitement the night before, Nomi had had trouble sleeping and had awoken with the sun. Elvis had been eager to go out on a walk, so Nomi had grabbed his leash and was now on her way to the woods. It was February, there were still patches of snow on the ground, and she had not been in the woods in a while. But it was going to be a clear day, and she could already feel the sun warming her as it rose higher in the sky.

She wanted to visit that cabin again and read more of Jonah's books. It made her feel closer to the nephew she had never really known. Jude had been concerned about him; she was eager to get to know them both better, even if posthumously.

As she walked, Nomi heard the dripping of snow and ice melting around her. Spring would come in due time. She imagined the sap rising in the tree trunks standing in their sleep, like a stretch and yawn, as they slowly woke from their slumbers.

The cold would pass, what was frozen would thaw, seeds dormant through the cold of winter would send signs of life shooting up through the earth and grow buds to flower and open to the sun. Winter was part of the cycle, a necessary part of the flow of life, not the end of it—even if sometimes that was hard to believe.

The cabin was just as she'd left it. Perhaps no one else knew of its existence. And with Lisa's condition deteriorating rapidly, John had not even asked her to bring him there yet. Elvis scratched at the door. Nomi lifted the latch and the door opened inward. Elvis went straight to his bone and started gnawing.

Nomi closed the door behind her. It was a bit warmer inside than out, but not much. She looked through some books, rubbing her hands together every once in a while to stay warm. She returned the books to the shelves and spotted what looked like a scrapbook. She opened it, finding page after page of clippings from newspapers about global warming, reporting on natural disasters, and predicting the end of the planet. In the front, there were verses from Genesis, the story of the Flood, handwritten—by Jonah?

> *And God saw how great human wickedness was on earth, and how every plan devised by the human mind was nothing but evil all the time. And God regretted having put humans on earth, and God's heart was saddened. God said, "I will blot out from the earth the humans I created—humans, together with beasts, creeping things, and birds of the sky; for I regret that I made them."*

Jude's dream had reflected reality. This is why Jude had been concerned. Jonah had not been able to see the rainbow Nomi was now beginning to make out on the horizon.

IT WAS ALREADY nine am when Nomi arrived back at the house. Ruth had awoken on her own and was going to the dining room for a Zoom class.

Diane would likely have started her workday at the center at nine. Nomi went out to the porch and called her number.

She looked out at the back of the property while she waited for Diane to answer. The trees were still bare, but in a few months, there would be leaves, then fruit. Blueberries, too. Would she be here for that harvest, or would she, Elvis, and the baby already be back in Israel on the kibbutz? The housing committee chair had said she had six months. What if the adoption process took longer? Surely, they would extend the deadline for that. Or find her and the baby a different house.

"Good morning, Nomi," Diane said. "How are you? And Ruth?"

"Good. Very good. Ruth is doing well, considering. She's a delight. I'm so glad I did this. It's just what we both needed."

A squirrel ran down the trunk of an oak tree with an acorn in its mouth.

"Yes. I hear the same from her. How wonderful it's working out. I'm grateful you took her in."

Nomi did not want to disturb Diane. She thought she heard typing in the background. Or maybe she just sounded distracted.

"Do you need anything, or were you just checking in? How are the birthing classes going?"

The squirrel was now perched on the rim of the well, opening the acorn.

"Great. I think she'll do just fine. And it's special for me, too. I've never done this before, you know."

"Yes, I do know. I hope it isn't too much for you." She paused. "Emotionally, I mean."

Nomi shook her head, answering the question for herself before she did for Diane. "No, no. Just the opposite. You see, we were talking." She took a breath. "Ruth asked me to adopt her baby. I thought about it, and I think it's a good idea." There. It was out.

There was quiet on the other end, and Nomi wondered if they had gotten disconnected.

"Really . . ." Diane finally said, between a question and a statement. "Are you sure?"

"Yes. I gave it a lot of thought. It makes sense. I can take him back to the kibbutz. Life is paradise for kids there." Once they stopped having the kids sleep in the children's house, it really became an ideal place to raise a child. "He'll have a good, secure life. And Ruth can rest assured he's in loving hands."

"Nomi—"

"We'll stay in touch, and Ruth can even visit. She told me she wants to see Israel. She's never been. Maybe she can come live there one day. Or I can bring the baby here to visit." She could handle the travel committee now; they'd have to agree. "We'll figure it out. It's what we both want. I don't want to be alone for the rest of my life."

"I hope you won't be," Diane said. "You may find love again. And if you do, having a young child will not make that easier."

"I'm not looking for romance right now." Nomi noticed the squirrel had gone.

"That may change." Diane sounded curt.

"Maybe." Nomi tightened her grip on her phone. "I'm thinking about now, Diane, and I'd like to do this." She thought of her conversation with Ruth, of the pleading look in her eyes. "There's a Yiddish word. *Bashert.* Do you know it? This was meant to be."

"Ok. I understand it's what you want." Diane sighed. "But it's a long shot. How old are you?"

"Sixty—"

"Oh, really. I thought you were a bit younger—"

"A young sixty. And healthy. I thought about that. I'd likely see him through college at least."

"Listen, Nomi. I'll be frank. You have three strikes against you: your age, your widowhood, and your place of residence. Plus, even if they say it's not out of the question, there's a process. Interviews, recommendations. References. It would not be a done deal."

"I understand that. But still . . ."

Diane paused then sighed again. "I'll make some calls and see what I can find out."

"Ruth and I would be so grateful." Nomi realized she'd been holding her breath. She let it out, slowly.

"Okay. It's a lovely idea, but don't get your hopes up. I'll be in touch. I have another call now—I must go."

"Goodbye. And thank you," Nomi said.

She looked out the porch windows. Squirrel was back again. With a friend.

Then she said another, quiet, "Thank you," to the God she felt coming back into her life.

CHAPTER 27

NOMI DIDN'T MIND waiting for Diane to call back. No news was good news. And for the next two weeks, when she returned from her walks with Elvis, she checked the mailbox to see if there was a package from Amazon, or a note from the post office to come pick one up, but nothing. There had been an email saying delivery had been a bit delayed, but the package should arrive any day now. She wanted to know what had happened to Izaak.

While her coffee was percolating, she went to the porch and brought Batja's diary to the kitchen table. She flipped through the pages again and picked up the photo of her sister with her buzz cut, on her knees among the blueberries, her hands in a namaste gesture. Her own thank you to the God she did or did not believe in. What was Jude trying to tell her?

The coffee was bubbling up. Nomi went to pour herself a cup. She added hot milk and was about to sit down when an old compact disc player on a shelf caught her eye. There was a disc already inside the player, an album by the Israeli singer Arik Einstein, one of her personal favorites.

Nomi had introduced Jonah to some of her choice Israeli singers when he had visited; he had taken a particular liking to Einstein, so she had given him a few discs for his continued travels, and even translated some of the songs for him. This was one of those discs. It touched her to know she had influenced him even in this small way.

She pressed play and sat down with her latte. When the song "And to Die" came on, she closed her eyes to listen more carefully. It was originally a poem, written by Abraham Chalfi, which Einstein set to music. She had always loved this raw meditation on mortality and human existential loneliness. Considering Jonah's reading material, it made sense he was drawn to this song, which was even more poignant with both Einstein and Chalfi now, like Jonah, no longer among the living.

"And to die, to die in secret, here in this room . . ."

As she listened to the lyrics now, they seemed more depressing to her than she remembered. Perhaps Chalfi had been mentally ill, even contemplating suicide.

Had Jonah been listening to this disc, this song, the night of his and Jude's deaths? Maybe they had been listening to it together. That was just too sad.

As the song reached its last stanza, Nomi sat up in her chair and clasped her mug to her chest. She remembered the words; they felt especially relevant now.

For everything, everything is but a song that always ends suddenly,
Between being and not-being, on an evening that annuls everything.
And I—I am just the son of a mother who died once.
Nothing more.

Nomi stood to change the disc, put on something more uplifting and stop the dark thoughts running through her head. She opened the disc's cover and found her translation of this song folded inside—worn and faded, but still legible. The words of the last stanza were underlined, in pencil that seemed much fresher than the pen Nomi had used those years ago. Like the pencil underlines in Batja's diary.

Chills ran all through Nomi.

Instead of putting the disc back, with trembling hands she returned the song to the beginning and pressed play. She sat again at the table to listen, looking at the photo of her sister in her Buddha-like pose and haircut. Who had taken the photo?

As Einstein sang that last stanza, Nomi looked into her sister's eyes. What had she been thinking when she had that picture taken? What had been going through her mind when she underlined those words?

CHAPTER 28

"COMING!" FRANK CALLED when Nomi kept ringing the doorbell. "Hold your horses!"

He opened the door and rolled around to the threshold. He was in his Harley sweatshirt again, but today with no bandana. Nomi had guessed he was bald, but it was still striking to see his hairless crown contrasted with the abundance of hair from right above his ears and downward.

"What's wrong?" he asked. "What's with all that ringing? You don't look so good."

"I haven't been sleeping well these past few nights. You said Jude was preparing for death. What did you mean?"

"Here. Come in and sit down," Frank said. He had his mask hanging from the armrest on his wheelchair. He put it on.

Nomi nearly always wore hers. This new Omicron strain was more contagious than the others. There was no end to this nightmare. And on the radio on her way over, Nomi heard Russia had invaded Ukraine. Batja's beloved Lwów, now Lviv, was under siege again.

She walked into the living room but did not sit.

Frank followed in his wheelchair.

She wrung her hands, trying hard not to crack her knuckles. "First, I should tell you, I'm pretty sure Jonah was suicidal. I don't think their deaths were an accident."

"*Their* deaths?" he whispered. "Jude's too?" He looked pained but did not so much as flinch, nor did his eyes reveal shock or even surprise.

"I don't know. I keep turning it over in my head. I have this awful feeling about it. Did you know about Jonah's mental health? Did Jude tell you?" Nomi closed her eyes and took a breath. "Did she suspect he might do something like that?"

Frank shook his head, his ponytail swinging. "She didn't tell me anything. When I asked questions about Jonah, she was evasive, protective of him. I had a feeling he wasn't stable, but I didn't press her. I respected her privacy."

Nomi paced Frank's living room. "Her privacy? We're talking about her life here. And her son's."

"She was devoted to him," Frank said softly. "I can't imagine her committing him to an institution against his will. That was not her way. And she took things on, as you must know. Especially other people's pain."

Nomi took the diary out of her bag. "I want to show you something," she said and opened the book to where she had returned the photo, back between the pages. She handed it to him.

He gazed at Jude. "She was so beautiful." His eyes filled with tears. "Just as I thought."

"What do you mean? Did you take this photo?"

"No, I didn't."

Of course, he didn't. He had never even been to the house. Jude had never brought Frank to her house not because she was hiding him from Jonah, but because she was hiding Jonah from him. This was clear to her now.

"And I mean, that look on her face," Frank added. "Don't you see it? She reached nirvana."

"Nirvana?" She knew the word, but what was he saying?

"Yes. Her soul learned all it needed to learn in this life."

"How can you be so sure?"

"Look at her. That's why she cut her hair, too. It was only a few weeks before she died. She was letting go of attachments. It made her happy. Honestly, during those last weeks she was the happiest I had ever seen her. It was like she was already on her way to that other place." He sighed. "She was lighter, like a cloud. I felt like I was with an angel. Looking at her now, I am certain she was enlightened."

Nomi took the photo from Frank and looked again into her sister's eyes. She did look like an angel. And her smile did radiate inner peace. It was the look Krakauer had described on McCandless' face as well. Being a cloud did not have to mean nothingness. Or nothingness did not have to be bad. Even for Avi, perhaps.

She placed the photo on the table.

Jude had been at peace, but why did *she* not feel at peace knowing that? "But that doesn't diminish the tragedy of the whole story. I can't accept this was the way it was meant to be."

He looked at the photo again. Lovingly. "Jude tried not to fight against fate. A big theme in her life, especially those last weeks."

Nomi was tired of this talk of accepting fate, embracing it, even. Who decided this was Jude's fate?

True, Nomi did not know what it was like to have a child. She did not judge her sister for protecting her son. But she did blame her for not doing all she could to save both their lives. Batja had tried, at least, even if she had not succeeded.

And if there had been any way to save Avi, Nomi would have at least tried. What had happened to her sister the fighter? Where had her warrior spirit gone?

Nomi was relieved Jude had died in peace. But she was going to go down fighting.

"Frank . . ."

"Yes?"

"Do you really want to ride a motorcycle again?"

Frank's eyes showed he was grinning. "Yes, I do. Why?"

"If that's what you love, then do it. I'm going to help you."

CHAPTER 29

NOMI REALIZED SHE had to confront David. It was time.

Avi was gone. As much as she wanted to feel him still with her, he was not. She could not ask why he had done what he did. But if David was still alive, perhaps she could at least ask him.

When at last Nomi mustered the courage to tell John the story, he was sympathetic, of course. He agreed to help locate David, which did not take long; he was still living in Massachusetts, in their hometown, in fact. He had taken over his father's business. Wholesale. He must have been doing well to afford living in that neighborhood. Or married well. Or both. Even if he didn't have two post high-school degrees, he was living the life her parents had wanted her to live. He would have been a good catch in their eyes.

Nomi couldn't decide whether to call. She put his number into her phone and tapped it, then quickly disconnected. This went on for over a week. She didn't know what she wanted.

It was that feeling of knowing there was a mess in a drawer she had yet to clean, but instead of cleaning, she had closed the drawer. If she couldn't see the mess, did it exist?

But she had to open it.

So, a few days later, there she was, sitting behind John on his police motorcycle, with Frank in an attached trailer. Nomi had asked John if he could rent a handicapped equipped trailer for the day, and they had shown up in front of Frank's house to surprise him. His eyes had filled with tears. Frank was a crier, a trait Nomi found endearing and assumed Jude had, too. He looked blissful as they rode, his eyes closed, feeling the wind on his face.

She had been planning to ride behind them in her truck, but John suggested she come along with them on his bike. He was a safe and careful driver, he explained, and he had an extra helmet and jacket for passengers. She trusted him. Still, there were other drivers on the road, too.

He had revved up the engine, and she had held her breath, closed her eyes, and prayed. But soon she realized not seeing was scarier.

Nomi held on tightly around John's middle. In the past, she would have been terrified at the thought of riding a motorcycle. Now she wasn't. She knew John's uniform had something to do with that, but it was also the person inside it—and she was feeling unusually brave since she had come down from that fire tower.

David had been surprised to hear from her but was pleasant enough. He said he was glad she had called; he had things he wanted to say. He sounded sincere. But then again, he had always been a charmer. She did not want to take any chances. She wanted her new friends with her, in case she needed help. Without hesitation they agreed to join.

Ruth had wanted to come, too, but Nomi thought it might trigger her own trauma. She'd be better off staying home and not falling behind in her schoolwork so close to her due date. Nomi would feel her support from afar and fill her in when she returned. Ruth resisted but eventually agreed.

They exited the highway into the suburb where Nomi had lived as a child. She loosened her grasp on John's middle just a bit and relaxed enough to look around as he maneuvered the suburban streets. The town had changed considerably. Starbucks had not even existed in her day. Now, Nomi saw two. And the one where she was meeting David would make three.

The houses looked bigger. Returning as an adult, she had thought things would look smaller. But everything in the U.S. looked huge to her now, after having spent so many years in Israel—where buildings, trees, mountains, even serving sizes, were scaled down, as if to fit inside the country's tight borders.

On the kibbutz, a house like one of these grand suburban Tudors could stand on a plot of several homes. Jude's house was just as big, but its modest farmhouse character made it feel less palatial; because at least half the house was partitioned off, Nomi forgot it was even there most of the time.

The suburb had also become more Jewish. Or perhaps just more overtly so. In the sixties and seventies, just a few decades after the Holocaust, the Jews kept their Jewishness quiet. No men walked around with *kippot* on their heads, and there were no kosher restaurants. There were synagogues, but they had not drawn attention to themselves.

Now, riding through her childhood streets, she saw proud signs advertising kosher restaurants, Jewish community events, and synagogues of various denominations. There was even a building with a sign out front saying it was a community mikveh. That was something she would never have seen in this place forty years before. Jews back then hid anything that might draw anti-Semitism; immersing monthly in a ritual bath after menstruation could certainly be ammunition for the modern equivalent of a blood libel, a pogrom, even an *aktion*, they had feared. Or a witch hunt.

Nomi thought of Batja's description of their life of wealth and privilege in Lwów before the Russians, and then the Nazis. This was the unsaid message of her own childhood: *Don't flaunt your Jewish identity. We know we're better than the gentiles, the "goyyim," but don't let them know we think so, or we'll all regret it.* And end up like Batja.

John pulled up in front of the Starbucks David had recommended and went around to unfold Frank's wheelchair and help him out of the trailer. Nomi was relieved to have arrived in one piece, but also anxious about seeing David, wondering if she had made the right decision arranging this meeting.

They found tables outside, near the opening of an area partially enclosed with plastic, and with outdoor heaters. Given Covid and Nomi's need for an easily accessible quick exit, this was the safest option. They had come early on purpose. Nomi would sit by herself, and David would not realize she had brought friends.

David soon walked in, also early, and Nomi's chest tightened.

He was carrying two drinks on a tray and spotted her immediately, despite her sunglasses. He had aged. He still had a full head of hair, but it was thinner and almost completely gray. He had been lanky as a teenager, but now his physique was thicker all around. Not overweight, but healthily padded. His nose had grown a bit longer, and there were wrinkles around those blue eyes she had once found so mesmerizing.

"You look great, Naomi," he said, as if he was just meeting up with an old girlfriend. Then he threw her one of those toothy smiles that used to make her feel special. Only now it made her stomach turn. "I would have recognized you even if I hadn't known you were in town. You've barely aged." He put the tray on the table. The latte Nomi had ordered was there. He must have seen her name on the order—had he noticed the missing A?—and said he would bring it.

Was she supposed to follow his lead and act like this was just a pleasant reunion? "It's the sunglasses," Nomi said, taking them off. "See. Plenty of wrinkles." Too unsettled to drink, she wrapped her hands around the glazed white ceramic of her mug to warm them.

David pulled out his chair and sat down. His expression and the way he carried himself were different. Sad and serious, even. His cocky look was gone. "I don't see plenty. Maybe just a few. Enough to make you look wise but not old. Kibbutz life must be good for you. I heard you went to Israel and married a *kibbutznik*."

Nomi did not tell him about Avi's death; bringing her relationship with Avi into this discussion would only taint it more. It may not have been perfect, but even mentioning him here felt disloyal, unfair. Just plain wrong.

"That was brave of you, to pick up and move to Israel on your own. But you were always strong."

Had she been? Not from what she remembered.

"Honestly, you look amazing. But I always did think you were beautiful. You must remember that." He took a sip from his espresso.

Nomi scowled at the thought of their shared memories. "I do recall your telling me that. You may have even said you loved me, that last night we were together." She paused and looked him in the eye. "When you raped me." There. She had said it.

David flinched, and Nomi looked over at Frank and John's table. They exchanged glances. John gave her an encouraging nod. Frank, a thumb's up.

"I deserved that. But your memory is correct. I did say that. I meant it, even if I didn't know then what love was. Or how you treat someone you love. I worshipped you, Naomi. I was not a liar. I was an impulsive horny jerk, but I was not a liar. I thought you loved me, too. And that's what people in love did, I thought. Make love."

"But that's not what we did, David. That was not making love. When you love someone, you don't hurt them." Even as Nomi said those words, she knew the truth was not that simple. But she kept at him. There was no excuse for what he had done. "Thank God I do know what making love is, and that was not it—"

"Yes—"

"That was rape, David. I told you to stop. I told you I wasn't ready. But you didn't listen. Why didn't you listen?" She cracked her knuckles and peered at him.

David did not avoid her eyes. "I thought you wanted to anyway. I know I should have listened to what you were saying, but it felt so right. I was being the man, taking control. Everything I thought I was supposed to do. I was so turned on that you were turned on, I guess I didn't want to hear what you were saying. And I had too many beers—"

"That's no excuse—"

"I'm not making excuses, but letting you know what was going on for me. Stopping would have been the right thing to do. But it was more than I could manage in the moment. I was a kid in a man's body. I didn't have the wisdom I have now. Or the self-control."

"But you raped me, David." That was all she could think to say, all that mattered.

"I know that now, Naomi. I even knew it later that night, after you asked me to drive you home and did not say a word the whole ride. And then refused to take my calls. I knew I had messed up big time. I wanted to take it back. That's why I kept calling you. To say I was sorry."

Even if David was remorseful, Nomi needed to say her piece. "You couldn't take it back, David. You violated me and you scarred me for life. I don't go into public parks by myself or walk alone at night. It's no accident I live on a kibbutz. I feel safe there. When I enter any closed space, the first thing I do is look for a way out." She glanced over at the exit now, too. "Why do you think I chose this table?"

She looked again at her friends' table and caught John's eyes. Their softness calmed her.

David looked down into his lap. "I'm so sorry, Naomi. I don't expect you to forgive me. But I do want you to know I regret what I did. I know this won't make you feel any better, but I, too, had a really hard time after that night. At first, I was angry at you. I felt rejected and abandoned."

"Angry at me? You had no right." Tears rolled down Nomi's cheeks. She looked at her drink and, feeling nauseous, pushed it away.

"I know. When I started to understand what I had done, I carried a lot of guilt. And rightfully so. I did a terrible thing, and I began to see myself as a terrible person. I gave up on myself, got into drugs. I was in a very bad place."

"Am I supposed to feel sorry for you?"

David shook his head. "No. I just want you to know that I was not proud of what I did. And I'm glad I hit bottom because it made me get help." He moved his chair closer to the table, closer to her. "In rehab, I had intensive therapy and began to understand some of the roots of my behavior. I am a better person now, Naomi. But I never got over the guilt. Now, maybe after seeing you and apologizing face to face, I can close that circle."

Nomi moved her chair back ever so slightly and composed herself. "I don't know if you have the right to close any circles. I am glad to hear you're sorry and you realize what you did was wrong, that it was rape. But it's not my job to absolve you or release you." She realized her hands were shaking. She held them together on her lap. "I came here to close a circle for myself. To confront you and let you know how much you scarred me. To face the beast, so to speak."

David recoiled. "Wow, that hurts. But I deserve it. I was a beast. But I hope you can see I'm not anymore. I've been drug-free for thirty years. I even settled down. I think you'd like my wife. She reminds me of you in some ways."

"How so?" She wondered how else David remembered her, what he had seen in her. He said he had worshipped her. Why?

"She's focused, keeps me organized and on track. My better half, as they say." He let out a short laugh then looked down into his coffee cup, as if into a glass ball bringing him back to their past. "She's smart and good. And strong. Like you were. But it's more than that. She helps me find meaning in life, and she's always trying to improve herself, be a better person. I admire that in her, and I did in you, too. I tried to follow your example back then, but I failed miserably. I think I'm doing better at it now. I certainly am trying."

Nomi felt her nose turn warm and her eyes start to water again, but this time the emotion was different. "Thank you for that, David."

She had been afraid to revert to who she was before she had left, but maybe there was nothing to be afraid of. Perhaps who she was now, even who she aspired to be, had always been there inside her. And maybe the aspiring is what it was all about, anyway, the ability to keep getting up again after a fall—whether caused by others or even herself—a stronger, more resilient, more compassionate, more grateful and better person than she was before.

"And I can see you're trying."

"It means so much to me to hear that from you, Naomi. It's really what I live for these days, to prove myself worthy of this second chance I got in life. For my family." He put his hand into the breast pocket of his shirt. "I want you to see them. Can I show you a photo?"

Nomi nodded and reached out her hand. She did not want to see David's family, but this time, at least, he had asked her permission. There was no crime in his wanting to show the inner work he had done, how much he had changed, the life he had built as a result. He had no idea about her life, all her losses and pain. He just pulled out his wallet like he had his erection that day—with no bad intentions yet causing harm nonetheless—and handed her the photo.

As David drank the rest of his espresso, Nomi gazed into the eyes of his wholesome wife—he was right, in another life they could even have been friends—with her pack of kids and grandkids. And it did hurt. But at the same time, Nomi felt her heart open just a crack, not only to let in a bit of compassion for herself, but to let some out for David as well. It did not give her pleasure to imagine him beneath a pile of stones; it just made her sad.

As much as Nomi wanted life to be fair, as much as she wanted the world to be neat and orderly, for blame to be easily placed, for people to fit into boxes of good and bad, the world was not like that. Gray areas confused her; they were messy and not secure. But that was life. She, Avi, Jonah, Jude, Ruth, Ruth's parents, Nomi's own parents . . . Everyone in her life. Even David. They were all just doing their best at living in this unfair and chaotic world.

Nomi finally put her drink to her lips. It was lukewarm, but it would have to do.

CHAPTER 30

NOMI WAS IN the kitchen fixing lunch. Ruth was the one who usually prepared their meals, but she was starting to look uncomfortably big. Nomi wanted Ruth to feel nurtured and held; she deserved pampering.

Nomi's phone rang. She glanced at it on the counter, to see if she wanted to answer. It was Diane. Nomi quickly dried her hands with a kitchen towel and grabbed it, her heart racing.

"Nomi?"

"Yes." She tried not to sound too eager.

"Where are you? At home? With Ruth?"

"Yes. Just fixing us some lunch. Ruth's on a Zoom class. Why?"

"You may want to sit down. The news is not good."

Nomi sat down at the table, in a daze. "Okay," she almost whispered.

"I'm sorry, Nomi. But I spoke to my connections at Child Welfare. They would not authorize your adopting Ruth's baby. They won't even let you apply. You simply don't meet their criteria."

Nomi clutched the closest chair. "But—"

"I told you it was a long shot."

"You did. I know. But I still thought—"

"Listen, Nomi. Please accept this. If you want to contest, it could mean a long process not best for the baby, and it would cost a fortune in legal fees."

Nomi collapsed onto the chair. Her spirit deflating like a punctured balloon. "But it's what Ruth wants."

"Ruth has the right to keep her own child if she can take care of him properly. But she can't decide who the state gives the child to if she puts him up for adoption. She can give her preferences, but she doesn't have the final word."

Nomi pressed her slippers against the terra cotta floor. "That doesn't seem fair."

"Fair or not, that's the way it works. I really am sorry, Nomi."

"How much would a lawyer cost?" Nomi held her phone against her ear with one hand while biting on the knuckles of the other.

"Do you have the money to pay a lawyer?"

Nomi had only a few hundred dollars of what the kibbutz had given her, and Jude's bank account didn't have much more. Her money and her time were running out. "No. I don't."

"So let it go. It was a beautiful gesture, and I'm sure Ruth appreciates it. You've done so much for her already. The baby will be fine. There are waiting lists of couples who want this baby. And Ruth is smart. Maybe her family will take her back, if that is what she wants after the baby's born."

Nomi took a sharp intake of breath.

"If not, she'll find her way. And we'll help her," Diane added.

Nomi's head was spinning. What an old fool she'd been. She had never been the smart one. She knew that, even if her parents had made her believe she was, and even if David thought so, too. It had been sweet of Diane to humor her fantasies. But she was telling her now to come back to reality.

CHAPTER 31

Lisa is gone.
Small visitation, funeral.
Just family.
Because of Covid.
Thought you'd want to know.
She is finally at peace.

NOMI READ THE message a few times and let out a sigh. Lisa's suffering was over. But she could have had many more wonderful, rich years. Her grandparenting stage had just begun. She could have worked in teaching for at least another decade before retiring—if she had even wanted to retire at all. Avi had still been working the tractors when he got Covid. Now, just like her, John was left alone.

In Jewish tradition, there is a seven-day shiva when people visit the mourners as they sit on the floor or on low benches, their clothing ripped and the mirrors in their homes covered. This was meant to be comforting for the bereaved. But Nomi had not wanted it, had not wanted to be around people. Avi's parents had sat shiva in their house, and she had been expected to join them. But she had refused. She only wanted to be with Avi. Since that was impossible, she had just wanted to be alone.

She wondered what John wanted.

What would you like from me? A visit, after the funeral? A walk in the woods? I do know how hard it is. I've been there. Still am.

John did not know about Avi's deception. She might tell him, but not while he was mourning his own beloved. Anyway, it did not change how much she missed her husband. In some ways, it made her miss him more. He had died with a secret. It would remain a mystery, and her wound open and sore.

John did not answer her message.

She waited. She had wanted space and time, so she knew to give him both. Finally, a few days later, he did write back.

A walk in the woods sounds nice. I'll be in touch.

IT WAS A cloudy February morning. Nomi wondered if taking a walk was a good idea. But John had texted the night before to say he'd be there.

She had just finished packing a picnic breakfast when she saw him pull up to the house. She put the thermos of coffee—black, like John liked his—and egg, lettuce, and tomato sandwiches, in her backpack, put on a hat and gloves, wrapped a scarf around her neck, and went out with Elvis.

John had taken a couple weeks off to plan the funeral, sort through Lisa's things, and take care of what he had months before called the bureaucracy of dying. When he had mentioned that to Nomi, she had not known how close to home it was for him, too.

John was not in uniform. Instead, he was wearing jeans with a leather jacket and hiking boots. He was parking his motorcycle when she came up behind him. He took off his helmet and put on a woolen hat from his coat pocket.

"I'm so sorry," Nomi said. John's back was hunched despite his muscular physique. She touched it. Lightly.

He turned around to meet her eyes. His looked bloodshot. Either he had not slept much or had been crying. Or both. "This sucks. Death sucks."

"I know. Life in general sucks. Let's start walking."

They walked in silence; the winds were strong, so it would have been hard to talk anyway. It started to drizzle, but neither of them seemed to mind.

Elvis was in the lead, as they followed the trail, the wind blowing through the trees like a howling dog. Crying for them both, it seemed.

When they reached the turn-off to the cabin, Elvis veered from the trail, sniffing the ground. John looked at Nomi questioningly. Nomi started after Elvis. John walked alongside her.

"Where are we going?" he asked—the first words either of them had uttered since the walk had begun. His cheeks were wet with tears, most likely not just from the cold winds and light rain mixed with hail.

"To Jonah's cabin. It's this way. Let's go there to dry off and warm up. I packed us breakfast."

"Right. I meant to go there, should have. I've been lying down on the job, I'm afraid."

"You've been busy, John," Nomi said, throwing him a sympathetic look. "With more important things. Besides, you go way beyond doing your job. You've been such a big help to me since I got here. I wish I knew what to say to make you feel better."

"I'm not sure I want to feel better," John said as he walked, his gloved hands in the pockets of his jacket, his head drooped at the neck. "Lisa deserves at least that. And it feels like a tribute to our love in some way, too. Like proof it was worth all this suffering." Lisa had known he would be stoic.

"I get that." Nomi shivered. "Thank you for articulating it." She touched John's arm, and they both stopped walking. He lifted his head and looked at her. Their eyes locked. "And, honestly, there *is* no feeling better. Every day is a struggle. I take one day at a time. And even that sometimes feels like too much."

When they reached the cabin, Nomi opened the door and gestured for John to go in. Elvis entered first, sniffing around the floor, until he found his bone, which he took in his mouth and carried to his favorite spot on the rug. John followed Elvis, and Nomi closed the door to shut out some of the damp cold. This was the first time she had been here with another person. It was nice; she felt comfortable and safe with John, even alone here. Yet, what could she offer him when she, too, was so empty?

Nomi sat to unpack their picnic breakfast. John joined her on the wooden bench. They were both shivering. Nomi poured black coffee into the thermos cup and realized she had not brought another. The sandwiches sat, untouched, in front of them.

She took a sip and made a face. So focused on wanting to comfort John, she had forgotten how important the hot milk was for her own comforting morning coffee ritual. She offered him the cup.

He shook his head. "Covid."

Nomi's face turned warm. She had forgotten in the intimacy of the moment. Even John was foregoing a mask although they were indoors.

"I'll drink from the thermos." And he did just that. He couldn't sit still for long, got up, took a book off the shelf, and flipped through it, then put it back and scanned the titles. "He had a nice little library here. This place is amazing."

Nomi took the scrapbook off the shelf and handed it to John. "Take a look at this."

John flipped through the book. "He was concerned about global warming. I knew that."

"Read the quote on the front."

John read it. "Okay. He was very concerned."

Nomi hesitated but decided to continue. "I want to share something with you. But I don't know if I should, especially not under these circumstances.

But I want to share it first because you're a friend, and second because of your professional position."

John didn't say anything, just nodded.

"Well, I guess I'll just say it. I trust you to do what you think is right." Nomi paused, then said softly, "I'm pretty sure Jonah took his own life, that it was not an accident, and I think he may even have meant to take my sister's life, too."

John looked intensely at Nomi. "Why do you think it wasn't an accidental poisoning? I told you water hemlock is often mistaken for wild carrots or turnips."

"I've been going through a book Jude was reading leading up to their deaths. She underlined things and left things between the pages of the book. Articles, photographs, and such."

"How do you know it was she who was reading it, and not Jonah?"

"It took a while for me to be sure, but now I am. I could tell from what she underlined and left between the pages."

"Okay . . ."

"It seems she was concerned about Jonah's mental health. And my mother confirmed that."

"Assuming it was actually Jude who was making these notes . . . Forgive me, but your mother is not the best source of credible information right now." John's tone was confident but not condescending or argumentative.

"Maybe not, but she said Jude told her she was worried about Jonah. I don't think she was imagining it."

"Okay, so maybe he was depressed—"

"Delusional, I think—"

"Again, maybe. But how does this prove he was suicidal? And that he would have taken his own mother's life? That's a very drastic and desperate thing to do."

"Sam said he didn't go out much. And Frank never met him, had never even been to the house. I assume that was because Jude didn't want him to meet Jonah. Did Lisa ever mention anything about this to you? If they were so close, maybe Jude confided in her, too." Nomi remembered what she had said about not expecting Jude to go first.

"If she did, Lisa never said a word to me about it."

So, if Lisa knew something, she had not told even John. Perhaps Jude had sworn her to secrecy.

"Okay. But there's that book Jude was annotating. She was quite concerned about Jonah. It took me a while to understand. The underlining, an article she had clipped about mental disorders—it was all referring to him. At first I thought they were about Frank."

"How do you know they weren't?"

"Maybe they were about both, then. But Jonah for sure. I just know it. There was a disc in the player, with an Israeli song. "And To Die." That's the name of the song. I'm telling you."

John stood and paced the cabin. "A disc? I don't understand."

"It's a song. It ends quoting *Hamlet*'s to be or not to be and talking about being the son of a mother who died, too. The disc was in the player in the kitchen."

"So, they were listening to a depressing song—"

"Someone underlined that last stanza. I'm almost certain it was Jude . . . In pencil, like in the diary . . ."

"Did Jude say anywhere explicitly that she was worried Jonah would take his own life? And hers?"

Nomi shook her head. "No."

"Cryptic notations from a dead woman, a disc she or her son may or may not have been listening to . . . they are not proof of anything. But if you insist, I can investigate further." He stopped in front of Nomi. "Is that what you want?"

"Is that what I want?" She echoed. What did she want? When had she ever asked herself that question?

"Yes. What do you want? It's up to you to decide."

"Me? But you're the one in charge here. You're the police officer. What is the official procedure in a case like this?"

John sat down next to Nomi. She felt a warmth from inside herself and from the heat of his body, yet she was still shaking. He took her gloved hands in his, which steadied them some, and looked at her intently with his eyes. She felt the slightest flutter in her lower belly.

"Listen, Nomi. I too was suspicious, I admit. And I agree what you are suggesting is a definite possibility. But he is innocent until proven guilty, and as the officer in charge of the case, I do not feel compelled to pass this information to anyone. I'm happy for it to stay between us and between the pages of that book. But as the sister and aunt of the deceased, what do you want?"

What Nomi wanted was for John to tell her what to do. "Oh, I don't know, John." She squeezed his hands. She looked over at the bookshelf and then back at him. "Shouldn't the truth be known? Or justice served? What happened, however it happened, is just so tragic. I'm supposed to just leave it be?"

"What good would investigating this further do? Jonah is dead. Do you want Jude and Jonah in the headlines? Again? Accidental poisoning of mother and son was sensational enough. Let's say we find you are correct. Who would that information serve? It wouldn't change anything, practically speaking. It would only put an ugly end on the story of both their lives."

"I hear what you're saying."

"Then, if you really want my opinion, I say let them rest in peace. And this story, too."

Nomi realized this was what she wanted. Yet she wanted more than just to let them rest in peace. She wanted to do something, take some action to make life feel more hopeful, have some meaning.

The image of Frank riding in the trailer on John's motorcycle, his eyes closed, his face to the wind, came to Nomi. And then her sister with her buzz cut, kneeling in her blueberry patch, her hands in a namaste gesture, thanking the Universe for that very moment, if nothing more.

"Oh, John. That's what Jude would have said, I think. But I can't just accept that as the end of the story. There must be more, but I feel so defeated. Coming here, to this place, gave me some direction and purpose. And then taking in Ruth gave it meaning, even. Doing something useful and helpful. But even that turned out to cause heartache." She looked down into her lap, where their gloved hands were still clasped.

John let go of one of her hands and gently touched her chin, slowly lifting her head so he could look into her eyes.

"How so?" he asked.

John's expression and tone were so sympathetic, Nomi let the story out. "Ruth asked me to adopt her baby. At first it sounded crazy, but the more I thought about it, the more I wanted to do it. I got attached to the idea." It felt good to be unloading this, despite her shame at having dared to even hope it could happen.

John did not laugh, or even snicker. She was grateful for that.

"But when I inquired about it, I discovered it was just a fantasy. The state would not let me, a single sixty-year-old woman who lives in Israel, adopt a newborn baby here in the U.S."

"I'm sorry."

"Oh, John. I feel so silly. It was a foolish idea. But I wanted it so much. I'm lonely, and I'm so tired of having my heart broken." Nomi's voice cracked.

"Me, too." John sighed and shook his head. "I don't know what I'm going to do without her."

Nomi and John found themselves hugging—Covid be damned. Nomi put her head on John's shoulder. It was broad and firm like Avi's, and when she closed her eyes, she was back in her cozy little house on the kibbutz with the love of her life.

She began to weep. She wanted to stop, to be there for John, like she had intended, not asking for a shoulder to cry on.

Then John was crying, too, their chests heaving in unison, their tears mixing on their coats.

Thunder sounded outside like the divine heart breaking, and an icy rain started coming down hard against the cabin's roof and walls. Despite the promise of the rainbow, was even God unable to contain the flood? But at least the *Shechina* was crying with them.

CHAPTER 32

BACK AT HIS motorcycle, after the downpour had eased, John said he had something for Nomi. He reached into his pants pocket and took out a small jewelry box. "It's from Lisa."

Nomi opened it. There was a golden cross inside. Just the cross. She smiled. "Lisa said it's a sign of hope. God's reconciliation with humanity."

"Yes, it is."

Nomi removed the cross from the box. It was on a chain.

"May I?" John said. "Would you like me to put it on you?"

Nomi stepped back. "Are you kidding? I'm Jewish. I told her I'm the Star of David type." She showed him her necklace. "But I guess the dead get the final word."

Except Avi, who had still not sent her the sign she wanted. Or . . . could it be? No. It couldn't. "But seriously. I can't wear that. I will cherish it, though."

"Yes, of course," John said, trying to smile. "I wasn't thinking."

Nomi had not meant to insult him, or Lisa, but, surely, he understood wearing a cross was out of the question. She returned the necklace to its box and put it into her jacket pocket.

John put on his motorcycle gear, got on his bike, and rode off, but not without turning around to wave before he was out of sight. Crying together had been a catharsis for her, but he still looked so sad. She would be sure to call him later. His wound was so fresh, while hers was beginning to heal. Painfully slowly, but still. She would recommend he switch to her and Frank's support group now, the one for bereaved spouses instead of caregivers. The sequel.

She went to check the mailbox. The book had finally arrived.

Nomi walked back to the house, her feet dragging. Anticipating reading the book did not even lift her spirits. The gesture from Lisa had cheered her a bit, but now it saddened her more. Lisa, like Avi, was tragically gone. All that was left of her for Nomi was what she had in her pocket, something she couldn't even wear.

Ruth was sitting at the table eating cereal and milk. Nomi remembered their conversation about God helping her choose her cereal, and how she felt God guiding her to ask Nomi to adopt her baby. Nomi had not told the poor kid about Diane's phone call. She would have to, she knew, but she had no idea how.

"Good morning!" Ruth said, full of cheer, barely looking up. She had her curls gathered into a steel-wool-like paintbrush on top of her head. Her face was filling out as her due date drew closer. "It must be cold out there. And wet. What were you doing?"

"It is nasty out there. But Elvis needed a walk, and John needed company."

"Right. How is he?"

"Sad. Very sad."

Ruth looked up, and into Nomi's eyes. "Of course, he is." She lowered her gaze to Nomi's midriff. "What do you have there?"

Nomi winced. Would she dare show Ruth the cross? If it made her uncomfortable, what would a rabbi's daughter think of it? Then again, she was doing pagan Jewish priestess rituals.

"You ordered something from Amazon?" Ruth asked.

Nomi let out a breath. She had forgotten about the book. "Yes. A book." Now she could put off talking about Diane's bad news.

She walked over to the kitchen counter and chose a sharp knife. She cut the cardboard wrapping. "You know that diary I was reading, the one written by the woman in hiding with her son? The one I think Jude was reading when she died?"

Ruth nodded.

"Well, it turns out it was republished by a big house. A new edition. I ordered myself a copy. I was hoping it might have more information about what happened to the son."

"Cool. Let me know if you find anything."

Ruth drank the cereal milk straight from her bowl and brought the empty dish to the sink. She turned on the faucet to rinse it. "Reminding you about the childbirth class later," she said, raising her voice to be heard above the running water.

"I didn't forget." Nomi looked at Ruth. Her belly was bulging, more like a watermelon than a honeydew now. She was carrying all in front; from the back you couldn't even tell she was pregnant—as if the bulge could just disappear and Ruth's life return to normal. Nomi knew how deceptive that was. Hers had never gone back to normal, and she had not even had to carry and give birth to her rapist's baby. Although part of her now wished she had.

"It's hard to believe it's almost time," Ruth said, looking at her belly. "The baby's getting restless. And too big. He can hardly move in there."

Nomi pulled the book from its package and turned it over in her hands. On the cover was that same photograph of the crawlspace where mother and son had hidden. "Like Batja and Izaak, the mother and son in the diary. She couldn't stand in their hiding place, and he could only stand hunched over."

"You sure know how to bring down a gal's mood," Ruth said, placing her bowl on the dish rack to dry.

"They lived in there for almost two years," Nomi continued. She could not act chipper. "It's unbelievable what people can handle."

Ruth dried her hands with a towel. She turned to face Nomi with her dark eyebrows furrowed, creating lines along her forehead. "Well, it certainly does put things in perspective. I thought it was the end of the world after I was raped. And then when I discovered I was pregnant, I didn't know if I could manage. But I'm almost at the end, and thanks to you and the center, it hasn't been so bad . . ."

Nomi didn't know what to say. She couldn't pretend life was rosy—or even fair, for that matter.

Ruth filled the gap. "Are you okay, Nomi? Did you find out anything more about the adoption? Does Diane know about the process? How to make it happen. You spoke to her, right?"

Ruth needed to know the truth as soon as possible. Nomi took a deep breath. "Come sit with me at the table," she said, trying to emulate how Diane had broken the news to her. She made a move to sit.

"No thanks," Ruth said, her face clouding over. "I'd rather stay where I am."

The belligerence in Ruth's voice concerned Nomi. She had not experienced it before, but she knew Ruth had it in her. "Just tell me what she said."

Nomi released her hug on the book and it hit her thighs with a thump. "It's not going to happen, Ruth. I'm sorry. Diane says the state would never allow it. They have couples waiting in line for your baby. Nice young couples who live here in this country."

Ruth frowned. "That's crazy. Shouldn't I be able to decide who gets my baby?"

"In a private adoption, maybe, but even then, there are social workers involved. But in a situation like this, we have no chance. And neither of us can afford the legal fees of a private adoption or lawsuit. We'll have to trust your baby will be in good hands and put this behind us."

She approached Ruth, stroked her arm with one hand—the other was still holding the book—but Ruth jerked away. Nomi's hand fell.

She tried again. "You have your whole life ahead of you. Just think how happy you'll make a couple who can't have a biological child but also can't afford a private adoption."

Ruth shook her head, slowly, and then increasingly faster. "I don't think I can do it, Nomi. I don't think I can give up my baby to just anyone. It's like sending him into the wind. I want to know how he is. I want to be able to see him. I need to know he's okay." Her voice was shaking, her shoulders trembling.

"We can find out about open adoption. Diane mentioned that. You'll see. It will be for the best." Nomi wanted to believe that.

"How can it be best for a child not to be with his mother?" Ruth said, her nostrils flaring, making her beaded nose ring stand out more. "Or for his mother not to decide who raises him?"

"I don't know. But that's what the professionals are for. There are rules and regulations." How could she of all people have forgotten that? She had tried to truly think out of the box for once in her life and look where it had gotten her.

Ruth started out of the kitchen. "I need some air. I'm going for a walk."

Nomi put the book on the kitchen table and went after Ruth. "I'll come with you. Wait."

"No. Please. I want to be alone."

Nomi followed Ruth to the front door. Reluctantly, she let her go, but not without handing her a coat and hat. She followed her outside, holding out a scarf to protect her from the wind. Ruth needed her space, but she also needed a parent. Nomi would have to wait for her to calm down, and then they could discuss this rationally.

Nomi returned to the kitchen and made a pot of hot cocoa. It was all she could think to do while waiting. They would sit and drink something sweet and warm together, and she would try to talk her through this.

With a mug-full of the steaming hot drink, Nomi sat down at the kitchen table to collect her thoughts and devise a plan.

If Ruth did not return in an hour, she'd go out looking for her in the truck. And if she did not find her quickly, she'd put a call in to John. He'd be sure to find her on his motorcycle. Most likely, she just needed time alone.

It helped to focus on comforting someone else. She understood what a blow this was for Ruth. For her, too. But they were stuck; there was no way out of the box they had been cornered into.

CHAPTER 33

HER THOUGHTS ON Ruth and her hands around her mug of cocoa, Nomi remembered the book on the table next to her. She opened it to the foreword.

Dear Reader,

The last time I saw my mother, she was in and out of consciousness. She had not eaten in days, and she had barely agreed to take food before that. She wanted me to have it. She gave me pieces of raw potato, only a few bites a day, and she took only one bite, saying adults don't need as much food as children because they are not growing. Then the food ran out. That last night we were together, my mother used whatever strength she had left to push me out the trap door of the crawl space and tell me to run.

"Run, Izaak, run." She kept saying. "A Jewish boy must know how to run!"

She closed the door from inside. It was a night with no moon. As dark as death. I banged on the door, begging her to let me back in, but she refused. She kept up her refrain: "Run, Izaak, run!" while I began to run. Her voice became lower and lower, until I heard it no more. At least not coming from inside our box. It was inside my head. To this day, I hear my mother's voice whenever I need courage.

I ran to the woods in the cover of darkness, without shoes on my feet. I was terrified and distraught, but it did feel good to be free, to feel the open space. To not be boxed in by walls, to stand up straight and run and run and run with nothing in my way. My mother and I would describe the outside world often when we were in the box. She did not want me to forget the beauty God had created. It was not God's fault humans were destroying it with bombs and fires. It was not God's fault humans were killing one another with guns and gas.

I fell asleep that night when my legs would no longer carry me. I awoke in a bed of leaves. The air felt like spring. I stayed hidden during the daylight hours in leaves and ravines, in caves I created from rocks and branches. When I felt it was safe to go out—a sixth sense I developed like the animals, my neighbors—I foraged for nuts and berries and killed whatever I could find. I was a city boy, so I didn't know what was safe to eat. But I was so hungry, I would eat most anything. God was protecting me.

When darkness fell each dusk, I risked being caught by rummaging through garbage bins. I found a pair of old shoes, almost my size. They were better than nothing. My best meals were when I snuck into barns and animal pens to eat from their scraps. I did not speak. There was no one to talk to. I knew it would not be hard to play dumb if I was caught by the Gestapo. I was not even sure I could still talk.

And then it happened. I saw the bombs falling like stars from the sky. I wished on them for my parents to be alive, for us to be together again. God was finally rebelling against humanity. Breaking the promise my mother told me God had made to Noah and his family when they emerged from the ark. God had finally had enough, could not sit back anymore and watch what we were doing to the world.

The bombing went on for a long time. I lost track of the days. But when things finally went silent, I saw others popping out of their hiding places in the woods like flowers sprouting in spring. We started walking, as if in a parade, gathering more people as we walked, to see what was left of the world.

I followed some adults to a building where survivors were gathering, to see if I could find my father. I needed to find him so we could go back and free my mother from hiding, give her food and water, and tell her the war was over. I did not know how to find the Zacharczaks' house. I had run and run and never looked back, as my mother had told me to do. I went to the building every day, looking for my father. But he never came.

Finally, a man took pity on me. He asked me who I was looking for. I told him. He said he had known my father in the Resistance. "Look no more," he said, his face full of compassion and sorrow. My father had been captured along with a group of Resistance fighters in the woods. They had all been shot right before his eyes. This man, Eliasz, not a Jew but a Communist anti-Fascist, had survived only because the Nazis had mistaken him for dead. He took me into his care. He helped me look for news about my mother, but there was nothing, so we had to assume she was dead. She would have searched for me otherwise. Eliasz looked out for me until he could get me on a boat to Palestine, which later became Israel, where I still live to this day. I never saw Eliasz again.

I knew I had an uncle in Palestine, Jozef, and I was hopeful I'd find him and he would adopt me. But the only Jozef Gutowicz (my mother's maiden name) they found in state records had died of malaria, as my mother had feared. I was taken to a youth village, where I lived until I was drafted into the army. And even while serving, I had a home to return to at the youth village when on leave. I am forever grateful to the dedicated staff who welcomed us orphans with not a relative alive to look out for us.

All my family in Europe were murdered by the Nazis. I was an only child, my parents' treasure. They wanted more, but the Russians came, and then the Nazis. My grandparents were taken in one of the first "aktions" of the Nazis in the ghetto and were gassed upon arrival in Auschwitz. I discovered this when I went to check the archives in the Yad Vashem Holocaust Memorial in Jerusalem. My aunts, uncles, and cousins, too. Not one remains.

Unfortunately, I was not able to carry on my family's blood line. Perhaps it was those years of living like a rat in a box and then like a wild animal in the forest that affected my fertility. But I am giving back to humanity by running the youth village where I spent my teenage years. It is now a village for youth at risk. I do this work in tribute to Pan and Pani Zacharczak who gave their lives so I could live.

These selfless souls made it to their hiding place in a hole in the ground beneath the barn of farmers a few kilometers from their home. Those farmers were hiding several Jews and said they had room for the elderly Catholic couple, too. But the Nazis followed them the day the Resistance came to escort them into hiding, and the Zacharczaks, all of those who were hiding there, the farmers who were hiding them, and the Resistance fighter, were shot on the spot.

Not a day went by when I did not think of my mother. She would have been proud to know I came in first in the national chess championship for my age group and went on to play internationally. I heard her inside my head, helping me with every move, not only when playing chess. She has been my guiding angel since the last day I saw her.

One year, the 12th graders from the youth village were due to go on the usual senior trip to Auschwitz. This is before beginning their army service. They visit the most horrific death camp of all. I had never wanted to go with them. I did not want to go back.

Then one day, years later, I received a letter from Yad Vashem informing me of their plan to honor the Polish gentiles who had hidden Jews, with a memorial monument in what was once the Lwów ghetto. This was to be in a ceremony in what was now Lviv in independent Ukraine a week after the trip was to end. Pan and Pani Zacharczak's names would be included in the list of names on the monument. I decided to go on the trip and attend the ceremony with my beloved wife, Penina.

After the ceremony, I went to place a flower on the names of Pan and Pani Zacharczak and stood in silence to pay them tribute. When I opened my eyes, Pani Zacharczak herself was standing before me. Only that was impossible; I'd been told she'd been shot. And even if she had somehow survived, at least fifty years had passed since the war had ended, and Pani Zacharczak had been in her seventies back when we hid in their attic. It had to be a ghost.

"Who are you?" the ghost asked. "And why did you place a flower next to those names?"

"Don't you remember me? It's me, Izaak, only I go by Yitzhak now. I live in Israel. You saved me. I owe my life to you, dear Pani Zacharczak!" I fell on her shoulder in tears.

Pani Zacharczak's ghost held me until I stopped crying. "Dear man. I am not Pani Zacharczak. I am her daughter, Elza. I thought you were dead."

"No. I left the hiding place. My mother pushed me out and told me to run. I survived in the woods."

Now Elza started crying. "My parents' deaths were not in vain."

She held me at arm's length and looked me up and down, like a proud mother. "We never met because my parents forbid us coming to the farm during the war. They did not explain why. They said it would be better for everyone and to trust them. I had a feeling they were hiding Jews, but I did not dare suggest it. If I knew and was captured, I might talk and endanger others. I knew how the Resistance worked. But I did not realize I would never see my parents again. It was only after the war I learned they had hidden you and your mother. They were so brave and selfless. That is how they raised us, to look out for others. Finally, they are being recognized for their heroism."

Elza invited me and Penina to her home. She said she had something for me. After she poured tea, she brought me a worn leather journal. It was my mother's diary. "Here is the original. You must have wondered what happened to it."

I was confused. What did she mean? "I'm sorry. I don't understand. The original?"

She looked at me quizzically. "You didn't know about the book?"

I told her I had no idea. She explained she and her brothers had cleaned out the house to prepare it for sale and found my mother's diary. From the last entry, they thought my mother had taken her own life and mine as well. There were no bodily remains, so they assumed our bodies had been taken away, or that my mother had brought me to the forest and slit our wrists.

She brought the journal to the city archives—Lviv was part of the Soviet Union then—where a copy was filed away. Later, she heard from an American woman who was writing her dissertation on women's Holocaust diaries. She asked for Elza's permission to have her own translation published by a small press specializing in Holocaust memoir and diaries. And that was how my mother's journal was originally published.

Elza told me to keep the diary. I emailed the publisher in the U.S. and received a reply they had gone out of business when their founder and editor, himself a Holocaust survivor, died, but they had copies of the book in storage and sent me a complimentary one. They suggested I go to a mainstream press with my story and ask them to do a second edition with a foreword by me.

So here it is.

I dedicate this book to my parents, Jakub and Batja Gonczarska, and to my saviors, Thomasz (Pan) and Sylwia (Pani) Zacharczak, and to Eliasz, too. In their memories, I dedicate my life to helping youth at risk. Every life is precious. As Ethics of our Fathers says: If you save a life, you save an entire world.

Yitzhak Gonen (Izaak Gonczarska), Kfar Hoshea, 2010

Batja had not taken her son's life! She had not given up hope!

Nomi felt as if Izaak, Yitzhak, was speaking directly to her as she closed the book. He too lived in Israel. He, too, could not have biological children. Instead, he ran a youth village for teens in need. He would be in his seventies, less than ten years older than Avi would have been. She wondered if he, at least, was still alive.

She heard the front door shut and Ruth coming back in. Nomi quickly got up to meet her. She would reheat the cocoa, they would talk, and they had a childbirth class to attend.

CHAPTER 34

NOMI WAS WOKEN by cries from Ruth's room, the room that had once been Jonah's. She turned on the light and checked her watch. It was two am.

Ruth was sitting up in bed, holding her big round stomach, her curls matted to her head and her eyes wide with fear. She was covered in sweat and gritting her teeth.

"Already?" Nomi asked, frozen on the threshold.

"Yes!" Ruth screeched. "And we didn't even have our last childbirth class yet. I don't have a bag packed for the hospital. This is too soon."

Nomi tried not to panic. She, too, had been counting on the last class to help her feel ready to be Ruth's birth coach. She went to Ruth's bedside and breathed in and out like she was the one in labor. "Let's time the contractions, like they taught us in the first class."

Ruth scrunched up her face and let out a yell. "Here's one now!"

Nomi looked at her watch. Ruth stopped screaming, and Nomi started timing. Five seconds, six, seven, eight, nine, ten . . . One minute passed. Then two.

"Here comes another one! This hurts like hell."

"Two minutes? But they said to go to the hospital when they're four minutes apart."

"Tell my baby that. I said he wanted to get out," Ruth whined between breaths.

"I'll throw some of your things into a bag. Don't worry. Everything will be fine." How many times had she said that in the past few weeks?

Nomi helped Ruth out to the truck. She could barely walk, and they had to stop each time a contraction came on. Elvis followed, circling them quizzically. The dark and quiet were ominous. What had she gotten herself into?

Nomi helped Ruth climb into the back seat, interrupted mid-climb by a contraction. She could not get comfortable and chose a position on all fours, rocking back and forth.

"It's not safe to drive this way," Nomi said. "You need a seat belt."

"There's no way I'm getting into a seat belt like this. What do you know about how this feels? You've never even been pregnant!"

Ruth was right. What did Nomi know about giving birth? What had she been thinking?

She went to the driver's seat. Elvis tried to climb in after her. She couldn't bring the dog to the hospital. Could she just leave him here alone? How long would they be? "You can't come with us, Elvis. Go back home." But Elvis stayed by the car, whimpering.

Nomi, with a shaking hand, put the key in the ignition. She turned it away from her, but the motor didn't catch. She tried again. Still, it didn't catch. She tried a third time. Still nothing. It had never taken more than three attempts.

With Ruth moaning and panting in the back, Nomi took a deep breath and tried, for Ruth, to get calm. She must be doing something wrong, because of her nerves. She turned the key again, but this time it didn't even roll. Nothing.

"Here comes another one!" Nomi heard Ruth screaming behind her. "Let's get going, Nomi. Please!"

"Shit! This is not the time for you to die. You stupid truck!" Nomi banged on the dashboard. That had worked before. She turned the key again, but still nothing. Elvis barked, but even that did not work this time.

If only Jude was here, she'd know what to do. She'd stay calm, and she was a nurse for God's sake. She could even birth this baby.

Nomi was useless, an imposter, sitting in her sister's clothing in her sister's truck next to her sister's house, with her sister's dog whimpering beside her. And even her sister, Yehudis Gittel, everyone's fucking Glinda the Good Witch, had not managed to save her own son! *How did I get stuck in Hicksville Massachusetts with a pregnant teenager who's about to give birth in the back of a broken-down truck?*

Ruth started to yell. Nomi got out and opened the back door. Ruth was lying supine now, with her knees up, holding her stomach. Nomi timed the next contraction. This one was one minute and thirty seconds!

"Hang on," Nomi said, trying not to show her alarm. "I'm calling Sam." At least Sam had given birth a few times. Nomi had only seen it in the movies.

"Please," Ruth said between pants and shivers. "I don't think . . . we have . . . time. I'm scared."

"I'm here with you," Nomi said, taking out her phone with one hand and stroking Ruth's arm with the other. "We'll figure this out. And Sam will know what to do. I'm sure."

Nomi felt terrible waking Sam and Jeff, but she had no other choice. She could call an ambulance, but the closest hospital was at least half an hour away. She called Sam's cell phone, hoping not to wake the whole house.

"Nomi? What's going on? Are you in trouble?"

Nomi walked away from the truck for a moment. "Yes . . . Ruth's in labor . . . and Jude's damned truck won't start." She was practically hyperventilating.

"I'll be right over. You can have our car for as long as you need. We've got our truck, too."

"And you'll watch Elvis while we're gone?" she said, looking at the pathetic dog.

"Of course."

Able to breathe again, she thanked Sam, adding, "You're an angel."

But when Sam arrived with the car and keys, Ruth was sitting in the back of the truck with her legs bent against the front seat and her hands pressed firmly at her sides.

"There's no time to get to the hospital," Sam said to Nomi. And then to Ruth: "Should we bring you inside?"

Ruth was panting. "No . . . I need to push . . . Now!" She squeezed her eyes closed, her face red as a radish.

"It's not common for a first birth to be this quick, but it can happen," Sam said to Nomi. "Your baby sure wants to meet you!" She encouraged Ruth.

Sam brought a blanket from her car, climbed into the back of the truck, and helped Ruth slide around and come out, so she was half-squatting on the ground. Sam sat at Ruth's feet and told Nomi to lean against the truck and support Ruth from behind.

"You'll have more resistance this way," she explained to Ruth, "and gravity on your side, too."

Nomi looped her arms into Ruth's armpits, as if in a wrestle. "How are you holding up?" she whispered into Ruth's ear.

"Okay . . . but terrified." Ruth panted three times and let out a breath. "What if the baby . . . has red hair?" Her face was scarlet now, covered with droplets of sweat dripping from her curls.

"What do you mean?" With the sleeve of her jacket, Nomi blotted the sweat from Ruth's forehead and temples.

"HE has red hair!" Ruth screamed as she pushed, the words melding with her cries of pain. Nomi suddenly understood.

As Ruth pushed against her, Nomi pushed back against Ruth's pelvis, as though with her own force and will, she could push the baby out.

Between pushes, Ruth added, "I made a pact . . . with God," and exhaled a few times quickly. "If the baby has red hair . . . it's a sign I'm meant to give him up." She exhaled again a few times. "But I don't know . . . if I can."

Nomi felt Ruth's sweat on her own cheek, dripping down into her fleece jacket collar and drenching her neck. Their heads were side by side, like Siamese twins. "Oh, honey. You don't have to keep a pact with God. Since when has God kept promises? I'm not even sure God really made any promises. Not in real life."

Nomi felt Ruth push again, and Nomi joined in, pushing and panting.

"Good point!" Ruth screamed.

"I see him coming!" Sam called. "Just a few more pushes!"

"I don't think . . . I have it in me," Ruth cried. "I can't do it!"

"Of course, you can," Nomi said. "You're a priestess. The daughter of a warlock. You can make magic. You believe in miracles. Remember?"

"I do!" Ruth yelled as she pushed again, and again, with Sam kneeling at her legs waiting for the baby to crown, and Nomi supporting her from behind.

"He's here!" Sam called. "A beautiful head of dark curly hair, like yours."

Ruth's cheeks returned to their olive tone, her eyes wide with wonder and relief. "We did it!" she cried, tears now running down her cheeks.

Nomi realized she, too, was crying. If she believed in miracles, this would be one of them.

CHAPTER 35

IT DID NOT surprise Nomi when Ruth told her she had decided to keep the baby, but she felt at a loss how to help. Ruth would need support. Nomi wanted to try to talk some sense into Ruth's parents. Her father seemed like a good man. Insular and intolerant, but not malevolent. No one had given him a chance. He did not know about the rape. Perhaps they had been premature assuming he'd let his daughter down.

Nomi hoped she would find Ruth's father at the Chabad House where he lived and worked, and where Ruth had grown up. She knocked on the door to the synagogue section of the building, which was on the first floor. The family lived on the second.

"Come in!" came a voice.

Nomi put on her mask, opened the door, and looked inside. Ruth's father was sitting on one of the metal folding chairs around a long table. He was studying from a large volume, perhaps the Talmud. He was dressed in black, like he had been on the Sabbath, but with an everyday suit instead of a silk one. He twisted one short sidelock around his finger, while he followed along with another finger where he was reading on the page.

"Can I help you?" He looked up slightly.

"I hope so," Nomi said, still in the doorway. "I was at your service, when you talked about the golden calf and told the story of the man on the sinking ship." She decided not to remind him of the incident with her kaddish.

He lifted his head but had his finger holding his place on the page. "Ah. You must have been the one saying kaddish. From the women's section." Apparently, he did not need a reminder. "I hope you were not offended. But it's not a woman's place to say kaddish. There is a certain order to things. A woman's place is in the home, and her voice should not be heard singing or chanting in public. It's immodest, a breach of *tznius*."

Nomi was all for order, just not this kind. But she had not come to argue. She suddenly felt self-conscious about the jeans she was wearing, had not thought to dress differently for this visit. She was not coming for a religious service, after all.

He took his finger from the page and folded his hands on top of the open book. "But I looked for you after the service was over, to tell you I would be happy to say kaddish for your loved one."

"Thank you. It's for my late husband, and my sister and nephew. I like saying kaddish for them myself, but maybe it can't hurt to have more people doing it. I'll give it some thought."

"Good. I also wanted to invite you to *Shabbos* dinner. But you were gone. We welcome everyone here. There are just certain ways the *mitvos* are done. It's for a higher purpose. The way *Hakadosh Baruch Hu* wants us to act."

"Yes, I understood that from your sermon."

He closed the book but was still not looking her straight in the eyes. "So, what did you think?"

Nomi hesitated to enter, but perhaps more out of habit than actual fear. She wasn't sure, but she felt a shift inside since meeting with David, even if a subtle one. She took a few steps into the room. "About what?"

"My little *vort*. My words of *Toyra*. Were they to your liking?"

"I liked the message, but I have some questions."

"What do you think the message was?"

Nomi considered this for a moment. "To help ourselves and recognize God's hand in our lives even when it's not obvious. And not miss opportunities to save ourselves, opportunities for growth."

He lifted his head more and looked at her out of the corner of his eye. "And you agree?"

"Yes. Your talk was helpful for me. It took a while to internalize the message, but once I did, it saved me in a moment of despair."

Ruth's father closed the book he was studying and smiled. "That is a good thing. You are Jewish? You know the kaddish, at least."

"Yes. I live in Israel. But I grew up around here." She looked out the window. "My parents were not so religious. They did identify strongly as Jews, though. Culturally. And we did go to synagogue on Rosh Hashanah and Yom Kippur, do seders, celebrate Chanukah. I went to Hebrew school, too."

The rabbi stroked his beard. "Are you here to learn more? We have classes. And if you come again this Friday night, you'll eat dinner with us, like I said. Did you keep *Shabbos* when you were growing up?"

"Not like you do. We didn't go to services as a family, except when there was a special occasion. But I did go on my own more often. I liked synagogue. We did light the Shabbat candles, say kiddush, eat challah, and eat Shabbat dinner together as a family, though. But after dinner, we'd go to the movies, watch television, go to parties. We weren't strictly observant."

Finally, he looked straight at Nomi. "But you're interested in that now?" His tone was hopeful. "Is that why you're here?"

It was true she had always wanted to be more religious than her parents, but not like this man. And she was on her way back to the kibbutz anyway. She hesitated.

"Did you come here for help to live a life of *Toyra* and *mitzvos*?"

Ruth's father was good at his job; he lured you in with his confidence and charisma when he was up on the pulpit, and sitting here, with his persuasive forthright manner. She'd have to be careful. Although he was barely looking at her. She reminded herself of her reason for coming. This was no time for a religious "return."

"No. That's not why I'm here. I came because I wanted to bring you good news. I had someone waiting for me at home for Shabbat dinner when I left so quickly that Friday night. That's what I came here to speak with you about."

"Who? News? Come sit down," the rabbi said, gesturing to a chair across the table from him. "But leave the door open a drop, please. It's forbidden for me to be alone in a room with a woman with the door closed. It's *asur*. We call it *yichud*."

The rabbi saying this suggested he did not trust himself, which made her more uncomfortable than if he had said nothing and let her close the door. Nomi understood now why he had avoided looking her directly in the eyes at first. Is that why he had been unable to see his own daughter?

Still, Nomi left the door partially open, even if just to assure her own easy getaway. She walked over to the table and sat down. "I know your daughter, Ruth."

The rabbi, who had put on his mask, looked closely at her now. "Rutie? Really? Where is she?"

"Not far from here, actually."

"So why doesn't she come home? Why did she run away? Her mother said she called to say she's okay but doesn't want us to come looking for her. She couldn't live like us anymore." He pulled at his beard; his hands were trembling.

"No, she can't."

He squinted. "What is the good news you're bringing?"

"You're a grandfather," Nomi said.

The rabbi furrowed his brows. "I don't understand."

"Ruth had a baby boy. Both are well. They're living with me for now."

His forehead crinkled as his eyes opened wide. "A baby? Did she elope? We don't do that kind of thing. She needs a proper *chasana*. What are you saying?"

"Your wife did not want you to know this, but Ruth was raped. By one of your big donors, a man you've had stay over at your house many times."

"No." He shook his head, one of his sidelocks coming out from behind his ear. "There must be some mistake."

"There is no mistake. Your wife sent Ruth away so you wouldn't find out."

The rabbi was still shaking his head, only now with more fervor, and he was holding his beard like a security blanket. "I don't believe you. How do I know you're not lying to me? Do you have proof?"

"Of what? Here's a photo of her with the baby, if that's what you mean." Nomi showed Ruth's father the screen saver on her telephone. The rabbi examined the photo. His eyes welled up with tears. Was he happy? Sad? Both?

Nomi put the phone in his hand. Gingerly, he brought it closer to his face, examining it like a holy object. He touched the screen gently with his finger. Then he looked up at Nomi through his watery eyes.

"I meant proof of who the father is," he whispered.

"No. You'll have to believe your daughter. She says he came to her bedroom while everyone in the house was sleeping. He threatened her, forced her."

"Why didn't she call out to us?"

Of course, he, too, knew the biblical verses. "She didn't want you to see her like that."

Ruth's father placed Nomi's phone on his book and put his face in his hands. "The poor *mamelah*. Why didn't she tell me?"

"She told her mother, and her mother told her to leave."

The rabbi looked up from his hands. The expression in his eyes grew grim, as if mentioning his wife brought him back to his senses. "Yes. She can't be here. It would ruin everything we've built."

"But I thought—"

"You thought wrong. How do we know it was . . . as she says?"

"Don't you believe your own daughter?" Nomi asked, raising her voice. She didn't want to be disrespectful, but how could he squander something as precious as a child?

He paused for a few moments, and Nomi thought he might be coming around.

"I can't have her come home with a baby and without a husband. I must be an example. My family must be an example." He banged a fist on the table. "I have my boundaries, and this crosses them. She knows that. That's why she left. She's been pushing those boundaries, rebelling against our ways for years. She knew it was for the best."

Ruth too had said it was for the best. But Nomi was not sure she agreed. She stood up suddenly, leaning on the table, and looked at the man before her. Rabbi or not, he had less authority on this matter than she did. "Listen, Rabbi Schwartzman. I understand the difficulty in this situation. But she's your daughter, and he's your grandson. And even if she does not agree with your way of life, she did not deserve to be raped. No one deserves that."

The rabbi stared out the window, as though she wasn't there.

"Where are they?" he finally whispered.

"We live a short drive away. Will you at least come see her? Meet your grandson?"

The rabbi sat stroking his beard. Nomi did not press him.

"Was there a *bris*?" he asked.

Nomi got up from her chair and stood straight and tall, her feet planted firmly on the parkette floor. "The baby was born only a few days ago. That's why I came to you. Do you know someone who can do it?"

Ruth's father stood, too. "I'm a *moihel*. I will do it. It's the *haluchah*. He's flesh of my flesh. With no father, the obligation falls on me to bring him into the covenant. You must know that's what *bris* means, right?"

"Yes, I do. But we say brit in Israel."

"*Eretz Yisroel*, the Holy Land . . . One day I'll get there, I hope . . ." His tone was wistful as he stroked his beard again. "What day was the baby born?"

"Thursday will be the eighth day."

"I'll come to you then. In the morning," he said, taking a pen from a mug on the table. He took a slip of paper from inside the book, a place holder. "Give me the address."

Nomi gave him her address and walked to the door.

"You said you had questions, too, about my words of *Toyra* on *Shabbos*."

Nomi stopped and turned to face him. "I was thinking about the golden calf, about what you said. Ruth told me you believe a mezuzah can protect you. How can a mezuzah have power if a statue can't?" She looked at him squarely. "I want to know if you believe in miracles."

"Yes, I do," he said. "But it only works if we believe. *Bnei Yisroel*, the Israelites, they did not believe. They gave up hope *Moishe Rabbeinu* would come down the mountain. Theirs was an act of despair, not hope. Their faith was gone. That was their *cheys*. That is when they lost their way."

"Thank you, Rabbi," Nomi said. "I'll see you Thursday. For the brit."

"It's a joint project, life. Us and *Hakadosh Baruch Hu*. We must send the energy up for it to come down. That's why we call it a covenant," she heard him add as she walked out the door.

CHAPTER 36

RUTH'S FATHER SHOWED up at eight am with a black leather bag, where Nomi assumed he kept his circumcision tools for the brit. She could not tell what he thought or believed about what had happened and who was to blame. He looked around as if wondering where to begin. A man with a mission.

He spotted Ruth. She was sitting on the couch in the living room nursing the baby to try and calm him before the ceremony, biting her lip from the pain of her sore nipples. Her father stood in the foyer, taking in the scene. His stolid expression turned soft, and he slowly walked toward his daughter, stroked the baby's dark hair. He was shaking.

Nomi reached for her mask, but when she realized neither of them were putting theirs on, she kept hers off, too. They were family now.

"He looks like your new baby brother," Ruth's father whispered.

"How is *Muter*?" Ruth asked.

"Strong, as usual," he said, looking down. "She keeps everything going. Such reserves of strength, it amazes me." He looked up at Ruth. "My poor *kinder*. It was Druckerman, wasn't it?"

Ruth nodded.

He kissed her forehead, smoothed her curls. "The *hazer*. I won't let him back in our house. Never. I promise. He's dead in my eyes."

Nomi wanted to intrude, to suggest pressing charges. But that was not for her to decide. It was Ruth's decision whether she wanted to put herself and her family in the headlines. Just as John had said about Jude and Jonah.

"Really?" Ruth looked suddenly childlike sitting next to her father. And her voice sounded ten years younger. "But *Muter* said you wouldn't be able to keep things going without his money."

He scowled. "Your mother doesn't know everything. I'll find a way. How could I take money from such a man? And don't worry about the baby. You can come home, both of you. I have a plan."

"A plan?"

"I've thought this over—"

"Thought what over?" Ruth asked. She looked genuinely puzzled.

Nomi, too, wondered what he meant.

He put his bag down on the coffee table with a thump. "Let me have my say." He sat down beside Ruth.

"Okay, *Tatte*. Go ahead. I won't interrupt."

"I have a match for you," he continued in a definitive tone. "I spoke to Rav Lefkowitz in Brooklyn. He found someone. A good young man. One of his star students. But he has a past, too, so he can't be picky. He's agreed. He'll keep it quiet. It's all arranged. Your mother and I have been saying we sent you away to Brooklyn for seminary, to get you back on the *derech*. No one will suspect anything."

Nomi looked at Ruth. Her eyes and mouth were open wide.

Her father was looking over her head, at some point past her. "It was no secret you were a rebellious child. We said we needed to get you out of this environment, that it was bad for you. So, now you'll come home married and with a new baby. Totally reformed. Everyone will be happy."

Ruth's mouth and eyes closed partially and softened, but her tone was firm. "I love you for trying to fix this, *Tatte*, but it can't be fixed that way. I'm not marrying anyone now. He may be a good match, but I don't want an arranged marriage. I want to fall in love. I'll manage on my own 'til then."

"Maybe you'll fall in love with this young man, like I did with *Muter*. Give it a try."

"No, *Tatte*. Look at me." Ruth handed the baby, who was now asleep, to Nomi and stood, her abundant wild hair adding inches to her height, her shirt buttons still open to the waist revealing the cleavage of her dripping breasts. Milk was soaking through the material of her shirt. "I don't belong. I never did."

Ruth's father did not turn away. He looked at his daughter, straight at her, as if really seeing her for the first time. His shoulders and face sank. "I'm sorry, but you can't come home like this. You must understand."

"I do, *Tatte*. I can't live a lie, and I don't want to live like you do. I don't blame you. I would like you to visit. You are my parents, and the grandparents of my son. When I figure out where we're going to live, I'll let you know."

"We'll help you, *mameleh*. I'll give you money. We don't have a lot—"

Nomi did not have a lot either. But she did have her sister's house. As she watched this scene unfold, she knew what she had to do. "I'm going to help, too. I've decided to sell my sister's property. The house, the land. I don't need it. The kibbutz will take care of me. I get everything I need there. I want to give you the money. It'll help you get through college, pay rent and for day care. Get you on your feet."

Ruth sat down next to Nomi on the sofa and tried to smile. She looked troubled.

"Why do you look sad, Ruth? I thought you'd be thrilled."

Ruth put her hand on Nomi's shoulder. "I'm grateful beyond measure for this. But honestly, I was hoping you would just decide to stay." She looked down at the baby in Nomi's arms.

Nomi's heart was full but aching. Ruth's hand on her shoulder felt fragile yet steady. Ruth looked up at Nomi with those pleading eyes Nomi had such trouble resisting. But there was only so much she could do.

"Oh, Ruth. I've lived on the kibbutz since I was your age. I wouldn't know what to do with myself here. This is Jude's life, not mine. I realized that when you were in labor. I panicked, felt out of my element. It's time for me to go home."

"I thought we had built a home *here*. Together."

"Oh, we did, honey, and it's been special. I will always cherish that. But now it's time for me to move on with my life."

Ruth looked like she was about to cry. "You won't leave just yet, will you?"

"No. Of course not. I'll help you get used to having a baby. I'll need to sell the house, and we'll need to find you an apartment. Maybe in a bigger town, where there are other young parents with kids, near a park, a daycare center in walking distance. Unless you learn to drive . . . Then we can get the truck fixed up for you . . ."

As Nomi painted this picture of the life Ruth had ahead of her, it was hard to extract herself from it. But Diane had confirmed it; any slight chance she may have had for a family of her own was gone.

Ruth looked again at her baby, who was still asleep in Nomi's arms. She took his tiny fingers in hers. "You will come visit us, won't you?"

Nomi thought of the kibbutz travel committee. "I'll try. And you can come visit me, too. The kibbutz is a great place for kids."

"Maybe I can come with you," Ruth said, her face lighting up. "To the kibbutz. To live."

"I thought of that, Ruth. Believe me. But getting membership these days is nearly impossible. Unless you're family. That's why I thought of selling the house. If you can't come with me, at least I can help you build a life here."

Ruth looked pensive. "I would refuse to accept your offer, but I'm in no position to do that. So, all I can do is thank you."

Nomi leaned over and embraced Ruth, then caressed the baby's cheek, so soft it took her breath away. "Please don't refuse. It does me good to do this for you both."

"I want to thank you, too," Ruth's father said. He had been sitting quietly, watching. Seeing. "That is a very generous offer. A mitzvah." He stood. "Now, I came here to perform a mitzvah, too." He went over to Nomi and held his hands out for the baby. Nomi looked at Ruth, waiting for her approval. Ruth took the baby and transferred him to her father's arms.

He scanned the room. "Where should we do it? We need a good, stable chair." He stood and took his bag from the table.

Nomi led them to the dining room and pulled out a chair from the head of the table. It was heavy and had armrests and a sturdy back.

"Yes, that will do just fine," Ruth's father said. "Now for a cushion."

Nomi took a seat cushion from one of the other chairs and gave it to the rabbi.

"We're ready, then," he said.

"Wait!" Ruth grabbed the baby from her father, who was too startled to react. The baby opened his eyes, woken by his mother's fear. "I'm having second thoughts."

Nomi was slightly startled. Then she sighed. "I thought you wanted this, Ruth. I wouldn't have asked your father to come if I didn't know you wanted a brit."

"I'm scared. Are you sure it's okay? He's only eight days old. Can't we wait a little longer?"

Nomi looked at the rabbi.

"Of course not, *mameleh*," he said. "You know that. What's gotten into you? Now is the time. Since *Avram Avinu* Jews have been circumcising their baby boys. On the eighth day. All Jewish mothers get through it. You'll manage, too, I'm sure. You're brave enough."

"I don't know. Before, it seemed like the right thing to do. But I just don't know . . ."

"Of course, you know. It's not even a question." He opened the clasp on his bag.

"I can't do it. I just can't." She clutched the baby close to her chest. "It's barbaric. What's the point?"

"Rutie." The rabbi's face was turning pink. "How dare you use that word about a mitzvah."

"Really, *Tatte*. What will happen if I don't do it? Isn't there a better way to show my faith in *Hakadosh Baruch Hu*? I don't believe this is what *Hashem* wants me to do."

The rabbi's face was red now. "Of course, it is. It's in the *Toyra*. It's a commandment. It's not for us to ask why." He was spitting out his words, gesticulating with his arms.

But hadn't he told Nomi life was a partnership between the divine and humanity? Like the Star of David.

"Remember what happened when *Moishe Rabeinu* hesitated to give his son a *bris*!" the rabbi scolded.

Nomi remembered that story from Hebrew school. Tziporah, the Midianite wife of Moses—her father, Jethro, was a pagan priest—jumped in to circumcise their firstborn son in Moses' stead.

"I guess I'm not as brave as Tziporah, *Tatte*."

On the contrary, Nomi knew Ruth was the epitome of bravery. Especially standing up to her father this way. But Nomi was on the rabbi's side; she had summoned him. Circumcision was sacred. Ruth was a priestess, like Tziporah. Shouldn't she of all people want to perform this rite on her son?

"Here, give me my grandson," he said, stretching out his arms to take the baby. "No one's asking you to do it yourself. You don't even have to watch. You can go to the other room."

Slowly and hesitantly, Ruth held her arms out to her father with the baby, who was crying now from the commotion. "No. I won't do that. If you're going to cut my baby, the least I can do is stay here with him."

Nomi remembered what Ruth had said about not abandoning her child. She was not only brave; she was a parachute. She would have her son's back.

The rabbi took the baby and gave him a kiss on the forehead, like he had to Ruth when he came in. The baby calmed down.

"We need a *sandak*," he said and turned to Nomi. "You'll have to do." He handed her the baby.

Nomi knew he meant because she was not a man. But he did not silence, shame, or oust her for being a woman. Ruth was right, he was a complex human, not as narrow as he appeared to be. And more flexible, too. Ruth had said he was both strict and soft.

"You hold him while I cut."

Nomi took the baby in her arms and sat on the designated chair.

She watched as the rabbi recited the blessing in a singsong: "*Baruch Atah Adoinai, Eloheinu Melech Haoilam, asher kidishanu bimitzvotav vitzivanu al hamilah.*" Blessed are You, Lord our G-d, King of the Universe, who has sanctified us with His commandments and commanded us concerning circumcision.

Ruth covered her eyes, but Nomi did not even turn away. She watched the rabbi examine his scalpel and put his finger to the blade to check its sharpness. The baby had gone back to sleep. So innocent, so vulnerable. In a moment, he would be shocked out of his bliss, the first of many hurts, wounds, and scars for the rest of his life. Might as well start now.

But just as Ruth's father was about to cut, she, like the biblical Abraham's angel, swooped in, grabbed the rabbi's arm, took the knife from his hand, and threw it to the floor. "No, *Tatte*! You will not cut my child."

Then, reversing Tziporah's act thousands of years ago, she took her baby in her arms and covered his face with kisses and tears.

Ruth's father, as if in a trance, continued with the ceremony, but without the cutting: "*Baruch Atah Adoinei, Elohim Melech Haoilam, asher kidishanu bimitzvotav vitzivanu bibrito shel Avram Avinu!*" Blessed are You, Lord our God, King of the Universe, who has sanctified us with His commandments and commanded us with the covenant of Abraham our father. He was crying.

The rabbi passed a prayerbook to his daughter and pointed to the line she was to say next. Ruth gently pushed the book away and recited from memory but with feminine God language: "*Bruchah at Yah, Ruach HaOlam, shehechianu vikiyemanu vihigiyanu lazman hazeh,*" thanking a feminine God for bringing them to this moment. Then she took the book from her father and held it in front of Nomi for her to read.

"*K'shem shenichnas labrit, ken yikanes l'Torah, l'chuppah, ulimaasim tovim,*" Nomi recited. Just as this baby has entered the covenant, so may he enter Torah, marriage, and good deeds.

Ruth's father then recited a few more lines in Hebrew, barely audible because of his weeping, and turned to Ruth. " . . . *ukrah sh'mo biYisroiel* . . . What is his name?" he blurted out.

"Avraham," Ruth said, looking at Nomi.

Nomi was moved beyond words. She brought both mother and baby into a bear hug. Avi—who himself had been named for his uncle, murdered by the Nazis when he was only a baby—may have spread his seed around northern Israel, into the uteruses of scores of anonymous women, but his name, and the name of his biblical namesake—another spreader of seed, who not only cut his son's flesh, but cut his own, too, in the name of God—belonged on this not-yet-wounded child.

There would be time for that. But at least it could be done without intention.

RUTH'S FATHER LEFT, out of sorts, but seemingly resigned to what had transpired. He even said he would come back to visit.

Nomi called Diane to tell her the baby's name and their plan. "We're calling him Abe."

"That's a beautiful name, Nomi. You must be so touched."

"Overwhelmed with gratitude, really. And Ruth will stay with me for now. Until I sell the house and we find a suitable place for the two of them to live. I'm giving the money from the sale of the house to Ruth."

"That is very generous of you. But—" Diane said after a brief pause.

"Don't try to talk me out of it. I know what I want now and what to do to make it happen." She had been happy in her life since moving to Israel but had allowed things to happen to her. Not this time.

"Okay. Do you have a U.S. bank account?" Diane asked.

"Yes. I have Jude's."

Then she remembered; until now she hadn't thought of it, since Jude had so little money in her account. She was not even supposed to have a foreign bank account or money separate from the kibbutz at all. If she sold the house, the money would go to the kibbutz, unless she gave up her kibbutz membership. So long as she was a kibbutz member, all her money went into the kibbutz's collective pot. Even money she earned abroad, even money she inherited abroad. Those were the rules. Good for the collective, but not for her. And not for Ruth.

She had enough of the kibbutz and its rules! But who else would take care of her? Where else could she feel so secure? She may not entirely belong, but she was not a total outsider, either. She had been there for so many years, and they had all loved Avi. They were her only connection to him. He was buried there. And at least there she had the fields and orchards, which she missed; that was something she could care for. What other purpose did she have on this earth?

Nomi explained her predicament to Diane and disconnected the phone. But what would she tell Ruth? She would understand, of course; she had not been expecting money from Nomi. Although she had said she was hoping Nomi would stay.

She could leave the kibbutz and stay here with Ruth. After all, Israel had been a refuge, but despite her expectations, it had never felt like home. Ironically, the place that was in some ways her homeland also made her feel in exile, having been as good as banished from her childhood home. And there was her mother, who had no one else.

But what would Nomi do here? This was Jude's life, not hers. She missed Israel, and even the kibbutz, as flawed as it was. Or was it her life with Avi she missed? Where was he? She needed him now, her guiding angel.

That night, Nomi lay on the couch, unable to sleep, wondering how to tell Ruth she would be letting her down once again. She remembered what Ruth's father had said about miracles and sending up energy. She had not tried in months to summon Avi to her dreams, had given up hope of it working, feeling foolish for even thinking it could work. Perhaps it wouldn't hurt to try again now.

"Avi, please," she whispered as she drifted off to sleep. "If you are out there somewhere, please help me figure out what to do. I want to help Ruth and baby Abe. I feel so lost and alone."

Nomi slept restlessly that night. There was a howling wind outside which Elvis answered with his own howls. At some point, she did enter a deeper sleep, but when she awoke, there was nothing from Avi. She did have a snippet, though, from a longer dream she could not recall. All she could remember was one scene, and a strange one at that. She wondered where it came from.

It was of a woman holding a baby, but she was too old to be the mother. And she was surrounded by other women, who were exclaiming something to her in unison, but she could not make out what they were saying, except something about the number seven.

After a walk with Elvis, Nomi told Ruth about the scene from the dream, over breakfast. Baby Abe was sleeping beside them in a rolling bassinette Sam had brought over, along with other baby items and infant clothing.

"Sounds like the last scene of *Megillas Rus*," Ruth said.

"The story of Ruth and Naomi? From the Book of Ruth? I'm not sure I remember the last scene that well."

"Let's look at it together then," Ruth said, taking out her cell phone. She typed something in and read aloud:

"So Boaz married Ruth. She became his wife, and he came to her—"

"That's a euphemism for sex, you know—"

"Yes, I know." Ruth nodded and continued reading. "So God let her conceive, and she bore a son. And the women said to Naomi: 'Blessed be God, who has not withheld a redeemer from you today! May his name be perpetuated in Israel! He will renew your life and sustain your old age, for he is born of your daughter-in-law, who loves you and is better to you than seven sons.'"

"Wow! That's it. Seven. Unbelievable."

"Well, there's more." Ruth continued reading. "Naomi took the child and held him to her bosom. She became a foster mother, and the women neighbors gave him a name, saying: 'A son is born to Naomi!' They named him Oved; he was the father of Yishai, father of David."

"David . . ." Nomi made a face, but her stomach did not turn at the mention of his name.

"Yes. King David. There is a tradition that the *Mashiach* will come from David."

"Yes, there is." The Messiah coming from David. Could redemption come from a place of pain?

And that is when the vision came to her. Like in the game she'd been playing with herself for years, imagining other people's families, she saw a clear picture in her head of two women—one old enough to be the other's mother, even grandmother—and a baby. They were living on a farm, surrounded by other women—some pregnant, some not—working in the fields, cooking, reading, playing board games, doing puzzles, lounging.

This time it was not someone else's family. This time it was her family.

Once again Nomi had found herself inside one of Jude's dreams. But this one had been a waking dream, an aspiration her sister had been unable to fulfill. But Nomi could. She would turn Jude's dream of a halfway house into a reality. She and Ruth, with baby Abe to nurture like a precious seedling. Along with other precious souls, although those already wounded—helping them heal with good food, company, and work—teaching them to plant, harvest, and experience the inevitable natural cycles of life. To let time, care, and love work their magic. Like Avi, her angel, had done for her.

Angels are not perfect, just there at the right time and place to do God's work on earth. Another myth shattered. She could live with that.

CHAPTER 37

BILL THE CAR mechanic, and his son, Bill Junior, had come to pay a house call after the baby was born, and fixed the ignition there on the spot, refusing to take a cent. Bill told her she could pay if she decided to bring the truck by for a proper tune-up but not to worry about it until things settled down and she knew her plans.

Well, now she did know her plans. For Ruth and Nomi to use the truck, together. Both women were officially moving into Jude's house, and Ruth was going to take driving lessons.

Nomi left the truck and the keys inside the shop with Bill. Bill Jr. was outside, working on a car with its hood up. He was wearing a down jacket, jeans, heavy leather boots, and his signature Red Sox hat, and he was sporting a moustache with no beard. She noticed some motorcycles parked in the lot and asked him if he fixed those, too.

"Yes, ma'am." His hands were soiled with grease. "They're a big thing 'round here, as you must've noticed. I'm a biker myself." This surprised Nomi, because of the baseball hat. Although, slowly, she was learning not to make those kinds of assumptions.

She went over to the motorcycles. Bill Jr. stopped what he was doing and came to join her.

"Do you know anything about bikes for paraplegics?" she asked, running her hand over the handlebars of an especially nice-looking Harley.

"Yes, I do. Why d'ya ask?" He spun his wrench around his finger.

"I have a friend who was paralyzed in a bike accident. He'd like to ride again. Can you convert his old bike into one he can ride now?"

"Frank?"

"Yes. Of course you know him. Small town."

"You're sure he's interested?"

"That's what he said."

Bill Junior frowned. "That accident with Susan was just terrible. A biker's nightmare." Then he grinned. "It'll be nice to see him on a bike again. Just bring 'er in, and I'll give you the best deal I can. For Frank. It'll be my pleasure."

Nomi said she would do that and asked how long it would take for the truck to be ready. At least a couple of hours, he said, so she texted John to see if he was free for lunch.

Meet you in fifteen minutes, he texted back. I'm starved and was planning to call you today, anyway. I have something to show you.

Nomi put John's usual black coffee with ham-and-cheese-sandwich-on-a-Kaiser-roll on the table at his place across from her outside the coffee shop. It was the first time in her life she had ordered such a thing, even if she had no intention of eating it herself. She had already started eating her toasted bagel with cream cheese and tomato.

John emerged from the police station with a paper in hand. He sat down in front of his sandwich. Nomi noticed his hair was starting to grow in from his buzz cut, now that Lisa was gone. It was thinning on top, and it was the color from their wedding photo but mixed with gray.

"Is that what you wanted to show me?" she asked, indicating the paper he was holding.

"Yes. They were able to get into Jude and Jonah's computers. You were right about Jonah." He placed the paper on the table.

Nomi put down her bagel and picked up the paper. "I'm afraid to look."

"Apparently, he had an alias on Facebook and was posting all kinds of conspiracy theories. The posts start by being just gloom and doom, but leading up to the poisoning, they start getting delusional. He was obviously not in his right mind. It's just so tragic Jude didn't reach out to anyone for help. She almost reached out to you, but, apparently, she thought twice about going through with it."

"What do you mean?" She looked down at the paper. It was a printout of an email. From Jude.

"They found this email, written to you, in her unsent drafts. They said I could show you a printout. So here it is."

John took a bite from his sandwich and Nomi began reading.

> Dear Naomi,
>   I am reaching out to you, my only sibling, wondering what to do. I know you are far away and probably can't do anything to help, and maybe that is why I feel safe confiding in you. So here it goes . . .

Is that why Jude had felt safe confiding in their mother? She was her own kind of far away. Nomi continued reading.

> Jonah was never an easy child. He was extraordinary, but not easy. And he was my only child, so I had no way to compare. Which is fine. I had no need.
>   From the time he was able to walk, he brought home wounded baby birds and sick kittens. He was so sensitive he couldn't even watch some

children's films. Dumbo had him in hysterics. When we read Charlotte's Web he was undone for weeks after. So much was too much for him. Everything hit him hard. He didn't have the kind of defense mechanisms others create to live in the world. He was overwhelmed by everything.

His teen years were difficult, but not in the way mine were. I rebelled against Mom and Dad and the bourgeois suburban life they led. I went my own way. But Jonah rebelled against the world. He couldn't settle down. He was always on the move, mostly off the grid but coming back into society to replenish his supplies. He would come back home—yes, my home was always his home, too—to live and work, and he would sometimes ask me for money when he was in need. I was happy to give it to him. Then he'd go off again.

Jonah was never violent, and he never abused drugs. He smoked weed, I know, but only to calm his nerves. He was not addicted. It did him good. In high school, he took medication prescribed by his psychiatrist for a while, but he hated how it made him feel. Or, more accurately, it made him stop feeling, he said. He did not want to stop feeling. So, then he refused to take it. When the feelings got too big, or the stimulation too much, he retreated into himself. He seemed to have it under control.

When Covid hit, he came home, and fell into a rhythm here. He went between the house and a cabin he built for himself in the forest, where he would go to read and smoke weed.

It made sense Jude knew about the cabin.

He would walk Elvis at least once a day to the cabin, forage and hike the trails, so I was not concerned about him not getting out enough. It was more than so many people around the world were able to do during that time.

And he had his computer. He spent many hours in front of the screen when he was indoors, connecting with people from around the world. On social media and Zoom. He was interacting. Lockdown was not a big change for him. Isolation had always been his way of protecting himself.

Jonah, my poor son, was grieving for the state of the world, but not in a way that worried me. For a while he channeled his grief into activism. He raised money for Greenpeace on the phone, wrote letters to public officials and posted a lot on social media.

But then there was a shift. George Floyd's murder devastated him. He saw the video, and it did him in. It was all just too much. Global warming, Trump, George Floyd's murder, the pandemic. He retreated into himself even more.

He fell into a deep depression. He came out of his room less and less often, except to use the bathroom. I had to bring him food or he would have starved. He forwarded me information from the internet about how the world was coming to an end. Some you could call conspiracy theories, while some were about real threats, like climate change. That was excruciatingly painful for him—watching humanity destroy the world. That is how he put it. He would weep about global warming.

Things turned around a bit when Biden and Harris won. He started to come out and talked about a future for himself and the world. There was a vaccine, the Democrats were in office.

He's tried to pull himself out of his darkness. He's started going out to the cabin more again, foraging, walking in the woods, eating his meals with me in the kitchen. We went out together to the blueberry patch a few days ago and cut our long hair short, almost to the scalp. The two of us, to let go of attachments. It was a magical day. He has even started talking about travelling again. To India. Maybe I can take some time off and visit him there. I am trying to be hopeful but without being attached to any of my feelings. Not even hope.

Even with the vaccine, Covid seems here to stay. And Trump is gaining footing again, preparing for the next election. And the Supreme Court is stacked against liberal values. But most of all, the world is not acting fast enough to stop global warming. Glasgow was a big disappointment for Jonah. It was not enough, he says, and he does not want to be here to watch the world burn. It worries me when he says that.

It has been torturous to watch my son suffering. I feel so helpless. Especially with the pandemic, lockdowns, the world seemingly attacked from all angles: nature and humanity, and the interplay between the two.

There is a difference between surrendering to one's fate and despairing. The former I am ready to do, not the latter. But Jonah is different. He has his father's genes, too, and he reminds me more of him as he gets older. That concerns me.

I am writing to you because I suspect Jonah might take his own life, and perhaps even mine, too. I've tried to get him to go back on meds, but he adamantly refuses. And I cannot go through with committing him without his agreement. That would break him. I cannot do that to my son. I have decided to put my trust in the Universe and accept whatever happens to him, to me. To us.

He is my only son, and I am his only mother. He is just the child of one mother, who will die. Nothing more.

As Nomi had suspected, it was Jude who had underlined those words in the translation of the poem, the song-lyrics, she had found in the disc's cover.

I could call the police. One of my patients has a lovely police officer for a husband. He would surely help.

Nomi looked up at John. He was watching her read. "She almost reached out to you, too, I see."

"I would have tried to help, if she had let me," he said softly.

"I know, John. She knew that, too."

My son has never threatened me, but he has spoken of a desire to end it all, and of his worry about leaving me behind to face what he believes is to come. He never did anything violent to me or others. Just the opposite. Violence makes him physically ill. It's not like that. But as much as I know my son and believe in his good pure heart, and as improved as his state does seem to be now, I am alone with him here in this house, and I do wonder sometimes if he might snap.

I read that sometimes when someone suffering from mental illness seems to be doing better, seems less depressed, is getting out more, they are actually more likely to act on their suicidal thoughts and perhaps even hurt others, even those they love. I don't think my son would do anything he thought was causing me harm, but I do question his ability to judge when he is in his dark place.

I am reading a book now, a diary of a mother in hiding from the Nazis with her son. She killed him, Naomi, to prevent him from getting into the clutches of the Nazis. Like the first woman who lived in my house killed her own daughter, out of despair of this world that can sometimes seem just too horrific to bear. If mothers can take their children's lives to save them from a more horrible death, or even life, a son can take his mother's life to save her from a world he believes is on the way to destruction.

I have had a good life. I don't regret a thing. I would be sad to leave it and the physical body which has served me well. But we all must do that some time. I am willing to accept my time when and however it comes.

If Jonah and I are both gone, you will inherit all I own. Our mother is in no condition to deal with the house. Besides, the state would take everything and put it towards her nursing home, instead of Medicare paying for that.

Nomi looked up again. "Oh, John. She did suspect he might take both their lives."

He nodded. "Keep reading."

I know you are a kibbutznik and have chosen the communal life I, myself, could not manage to uphold. I am so proud of you for that, little sister. You are more courageous and idealistic than I proved to be. But I had a child to raise, and then our parents here to take care of.

Becoming a parent made me realize how hard it is. We make decisions every day that affect our children's lives and our own, and the relationship between the two, in ways we cannot foresee or understand—and our decisions are not always altruistic. After all, we, too, are humans with needs and issues of our own. Once I experienced that myself, it was easier for me to forgive our parents. But you never had children. Perhaps that is why you have been able to stick to your ideal vision of a just, unambiguous world. Part of me envies your free spirit and ability to hold on to that vision.

Jude had considered *her* a free spirit, an idealogue? Strong? Jude had envied and looked up to *her*? Nomi read this paragraph again to be sure. She didn't know if she agreed with her sister. But she was, indeed, stepping out of her comfort zone now, getting stronger and more independent, and it felt good. And with Ruth and baby Abe in her life, she was beginning to see what Jude had, about parenting, and having compassion around it. But the complexity of life was not something to apologize about, she was also learning.

If you should inherit my estate, I hope you won't feel burdened by it. I know I turned into the more bourgeois sister of the two of us. If you choose to put the money into the kibbutz, that is fine. And if you choose to start over here now that Avi is gone, that is fine, too. Especially if our mother is still alive. I trust you to do what you think best.

No sage advice, no Buddhist aphorisms. Jude trusted *her.*

> We never know what will come from what life sends our way. As the Buddha says: "Every experience, no matter how bad it seems, holds within it a blessing of some kind. The goal is to find it."

Well, she was still Jude, after all.

> Love and Peace,
> Jude

Nomi looked up again at John through watery eyes. What a gift this final communication was.

"Wow. What a letter. Thank you, John."

"My pleasure." He grinned.

They were outside, eating. No masks. She liked seeing his smile.

"So, what do you think? Does this mean you do need to pursue this angle?"

"No. It does seem likely he took his own life, but there is nothing in this letter or in his posts or correspondences to indicate he meant to poison Jude, even if she suspected he might. It is a definite possibility, but there is no proof."

She looked down at her coffee, tracing the rim of her mug with her finger. "Does that mean we'll never know for sure?"

"Probably not."

"Will you close the case?" she asked, looking up at John.

"With your permission, yes." He nodded.

"You have it, then. Perhaps it's better this way. Not knowing." Although Nomi did know in her heart what had happened and assumed John did, too. How tragic Jude did not know that Izaak had survived, that Batja, like Abraham in the biblical story of the almost-sacrifice of Isaac, had not put her hand to the child.

"Perhaps." He indicated the paper. "You can keep that. Jude did not press send, but I think she wanted you to read it."

"Yes, I believe she did. At the right time."

Nomi folded the paper and put it carefully into her backpack.

While they finished their food and drank their coffee, they talked about her plans. She had already called to tell him of her decision to stay, a decision she had made without Jude's advice. Of course, he had said he would be happy to help her with anything she needed. He sounded pleased with her decision.

She thought of the first day they had met—even then she had been intrigued—followed by all those breakfasts at this same spot they were sitting now, then riding on his motorcycle with her arms around his middle, crying in his arms that day at the cabin. She would be fooling herself to say she did not want to spend more time with him.

On her way to the car, Nomi stopped in at the locksmith, who said she'd come over later that afternoon.

With all three floors open, there would be plenty of room to make her and Jude's vision come to life.

Chapter 38

WHEN THE LOCKSMITH left, Ruth was nursing baby Abe on the couch. It had taken mother and son a few weeks to get the hang of breast feeding, but they were doing fine now, and Nomi took on one nighttime feeding with a bottle of pumped breastmilk so Ruth could get at least six hours of sleep in a row. The three of them were already in a rhythm that felt not only manageable but lovely.

Nomi did not even feel envious of Ruth's chance at maternity; perhaps because this felt like her chance as well.

"I had the locks changed," she said, dangling a set of keys in front of her. "I'm going to have a look. Do you want to join me?"

"Sure. Abe's nodded off. I'll put him in his seat."

Ruth detached the baby from her nipple, with just the slightest cringe, put him down in his car seat—which doubled as a carrier—and followed Nomi into the kitchen. Elvis appeared, too, panting his eagerness to join in the adventure.

"Where should we go first?" Nomi asked.

"Upstairs."

Nomi put the key into the lock. It fit and worked. She turned the knob, and the door opened onto a small storage room, a second foyer off the back door, locked and boarded. There were boxes piled under a staircase leading to the second floor. Nomi opened one. It was full of books. She opened another. It contained an assortment of yellowed newspaper clippings and photographs she would examine later. She wanted to go upstairs.

The staircase was steep. Wooden panels creaked beneath their feet as they ascended, Ruth carrying the baby and Elvis taking up the rear. At the top of the steps was a hallway with a row of bedroom doors on each side.

Nomi went from room to room, checking each one. They were all sparsely furnished, with a bed, dresser, and writing desk. She pictured the rooms full of young women like Ruth, all looking for a place to call home, at least temporarily.

She folded her arms and smiled. "We can liven it up a bit, but this will do just fine."

Ruth had put the baby carrier on one of the beds and was walking from room to room. "It's perfect!"

"Let's go down to the cellar now." Nomi felt pulled to there. After over four months, she was eager to see the house from top to bottom.

Once back in the kitchen, Nomi closed one door and unlocked the other, revealing a ladder leading into what John had called the Indian cellar.

"I'll stay up here with Abe," Ruth said. "You go without me. I don't think I should take the baby down there until we know what to expect. You know, because of the noise."

"Are you afraid of ghosts or a wild animal?" Nomi half smirked.

"Both."

"Well, I assume it's nothing too dangerous. Probably mice. At most squirrels or a racoon. Maybe rats." She said this to assure herself as much as Ruth.

"We'll stay up here," Ruth said with a grimace.

"Come on, Elvis," Nomi said. She would not go down alone.

Gingerly and with her heart beating rapidly, Nomi descended the ladder, chanting "Lions, and tigers, and bears, oh my! Lions and tigers, and bears, oh my!" She found herself in a small room with empty shelves lining the walls. The air was cold and damp, and there was a strong smell of mildew.

"Elvis!" she called up the ladder. "Come on, boy."

Elvis let out a whimper and practically jumped down the ladder into Nomi's arms. She fell to the floor with him. He started sniffing the mouse droppings forming a line leading beneath the wall on the porch-side of the house. He stopped at the wall, continuing to sniff and whimper.

"It's just mice!" she called up to Ruth, vindicated.

Already on her knees, Nomi got into crawling position and went to get a better look. This part of the wall did not reach the floor, leaving a space large enough for a mouse. The droppings continued underneath. She put her hand in the space between the wall and the floor, and the wood moved above her hand.

Nomi grabbed onto the loose piece of wood from underneath. It was a small door but with no handle or knob, so looked like part of the wall. Nomi pulled it toward her; it opened upward, revealing a crawlspace beneath the screened-in porch. It looked like someone had dug it out.

"You won't believe what we've found!" Nomi called up to Ruth.

"What?"

"It looks like a hiding place!"

Nomi stuck her head inside. It was darker, and even more cold and damp than the cellar. A more secure hiding space in case of attack, she assumed.

"I'm going in," she said to Elvis. "Are you coming, boy?"

The dog put one paw in and then pulled it away. Coward.

Nomi crawled in, feeling her hands and the knees of her jeans becoming soiled with dirt. She reached her arm up to feel how high the space was. She could not even straighten her arm. Is this how it had felt for Batja and Izaak in their hiding place? It had likely been even smaller, and between the attic and the roof, so they were more exposed to the cold and heat. Although at least they had proper walls and a ceiling. This was literally a hole in the ground.

Nomi felt closed in and wanted to exit. Not long ago, she would not have had the courage to be here at all. Yet now that she was here, she felt drawn to stay, to try to imagine being cooped up in a space like this for months. Years, even. She felt around for a dirt wall, and once she found one, she sat, her back against the cold earth, trying to feel how it might have been for Batja. It was unthinkable. Unimaginable. Life does that, she thought, forces us to stretch ourselves beyond our wildest imagination and comprehension.

Something tickled Nomi's arm. She jumped and let out a yelp. Then something cold touched her cheek. It was Elvis. He had joined her and was nuzzling up against her. At least, like Batja, she was not alone.

Nomi closed her eyes and took in a few breaths. For Batja, surely, her "box" had been both a refuge and a prison. Boxes can be that way, protective but also limiting freedom and the ability to expand. She had spent her whole life in various boxes—some self-imposed, some imposed by others; some she still clung to for their security and structure, and some she was ready to let go.

She opened her eyes, now adjusted to the dark, and noticed the pile of slate pieces in the corner. She crawled over and picked one up. She ran her hand along its surface. There were indentations in it.

Nomi remembered the exhibit of colonial clothing and artifacts at the Witch Museum. In a display case with children's clothing, some wooden toys, a metal lunch box for school, there had been also a slate like this one. Paper was scarce, so children had learned to write on slates. And even adults—those who were literate—used slates or birch bark mostly, not paper, and sparingly.

Only now Nomi—feeling foolish—remembered she had a flashlight on her cellphone, in the pocket of her jeans. She took it out to see if there was anything written on these slates to make them worth lugging up the ladder. The screen lit up as she touched it, and she was able to find the flashlight function. She shone the light on the slate in her hand.

On the charcoal-gray surface, instead of writing, there was an image, a depiction, not with chalk, but etched into the slate. The person who created it clearly had talent. It was a woman holding a baby. By the neck. And shaking it. Both were crying. It was representational but distorted and frightening.

Nomi's heart was pounding loudly in her chest. Was it possible these slates belonged to Leah Marshall?

She was likely illiterate, but if this was hers, she was a natural artist. It must have been frustrating to have such talent yet be confined to caring for the children and maintaining the home—weaving, spinning, cooking, cleaning. Especially back then, when there was no dishwasher, no supermarket, no washing machine—not even electricity or running water.

Nomi placed the slate on the floor and picked up the next. She shone her flashlight on this drawing. It was of a woman, naked, with bulging breasts and a protruding stomach, tears dripping from her eyes. There was still some longing there, seeing a pregnant woman, but with Ruth and Abe in her life now, it did not hurt like it used to. And judging from this drawing, the woman—Leah, if these were her drawings—did not even want another child.

The grotesque style of these drawings supported the historical record; this woman was mentally ill. Anyone with a tendency towards mental illness could have fallen into depression or psychosis under those conditions, like Jude had written in her email about Jonah. If it was Leah, perhaps she had come to this place for quiet time with herself, some space to create and express. A hiding place from her own life. Or perhaps a sanctuary. And a place to vent to God.

The third slate was of a man and a woman—he was on top of her; she was screaming. Nomi covered the picture with her hands. It brought her back to David shoving himself inside her, filling her with an enormous rage that built up in her belly, until she felt a powerful urge to push—giving birth not to a living being, but to an ear-splitting scream: for Leah, for Despair, for Batja, for Izaak, for Jude, for Jonah, for Frank, for Susan, for Ruth, for John, for Lisa. And finally, for herself.

"Nnnnnooooo!"

As if in response, Elvis howled along, calling their dissent out into the Universe.

But just as suddenly, remembering Ruth above them, she stopped. She would not scream for baby Abe. Ruth had not let her father put his knife to the child. She had broken that cycle. This baby would, at least for now, remain whole.

CHAPTER 39

THE ICE WAS melting, the sun was out. Nomi heard birds chirping outside, gathering around the bird feeder, full of seeds. She had filled it when she was cleaning the back porch in a surge of energy to make the house home. Her home. The first home she had owned and made her own.

She had been out on a walk with Elvis earlier that morning. Skunk Cabbage plants were starting to come up around the wetlands on the bank of the stream near the footbridge, their maroon leaves spotted with green, cradling a spadix that reminded Nomi of photos she had seen of the enlarged Coronavirus. Spring was finally on its way, and hopefully Omicron was on its way out, but she knew better than to think this meant saying goodbye to the virus completely.

Life was just not that gracious. Russia was still in Ukraine, with reports of massacres surfacing. History repeating itself. Hope was a necessity, but so was vigilance. Nomi would never be as free-spirited as Jude imagined she was. And that was fine. She was finding her balance.

Nomi had Abe, fresh from a feeding, in his carrier. She brought him out to the truck and snapped the carrier into its frame on the seat. She was taking him to visit her mother. His great-grand-godmother. Or was it grand-godmother? Nomi wasn't sure of her—and therefore her mother's—relationship to this baby. Nomi was old enough to be the baby's grandmother, yet she felt an almost maternal attachment. He was both godson and grand-godson. Maybe she'd ask him to call her his fairy godmother. Or angel godmother. Or maybe just *sandak*.

She drove more carefully than usual, aware of the precious cargo on the seat beside her.

Nomi carried baby Abe into her mother's room. She was sitting in a chair, looking out the window. Nomi placed the baby carrier on the table, and her mother turned to face her. She already had a mask on. One of the nurses must have just been around.

"Judith. Who is that?" she asked, looking at the baby.

"This is Abe. Avraham. Abraham. He was named after Naomi's Avi. *My* Avi. Mom, I am not Judith. I'm Naomi." She pulled her mask down for a moment to show her mother her face. "I'm here now. I came from Israel."

Her mother's eyes opened wide. "Naomi? From Israel? You and your Israeli husband had a baby?" Nomi did not tear up at her mother's mistake. "That's wonderful news! Let me see the little thing."

It felt good to have her mother's approval of her as Naomi—even if she was only half-aware of who she and this baby were. She unclipped the straps and took Abe from his carrier. He had a full head of hair, and his cheeks had become almost pudgy since the birth. She brought him over to her mother, whose eyes brightened at the sight of the infant. She put her finger next to his tiny ones, and he grabbed it.

"No, Mom. This is not my baby. He's my god-baby. I was the *sandak* at his brit. And Avi is not alive anymore. He died of Covid a year ago. I told you that on the phone. This is the baby of a young woman, around the age I was when I left home, who was raped. She became pregnant with his baby. I'm helping her take care of him. They're living with me, in Jude's house."

"Ah, so this is all Judith's doing. Another one of her do-good schemes."

"No, Mother. This is *my* do-good scheme. Jude is not here anymore either. Neither is Jonah, her son, your grandson. My nephew. I am sorry to have to break this to you, but they're gone."

"I don't understand. Gone? What do you mean?" She was shaking her head in distress.

Nomi's original instinct not to tell her mother of Jude's and Jonah's deaths had been a good one. Why upset her mother? Her state was fragile enough. "Judith's not here, that's all. Naomi, your long-lost daughter has come back. She'll . . . I'll take care of you while Jude's gone."

Nomi's mother's eyes brightened. "That's good. Naomi was always a good girl. Didn't cause trouble, like her sister did. Until she left. That broke my heart."

Nomi put her hand on her mother's shoulder. "Look at me, Mom. I am Naomi."

Her mother looked at her, blinked, and shook her head. "I don't know. Naomi is younger than you are."

"I was then. But I'm older now. Wiser. I know it hurt you when I left without a trace. I'm sorry if you felt abandoned. But you really hurt me, Mom. I needed you and Dad, and you let me down. I did nothing wrong. I was a victim, not a criminal. I was traumatized enough. I told you I didn't mean to . . . They call it date rape. I needed your support."

Her mother was shaking. "I didn't know what to do, Naomi. I didn't understand . . ."

Baby Abe began to fuss, so Nomi put him over her shoulder and rubbed his back. "I didn't either. I realize that now, Mom. We didn't know how to talk about what happened to me."

The baby was still uncomfortable. Nomi bounced, hoping that would calm him.

"It was rape, even if he does not deserve to be stoned. I don't, either. I don't need to blame or be blamed anymore. I can live in that gray area." It was a relief to say that, to feel that. "But you did blame me, Mom. You blamed your own daughter for something not her fault. You were not my parachute, Mom. You were not there to open for me."

Her mother shoo-ed Nomi away with a wave of her hand, like a pesty fly. "You're not making sense, Naomi. About stoning and parachutes. You're breaking our hearts, running around with no-good boys. You're smarter than that."

Nomi looked at her mother. She was frail and confused, moving between past and present, reliving Nomi's disappearance, bringing Nomi back in time as well, to that most wounded place she, even now, had yet to truly heal.

Nomi closed her eyes. She was in her parents' living room, scared for her future, pleading for their help. "I'm trying to get your attention, Mom," she heard her seventeen-year-old-self saying. Only the words were coming from her mouth, now, the words she wished she had said back then. "You have me pegged as the good girl. I don't want to be put in a box. Or maybe part of me does, but part of me doesn't. There's a side of me that wants room to grow, and you're stifling that instead of nurturing it. I want you to see I'm more than how you see me. And less, too—"

"Less?" Her mother looked even more puzzled.

"I don't want to have to live up to your expectations. Don't you understand? You don't see my sister or me for the complex people we are. Judith is the stupid, irresponsible, flighty one. You're writing her off before she has a chance to mature into adulthood."

"Judith?" Her mother was twisting her loose-fitting rings around her fingers.

"And I have so much promise in your mind, that any sign of being human, of being a teenager, throws you for such a loop you can't even stand to look at me now. I am the smart one, the dependable one, the one who doesn't get into trouble. So, now that I did, it's turned your world upside down." Nomi cracked her knuckles as she held the baby in her arms.

Baby Abe. Nomi closed her eyes, took a breath, and opened them, bringing herself back to the present. She was a sixty-year-old woman holding a baby, talking to her almost-ninety-year-old mother. "You were so busy mourning the loss of the daughter you thought you had you couldn't be present for the daughter who so desperately needed your help."

"I'm sorry," her mother said, looking into her lap.

Nomi glanced at her mother, then did a double take. Had her mother just apologized? To her? To Nomi? Whether or not she was lucid, she *had* said she was sorry.

"But you never came back," her mother continued. "You didn't give me a chance to change things between us. Judith did but you didn't."

So much time had passed that could never be brought back. Nomi felt overcome with emotions.

"I'm sorry, too, Mom. I really am. You're right. I should have come back, at least to visit. But I am here now."

Baby Abe let out a long burp. Nomi only realized how her own muscles had tightened, as they released and relaxed along with the baby's.

Her mother looked at her again with what Nomi sensed was true recognition, even if fleeting. "Yes, you are, Naomi. You are here now. You came back. Thank you."

"No, Mom. I want to thank you."

"Thank me?"

Nomi held baby Abe with his face against her chest now, his miniature heart beating rapidly with hers. "I took your advice. You said I should find someone to take care of. So that's what I did. And you were right, Mom. It feels great. It's just the salve I need now that Avi's gone. I wanted to thank you for that."

"You're welcome," her mother said. "I guess I'm not a complete failure of a mother, like I thought."

"I guess not."

With those three words, Nomi let go of over forty years of resentment and anger. Jude would have been proud.

"And my name is Nomi now, Mom, without the A." It was Avi who had taken the A out of her name all those years ago. Now it was time for her to let go of it as well. "Nomi," she said again. Only now it sounded like an invitation too, not just a name.

"Nice to meet you, Nomi," her mother said, slipping back into her fog. Nomi was grateful for the minutes of lucidity her mother had found for her. She knew it had not been easy.

Nomi put her arms around her mother, with the baby wrapped inside their hug. A circle literally closing as three, maybe four, generations embraced.

CHAPTER 40

NOMI BROUGHT THE baby back to Ruth to breastfeed. Within seconds, Abe was attached to her nipple and sucking away. She did not cringe at all. The painful period had passed.

Nomi went down to the cellar and came up with the slates in her hands. She wrapped them in one of Jude's hand-knitted blankets and headed for the front door.

"Where are you going with those?" Ruth asked.

"I'm bringing them to John. He'll know what to do."

Nomi sent a text.

John answered she should come to the station.

"These are incredible!" John exclaimed. His hair was now completely grown in, enough so, it seemed, that he had gone for a proper haircut.

"You think so too? Do you think they could have been Leah Marshall's?"

"I think it's a very real possibility. And I know just who to show them to. A local historian whose specialty is that period. She works for the county's historical society. Why don't you get us both sandwiches to-go while I finish up my work? I'll meet you next to my motorcycle."

"Great!" With her phone, she took photographs of the slates and asked John to print them. "A memento."

Nomi waited outside, sipping coffee, with their usual sandwich and bagel in a paper bag by her side. She was no historian, but she knew those slates had to be an important find. Perhaps they would even help people understand Leah, too, had been a victim. It was possible to be a victim and a perpetrator at the same time.

As she finished her coffee, John came out of his office, handed her the photos in a plastic sleeve, and they left on his motorcycle.

John had phoned the historian to make sure she was available. He told her he had a surprise.

She was in her office. John introduced them. Her name was Amy, and she looked a bit older than Nomi, with short gray hair, reading glasses, and a classic crewneck cashmere sweater and pleated corduroy pants. She had a box of disposable masks on her desk; she was wearing one.

John explained Nomi was living in the old Marshall farmhouse, and was Jude's sister, from Israel.

"I'm so sorry for your losses," Amy said, while she put on gloves to examine the finds. Her North Shore accent was as strong as John's. She took the slates from him. "Your sister was one special woman."

"Yes, she was," Nomi said, nodding.

Amy turned the slates over, one by one, examining the drawings with a magnifying glass held up to her reading glasses, exclaiming here and there as she looked with wide eyes. Nomi shifted in her seat.

"Amazing!" she finally said. "I can't believe what I'm looking at. And so well preserved."

"They were in a damp cellar. Or more like a hole in the ground next to the cellar," Nomi offered.

"That explains it. I'll have to check them for authenticity and date them. And I'll need to see exactly where you found them. But if these are what I think, they'll bring a significant revelation about the Leah Marshall case. Or more like proof of what I suspected all along."

"Which is what?" Nomi asked.

"The court proceedings and decision state she tried to kill her husband, not just her child. There is a vague phrase saying she claimed her husband mistreated her. But no more. These drawings explain what she meant. At least part of it. She was an upstanding church member when the family first arrived. But with her second-to-last child, she started to become what they called melancholy."

Amy pushed her reading glasses down her nose and looked up at Nomi. "Judging from the town records, Despair was born not more than a year and a half after the sibling above her in age. Which means poor Despair was conceived while Leah was in the depths of a postpartum depression. The story these slates show is her husband forced himself on her, that she did not want another child."

"He raped her," Nomi stated. Even if the Bible didn't recognize marital rape, or have the language for it, that didn't mean it didn't exist.

"Not only that," Amy added. "When she started to rebel, the court had her chained to a post and whipped. At her trial, she admitted to killing her baby daughter and said she only did it to free her from further misery. And the court sentenced her to death, despite her apparent insanity. They hanged her. She went willingly to the gallows."

"That's so awful." The baby's death, the mother's hanging. Certainly, no sane mother would kill her own child. And once Leah did kill her daughter, of course she went willingly to her death. How could she want to continue living after that? Jude had felt similarly about committing Jonah to an institution, which for him would have been worse than dying.

"I've always felt they used her as an example for other women, in case they were also thinking of rebelling." Amy sighed. "A deterrent."

"Like with the witches," John said. "Salem has a strong history of such deterrents. Like Hester Prynne's A."

"That's what we're infamous for here in Salem, I'm afraid. A heritage I'm not proud of. But it's my job to gather the information and tell the story, even if it's not pleasant." Amy picked up her cell phone. "And now, I should start making some calls."

"Will you keep us posted?" John asked.

"Of course. It's Nomi's find." She turned to Nomi. "I can't thank you enough. This will be a great contribution to restoring a bit of Leah's honor. Or at least arousing a little compassion for her. It will change forever how people look at a certain historical moment."

Sometimes there was reason not to leave the dead buried.

"I know this is nothing like what archeologists find back where you come from, but for us, this is the equivalent of ancient history."

"Do you know where Leah was buried?" Nomi asked on the way back to John's bike. "She wasn't cremated, was she?"

"No. Just the witches were. She was buried in one of the old cemeteries. I can take you there now."

"Perfect. I want to leave her something. And we can have a graveyard picnic."

The cemetery was overgrown with weeds, and the gravestone was simple, mossy, and blackened. It read: *Leah Marshall (1603-1638). Possessed by the Devil. May Her Soul Rest in Peace.*

Nomi took the photographs of the slates out of her bag. She placed them on the grave. She was not the only one who had decided to leave something. There was also a laminated note.

Poor Leah. In another time, in another place, you might have gotten help before it got so bad you killed your own child, my great-aunt (many times over) Despair. At minimum, you would have simply gone to a mental hospital or jail for the rest of your life, instead of being hanged. To me, and my family, our ancestor will be Leah Marshall— the tragic victim of mental illness, abuse, and distorted religion. But to history, my great-grandmother many times over will always be Leah Marshall the murderer. I wish I could change that. But if you hadn't lived, I wouldn't be here today. Thank you.

Of course. Leah had seven other children. Nomi hadn't considered there would be descendants. What a legacy to bear.

Nomi could not bring Jude back. She could not bring Jonah back. She could not bring Leah or Despair back, or Mary Dyer. And she could not bring back all the witches and warlocks hanged in the name of God. She could not bring Lisa or Avi back, either. But she could do her small part in this place where she had landed—call it her exile or her refuge—to help end this cycle of intentional and unintentional abuse, and hopefully even ease some suffering.

CHAPTER 41

NOMI CALLED PEST control. A man named Steve said he could catch the mice—and whatever else was down there—and take them into the forest, not kill them. That was a relief for both Nomi and Ruth, who did not want to take part in more killing in the house.

But after it was all done and Steve had left, Nomi and Ruth, sitting on the porch with the baby, heard the scratching noise again.

Nomi called Steve and asked him to return, which he did, just minutes later; he had been outside in his truck eating his lunch and making some calls before driving out to the forest to release the mice, who were in cages in the back of his truck. Nomi followed him down to the crawl space, and they both agreed there was nothing left down there. At least nothing they could see.

"Maybe it's just your imagination now," he suggested, as they climbed back up the ladder. "Like a phantom noise. I've heard about that when someone loses a limb. Maybe it can also happen when you're used to hearing a noise. You keep hearing it."

"Maybe," Nomi said, and saw Steve out, again.

Ruth was still nursing the baby on the porch.

"He called it a phantom noise. He said I'm just used to hearing it, so I'm imagining it now."

They heard the noise again.

"But I hear it, too, Nomi," Ruth said, a quiver in her voice.

They looked at each other.

"And if it was mice, we wouldn't hear it this loudly from up here," she added.

"Good points." Nomi shivered. "But I suppose we could both be experiencing the same psychological phenomenon."

"Like when women living together get their periods at the same time?" Ruth looked incredulous.

"Something like that."

Ruth scowled. "Or maybe it *is* a phantom. The spirit of Leah Marshall. I told you that the day we were at the Salem Witch Museum. Remember? You didn't take me seriously."

"Should I?"

"Yes. It seems to me the only possible explanation. I think it's time we do an exorcism," Ruth said, without even a hint of a smile.

"You can't be serious." Nomi had done things she could never have imagined since she landed here in witch-territory. But an exorcism? "You wouldn't do a brit, but you'll do an exorcism?"

Ruth looked annoyed. "I am totally serious. There are records of Kabbalists doing exorcisms in Sefat not long before the witch craze here."

"Interesting. So, the Kabbalists were warlocks?'

"In a way. Even more than my father is, for sure. Besides, this is a harmless ritual. If it works, great. If it doesn't, no big deal. Totally different than cutting off a foreskin."

"I get your point."

Ruth covered the baby's ears and made a face. "Very funny. But little Abe here does not appreciate your pun."

"Oh, Ruth. Really. That was not at all intentional."

"Good. Well, do you know any other way to convince her spirit to leave? It's worth a try. Especially with all our plans for this house."

Nomi did believe in angels. She even believed in the *Shechinah*, now, if that meant a God who still believed in her. Ghosts, however, was going too far. But perhaps doing a ceremony would put an end to whatever was making them hear phantom noises in their heads.

"Do you know how?" she asked, lowering her voice.

"I think I could figure it out. I saw a bunch of books in the museum gift shop on witchcraft. I'll bet they have information on exorcisms there. On the internet, too. And I can get ideas from my Priestess community to add some Jewish twists."

Nomi said she would help Ruth, but not because she believed. It just couldn't hurt to go along with it.

They drove to the museum and bought a couple of books on witchcraft with chapters on exorcisms. Ruth noticed a pentacle necklace like the one they had seen at the Witch Trial Memorial, with an explanation of its significance.

"The pentacle is the symbol of the Wiccan faith," Ruth read from the box. "And the pentagram star, a talisman that wards off evil spirits and is used for home protection." She looked up at Nomi. "Like the mezuzah. Perfect for our ceremony."

Nomi bought Ruth the necklace.

When they got home, Ruth took the books and the baby to the porch to start reading. Later, she said, she had a Zoom meeting scheduled with one of her teachers at the Priestess Institute, who would instruct her on some of the Kabbalistic methods of exorcism.

Over dinner, Ruth reported the main idea of an exorcism ceremony, both in Kabbalah and in the Wiccan tradition, was to speak to the ghost, tell the spirit it was being felt, and then give it permission to leave, or even compel it to do so. In Kabbalistic circles, this was called enacting a *tikkun*, a repair, so that the trapped soul could be cleansed and go to the afterlife, or even be reincarnated.

Ruth said she would take pieces from both traditions to create a ceremony, with some of her own additions as well. In both Kabbalistic and Wiccan circles, the practice was to call in a seasoned exorcist, but Ruth said she preferred to do it herself rather than rely on an intermediary. She would handle everything, she said, and Nomi would not have to do much more than show up. Unless she wanted to.

Nomi said she'd give it some thought. She, too, was trying to trust her own instincts rather than depend on others.

"What is most important is intention and stance," Ruth explained. "Leave your skepticism at the door and be firm, they say. The spirit can tell if you are ambivalent. It'll take advantage."

Ruth's father had said something similar about the importance of belief. Nomi would try to suspend disbelief, as challenging as that was.

ON THE MORNING of the exorcism, Ruth brought in buckets of water from the well in the backyard and poured them into the bathtub. She invited Nomi to join her in a ritual washing, for purification before the ceremony. She had read this was vital for preparation for the event.

When Ruth had asked her if she had any other amulets besides the pentacle, Nomi remembered what Lisa had said about the cross' significance. A redemptive message about God's grace and mercy seemed appropriate in the face of the Leah Marshall story. And she had been a devout Christian, after all.

But Nomi had not been expecting to be the one wearing the necklaces. When Ruth put them on, baby Abe started pulling at the pendants and chains.

"Here. You wear these," Ruth said, handing her the two necklaces.

Nomi resisted, but when Ruth insisted, Nomi figured she could, just for the ceremony. No one else would see but Ruth. Besides, Ruth said they would leave them down in the cellar after the ceremony, as a preventative measure.

And so, Nomi found herself climbing down to the cellar with the pentacle necklace and Lisa's cross hanging from her neck along with her Star of David. Ruth followed her with Abe sleeping in the baby sling on her chest.

This was Ruth's first time in the cellar. She looked around in amazement, a serene expression on her face. "I feel her here. And Jude, too. Do you?"

"I've felt Jude in the house since that first day I arrived," Nomi admitted. "But not as a ghost. More like a presence. Like she left her residue behind."

"How is that different than her spirit being here with us?"

"I don't know. I'm just not convinced." If she could not even feel Avi's spirit with her, how could she feel the spirit of Jude or a woman she had never met?

"Well, I am. So, let's do it."

Nomi followed the stage directions Ruth had given her. She went on her knees and crawled into the space where she had found Leah's slates. That was to be her station, Ruth had said.

Ruth, with baby Abe in his sling, stood in the cellar on the other side of the threshold of the hole, handing Nomi supplies through the opening.

Nomi placed tea lights in small dishes around the cave and waved burning palo santo wood, sage, and mugwort incense. To dispel negative energy, Ruth told her. Nomi was trying not to be skeptical, but it was hard to believe in this whole display.

Meanwhile, Ruth spread salt on the threshold, encouraging Leah's ghost to pass through. With a garden spade, she dug into the dirt of the makeshift doorpost and stuck a mezuzah inside, to prevent Leah's spirit from returning once it left, like the necklace amulets would do.

Then she chanted the Hebrew incantations inviting in the Sabbath angels on Friday nights and inviting in the archangels before sleep:

"*Shalom aleichem, malachei hasharet, malachei elyon, mi-melech malachei hamilachim, Hakadosh Baruch Hu,*" Peace unto you, Angels of Service, Angels of High, from the most regal, Holy Blessed One, she called. "*Liyimini Michael,*" To my right Michael, pointing to the right. "*Ulismoli Gavriel,*" And to my left Gabriel, pointing to the left. "*Mimuli Uriel,*" In front of me Uriel, putting her hands out in front of her. "*Umeachorai Raphael,*" And behind me Raphael.

She put her hands back behind her and then brought them up over her head. "*U'mealei,*" and above me, "*Shechinat-El,*" she added, invoking the divine feminine presence, in a clear and powerful voice.

Then Ruth named the spirit.

"Leah Marshall!" Ruth called, with Nomi listening from inside the womb-like shelter Leah Marshall herself may even have created.

"We know you're still here! We feel you. We hear you etching on your slates."

A scratching noise startled Nomi and she looked around with her heart racing.

"She's still here all right," Ruth called to Nomi.

"Leah, we need to talk," Ruth began, enunciating each word slowly and clearly. "We know what you went through, and we sympathize. We were lucky to find help and support. But you weren't. Nomi's nephew Jonah wasn't either. But we hear your pain. And your descendants do, too. They know you would not have killed your daughter if you had seen another way."

Nomi took a breath. All was quiet and still. She did not even hear a peep from the baby.

"The world is changing," Ruth continued. "I know it seems grim sometimes. I know you were in despair—as you named your daughter. But we know there are angels all around us. Maybe you had some, too, but just couldn't see them. But we do. We won't give up hope."

Nomi closed her eyes. Ruth's melodic voice was lulling her into a trance.

"We want you to know you can go now. You don't need to linger. We'll take it from here," she said. "We will be your *tikkun*. Trust us, spirit of Leah Marshall, you can go."

While Ruth chanted, "Go, Leah, go . . . Go, Leah, go . . . Go, Leah, go . . ." in a hushed voice, Nomi imagined Leah, and all others who were hanged in this place in the name of God, floating not down, but up, with open parachutes attached. As if on the wings of angels, ascending a ladder to heaven. She sat with that image for a time she could not measure. Energy going up so energy could come down, and magic could happen.

Then Ruth recited a prayer Nomi knew from the Friday night service. Ruth had told her it was also a Kabbalistic incantation to summon divine intervention: "*Anna bikoach gedulat yeminchah tatir tzerurah . . . Shavateinu kabel ushma tzaakateinu, yodeah ta'alumot.*" Please, by the great power of your right hand, set the captive free . . . Accept our prayer, hear our cry, You, Knower of Mystery.

The noise returned. At first it was the usual rapid, frantic scratching. Then it slowed, with more space between the sounds. Like labor in reverse.

"Wait! Before you go," Nomi whispered. "Please, tell Avi I'm still waiting for a sign, a message. And tell Jude I listened to her advice. Not all of it, but what was right for me. I know she's here, too, guiding me. As an angel, not a ghost. My fourth imperfect angel. She brought me here, to this moment."

There was silence.

When it was clear the scratching noise was gone, Ruth recited the priestly blessing:

> *Yivareiyich Adonai viyishmireiyich*
> *Yaer Adonai panav eleiyich viyichuneiyich.*
> *Yisai Adonai panav eleiyich*
> *Viyasem lach shalom.*

> May God bless you and keep you.
> May God shine light on you and be gracious to you.
> May God turn toward you
> and grant you peace.

And together, they said, "Amen."

Ruth stood tall, took a shofar out of her shoulder bag of supplies, put the ram's horn to her lips, and blew a strong and long blast, which echoed off the walls, reverberating until it was gone. Nothing. Not a sound. Even baby Abe was too startled to cry.

"Are you ready?" Ruth called to Nomi. "It's time for the *shehechianu!*"

"Yes, I'm ready," Nomi said. Then she recited the blessing along with Ruth, addressing the womblike God, the one she now believed in, alongside the seed-planting God, as they were One after all.

"*Bruchah at Yah, Ruach HaOlam, shehecheyanu, v'kiyimanu, v'higiyanu lazman hazeh,*" they recited in unison. Blessed are You, Yah our God, Spirit flowing through the Universe, who gave us life, sustained us, and brought us to this moment.

"Rest in Peace, Leah Marshall," Nomi whispered, fingering the three pendants dangling between her breasts. "The world needs hope, not despair. And a little bit of magic."

CHAPTER 42

IT WAS A bright, clear day in early July. The mulchy smell of fresh earth and leaves filled the air, and the sun was shining after some good rain.

Good for blueberries, Nomi thought.

She was sitting with Abe on the screened-in porch. The baby was in his bouncy seat, cooing and playing with his teething toy. They were watching two cardinals build a nest where some branches of a crabapple tree came together to form a perfect spot, holding the nest like in the palm of a hand. The birds had been working on it for days, and the nest was almost complete. Abe's eyes followed the birds, and he made noises when they did, mimicking their chirps and tweets, whereas only weeks before, he had barely noticed.

Nomi had not seen cardinals in Israel. Watching them was another one of her fond childhood memories, as well as other local species like blue jays and robins. The birds reminded her of a time long gone. The baby birds in this nest would one day be pushed out, too, by their parents, and the nest itself would be abandoned and destroyed by the elements. Her heart went out to the baby birds, and to their parents, but it was just the way things were.

Nomi had been reading up on local birds. Jude had kept a bird book on the porch, and Nomi took up birdwatching with the baby while she read aloud to him about the different birds they saw. He was not old enough to understand, but he seemed to enjoy watching the birds and hearing Nomi's voice. She loved observing his developing reactions to his environment, and she found the details about the birds fascinating and relevant.

She opened the book to the page on cardinals.

"Cardinals are one of a smaller number of species where male and female build their nest together," she read aloud. "In most species, the male builds the nest to attract the female. But cardinals build the nest together, as part of their courting."

Nomi wondered what they did if their eggs did not hatch. Did they stay together in the nest, or did the male seek a partner who might be a better egg-layer?

She read on: "Cardinals are also a monogamous species. They mate for life."

"Mate for life," she said to the baby. "What does that mean? For both their lives? Or just one of their lives? If one dies, does the other seek a new mate? Or does it spend the rest of its life mourning?" She put her finger on the baby's nose, and he gurgled. "What do you think?"

Baby Abe moved his arms and legs around, blowing spit bubbles.

"You don't say. Well, I wish I understood you, because it's a mystery to me. Do you think there are any species where the female builds the nest to attract the male? Or maybe even some where the birds live in separate nests? Especially if they're beyond egg-laying years."

Did birds ever mate for companionship, or was their relationship just about laying and hatching eggs? These cardinals looked like they were enjoying each other's company.

Nomi heard the porch door creak open, then spring shut. She looked up from the bird book. "Good morning, sleepy head," she said to Ruth.

"Morning." Ruth looked quizzically at Nomi. "Where'd you get that shirt? I didn't see it in Jude's closet. Or Jonah's."

"It was Avi's work shirt. My favorite, the only article of his clothing I brought with me. He was wearing it the day of our first unofficial date. It's lasted all these years."

"I like it."

"Me too. This is the first time I've worn it."

She rubbed the material of the sleeve, soft and thin from years of wear. She could practically feel the contours of Avi's arm beneath her fingers. Her stomach tightened, but she took a breath and let the sorrow pass. "And speaking of being about time, I'd like to take Abe out to the blueberry patch. I have a feeling they're beginning to ripen. It may be time to start advertising for pick-your-own. Do you want to join us?"

"Sure. Then, when he's napping, I want to go online and look up places to study in the fall. In addition to the Priestess program."

"You were accepted?"

"Yes. It's official. I've enrolled in their online certification program. But I'd like to go to cooking school, too. Abe should be old enough for daycare by then."

"Both of those ideas sound perfect. And I can pitch in with Abe. I assume you'll have some night classes, too. Don't worry about a thing. We'll work it all out."

"We?" Ruth's eyes brightened.

"Yes. I don't want you to think of yourself as a boarder here. This is your home. And even if I couldn't formally adopt Abe, I am his *sandak*." She was not going to let this lifeline pass her by. "Consider me your partner in parenting."

"You know that's what I most wanted."

"Yes, I do." They smiled at each other.

Ruth picked up the book. "Maybe you also want to take some courses. You never did go to college, did you?"

"Nope. And that's a lovely idea. Permaculture and organic farming. And psychology, too." Maybe even courses in gardening therapy if there was such a thing. If not, she'd invent it. She didn't need to meet teachers' expectations anymore.

When she had shared with Diane her plan to take in more women and start a therapeutic farm for rape survivors, Diane said the idea was especially relevant now that the Supreme Court had overturned Roe vs. Wade. Even if Massachusetts was a liberal state, there could be women coming across the border from around the country for help.

Diane also told her the money they had raised for that community garden Joan had mentioned, plus other money they had raised for a halfway house, could go toward the project. So, there would be payment involved. Not only to compensate for the women's expenses, but also to pay Nomi a salary. It would be a paid vocation, not volunteer work.

Plus, Amy had called to say the slates were authentic, and Nomi would be receiving monetary compensation for this important find. That should be enough money so she could even go back and visit Israel and Avi's grave, maybe even bring Ruth and baby Abe along. Moving back there one day was not out of the question, either. But for now, at least, this was home.

"We can be dorm mates. Only the dorm will be right here," Ruth said, twirling around the porch. She scooped the baby from his bouncy seat and kissed him on the cheek. Her face changed to a sour expression, and she pinched her nose. "I think he needs a diaper change. We'll be right back."

Nomi went to put on her boots and bring her coffee mug to the kitchen. John's number was still hanging on the refrigerator with a magnet, although she had saved it in her cell phone not long after they'd met. She had not noticed, however, what it said on this magnet:

> The master key is the broken heart.
> — Baal Shem Tov

That was it. The lost key to this next life stage was the broken heart she'd been carrying around all this time. Without it she would never have made it to this moment. Her broken heart had now become an open heart.

"Thank you, Avi," Nomi whispered. "I feel you now. And I hear you now, too. I'm sorry. I wasn't listening hard enough."

Now that she trusted herself, it was easy to see how Avi had been with her, supporting her all along.

Ruth came out of her bedroom with baby Abe in her arms. Nomi had already put on the sling and reached out for the child, who slid happily into place, kicking his legs, and waving his arms in excitement. With baby Abe against Nomi's breasts, they walked out the back door and onto the grass. Elvis was there to greet them. Nomi felt the sun's warmth inviting her body to wake like a flower opening.

They reached the blueberry patch with Elvis following and walked along the rows of bushes, examining the plants. Clusters of blueberries stood out among the smooth pointed green leaves. Their color was still a crimson purple, with patches of green, but it would only be a matter of days, maybe a week, before some would be plump and blue and ready for harvesting.

The thought made Nomi's heart quicken, as she pictured people coming from near and far, filling their wicker baskets with the tart-sweet fruit.

She took her cell phone out of her jeans' pocket and texted John:

Blueberries are almost ripe for harvesting. Join us next Sunday for a first harvest and blueberry buckwheat pancakes?

She would invite Sam, Jeff, and Hope, too. And Frank. Blueberries were not the only things to ripen. Bill Jr. had finished repairing Frank's Harley and putting in hand controls and some other additions, including a compartment on the back of the bike to take a fold-up wheelchair along. Dying in peace was a blessing, but so was living every moment as if it was the last, savoring it and feeling it fully, like a perfect blueberry on your tongue.

Ruth came over, holding her cell phone in the air. "Let me get a picture of you two with the blueberries!" she called.

Nomi squatted on the ground, still moist from the rains. She brought her hands together into a namaste gesture in front of the baby, who was resting peacefully in his sling on her heart, and for the first time since Avi had died, she felt at peace. Sprinkled, even, with moments of joy. She felt her sister's spirit within and around her, informing her, guiding her, but not pushing. She was here, present in her own life, taking up space in the world, with her whole being planted firmly on the earth.

"Say cheese!" Ruth said, as she adjusted her cell phone camera.

Nomi took a deep breath through her nose, the scent of ripening blueberries flowing through her body. As she exhaled, she rubbed the material of Avi's shirt collar between her fingers. She would live life to the fullest—the bitter and the sweet—until their souls might, perhaps, one day meet again.

"Beautiful Blueberries," she said.

Ruth snapped the photograph.

Haviva Ner-David is an ordained rabbi and interfaith-interspiritual minister, with a doctorate in philosophy and an M.F.A in Creative Writing. She runs Shmaya: A Mikveh for Mind, Body and Soul, where she officiates ritual immersion ceremonies and offers group workshops. A certified spiritual director with a specialty in dreamwork, she works with individuals and couples. Rabbi Ner-David is the author of three published spiritual journey memoirs (*Life on the Fringes: A Feminist Journey Towards Traditional Rabbinic Ordination*; and *Chanah's Voice: A Rabbi Wrestles with Gender, Commandment and the Women's Rituals of Baking, Bathing and Brightening*), *Dreaming Against the Current: A Rabbi's Soul Journey*, and the children's book, *Yonah and the Mikveh*. She is also the author of a soon-to-be-published guidebook for engaged couples, *Getting (and Staying) Married Jewishly: Preparing for Your Life Together with Ancient and Modern Wisdom*. Rabbi Ner-David is involved in peace work, promoting a shared society of Jews, Christians and Muslims in Galilee, where she lives with Jacob, her life partner of thirty years, their seven children and their dog and cat. She also lives with a genetic degenerative muscular disease called FSHD, which has been one of her greatest teachers.

Visit Haviva's website at http://www.rabbihaviva.com.

Printed by BoD™in Norderstedt, Germany